The Club Series book seven

THE CONSUMMATION

Josh and Kat Part III

Lauren Rowe

D1153829

Chapter 1
Josh

I stumble out of Walmart (the only place open at eleven-forty-five that sells electronics) and cross the parking lot toward my waiting town car. I open the door of the black Sedan and hurl myself into the backseat. "Thanks for waiting, man," I mumble.

"Did they have what you were looking for?" the driver asks.

I hold up a plastic Walmart bag containing my new purchases.

"Where to now?"

I give the guy the address of Kat's apartment and he starts the engine.

As the car pulls out of the parking lot, I surreptitiously dig into my plastic bag and pull out one of my three Walmart-purchases: a bottle of Jack.

The driver's eyes flicker at me in the rearview mirror, but, thankfully, the guy doesn't say jack about my Jack. I lean back in my seat, the bottle of booze perched against my lips.

Man, I fucked up tonight. I had no idea not telling Kat about my upcoming move to Seattle would play out like fucking Armageddon. Watching Kat cry big ol' soggy tears, especially on account of something I did (or, technically, didn't do), ripped my heart the fuck out of my chest. Each tear that streamed down Kat's beautiful face felt like a knife stabbing me in the heart.

"I would have been bursting at the seams to tell you if the situation were reversed," Kat said in front of the karaoke bar, her eyes glistening. "You would have been the first person I would have called."

Up until that moment, I'd been thinking my tempestuous little terrorist was simply overreacting—letting her emotions and temper

1

run wild, as she's been known to do a time or two. But the minute those daggers left Kat's mouth, I knew they were cutting me so deep because they were the God's truth—and that if Kat were to buy a house in L.A. and not bother to mention it to me, I'd be crushed.

Which is exactly how Kat seems to be feeling right now: *crushed.* In fact, it seems like Kat might be thinking she's done with me for good, though that's not what she said when I dropped her off at her apartment. All she said before slipping inside her place was that she "needed a couple days to think and regroup" so she could "figure out if she was overreacting or not"—but the look on Kat's face as she closed her door made it clear she wasn't even close to deciding she'd overreacted.

"Okay," I said softly, even though all I wanted to do was plant a deep kiss on her mouth that would somehow erase her short-term memory from her brain. "Take your time," I said. "I'll call you in a few days." And I wasn't bullshitting her when I said that—I really wasn't—I truly planned to leave her alone. I mean, shit, God knows groveling never has been my style. But, fuck me, after only an hour alone in my hotel room, drinking whiskey and staring at the Space Needle—not to mention getting my ass chewed by fucking Adele—I just couldn't sit there like a flop-dick anymore. I had to do *something* to make her forgive me.

So I texted Kat a couple times, asking her to call me—but she didn't respond. So I bit the bullet and called her—let the groveling begin!—but my call went straight to voicemail. So, finally, I tucked my dick and balls firmly between my legs and left Kat a rambling voicemail that can only be described as "vaginal." But, still, I didn't hear a goddamned peep from her. Which is when a panic started descending upon me, a thumping need to make Kat understand I'm genuinely crazy about her, addicted, insatiable. *And that's when I got my brilliant idea.*

I pull my new portable CD player out of my Walmart bag and remove it from its packaging. It's quite a bit smaller and way more modern looking than the old-school boom box I'd envisioned when I stumbled into the electronics aisle at Walmart, but I suppose beggars can't be choosers, especially at just before midnight on a Friday night.

The sedan pulls up to the front of Kat's apartment complex.

"Just park in the driveway," I say to the driver. I hand him my phone. "Connect this to your stereo—I've got a song all cued up."

"Huh?"

"Blast the song I've got cued up on my phone."

The driver looks incredulous, not to mention annoyed. "It's past midnight, sir. We can't be blasting music in a residential area."

I shove a couple hundred bucks at the guy. "Come on, man, I've got a girl to win back. I fucked up and now I gotta make her forgive me."

The driver takes my cash. "The song's cued up?"

"Yep. Just press play at my signal—and then blast the motherfucker at full volume, as high as your speakers will go."

"Full volume? Sir, I really can't—"

I throw a bunch more bills at the guy. "Just do it," I bark. "I'll handle any complaints."

Without waiting for the driver's reply, I stagger out of the car with my CD player in one hand and my brand new Walmart-issued trench coat in the other.

I can't believe I'm doing this. Was there an exact moment when I handed Kat my dick and balls, or did I give her my manhood in bite-sized pieces, the same way I fed her a peanut butter and jelly sandwich in the sex dungeon? Well, either way, the woman's definitely got my crown jewels in a Ziploc baggie now.

I place the CD player on the ground so I can put on my spiffy new trench coat, and when I'm positive I'm sufficiently John-Cusack-ified, I take a deep breath, lift my makeshift boom box over my head, and signal to the driver to start the music.

Peter Gabriel's song "In Your Eyes" begins blaring loudly from the car.

I stand stock still, holding the boom box over my head. And I wait.

But no Kat. What the hell? Surely, she can hear the loud music—her apartment is one of the units closest to the street.

I continue waiting, holding the CD player over my head.

But, still, no Kat.

Shit.

A feeling of pure desperation floods me. Is she really gonna ignore me out here? I'm putting my fucking heart on the line for her.

3

But wait. What if Kat hears the song but doesn't put two and two together? What if she thinks it's just some drunken asshole, passed out in his car, playing the oldies station much too loud? I quickly stride back to the sedan and bend down to the driver.

"Hand me my phone," I say. "I'm gonna send my girl a text."

"You want me to disconnect it from the stereo?"

"No," I reply. "Keep the song going. I'll just reach over you real quick." The driver pulls my phone toward me, as far as it will go with the connection cord attached, and I lean over him and tap out a text to Kat: "Come out to the street, Kitty Kat. There's a hound dog out here with his tail between his legs." I press send on my message and quickly reposition myself with the boom box again.

A few seconds later, a shirtless guy with a beer belly marches out of the apartment building, a lit cigarette in one hand, a beer can in the other.

"What the *fuck*, man?" the guy shouts. "I've got a baby trying to sleep in there."

"I'm doing *Say Anything* for my girl, man," I say. "I'm in the doghouse."

The guy makes a face like I've just blurted I have no penis.

"Dude, I got no choice," I continue. "My girl's a fucking unicorn."

The guy nods and takes a long drag off his cigarette. "She likes that movie, huh? The one with the boom box?"

I roll my eyes. "She thinks it's 'romantic.'"

The dude laughs heartily and takes a few steps back, apparently ceding center-stage to me. "This I gotta see," he mumbles.

A brunette woman comes out of one of the apartments, a look of complete annoyance etched onto her face—but when she catches sight of me, her face melts. She quickly disappears into the apartment building and returns with another woman in tow, and when the second woman sees me, her face melts, too. Well, shit. I'm glad these two women think I'm so fucking adorable, but they're not my intended audience. Where the fuck is Kat? Could she be asleep already? Or maybe in the shower? Did she not see my text?

My arms are getting tired. I didn't expect to have to do this for so long.

I shift my weight. Shit. In the movie, the girl looked out her window right away, didn't she? What the fuck is taking Kat so goddamned long to come out here and put me out of my misery?

A guy's face appears in the window of the front apartment. He turns to say something to someone behind him and an instant later, a second face appears in the window, laughing at me.

Well, let them laugh. As long as Kat comes out here and sees me and forgives me for crushing her, I don't care if the whole world laughs at me tonight. All I care about is setting things right with Kat—making her understand my failure to tell her about Seattle had nothing to do with her and everything to do with me.

"Hey, sir," the driver says to me above the music. "You just got a text. I don't think she's coming out."

I lower my boom box and turn around to face him, my heart beating like a steel drum.

"She replied to your text," the driver continues. He motions to my phone.

I lurch over to the car and grab my phone, my eyes bugging out of my head.

"I'm not playing hard to get or being a terrorist," Kat's text says. "I can't see or talk to you tonight. Please just give me a couple days to think and regroup and figure a few things out."

Chapter 2
Kat

"Happy birthday to youuu!" everyone at the table sings and Colby blows out the thirty candles on his carrot cake.

"Thanks, everyone," Colby says. "The cake looks great, Dax."

Mom begins taking the candles off Colby's cake and cutting slices for everyone while Dax assumes ice-cream-scooping duties.

"None for me," I say when Mom offers me a thick slice.

"Are you feeling okay, honey?" Mom asks. "You look a bit peaked." She hands Ryan the piece of cake she'd offered to me.

"I'm fine. I just went a little crazy at the karaoke bar with friends last night," I say. "Shouldn't have had that last martini."

Mom shoots me a scolding look. "You weren't driving, I hope?" she asks. She hands a huge slice of cake to Keane.

"Nope," I say.

"And whoever was driving wasn't drinking?"

"Correct," I say.

"Never drink and drive," Mom says firmly. She slides a noticeably slim piece of cake to Dad. "Just get that Uber-thingy on your phone and they'll pick you right up."

"You mean the Uber *app,* Mom?" Dax asks, shooting me an amused look.

"Yep. It's called Uber. They'll pick you right up."

"Wow. Sounds neat-o, Mom," I say, returning Dax's smile. She's so cute.

"Did you hit 'em with your karaoke-specialty last night?" Keane asks. He puts his hand on his heart and breaks into a full-throated chorus of "Total Eclipse of the Heart."

"Of course," I say. I toss my hair over my shoulder. "And I *nailed* it, too."

6

"Aw, you cheated on me, Baby-Gravy?" Ryan asks. "I'm devastated."

"Sorry, Ry," I say. "The opportunity presented itself and I had to take it. I thought you'd understand."

"Well, I *don't* understand," Ryan says. "That's *our* thing, Kum Shot."

"Stop with the semen-nicknames," Mom says. "You know I hate that."

"Sorry, Mom," Ryan says. "But I think your disciplinary efforts would be better spent telling Ebenezer Splooge over there not to stab me in the heart with a rusty blade."

"Aw, come on," I say. "I couldn't let the moment pass me by. *YOLO,* brah. That's how I dooz it."

Ryan scoffs, utterly miffed.

"*YOLO,*" Dax mutters with disdain. "I wanna strangle the genius who came up with that."

"What's 'YOLO'?" Dad asks, happily chomping on his little morsel of cake.

"'You only live once,'" Dax answers, practically holding his nose.

"Oh, *carpe diem* isn't cool enough for the kids these days, huh?" Dad says.

"That's too long to text," Mom says, taking a bite of ice cream. "They shorten everything these days, honey. 'LOL! OMG!'" She throws up her hands, apparently imitating a spazzoid-teenager at a mall.

Derby Field! Namibia!, I think to myself, my heart panging.

"So who sang my part for you last night?" Ryan asks. "Whoever the bastard was, I guarantee he didn't even come close to doing *this.*" He breaks into singing the 'Turn around, Bright Eyes' part of the song with hilarious gusto.

I laugh despite myself. Ryan can always make me laugh, no matter how dark my mood. "You're right. The guy who sang it didn't even come close to doing *that.*"

"So who was this douchebag who deigned to poach on my sacred karaoke-territory?" Ryan asks, stuffing a huge forkful of cake into his mouth.

"Language, Ry," Mom says. "Please, honey."

7

"Just this guy I've been seeing," I say. "Sarah's boyfriend's twin brother."

"Whoa. That's a lot of possessive nouns," Keane says.

"The twin brother of Sarah's new boyfriend," I clarify.

"Yeah, I got it, Protein Shake. I was kidding," Keane says. He rolls his eyes. "I'm dumb but I'm not *that* dumb."

"Sorry," I say.

Keane winks at me, apparently not genuinely offended.

"You've been seeing someone?" Ryan asks.

I nod.

"What's his name?"

"Josh Faraday," I say.

"Also known as the one and only porn king 'Sir J.W. Faraday,'" Dax says reverently, and I swiftly glare at him, nonverbally telling him to shut the fuck up.

"What?" Mom asks. "You're dating a porn king?"

"*No.*" I shoot bullets at Dax, the little fucker. "Dax is just being a little shit."

"*Kat*," Mom says, rolling her eyes. "*Language.* Come on, guys. Not at the table. *Please.* Can we just pretend to be civilized through one birthday meal?"

"Sorry, Mom." I bat my eyelashes. "Dax is just being a little *pill.*"

"Thank you," Mom says. "That's my little lady. Keep it clean, people."

"Always, Mommy," I say sweetly.

"Always," my brothers chime in with mock solemnity.

"Hey, no porn kings, Kitty," Dad says. "You know that."

"Yes, dearest patriarch," I say. "I know the rules. We all do. No dating porn kings, porn stars, pimps, hoes, felons, junkies, or *strippers.*" On that last word, I shoot Keane a snarky look and he smiles broadly. We kids all know Keane's recently been raking in the cash (one dollar bill at a time) as the Morgan Family's answer to Magic Mike, but our parents certainly don't know that. "Don't worry, Pops," I continue. "This Josh guy isn't a porn king or a pimp. He runs an investment-something-or-other with his brother and uncle. He's a respected member of society, I assure you."

"Oh, is this the boy from Las Vegas you were telling me about?" Mom asks.

"Yeah," I say. "But he's not from Las Vegas, Mom—he's actually from Seattle, though he lives in L.A. now."

"Wasn't that guy supposed to come to dinner tonight?" Colby asks.

"Oh, that's right," Mom says. "I forgot about that. Why didn't he come?"

"Something unexpectedly came up at work and he had to fly home to L.A." Heat flashes into my cheeks at my lie. "He told me to tell Colby 'Happy Birthday' and that he's sorry to miss the party. He was especially sorry to miss out on your spaghetti, Mom—I told him it's legendary."

Mom smiles.

"Don't worry. I'm sure you'll meet Josh one of these days soon," I say breezily, smiling at Mom, even though my stomach is turning over. *Considering he's gonna be the father of your grandchild.*

"Damn," Dax says. "I was looking forward to seeing if J.W. Faraday is as pretty as his picture." Dax addresses the group. "I saw a photo of this guy the other day and he's even prettier than Ry, if you can believe it."

Keane scoffs. "Pfft. Nobody out-pretties our Pretty Boy."

"Fuck you, Peen," Ryan says. "I keep telling you: I'm not pretty, I'm 'ruggedly handsome.'"

"*Language*," Mom says. "Good lord, guys. You're a bunch of sailors. Where did I go wrong? And don't call Keane that name. It's disgusting."

"Sorry, Mom," Ryan says. He addresses Keane again. "*Eff* you, *Peen*elope Cruz. How's that, Mom?"

Dad belly laughs and Mom shoots him a scolding look.

"It's funny," Dad says sheepishly, still laughing.

"Well, I'm sorry Josh couldn't make it this time," Mom says, peeling her scolding eyes off Dad. "Please tell him he's always welcome here. I'll make my 'legendary' spaghetti for him whenever he's able to come."

"Thanks, I'll tell him." *Right after I tell him I'm pregnant with your grandchild.*

My eyes drift aimlessly around the table and finally land squarely on Colby's ruggedly handsome face. He's staring right at me

9

with flickering eyes, looking at me like he can see right through me—and the moment our eyes connect, my cheeks burst into flames.

"Sorry Josh couldn't make it tonight," Colby says evenly. "I know you were excited to introduce him."

"Oh, it's okay," I manage to say, tears pricking my eyes. "Maybe another time."

Colby holds my gaze for a long beat until finally shifting his attention to Dax.

"This cake is great, Dax," Colby says. He rests one of his muscled forearms on the table. "Thanks for making it."

"Actually, I was hoping the cake would put you in such a great mood, you'd let me borrow your truck tomorrow? I gotta haul some gear."

Colby chuckles. "Sure. But only for a couple hours. I've got stuff to do tomorrow."

"Thanks, bro."

"And thanks for the spaghetti, Mom," Colby says. "It was fantastic, as always."

"You're welcome, honey. I made extra sauce so you can take some home with you and put it in your freezer. The birthday boy always gets extras."

"Thanks, Mom."

"Can I have extras, too, Mom?" Keane says. "I've been living on Taco Bell."

Mom laughs. "Yes, I made extras for you, too, Keaney—and also for Kitty Kat. It's in the fridge with your names on it."

"What about me?" Ryan says. "You're not gonna give extras to your favorite kid?"

"You got extras last time," Mom says. "I'll make extras for you and Daxy next time. And, by the way, you're *all* my favorite kid."

"Keane got extras last time," Dax says. "He shouldn't get 'em this time."

"Hey, that's right," Ryan says. "And the time before that, too. Why does Keane always get extras?"

Mom grabs Keane's hand. "Because Keane always *needs* them."

We all roll our eyes and Keane shoots us a "fuck you" look. "Thank you for understanding that, dearest mother," Keane says, flashing a mega-watt smile. "You're an exceptional caregiver to us all."

We all roll our eyes again, even Dad.

Mom has obviously caught wind of all the eye-rolls going on around her. "Stop it, guys," she says. "I know Keane's a brown-noser—I'm not an idiot."

Everyone bursts out laughing, even Keane.

"But it doesn't matter. The boy needs extras. He can't even boil water."

"And who's fault is that?" Dax says. "Whatever happened to personal responsibility?"

"You're an enabler, Mom," Ryan says. "Plain and simple."

"Don't listen to 'em, Mom. You're doing great," Keane says.

Mom squeezes Keane's hand again. "Look, I'll be the first to admit I parent each of you guys differently. For each and every one of you, I'm the mother you specifically *need*." She looks at Keane adoringly. "And when it comes to extras, Keane needs them."

The table erupts.

"Enough," Mom says firmly. "No arguing about extras, guys."

We all grumble quietly for another long moment, especially Ryan.

"Hey, Ry, you can have my extras," I say. "I don't need 'em."

"Nah, it's okay," Ryan says. "I'll happily steal extras from *Pee*nelope Cruz with a clear conscience, but I won't steal 'em from Spunky Brewster. I'll wait my turn."

Mom's face lights up. "*Spunky Brewster*? Finally, a sweet one. Now was that so hard?"

Ryan's expression is absolutely priceless right now. "No, Mother Dear," he says piously. "It wasn't. In fact, it was really quite easy."

Mom looks at me lovingly. "I love it. It sure fits our Kitty Kat. I can't think of a better word to describe her than *spunky*."

My brothers are absolutely dying right now.

"Yep," Ryan says, his nostrils flaring. "That's our Kitty Kat for you: full of *spunk*."

Everyone at the table bursts into raucous, tear-filled laughter except for poor, clueless, adorable Mom who's obviously never heard that particular slang term for cum before.

"What?" Mom asks, her eyes wide. "What's so funny? Am I being dumb?"

"I'll tell you later," Dad says, laughing his ass off.

"Am I being dumb?"

Dad shakes his head. "I'll tell you later, Louise."

But we all know he won't tell Mom a goddamned thing. Not a single one of us, including Dad, would ever dream of throwing our hilarious Captain Morgan under the Mom-bus—he's just too goddamned entertaining.

"So when's your next gig, Dax?" Dad asks, obviously trying to change the subject. "Anything I might be able to catch?"

Dax wipes his eyes from laughing. "Uh, sure, Pops. Friday we're playing at that Irish pub downtown, and Saturday we're playing at a street fair in Bremerton..."

Normally, I love hearing every last detail about Dax's upcoming gigs, but at the moment I can't concentrate on what Dax is saying—not when my oldest brother is staring me down, drawing my attention like a magnet.

When my eyes lock onto Colby's, he makes a sympathetic face—and, just like that, my eyes water. I look away, my lower lip trembling. Damn, that Colby—even when Josh isn't here, Colby can sniff him out.

As if on cue, my phone buzzes with a text from Josh.

"Are you at Colby's birthday dinner?" Josh writes.

It's all I can do not to scream in frustration. For crying out loud, it was only last night I told Josh I needed a few days to think and regroup after being blindsided at the karaoke bar. What does he think has changed in twenty-four little hours? (Okay, yes, in point of fact, every goddamned thing in my life has changed in twenty-four little hours, thank you very much—but Josh doesn't know that. And, anyway, discovering I'm pregnant with Josh's accidental spawn has only made me feel *less* prepared to talk to him any time soon, not *more*.) Gah. If only I could talk to Sarah. She always helps me find clarity in the midst of any shit storm. Unfortunately, though, talking to Sarah isn't an option, at least not for a few weeks. She's starting her final exams on Monday and right after that, she's heading off to Greece to get engaged (unbeknownst to her).

I tune back into the conversation at the dinner table. Ryan and Colby are talking about the second season of *True Detective*.

"I agree it isn't as good as the first season," Colby says. "But I don't know why people are trashing it. It's still one of the best shows on TV."

"It's just that the first season was so *epic*," Ryan says. "Everyone's expectations were just so high after that."

Under-promise and over-perform. That's what Josh once said is one of his many life mottos. Is that what Josh was doing by not telling me about Seattle? Under-promising? I'm guessing yes. So, hey, maybe I should take a page out of Josh's under-promising playbook and hold off telling him about the accidental Faraday gestating inside me for a bit? Given the timing of when we were in Las Vegas together, there's no way I'm out of my first trimester yet, which means my chances of miscarriage are still relatively high (especially, I'd think, in light of my boozing and weed-smoking and Sybian-riding).

If nature winds up taking its course and this pregnancy doesn't stick, then I'd be awfully bummed if I'd stupidly told Josh about the situation early on. And on the other hand, if this pregnancy *does* wind up sticking—if I actually do wind up giving birth to Josh Faraday's lovechild—oh my fucking God—well, then, there'd still be no *rush* in telling Josh about it, right? Because if we're ultimately gonna have a kid together some time this year, there's no reason Josh needs to know about it tomorrow versus, say, in a month... right?

I suppose if I thought Josh would ask me to get an abortion, there might be a different analysis about timing, but I already know (based on a surprisingly deep conversation we had about religion and spirituality one night on the phone) that Catholic-raised Josh wouldn't ask me to do that; and, for myself, I've already seriously considered and rejected that option, anyway. Which means, under any scenario, it makes no difference if I tell Josh about my accidental bun in the oven now or a month from now.

A feeling of relative calm washes over me.

I think I just made a decision: I'll wait a month to tell Josh about the baby, just in case natural selection takes care of things between now and then. And in the meantime, I'll just try not to think about it (other than taking pre-natal vitamins and picking up *What To Expect When You're Expecting*).

Yep. That's the plan.

Okay.

Whew.

I take a deep breath and tune into the conversation at the table again, feeling oddly relieved.

"So it turned out it was just a little brush fire," Colby's saying. "And yet there we all were, geared up for the Apocalypse."

Everyone laughs.

"I always get so nervous every time you go out on a call," Mom says to Colby.

"I know, Mom. But I wouldn't wanna be doing anything else with my life. I love it."

"I know you do, honey. We're so proud of you."

I look down at my phone and stare at Josh's text, the one asking if I'm at Colby's birthday dinner. I suppose I should answer the guy.

"Yeah, I'm at the party," I write. "Sitting at the dinner table with everyone right now, as a matter of fact. We're eating Dax's carrot cake, which is utterly DELICIOUS, bee tee dubs. Too bad you had to miss it." I press send on my text and look up from my phone. "Hey, Mom, can you cut me a little slice of cake, after all?"

"Sure," Mom says. "Does that mean you're feeling a bit better?"

"Mmm hmm."

My phone buzzes with Josh's reply: "I wanted to be there, but you UNINVITED me." He attaches a sad-face emoji.

"Are you in L.A.?" I write.

"Yeah. I took the first flight home this morning." Another sad-face. "Did you tell your family why I'm not there?"

"No. I told them you had to return to L.A. for work."

"Why didn't you tell them I'm a total asshole?"

"Because it's none of their business you're a total asshole," I write. "WHICH YOU ARE."

Everyone at the table laughs uproariously about something Keane is saying.

I glance up from my phone to find Colby staring at me, his eyes full of sympathy.

Damn, that Colby.

"Excuse me," I say, leaping up from the table. I sprint across the house toward my mom's office, intending to close the door behind me and continue texting with Josh, but my sudden movement has made me feel horrendously queasy all of a sudden, so I hang a sharp right and bolt into the bathroom.

Gah. Thar she blows.

Bye-bye, carrot cake.

Lovely.

So far, being a mommy is super-duper fun.

I rinse out my mouth and run cold water over my face and then sit on the edge of the tub, my head in my hands. I can't believe this is my life. I quit my job yesterday, thinking I was gonna spend the next year building a business—but, instead, it turns out I'm gonna spend the next *eighteen* years unexpectedly raising a *kid*. Without any desire to do so, I've trapped Josh exactly the way he's always feared some gold digger would do—and at a time when he's so unsure about our potential future as a couple, he didn't even tell me about his impending move to my city.

I put my hands over my face. This is a freaking nightmare.

My phone buzzes with an incoming text.

I wipe my eyes and look down at my phone, my vision blurred by tears.

"This 'total asshole' just booked you a first-class flight to L.A. on Thursday," Josh writes. "I get why me not telling you about Seattle hurt your feelings. You're entitled to that. But I'm not gonna let you torture me with it forever. Go ahead and 'think and regroup' all you want for exactly five motherfucking days, but that's all you get, Madame Terrorist. After that, I'm gonna fly your tight little ass down here and give you no choice but to forgive me."

15

Chapter 3
Josh

I crane my neck, scrutinizing the passengers filing through the gate, my skin buzzing with anticipation, my heart clanging in my chest. Not her. Not her. Not her. Did the entire city of Seattle board Kat's flight to L.A.? Jesus.

I can't wait another minute to see her. I'm wrecked. Out of my mind. These past five days, I haven't been able to sleep. Think. Eat. Laugh. I fully expected Kat to break down and call me at some point this past week—or at least *text* me—especially in light of all the ridiculously expensive flowers I've sent her every day—but she didn't. Nope. I didn't hear a goddamned peep out of Kat (unless, of course, you count texts that said: "Thank you for the beautiful flowers and for continuing to give me time to think and regroup."). Fucking terrorist. I've been physically sick with loneliness and yearning and regret all fucking week. If she wanted me to know what my life would feel like without her in it, well, now I know: it's fucking torture.

Not her. Not her. Not her. I'm dying here. I shove the bouquet of red roses I'm holding under my nose and inhale deeply, trying to calm myself down with a little aromatherapy. Where the fuck is she? She was seated in the first-class cabin on the plane—so she should be one of the first people off the flight. Is she waiting to de-board just to prolong my torture a bit more? Motherfucker, I'm *dying* here.

Oh, good God, no—I just had a horrible thought: could Kat possibly have missed her flight? Or worse, did she decide not to come to visit me, after all? Oh God, that would crush me. In all honesty, it might even kill me at this point—I'm just that desperate to see her.

All I did this past week was play and replay our post-karaoke conversation in my head—only not the real conversation as it truly

16

happened, but a revised, fantasy-version in which Kat said, "My heart's on the line, Josh," and I smoothly took her into my arms and replied, "My heart's on the line, too, babe." If only I'd said that, maybe things would be different now.

My heart stops. Oh, thank God. There she is. *Katherine Ulla Morgan.* The one and only. My unicorn. Long legs. Golden mane. Head held high. Just the sight of her jumpstarts my aching heart and makes me feel half-alive for the first time in five days.

"Kat!" I yell. I wave at her. "Kat!"

She looks toward the sound of my voice and her eyes light up when she spots me. Oh my God, I feel euphoric. She's here. Thank God. She didn't leave me for good. My heart can beat again. Everything's gonna be okay.

"Kat," I say when she reaches me.

But she looks upset. She's pressing her lips together. Her face is tight. Her eyes are moist.

I hand her the flower bouquet, wrap her in my arms, and kiss her deeply, crushing the flowers between us. Oh my fuck, she tastes like heaven. Minty. Like she just brushed her teeth. I press myself into her and devour her lips, feeling like a junkie who's finally, blissfully, *blessedly* getting his next fix.

When we finally pull away from each other, Kat's eyes are dark with desire and I'm hard as a rock.

"Josh," Kat breathes, her cheeks flushed. She licks her lips and tilts her face up like she wants another kiss.

I put my fingertip under her chin. "I know we've got a shit-ton to talk about, but *please* give me one night to—"

"We have nothing to talk about," Kat says curtly, cutting me off.

I shoot her a look of blatant skepticism.

"I'm serious, Josh," Kat says. "From this day forward, all I wanna do is be in the moment with you. No talking about the future. No talking about our feelings. Just kiss me and let's pretend this past week never happened."

17

Chapter 4
Kat

"Scrabble?" I ask. "Not quite what I was expecting as our first activity of the weekend."

Josh puts the game box on his dining room table and crosses his arms over his muscled chest—and much to my surprise, he's not flashing a smart-ass smirk. In fact, he looks completely earnest. "You were upset we never do normal, real-life stuff like play board games—so that's what we're gonna do. *All. Weekend. Long.* You want real life? You think I'm addicted to excitement, and not to you, personally? Fine. This entire weekend, I'm gonna be every bit as boring as Boring Blane or Cameron Fucking Schulz. No booze. No weed. No poker chips. No 'numbing the pain of my tortured soul.'"

Ah, there it is—he flashes the smart-ass smirk I was expecting a moment ago.

"From here on out," Josh continues, "I'm all about Scrabble and Monopoly and adamantly *not* trying to escape the pain of reality in any way."

My mind is racing with a thousand emotions all at once, but the one that seems to be rising to the top of the heap is *relief*. The entire plane ride to Los Angeles, I was stressed out, wondering how the heck I was gonna deflect attention away from my newfound aversion to alcohol—I *am* the Party Girl with a Hyphen, after all—and now, in an unexpected turn of events, Josh has just made club soda this weekend's beverage of mutual choice.

"But... we're seriously gonna play *Scrabble*?" I ask, dumbfounded.

"Yeah," Josh says, spreading the game tiles onto the table. "We're gonna find out if we're every bit as addicted to each other

18

when we're playing a board game as when we're saving the world or smoking weed or drinking martinis or fucking in a sex dungeon. I'm willing to bet anything we will be—but, apparently, you're not convinced. So, here we go."

"*I'm* not convinced? Are you on crack? You're the one who didn't want me to know you're moving to Seattle."

"Oh my shit. *Really*? That's the story you're telling yourself inside your head? That I 'didn't *want* you to know' I'm moving to Seattle? That's an interesting spin on reality—and when I say 'interesting,' what I mean is 'completely *delusional*.'"

I open my mouth to protest. Is he seriously picking a fight with me? We just walked into his house from the airport not five minutes ago and he's already laying into me? Why the hell did I come all the way down here to L.A. if he's just gonna 'dick it up' and not even *try* to convince me he's sorry for—

"*Babe*," Josh says emphatically, cutting off my internal rant. "I didn't *tell* you I was moving to Seattle, which is a whole lot different than me 'not *wanting* you to know,' because I'm a total flop-dick who's scared shitless about the intensity of my feelings for you."

My heart skips a beat.

A sexy smile dances on his lips. "I didn't *tell* you because I'm having a hard time believing feelings this intense could possibly lead to anything but a gigantic fireball in the sky that burns out as quickly as it ignites," he continues. "But, I'll be damned, no matter what happens, my feelings don't seem to burn out—not at all—they just keep on blazing hotter and hotter." He bites his lip. "And *hotter*."

If I were a cartoon character, I'd be saying, "Hummanah-hummanah-hummanah" right now. But since I'm a flesh-and-blood human, I just stare at Josh, my chest rising and falling with my sudden arousal.

Josh grins. "So don't say I didn't *want* you to find out. Big difference. Okay?"

I nod, my eyes wide. I want to tackle him. Lick him. Kiss him from head to toe. *Suck his dick*. But I don't move a muscle.

Josh settles into a chair and moves the Scrabble pieces around on the table. "Now pick your fucking tiles so we can play the game." He picks up the directions sheet from the box and studies it while I continue staring at him like a wide-mouth bass. "It says here each player picks seven tiles," he says.

My crotch is burning. My nipples are hard. That was the most incredible speech any man has ever given me—and he wasn't even buzzed or high or enacting some sort of fantasy role-play when he said it.

"We're *seriously* gonna play *Scrabble* right now?" I manage to say. My cheeks feel hot. My clit is buzzing. All I want to do is fuck the crap out of him.

"Yup. Sit the fuck down, Party Girl. We're gonna test my theory that you and I can have fun doing literally anything. Since playing Scrabble is my idea of the seventh circle of hell, I figure if we can have fun doing this, then I'll have empirically proven once and for all we can have fun doing *anything.* And if we can have fun doing *anything,* then I *also* will have empirically proven I'm not Garrett Bennetting you." He rolls his eyes with disdain. "Which, by the way, still pisses me off that you'd even think that for a minute."

I open my mouth to speak, but close it again.

Josh claps his hands like he's commanding a puppy. "Now, come on, Party Girl, sit down and pick your fucking tiles. Time to get your tight little ass whooped."

I sit down across the table from him and stare at him blankly.

"Pick seven tiles," Josh says, motioning to the scattered game pieces on the table.

I make a face like he's a total dork, but I do as I'm told.

After I've got my tiles lined up on my rack, I look up, blankly. "Okay," I say.

Josh's gorgeous blue eyes are fixed on me intensely. "Go ahead," he says, motioning to the table. "Play Scrabble."

"'Play Scrabble'?" I say. "I've never played this game before. I have no idea what to do."

"You've *never* played Scrabble?" he says, incredulous.

"We always played cards and video games at my house—not board games. You go ahead and I'll just do whatever you do."

Josh grabs the directions sheet off the table in a huff. "Well, shit. I dunno what the fuck to do—I've never played Scrabble, either. I thought you'd know, growing up in a real family, and all."

I bite my lip, trying not to smile.

Josh scans the directions for a moment, obviously completely annoyed. "Jesus, Kat, I figured you'd played *all* the board games." He reads again for a long moment. "Okay, well, it looks ridiculously simple. Seems like we just lay tiles on the board to spell words and rack up points for the letters. Nothing to it."

"Okay. You go first," I say.

Josh pauses briefly, considering the tiles on his rack, and then lays down three letters: *D-U-M*.

"Dum?"

He shrugs sheepishly. "I don't have 'B-S-H-I-T' on my rack," he says. His eyes flicker with apology. "I was a total *dumbshit* for not telling you about Seattle," he says softly.

I nod emphatically. "Yeah, you were."

"I know—I just said that," he says. "Okay, that's six points for me. It's your turn."

I assess the seven tiles on my rack and lay down three: *A-S-S*. "I don't have 'H-O-L-E,'" I say, smirking. "How many points does that get me?"

Josh is clearly stifling a smile.

"Come on," I say. "How many points?"

Josh looks at the directions again. "Three. But I think you should be awarded triple points for being one hundred percent right."

"Agreed. Okay, your turn," I say, jutting my chin at him. "Play Scrabble, Josh."

"I think I'm supposed to pick three more tiles to replace the ones I already played," he says. He picks up the directions sheet again. "Yeah. It says here we both pick tiles to replace the ones we've played."

We each pick three additional tiles and, after brief consideration, Josh lays his new word onto the board: *W-O-O*.

"Woo?" I ask. "Like 'woo-hoo!'?"

"No. Like, '*woo*,'" he says. "Like 'I'm gonna *woo* you, Miss Katherine'—like, you know, old timey *wooing*." He flashes a charming smile. "As in, 'You better brace yourself, Miss Katherine, because I'm gonna *woo* the fucking shit out of you.'"

"Oh my goodness, sir. You're gonna *woo* me *shitless*?"

"Yes, I am, m'lady."

"Well, sir, I'm not completely sure I'm ready to be wooed shitless, to be perfectly honest. What would people say?"

"You don't get to decide. You're gettin' wooed shitless whether you like it or not."

My pulse is pounding in my ears.

"Okay. Quit stalling," Josh says. He motions to the game board again. "It's your turn. Play Scrabble, Kat."

I bite my lip and look at my tiles, considering my move. But none of the letters on my rack are calling to me, so I begin rearranging the tiles Josh used to spell W-O-O.

"No, babe, you're supposed to use new tiles from your—" Josh begins, but he abruptly stops talking when he sees the word I've spelled with his tiles.

"Ow," I say softly, reading the new word I've created.

Josh's face twists with what appears to be sincere remorse.

"You *really* hurt my feelings, Josh," I say. "I felt totally rejected—like I'm in this relationship all by myself."

Josh opens his mouth to speak but apparently thinks the better of it. He begins furiously peeking at the down-facing tiles on the table, apparently looking for something specific, and when he's found his desired tiles, he lays a word onto the game board: *S-O-R-R-A*.

"Sorra?" I ask.

Josh shrugs. "I couldn't find a 'Y.'"

I bite my lower lip, simultaneously amused and touched.

"I'm sorry, Kat," Josh says softly. "I didn't tell you about Seattle because there's something wrong with *me*—not because there's something wrong with *you*. You're perfect in every way. I just... " He looks up at the ceiling, apparently searching for the right words. "I just fucked up, that's all," he finally says matter-of-factly. "Because *I'm* fucked up—more than you know." He pauses. "More than I even realized."

I bite my lip and nod.

"And, in the interest of full disclosure, this probably won't be the last time I fuck up, either. I'm not sure exactly how or when I'll do it again, but I most certainly will. And when I do, please, just try to be patient with me. I'm trying my damnedest to 'overcome' every single day—I swear I am—and, mostly, I succeed. But sometimes, I can't seem to get out of my own way."

I swallow hard, stuffing down the fierce emotion rising up inside me.

Josh exhales. "I'm really, really sorry, Kat," he says, his blue eyes begging for forgiveness.

Oh, his eyes. I could get lost in those beautiful blue eyes forever. I begin hurriedly peeking at the undersides of tiles spread out on the table, looking for specific letters. Finally, when I've gathered almost everything needed, I lay my tiles down on the table: *I-F-O-R-G-V-U.*

Josh cocks his head to the side, looking at my tiles.

"I forgive you, Josh," I say. "But I'm too impatient to keep looking for the rest of the tiles."

Josh lets out a long, relieved exhale, and before I can say another word, he swipes the game board off the table, scattering tiles all over the floor, pulls me out of my chair, and proceeds to maul me.

"I'm so sorry," he breathes between voracious kisses.

"I forgive you," I say, my body exploding with desire.

"I'm not Garrett Bennetting you."

"I know. I'm sorry I said that."

"Never," he murmurs.

In a frenzy of heat, he pulls off my clothes and guides me onto the table on my back and begins covering my body with greedy kisses. He's everywhere, all at once. His lips are on my neck, and then my breast; my nipple's in his hungry mouth; his fingers are brushing lightly against my thigh and then across my hipbone. I arch my back with pleasure at the urgency of his touch, his mouth, his lips.

"I've been wrecked without you," he whispers.

"Me, too," I say. I breathe in his intoxicating scent and shudder with desire. "I was miserable."

"I wanna be with you when I move every fucking day," he says, and my clit zings like Josh just sucked on it.

I moan loudly, already on the edge of ecstasy.

"I can't stand being away from you, Kat. It *hurts*."

My clit flutters and ripples wildly with anticipation.

"Please, please don't ever shut me out again," he breathes.

"Josh," I blurt, my excitement beginning to boil over.

His tongue finds my clit and I arch my back, shoving myself into him urgently. He groans loudly, obviously enjoying my reaction, and the sound of his pleasure sends me over the edge. I let out a low growl as my body begins clenching and rippling ferociously into his mouth, and he responds with noises that quite clearly convey his excitement.

When I'm done climaxing, Josh begins working his way from my crotch toward my face with his tongue and lips. I'm writhing, moaning, out of my head with desire—his for the taking, in every conceivable way. When I feel his hard-on slide inside me and fill me up to the brim, I explode and melt at the same time. I reach around him and pull him into me by his muscled ass, attacking him with deep and passionate kisses. I throw my legs around his waist and lift my pelvis, synchronizing my movement with his, moaning like a cat in heat as he fucks me.

Josh presses his lips against my ear. "My heart is on the line, too," he whispers as his body rocks with mine.

I gasp and claw at his back, pulling him into me as deeply as I can, my heart and body bursting simultaneously.

"I was wrecked without you, babe. Don't do that to me again."

He pulls out of me, turns my twitching, trembling body around, and bends me over the table. In a flash, he's inside me again, pumping into me while kissing the back of my neck.

My body's on fire. My heart's racing. For the first time since I peed on that goddamned stick, I feel like me again.

"Don't leave me," he whispers hoarsely in my ear.

"I'm not going anywhere," I say, gasping for air.

"Don't cut me off again."

"I won't," I grit out, just as another orgasm rips through me. "I'm all yours, Josh. Oh my God. I'm all yours. *Fuck*."

He comes behind me, clutching me fiercely as he does, his fingers digging deeply into my flesh, and then we both collapse onto the table into a mangled, crumpled heap, mutually gasping for air.

When we've quieted down, he slides into his chair, his chest still heaving, and pulls me into his lap.

My chest is pressed against his.

My arms are wrapped around his neck.

I rest my cheek on his shoulder, breathing deeply, fighting to quell my sudden urge to bawl and/or barf all over him.

Finally, when I'm pretty sure I'm not gonna cry or hurl, I lift my cheek and look into his sparkling blue eyes. "Was that one of our boring 'real life' activities, Josh?" I ask.

Josh laughs and makes a face like I'm a total smart-ass.

"So what other boring 'real life' activities are on tap for the weekend, babe?" I ask.

Josh strokes my hair for a moment. "Well, tomorrow we're going hiking in Runyon Canyon and then I thought maybe we'd do a little grocery shopping and stop at the dry cleaners on the way home." He smirks. "And then I thought maybe we'd play some late-night backgammon while guzzling club soda—and then maybe binge watch *The Walking Dead.* You know, just normal, real-life stuff boring people in normal relationships do. No saving the world, no cocktails, no poker chips." He shrugs nonchalantly, but there's a wicked gleam in his eye.

Clearly, he's daring me to say, "Never mind what I said in front of the karaoke bar—gimme more of the Playboy Razzle-Dazzle, baby!" But, obviously, I can't say any such thing without Josh hopping up to make me a stiff drink. "Hmm," I say. "That all sounds super fun. I'm totally on board. I especially like this no-booze idea—good thinking. Maybe Boring Cameron Schulz was onto something."

Josh scowls.

"But *maybe* we don't have to be *so* disciplined about experiencing real life," I continue. "Maybe it wouldn't hurt if we mixed a tiny bit of *fantasy* in with our real-life activities?"

Josh raises an eyebrow. "Well, gosh, PG, I wouldn't want you to compromise your core values or anything."

I narrow my eyes and flare my nostrils at him.

He smirks.

"What about this?" I say. "What if we skip any and all mind-altering substances for, oh, I dunno, let's say a month, just for kicks—*but* we also continue fulfilling items on our fantasy-list? Kind of a nice middle-ground-approach, don't you think?"

Josh considers. "Kind of arbitrary cherry-picking of what we can and can't do, I'd say. If we're gonna do fantasies, why not have a cocktail while we do 'em? I've got a great recipe for a basil and lime margarita—"

"No," I blurt.

Josh looks at me quizzically.

Damn. How the heck am I going to convince Josh it's completely normal I don't want to drink? It's so unlike me as to be worrisome, I'm sure. "Absolutely no booze," I say. "As a fun challenge—to prove we don't need it to have a great time. Doesn't that sound fun?"

"No. Not at all."

"Well, I think it would be good for us."

Josh makes a face. "Why, exactly? I'm not sure I understand your thinking on this."

I scoff like it's totally self-explanatory, even though I'm shitting a brick. "So we know we can generate fun and excitement all by our little selves, Joshy Woshy. So we know we're addicted to *each other*, organically, with or without having beer goggles on."

"Beer goggles?" Josh says, incredulous. "You seriously think I'm attracted to you because I'm wearing *beer goggles*? Are you mad?"

I giggle. "Well, no. I don't think that."

"That's utterly ridiculous," he says emphatically. He touches the cleft on my chin with his fingertip. "But, okay, my batshit-crazy little terrorist. Your wish is my command, no matter how bizarre. No more booze for either of us for a month. Happy?"

"Yes, thank you," I say, exhaling with relief. Wow, I really am diabolical.

"But poker chips are okay, right?" he asks.

I smile. "Yes. I think we should *definitely* reintroduce poker chips into our fun."

"Well, all righty, then. Thank goodness for small mercies." Without hesitation, he stands up from his chair, taking my naked body along with him, and carries me like a baby monkey across the house, making me squeal. In the middle of the hallway, he stops at a closet and bends down to rummage for something (still holding my body wrapped around his), and when he stands upright again, he's got a poker chip trapped between his teeth.

I giggle and extract the poker chip from his mouth with my teeth.

"Come on, my little sex slave," Josh says, licking his lips. "I predict you'll be wearing a pair of soft cuffs in your immediate future."

Chapter 5
Kat

"Who are all the guys who'll be playing?" I ask. "Will Reed be there?"

It's Saturday morning and Josh and I are zooming down the freeway in his Lamborghini, en route to a park where Josh is meeting his buddies for their regular Saturday-morning game of flag football—another in a long line of "this-is-what-real-life-would-be-like-if-we-lived-in-the-same-city" activities Josh has planned for us this weekend.

"No, Reed won't be there," Josh says, steering his car onto an exit ramp. "He's in London with one of his bands. But Henn will be there, plus a bunch of our old fraternity brothers. And lots of guys bring random buddies or brothers to round out the teams."

"I'm excited to see Henny," I say.

"He said the same about you. You sure you won't get bored?"

"Are you kidding? It's gonna be real life, right? *Exciting.*"

Josh chuckles. "Well, if you change your mind and get bored out of your skull, you can always jog around the field and get in a workout. I won't be offended."

"Great," I say, even though I have no intention of jogging around the field. If I did, I'd almost certainly have to dart behind a bush to barf my lungs out by the second lap. "I'm sure I won't get bored, though," I add.

Josh slows the car and makes a right turn, and then another, and, all of a sudden, we're in the empty parking lot of a massive football stadium.

"Hey, I know this place," I say. I've never been to this particular stadium in person, but I've watched enough college football on TV to know it's the famed Rose Bowl—the legendary football stadium where UCLA plays its games. "You and your friends are playing flag football at the freaking *Rose Bowl*?" I ask, incredulous. "How? Are we gonna climb the fence and sneak in?"

Josh chuckles. "No, we're not gonna sneak in—I rented the place." He pulls his car into a parking spot and kills the engine.

"You *rented* the *Rose Bowl*?" I ask, my jaw hanging open.

"Yup."

I can't believe my ears. "Do you regularly rent the Rose Bowl for friendly games of flag football?"

"Nope. First time." He grins. "Actually, I rented the place specifically for *you*, Party Girl."

"For *me*?" I look at him dumbly.

Josh reaches across my body, opens his glove box, and pulls out a laminated ID badge attached to a lanyard. "How else am I gonna play in the Super Bowl?" he asks.

I touch the edge of the badge dangling from Josh's hand to stop it from twirling and gasp when I'm able to read the card. It's a press badge identifying me as "Heidi Kumquat, Reporter for ESPN," bearing the photo from my Oksana passport.

"Oh my God!" I squeal, my cheeks flushing. Just from this press badge alone, I know exactly what imaginary-porno Josh and I are about to act out.

But just in case I had a sliver of a doubt, Josh promptly lays a poker chip in my palm. "Hey, Heidi Kumquat. Guess what?" Josh says, a naughty smile dancing on his lips. "I hear the MVP of the Super Bowl has a thing for blondes—and a *really* big dick."

Chapter 6
Kat

"God, they're manly, aren't they?" Henn asks, surveying the action on the field. "Neanderthals, all of them."

"You sure you don't wanna play with them?" I ask, linking my arm in Henn's. "It looks pretty fun."

"You think *that* looks fun? Ha! No, I came to this barbaric game just to see you, Kitty Kat." Henn beams a smile at me that melts my heart like butter in a microwave.

"Aw, thanks, Henn."

Josh races past us on the field, cradling the football in his muscular arm. He evades a potential tackler, and then another, progressing at least twenty yards before being stopped.

Henn and I cheer like crazy and Josh looks over at us, pumping his fist.

"So what's new, Henny?" I ask. "You been working a lot?"

"Yeah, I just got back from D.C., working on our little case with the feds." He snickers. "Agent Eric asked me if you're single, bee tee dubs."

"What'd you tell him?"

Henn motions to Josh on the field. "Well, duh—I told him you're madly in love with the greatest guy ever."

I bite my lip but I don't deny it.

Henn grabs the "press badge" hanging around my neck. "Speaking of which, what the heck is this? 'Heidi Kumquat, Reporter for ESPN'? Josh asked me for your Oksana photo but he didn't tell me why he wanted it. Are you two crazy kids finding new and creative ways to take ol' one-eye to the optometrist or what?"

I decide to ignore his question. "Speaking of people falling

29

madly in love, how's it going with Hannah Banana Montana Milliken?" I ask.

Henn's face lights up. "Oh my God, she's incredible. She keeps doing this bizarre thing no other woman has ever done in the history of time—she's genuinely *nice* to me. Like, all the time."

"Wow. Cray," I say.

"Un-sane," Henn agrees, smiling adorably. "Did Hannah say anything to you about how things are going between us?"

"Yeah, she said you're the man of her dreams."

"Are you teasing me right now? Kat, please don't tease me."

"Henn, I swear on a stack of bibles. That's exactly what she said. 'The man of her dreams.'"

Henn looks like he could keel over with joy.

"Aw, you so deserve this, Henny," I say. "I'm so happy for you."

"Motherfucker!" Josh yells on the field after unsuccessfully trying to catch a long pass in the end zone. "That was my fault, bro," Josh shouts to his quarterback, patting his chest. He begins jogging back toward the line of scrimmage, but makes a sudden, lurching detour toward me on the sideline. With a loud growl, Josh throws his arms around my waist and twirls me around, making me shriek. "Hey there, Heidi Kumquat," Josh bellows. He lays an abrupt kiss on my mouth. "You know I'm trying to impress you, right?"

"You are?" I ask demurely.

"Is it working?"

"Definitely."

Josh laughs and trots away, leaving me swooning in his wake. Or, wait, maybe I'm not *swooning*—maybe I'm just queasy from being unexpectedly twirled around. I clamp my hand over my mouth, suddenly feeling the urge to heave.

"Hey, you okay?" Henn asks.

I take several deep breaths, trying to calm my churning stomach. "Yeah, I'm fine," I squeak out.

"You look like you feel sick," Henn says.

I swallow hard. "I'm just a little hung over, that's all."

"Ah, gotcha." Henn returns his attention to the action on the field, apparently completely convinced by my explanation.

For the next thirty minutes, Henn and I watch the action on the field, cheering and screaming as Josh and his friends play flag football as fiercely as any gladiators in ancient Rome, and when the game is finally done, Josh jogs over to Henn and me on the sideline. I'm expecting Josh to pick me up and whirl me around like he did earlier, but, instead, he whispers something to Henn, winks at me, and silently heads toward a tunnel on the opposite side of the field.

"Where's he going?" I ask Henn, admiring Josh's supremely bitable ass as he jogs away.

"To the locker room," Henn says. "He asked me to bring you there in five minutes."

"Oh, okay," I say, trying my best to sound nonchalant.

Henn shoots me a snarky look. "Josh had a message for you, bee tee dubs. He told me to tell Heidi Kumquat he's such a huge fan of your reporting for ESPN, he's decided to grant you an *exclusive* post-game interview.'"

Chapter 7
Kat

"Bye, Henn," I say, hugging him outside the locker room.

"Enjoy your optometry appointment," Henn says, snickering.

"Hey, man," I say. "Regular eye exams are critical to maintaining peak visual health."

Henn laughs. "Oh my God. You truly are the male version of Josh, you know that?"

"You think?" I ask.

"Indubitably." He hugs me again. "Bye, Kitty Kat."

I watch Henn walk away, sighing with my love for him, and when he turns the corner and disappears from sight, I open the locker room door and step inside, my skin buzzing with excitement. "Sports Reporter Bangs Super Bowl MVP in Locker Room After the Big Game" has been one of my top fantasies for a very long time—a go-to scenario I've thought about many, many times while pleasuring myself. I can't believe Josh has gone to such lengths to deliver it to me.

I begin walking slowly into the spacious locker room, my stomach bursting with butterflies, my crotch swelling with each step I take. I turn a corner around a bank of lockers, and—*boom*—there he is: the Super Bowl MVP himself, bending down to put something into a locker, his back to me.

Holy Beefcake, Batman. Josh is dressed in nothing but shoulder pads and tight football pants. His skin is gleaming with grime and sweat. Good lord, he's hot as hell—testosterone on a stick.

My phone buzzes in my pocket but I ignore it. Whoever it is can wait.

"Excuse me," I say softly. "Josh?"

Josh turns around and my heart palpitates—he's raw masculinity in its purest form.

"Yes?" Josh asks.

"Do you have time for an interview?" I hold up my badge to him. "Heidi Kumquat, ESPN."

Josh smiles and runs his hand through his sweaty hair, flashing me his "THE GUN SHOW" underarm-tattoo as he does. "Sure thing, Heidi. It would be my pleasure."

I motion behind me to my imaginary cameraman. "This is my cameraman, Brad."

Josh's eyes sparkle with obvious amusement. He looks over my shoulder to where I've indicated. "Hey, Brad," he says. He runs his hands over his muscled chest like he's lathering himself in the shower. "Ask me anything you want, Heidi—I'm all yours."

Oh, man, my body's having a physical, chemical reaction to this muscled, tattooed, sweaty man. My brain knows this is make-believe, of course, but my body apparently didn't get the memo.

My phone buzzes with another text but I ignore it.

"All mine, huh?" I say. "I like the sound of that."

"*And* I'll do the interview for you, too," Josh adds, his smile widening.

I return his smile. "Lemme just do my intro for the segment."

I turn away from Josh and look into the imaginary camera behind me, holding a pretend-microphone up to my mouth. "Hey, everyone. Heidi Kumquat for ESPN. I'm in the locker room with Josh Faraday, the star wide receiver for the Seahawks and the MVP of this year's Super Bowl. If you watched the game, then you know Josh well deserved his MVP honors—he was utterly brilliant out there today. Every man watching him wanted to be him, and every woman wanted to fuck the living hell out of him." I turn around and face Josh. "Ready?"

Josh's eyes are burning. "Why don't you start by asking me why I missed that one easy pass in the end zone?"

"Why'd you miss that one easy pass in the end zone, Josh?"

"'Cause I was looking at you. As it turns out, it's awfully hard to concentrate on catching a ball when you're thinking about fucking the smokin' hot blonde standing on the sideline a few yards away." He snaps the waistband of his tight football pants and my eyes are drawn to the hard bulge straining just below his hand.

I primly clear my throat. "Well, that's sweet of you to say. But I'd really better get to my interview."

"Of course. You're a professional—I admire that. Ask me anything, Heidi. I'm all yours."

My phone buzzes with another text. Hastily, I pull my phone out of my pocket, silence it, and shove it back into my pocket.

"Sorry about that," I say. "Well, first off, let me say congratulations on being named MVP of the game."

Josh flashes perfect, white teeth. "Thanks. But, you know, it was a total team effort." He runs his palm across his chiseled abs. "Damn, girl, you're something to look at, you know that? You're the kind of woman makes an MVP wanna *fuck*."

"Oh my goodness, thank you," I say demurely. "I'm flattered, but I really can't flirt with you, Josh. I've got a job to do."

"*Flirt* with me?" He smiles lasciviously. "You think I'm hard like this because I wanna *flirt* with you?" He makes an extremely sexual noise. "'Flirt' isn't the 'f' word I wanna do with you, Heidi."

I take a shaky breath and hold my imaginary microphone to my mouth. "Um." I swallow hard. "To what do you think you owe your success this season?"

Josh begins stroking the hard bulge straining behind his tight pants, his eyes smoldering. "I'd say the key to my success this season was just taking it one game at a time." His voice suddenly drops to a husky growl. "Shit, baby, you're making me hard as a rock. I can't even think straight, looking at you." He takes a step toward me and snakes his arm around my waist. "You've got beautiful eyes, you know that? I can't wait to watch 'em roll back into your head when I'm fucking you to within an inch of your life."

"Thank you. You have beautiful eyes, too."

Josh presses his hard-on into me. "Ever fucked the MVP of the Super Bowl, Heidi?"

I pretend to put my microphone to my lips again. "The Patriots definitely fought hard—"

Josh abruptly grabs my imaginary microphone and throws it forcefully across the room, making me laugh. "Interview over, Heidi," Josh says. "Time for the Super Bowl MVP to fuck you."

There's a beat.

I glance over my shoulder at my imaginary cameraman. "Beat it, Brad." I wait a moment to allow my imaginary cameraman to exit the locker room and then turn back to Josh. "You were saying?" I whisper.

Josh skims his lips against mine slowly. "I was saying I'm the MVP of the fucking Super Bowl, which means I can fuck any woman I want in the entire fucking world—and, baby, I want you. *Right fucking now.*"

My heart is pounding like crazy. "Oh, you think I'm gonna spread my legs and fuck you for no other reason than you're the Super Bowl MVP?" I whisper.

Josh presses his hard-on into me and levels me with blazing blue eyes. "No, baby, you're gonna spread your legs and fuck me because you're gonna enjoy sucking my dick so goddamned much."

Oh, he's good. He's very, very good.

Without further ado, Josh grips my hair and forcefully pushes me down to my knees—damn, the Super Bowl MVP's a bossy motherfucker—and a grand total of two seconds later, I'm on my knees, voraciously sucking the Super Bowl MVP's dick, making myself come like a freight train. Shortly after that, I'm dangling from a pull-up bar, my thighs resting on the Super Bowl MVP's shoulder pads, my pussy deep in his mouth, my flesh rippling against his lips and tongue. And after that, yep, the arrogant but sexy bastard called it—I'm spreading my legs for the Super Bowl MVP while getting fucked *hard,* until my eyes are rolling back into my head.

"Good times," Josh says after we're both done and completely spent. He spanks my ass playfully. "You wanna join me in the shower, Heidi?"

"I'll be right there. I'm gonna check my phone real quick. I got a couple texts."

"Okeedoke," Josh says. He turns around, flashing me his YOLO'd ass, and practically skips toward the showers. "Hey, a bunch of guys went for burgers and beers nearby. You wanna meet up with them?"

"Sounds great," I say. I bend down to grab my phone out of my jeans on the floor.

"All my friends thought you were awesome, by the way," Josh calls over his shoulder. "A couple of them said before today they were already on the cusp of hating my guts, and now, after meeting you, they absolutely do." He laughs heartily.

But I'm not listening to Josh any more. I'm looking at my phone, reeling, trying desperately not to freak out that every single member of my family except Colby has been furiously trying to reach me for the past thirty minutes. What on earth has happened? And why everyone *except Colby*?

"Oh my God! Josh!" I shriek, clutching my throat. "I think something's happened to Colby!"

Chapter 8
Josh

"I'm here to see my brother Colby Morgan," Kat says to the woman sitting behind the desk in the hospital lobby.

Poor Kat. When she called her mom and found out what had happened to Colby, I had to physically hold her up so she wouldn't crumple onto the cement floor of the locker room.

"Oh, the firefighter," the woman at the desk says, clicking on her computer keyboard. She looks at Kat sympathetically. "I saw what your brother did on the news. He's a real hero. We're all praying for him and that little baby he saved."

Kat lets out a little yelp.

"He's in the burn unit, room 402. Do you know where that is?"

Kat shakes her head and a pained sound escapes her throat.

"Just go down this hall and take the elevators to the fourth floor," the nurse continues. "When you get off the elevator, check in at the nurses' station there and someone will show you to his room. It's a restricted area."

Kat nods, apparently unable to speak.

"Thank you," I say, answering for Kat. I put my arm around her shoulders and usher her toward the elevators. "Come on, babe."

Kat nuzzles her nose into my shoulder as I lead her limp body down the hallway—and by the time Kat and I reach the fourth floor, I'm just about carrying Kat's full body weight in my arms.

"We're here to see Colby Morgan," I say to the nurse at the fourth-floor desk, my arm around Kat's shoulders.

"Are you family?" the nurse asks.

"Yes, this is Colby's sister," I say.

"And you?" the nurse asks me. "Are you family, too—are you her husband?"

For some reason, I feel like this nurse just punched me in the balls. "No," I say, my throat tight.

"He's my boyfriend, " Kat chokes out.

I nod and pull her closer to me. That was the first time Kat's called me her boyfriend—but it's hardly the time or place for me to feel excitement about that milestone.

"I'm sorry," the nurse says. "Only immediate family is allowed in the room for now. There've been a lot of people wanting to see your brother—reporters, other firefighters, well wishers—even the Mayor came by. We're gonna have to stick to the rules, at least until we get clearance from the doctor."

Kat looks stricken. "But," she begins, "Josh is my *boyfriend*." She grips my arm.

The nurse shakes her head. "I'm sorry. Your boyfriend will have to wait out here until I get clearance for non-family members. There are a lot of people already in the room—you've got a big family."

When the nurse uses the word "family," Kat looks toward the hallway with undisguised longing.

"Go ahead," I say, squeezing Kat's shoulders. "Go be with your family, babe. I'll wait out here."

Kat looks like a deer in headlights.

"Go on," I say, stroking Kat's golden hair. "I'll be right here." The truth is I don't want to leave Kat's side—I want to go with her and hold her through whatever awaits her in that room. But, obviously, my only job in this horrible situation is to make this as easy on Kat as possible. "Go on," I say softly.

Kat hugs me and I breathe her in for a moment.

"I'll be right here if you need me," I whisper.

Kat nods and the nurse wordlessly guides her down the hallway through swinging doors marked "Authorized Personnel Only." I watch her through glass panes in the doors as long as possible, until, finally, she and the nurse turn a corner and disappear.

With a deep sigh, I wander down the hall and take a seat in the waiting room. Shit. I feel like I've let Kat down somehow. When the nurse asked if I was family—if I'm her husband—should I have lied and said yes? I really don't think I was imagining the pained look in Kat's eyes when I said no. Why the fuck do I feel like I've somehow fucked up?

An older gentleman with a young woman and toddler are seated across from me in the waiting room. The trio's got the exact same features—same eyes, noses, dark hair. They're like generational Russian nesting dolls—even a casual onlooker would know instantly the three of them are family.

Family.

The nurse asked me if I'm Kat's family and I said no.

I put my head in my hands.

I've got the distinct feeling I've fucked up somehow, but I'm not sure how.

Are you her family? Are you her husband?

I really don't think I was imagining the look of utter disappointment on Kat's face at that moment.

A tidal wave of loneliness rises up inside me—an all-too familiar emotion for me. My eyes water but I swallow hard and stuff it down like I always do. Fuck. This isn't about me. This is about Colby and Kat and her family.

What I need to do is make myself useful, however I can.

I bow my head, close my eyes, and clasp my hands.

Dear Heavenly Father...

I take a deep breath.

Dear Heavenly Father...

I lift my head and open my eyes.

Fuck me.

The only prayer that's coming into my mind is so full of motherfucking expletives, I can't imagine it would help Colby at all.

Chapter 9
Josh

For the past hour, Kat's been in Colby's hospital room with her family while I've been sitting out here in this waiting room, listening to "Hold Back the River" by James Bay on my phone, trying my damnedest not to cry or, worse, catch Spanish Influenza from the cocksucker who sat down two seats away from me in an almost-empty waiting room and proceeded to cough up his goddamned lung.

From what I've gathered, Typhoid Joe was deemed "too sick" to go into the room of whatever patient he came to visit in the hospital, but rather than go home and take some fucking Nyquil, he decided to sit two feet away from me and try to take me down with him. Motherfucker. Of course, I moved as far away from him as I could in the tiny room, but just the sound of his constant hacking is making me feel like I'm hurtling to my premature demise on a bullet train.

Or maybe I'm just losing my mind.

I pull my earphones out of my ears and, for the second time since sitting down in this waiting room, bow my head in prayer. *Heavenly Father who art in heaven, please, I beg you, stop fucking with everyone I—*

My phone buzzes with a text that makes me open my eyes.

It's Jonas. "I CAN'T SLEEP!" he writes.

"Why, hello, Jonas," I write, smiling at the screen. "Why can't you sleep, bro? Could it be... SARAH?"

"YES!!!!! Today's finally the day!!!!" he writes—and, of course, I know he's referring to the fact that today he's finally gonna take his "Magnificent Sarah" to the top of Mount Olympus, push the poor girl off the edge of it, and ask her to be his wife.

"What time is it over there?" I type.

Lauren Rowe

"Almost 4:00 a.m."

I look at my watch and do a quick calculation. They're ten hours ahead.

"Are you just getting to bed or just waking up?" I write.

"Been lying here wide awake for hours while Sarah's been sleeping next to me, blissfully unaware my every happiness hangs in the fucking balance today. FUCK ME! I can't stop thinking about my big speech."

"Your big speech?" I write, chuckling to myself. "WTF. No big speech required, bro. Just say, 'Will you marry me, Sarah Cruz?' Easy-peasy."

"No, you DUMBSHIT. Any man who says 'Will you marry me?' and nothing more when asking the woman of his dreams to be his wife is a DUMBSHIT of epic proportions. Either that, or he fundamentally doesn't understand what makes women tick."

"Jonas," I write, rolling my eyes. "Don't make poor Sarah listen to a long, drawn-out speech or she's gonna jump off the mountain before you push her off just to get the fuck away from you." I laugh out loud as I press send.

"I don't need your advice this time, Josh. I got this," Jonas replies. "I can't ask Sarah to marry me without telling her WHY I'm asking her to be my wife or I'd never be able to look myself in the fucking mirror ever again. She's the goddess and the muse, Josh. She deserves to know that—and to understand WHY."

"Dude. First off, the all-caps are totally unnecessary. You're hurting my ears. Second off, you're overthinking this. Make it memorable, sure. Sweep her off her feet, absolutely. But too much talking and poetry and babbling about 'goddess and muse' shit and she's gonna think you've got a fucking vagina."

"Josh, please trust me, just this once I know more about something than you do. SO FUCK OFF."

"Testy, testy," I write. "Okay, okay. I'm hereby officially fucking off. Hey, can you talk instead of texting? My fingers are getting tired."

"No. Sarah's lying on my chest, fast asleep. I don't wanna wake her. So enough about me and my soon-to-be-fiancée (I HOPE AND PRAY)." He attaches a praying-hands emoji. "How's everything with you?"

40

I sigh, considering my reply. On our flight to Seattle earlier, Kat and I agreed not to mention the Colby situation to Sarah (and therefore not to Jonas, either).

"Knowing Sarah, she'd drop everything and immediately fly back to Seattle to be with me," Kat said during our conversation on the plane. "I'd never do that to her—or to poor Jonas. He's been planning this proposal for weeks."

"Agreed," I replied to Kat. "We'll tell them both what's going on when they get home. Hopefully, by then, Colby will be up and around and feeling like himself again."

Kat looked out the window of the airplane, her beautiful face etched with anxiety. "I pray that's true, Josh."

I quickly tap out my reply to Jonas' question: "Everything's good here." I give him a quick update on the refurb-job I'm overseeing for our twenty gyms and also regarding the buy-out of our shares of Faraday & Sons. "Oh, and escrow closed on my Seattle house yesterday," I type. "I'm officially your neighbor. I clocked it the other day and it takes exactly eleven minutes to drive from my house to yours."

"Awesome," Jonas writes. "So when do you think you'll move in?"

"Three or four weeks at most," I write. "Don't forget to send me a housewarming gift. Patron is greatly appreciated."

"Pretty weird you didn't tell Kat you're moving," Jonas writes. "She looked really upset about it at the karaoke bar."

My stomach twists at the memory of that horrible night. "Yeah, thanks for blabbing about that, motherfucker. That was super awesome."

"How the fuck was I supposed to know you hadn't told Kat you're moving? And why exactly didn't you mention it to her, btw? I'm still not sure I understand your thinking on that."

"I just didn't wanna get her hopes up," I write, but even as I tap out the words, I know they're douchey.

"Well, mission accomplished, huh? I'd say Kat's hopes are definitely way, way down."

I roll my eyes. Does my brother really need to remind me how badly I fucked up with Kat? That's *my* job—to remind Jonas when *he* fucks up with women.

41

"Was Kat really pissed at you?" Jonas writes.

"Worse than pissed. Crushed," I write, my heart squeezing.

"Poor Kat," Jonas writes. "The Faraday brothers strike again."

"More like DAD strikes again," I write. "He's the gift that keeps on giving."

"No shit," Jonas writes. "I don't know how either of us is ever supposed to know what's normal behavior when it comes to women. You, especially. He fucked with your head the most."

"My head? No way," I write. "You got it way worse than me, bro. Ten times worse."

"I don't think so. He hated my guts, but he loved you. Is it better to be told you're worthless every fucking day of your life or that you're better than everyone else? Either way, you're fucked. At least I got to escape to the 'treatment center' for months at a time over the years. You were stuck there with him, day after fucking day."

I stare at my phone. I've never thought about it that way. Holy shit. I think Jonas might have a point. I was Dad's golden boy, his heir to the Faraday throne, and Jonas and I both knew it. All these years I've felt guilty to have garnered so much of Dad's favor and attention—but did I actually draw the short straw, after all?

"You might have a point," I write. "I never thought about it like that."

"I've got more than a point. I'm right as rain. I'm the smart twin, remember? Never doubt me."

"You wish."

"Hey, I'm not the one who didn't tell my hot girlfriend I'm moving to her city," Jonas writes. "DUMBSHIT."

I scowl at my phone. Jonas knows I've got no comeback to that. "Yeah, I fucked up," I write.

"So did Kat break up with you when she found out?" Jonas writes.

"No, but almost," I write. "I salvaged it. I made her play Scrabble with me until she forgave me."

"Scrabble?" Jonas writes.

"Fun game, as it turns out, if you get creative with your words."

"Hmm. I see what you mean. I'm already thinking about all sorts of four-letter words I could play."

"There you go."

"So everything's good now?" Jonas writes. "Kat's happy again?"

Typhoid Joe coughs violently across the waiting room and I momentarily look up from my phone. Fuck me. I hate not telling Jonas what's going on with Colby. I never hide stuff from Jonas. But there's no fucking way I'm gonna throw a dark cloud over the biggest day of my brother's life.

"Everything's great," I write.

"Good. Don't fuck it up again, Josh. Kat's a great girl."

"I'll do my best. The question is whether I can avoid fucking it up when I don't realize I'm fucking it up?"

"I feel you. Just think, 'What Would Dad Do?' and then do the opposite," Jonas writes. "That's pretty much my true north."

"Good advice."

"Hey, so what's up with the MacKenzie deal for F&S?" Jonas writes. "Last loose end. Dying to make that fucker go away."

"Dude. I don't give a shit about the MacKenzie deal or anything else relating to F&S," I write. "That place can burn to the ground as far as I'm concerned. Sayonara, fucker."

"I'd agree if it weren't for Uncle William. We can't leave him hanging. Plus, the payday on the buy-out's gonna be sweet if we set it up right."

I pause. Jonas is right. The MacKenzie deal itself isn't that rich, but we each stand to net close to half a billion in cash in the buy-out of Faraday & Sons by a huge conglomerate if we leave the company on strong legs, everything in place. "Okay," I tap out. "I'll work up the MacKenzie deal this week and put it to bed."

"Thanks," Jonas writes. "I'd do it myself but Sarah would kill me if I worked while we're in Greece."

"No. Don't do a fucking thing. Just get engaged and bang your new fiancée every which way for the rest of the trip. I'll handle it."

"Roger that. Thanks, Josh."

"Now get some sleep, bro. You've got a big day tomorrow."

"Today, actually. I'm ten hours ahead."

"Oh yeah. Well, get some sleep, either way," I write.

"I don't sleep, remember? Sarah says I'm a droid."

"Man, she's got you pegged."

"In more ways than one." He attaches a smiley-face emoji.

I roll my eyes. "Try to sleep for a bit, Jonas. You gotta be bright-eyed and bushy-tailed when you bore Sarah to fucking tears at the top of Mount Olympus."

"I'm not gonna bore Sarah to fucking tears at the top of Mount Olympus, motherfucker—I'm gonna bore her to fucking tears on the shore of the Aegean down below."

"Either way, you need to rest up so you can bore her to fucking tears EXCELLENTLY, wherever the fuck you do it."

"I sense mockery in that all-caps word."

"Correct, sir."

"Oh man, I'm so excited," Jonas writes. "I'm about to become the happiest asshole-motherfucker alive."

"So you keep telling me, Jonas. Over and over and over."

"Sorry. I'm just so happy. It's a new feeling for me. I don't quite know how to handle it."

I grin broadly at that. "I'm happy for you, Jonas. It's pretty crazy. I never thought I'd see the day when either of the Faraday boys would ask a woman to be his wife. You're shocking the hell out of me, actually."

"I'm shocking the hell out of myself. It's awesome! Hey, you think maybe you'll shock the hell out of us, too? And maybe soon?" He adds a winking emoji and a cat.

"Hell no. Asking any woman to be my wife isn't in my life plan, dude—even a woman as awesome as Kat. You'll just have to represent for both of us."

"With pleasure," Jonas writes. "I can't wait to call Sarah my wife."

I roll my eyes again. "Good night, Jonas. Have fun tomorrow (today). Text me right after you ask her. I'll drink a shot of Patron in your honor."

"I will. Well, actually, I won't text you RIGHT after I ask her, if you know what I mean." He attaches another winking emoji and a muscled-arm emoji.

I chuckle. My brother is such a dork. "Hey, Casanova," I type. "What's with all the emojis? I didn't know you even knew what emojis were."

"I didn't until recently, but Sarah uses them all the time. Funny, right?"

I chuckle. What has this woman done to my dorky-ass brother? Jesus God. She's made him even dorkier than ever.

"Get some sleep, Mr. Emoji," I write.

He sends me a thumbs-up emoji in reply and I laugh.

"Josh."

I look up from my phone to find Kat walking into the waiting room, her face stained with tears. I leap up from my chair, instantly twitching with dread. Oh fuck, please God, don't let Kat be here to tell me Colby's dead.

Kat beelines to me and, without saying a word, throws her arms around my neck, presses her body into mine, and loses herself to wracking sobs.

Chapter 10
Josh

I wrap Kat in a tight embrace and hold her to me for several minutes, kissing her hair, rubbing her back, my heart pounding in my ears, dreading whatever's about to come out of her mouth.

Finally, Kat breaks away from me, wiping her eyes. "Sorry," she says. She pulls me down to sitting. "I've been holding it together pretty well for my mom, but seeing your face made me lose—" She suddenly clamps her hand over her mouth.

"Kat?" Holy shit. She seriously looks like she's about to hurl. "*Kat?*" I ask again, my skin prickling. I've never seen someone react to grief by throwing up before.

Kat takes a few deep breaths and groans like she's eaten a piece of rancid meat.

"Are you okay?" I ask, the hairs on my arms standing on end.

Kat makes a face I can't interpret and takes another deep breath. "I'm okay," she mumbles.

Typhoid Joe across the room lets out a hacking cough and Kat grimaces.

"How's Colby?"

"The tests came back and it was pretty much all good news, relatively speaking. Broken leg, ribs, and collarbone. Ruptured spleen. Smoke inhalation—but not too bad, thank God. He suffered some burns to his left side where the beam was crushing him, but his turnout gear protected him pretty well. Could have been a whole lot worse. No head trauma at all, thank God." She takes a deep breath. "It's gonna be a long road to recovery—lots of physical therapy. But he's gonna pull through."

I exhale with relief.

"But the baby Colby went back in to save?" Kat says, tears flooding her eyes. "She just died in her mother's arms in the pediatric unit."

"Oh no," I say softly, my heart dropping into my toes.

"Her parents came to Colby's room to thank him for what he did to try to save her. He wasn't conscious so they thanked my parents." Tears are streaming out of Kat's eyes and down her cheeks. "They said they were grateful to my brother for giving them the chance to hold their little angel one last time and say goodbye. Oh my God, it ripped everyone's heart out, Josh. All of us were crying, even Ryan, and he never cries."

I nod, incapable of speaking.

Kat inhales sharply again and suddenly clamps her hand to her mouth. "Shit," she mumbles. She leaps out of her chair and sprints to the bathroom across the hall, her body jerking with loud heaves as she runs.

What the fuck? Kat's puking *again*? I've never seen someone react to grief by puking before—and this is the second time today (the first time being in the locker room immediately after Kat talked to her mom about Colby). Does she have food poisoning?

Typhoid Joe coughs loudly again on the far side of the waiting room, jerking me out of my thoughts, and I share a "this guy's gonna infect us all" look with the young woman sitting across from me.

After a few minutes, Kat returns from the bathroom, her face pale. "Sorry about that," she says.

"Do you always react this way to extreme stress?" I ask.

"What way—by crying?"

"No, by barfing."

Kat twists her mouth.

"Do you think maybe you have the stomach flu or something?" I ask.

There's a long beat. Kat takes a deep breath and flaps her lips on her exhale.

"Shit," she says. She shakes her head like she knows she's about to say something highly regrettable. "Life is so funny. Before today, I thought I had the weight of the world on my shoulders—I really did—or, I guess, on my *uterus*." She snorts to herself. "And now, all of a sudden, my supposedly huge problem doesn't seem like that big a deal."

Wait. Did Kat just say she thought she had the weight of the world on her *uterus?* I open and close my mouth, but I'm too freaked out to link coherent words together. Does that mean . . ?

Kat levels me with a firm gaze. "Yeah, I'm pregnant, Josh," she says evenly.

The room warps. I can't breathe. *No.* Blood rushes into my ears in a loud whoosh.

"I'm sorry to tell you so bluntly, but there's really no other way." She clears her throat. "I'm pregnant with your accidental Faraday." She shakes both fists in the air in mocking celebration. "*Yay.*"

There's got to be some mistake. Kat said she was on the pill. *Holy fucking shit, Kat said she was on the fucking pill!*

"I didn't do it on purpose," Kat continues calmly. "I swear to God, Josh, this isn't a case of a 'gold digger' trying to 'trap' you. It was a complete accident—an honest mistake."

My heart is palpitating wildly. I clutch my chest. I feel like I'm having a heart attack.

"I missed a pill one of the days we were in Vegas," she continues, "but only because the days and nights blurred together so much while we were there—remember that? And the minute I realized I'd messed up, I immediately took the missing pill. And I really thought everything was okay—I really did, Josh—but just to be sure, I took a pregnancy test a few days after I got home and it was negative, so I figured we were in the clear." She grimaces. "But then I started feeling sick and my nipples were sore and then I barfed out of nowhere so I took another test, and lo and behold..." She exhales loudly and shrugs. "I'm rambling—sorry. The bottom line is I'm pregnant with your mighty spawn and I didn't do it on purpose—I swear to God on a stack of bibles—and I'm really, really sorry."

I feel like I'm gonna hurl. This seriously can't be happening.

"I'm not looking to trap you into anything," Kat says, her blue eyes flickering with obvious anxiety. "Nothing needs to change between us. We'll just, you know, keep doing what we're doing—and, at some point, we'll, you know, happen to have a baby together."

I open and shut my mouth, willing myself to speak, but nothing comes out. That was the stupidest thing I've ever heard anyone say in my life. *Nothing needs to change? We'll just keep doing what we're doing and one day we'll happen to have a baby?* Did she really just say that to me? Is she high?

Typhoid Joe begins coughing and sniffling loudly and I look at the guy, willing him to keel over and fucking die.

Shit. This can't be happening.

I stare at the toddler sitting across from me for a moment. Kat's growing one of *those* inside her body—and it's a *Faraday*? I run my hands through my hair. This is a fucking nightmare—the one thing I was never supposed to do. Oh my God. How many times did Dad tell me not to make a Faraday unworthy of my name and bank account? A Faraday has to be *planned*. A Faraday has to be on *purpose*. "If you're not careful, you'll wind up having a crazy-ass kid like Jonas with some gold digger you don't give two shits about," my father used to say.

Kat clears her throat. "So are you gonna say something or what?"

The room is closing in on me. I can't breathe. I open my mouth and close it, yet again. *Fuck.* How many times did my dad make me *swear* I'd never bring an accidental Faraday into the world? How many times did he fill me with the fear of God about some scheming gold digger using a baby to trap me into making her a part of our "empire"?

Kat shakes her head, obviously annoyed by my silence. "Say something," she says softly. But when I don't speak, her entire body stiffens with defiance. "I'm not gonna get an abortion, if that's what you're thinking."

I don't know what in my facial expression made Kat think I was about to ask her for an abortion—because I wasn't. I went to St. Francis Academy growing up, for fuck's sake. Some things are just too deeply ingrained to change.

"Say something, Josh," Kat pleads, her eyes glistening. "You're killing me, Smalls."

"I..." I stammer. "I would never ask you to... get rid of it. That's not at all what I'm thinking."

"Then what are you thinking?"

Fuck me. I have no idea what I'm thinking, other than "How the fuck did this happen to me?" Every single fuck of my life, without exception, from minute one, I've practiced safe sex. Kat's the first woman I've ever fucked without a rubber—*ever*—and now she's *pregnant*?

"Hey, look on the bright side," Kat says. "It's still early yet. The pregnancy might not stick."

"What do you mean?" I ask dumbly.

"There's a relatively high chance of miscarriage during the first trimester," she says, shrugging her drooping shoulders. "Especially, I'd assume, when you ply the poor little thing with booze, pot, and blinding orgasms on a Sybian."

I put my head in my hands. Holy shit. This is a nightmare. I can't believe she forgot to take her pill. I trusted her and she totally blew it. All of a sudden, I can hear my dad's voice as surely as if he were standing an inch away from me, pressing his lips against my ear. *I'll get the last laugh on that gold digger's ass and disown you faster than she can demand a paternity test.*

"You're sure it's mine?" I blurt.

Kat clenches her jaw. "I'm sure."

"I'm sorry," I say. "I just meant... how far along are you? That's what I meant to ask. I know you were with Cameron the week before me, so..." I abruptly shut my mouth. Oh shit. She looks like she's about to stab me.

"It's yours, Josh." Her eye twitches. "That was a low blow."

"I'm sorry," I say, my heart exploding. "That came out wrong." I cover my ears with my palms. I can't stop hearing my father's voice screaming at me.

The toddler in the waiting room shouts something to his mother about wanting a box of raisins and she gently shushes him. Oh shit. I'm gonna have a kid who screams about raisins in a hospital waiting room?

When my gaze returns to Kat, she's looking at me with steely eyes. "Your father really did a number on you, didn't he?" she says.

I can't reply.

"So are you gonna say something besides asking me if it's yours?" Kat asks. "Because if not, I'm gonna head back into Colby's room and be with my family."

I swallow hard. "How far along are you?" I ask. "That's all I meant to ask, Kat. I wasn't implying..." I trail off.

"I'm about seven weeks, I think," she says. "Maybe eight. But the whole counting thing is kind of confusing—the minute you miss your period, you're already considered four or five weeks pregnant—but since I haven't been having periods, I'm not completely sure yet. I'll know more when I have a sonogram, probably next week."

A nurse walks by in the hallway, her shoes squeaking on the linoleum and we both look toward the noise for a moment.

"Cameron and I used a condom," Kat continues, sounding like she's ordering a hit. "And I was with Cameron way before the timeframe, anyway. I'm one hundred percent positive it's yours. But I'd be happy to take a paternity test if you have a shred of doubt. Actually, fuck it, I'll take one, anyway, just so you never have room to doubt." Oh man, she sounds like a cold-blooded killer right now.

"I know it's mine," I say. "I'm sorry. I didn't mean to ask that. It just slipped out."

Kat sniffs the air, utterly pissed. "You're entitled to ask. But I'm telling you there's no doubt in my mind whatsoever. You're the only man I've been with." She grits her teeth. "We're exclusive and I don't cheat. But, like I say, I'll get a paternity test. No problem."

I've got goose bumps. She looks really scary right now, like she's sharpening her blade to cut off my balls and smash them between graham crackers.

"I don't doubt you," I say. "I know you've only been with me. I've only been with you, too."

"I guess you're thinking I'm some sort of gold digger who's trying to trick you into marriage, just like your father warned you against." She rolls her eyes. "But I swear to God that's the furthest thing from my—"

"We should get married," I blurt suddenly.

Kat stops talking and stares at me, her blue eyes wide.

There's a long beat during which we could hear a pin drop if it weren't for the loud hacking noises coming from Typhoid Joe on the other side of the room.

"What?" Kat says. She looks at me like I've screamed, "I'm a merman!"

"We should get married," I say softly, my heart pounding in my ears, my stomach churning. Oh my God. I can't believe I just said those words. I feel like I'm gonna throw up. I wait for a moment, fully expecting Kat to burst into happy tears and shout, "Yes!" But she doesn't. She just glares at me silently, her blue eyes on icy fire. "Well?" I ask, unable to keep the testiness out of my voice. Why does she look like she wants to clobber me instead of kiss me? Honestly, she should be crying with gratitude and relief right now—she's the one who forgot to take her goddamned fucking pill, not me, so she's got no right to be thinking up ways to detach my balls from my body. "I just asked you to marry me, Kat," I say, my tone impatient. "I'm doing the noble thing here. I think you should at least do me the courtesy of a reply."

Kat smiles thinly—but it's clearly a "fuck you" kind of a smile.

There's a long, silent, excruciating beat.

To be perfectly honest, Kat's starting to piss me off. For fuck's sake, I'm a fucking *Faraday* and I just offered to marry her—how the fuck is she not leaping at the chance? I'm doing the right thing, without hesitation or waffling, despite the fact that, as I've mentioned to her *quite clearly*, marriage isn't something I've *ever* contemplated doing before this very moment *and* despite the fact that she's the one who fucked up here, not me. I'd say I deserve a fucking medal, not the daggers Kat's throwing at me with her eyes. If my dad were here watching this exchange, I can only imagine how that vein in his neck would be bulging with fury.

"You want me to reply?" Kat says coldly.

I nod—but by the tone of Kat's voice, I'm not so sure.

"Okay, then I will." She shifts her weight in her chair, obviously gearing up to decimate me. "Thank you for your *noble* proposal of marriage, good sir. That was an *admirable* thing to do. You really should feel quite *proud* of yourself for displaying such unimpeachable *integrity* and *bravery* in the face of such horrific and victimizing circumstances."

Jesus fucking Christ. Only Kat could make a whole bunch of words generally regarded as complimentary sound like a string of curse words.

"I didn't expect you to ask me to marry you," she continues. "Not in a million years. I'm genuinely impressed with how quickly you rose to what you perceive to be your *obligation*. Thank you for that, good sir."

I nod. That's right. I rose to my obligation. But I'm confused. Kat's words and body language are completely at odds. It feels like she's doing that licking-and-punching-my-balls-thing she always does. And why the fuck does she keep talking like she's in a miniseries on fucking PBS?

"*But*," Kat adds, her voice prim, "although I'm infinitely *grateful* to you for swooping in to *save* me from this incredible cluster-fuck of a situation that will surely heap shame and disgrace upon my family's good name, I think I'll have to politely decline your *kind* and *generous* offer, good sir." Kat grits her teeth again. "I think I'd rather take my chances, however slim, that there might be a man out there who'll one day ask me to marry him simply because he's fallen head over heels in *love* with me to the point of actually *wanting* to marry me, the crazy son of a bitch, despite the fact that, by that time, I'll be the mother of *another man's goddamned kid*."

I blink quickly. What the fuck did Kat just say to me? Motherfucker! Did Kat just break up with me to marry some other hypothetical guy—*and with my fucking kid in tow*?

"Excuse me?" I say, suddenly enraged.

"You heard me," Kat says, jutting her chin at me. "I said *no*."

"What the fuck, Kat!" I bark, rising out of my seat. I know I'm talking way too loudly for this small waiting room but I can't control myself. "You can't say something like that to me—I'm a fucking Faraday!"

Kat looks around the waiting room, obviously embarrassed. "Sit down, Josh. Jesus."

I glower over her for a moment longer, but then I sit, clenching my jaw.

"You can't say shit like that to me," I grit out in a hoarse whisper. "Now's not the time to be a terrorist, Kat. You're pregnant with my kid—so don't talk to me about running off into the sunset with some other guy. You're *my* Party Girl with a Hyphen and you're not marrying some other guy with my goddamned kid in tow." I take a deep breath. "Now I'm gonna ask you one more fucking time—and this is the last time I'm gonna ask you, so don't blow it." My nostrils flare. "Will. You. *Fucking*. Marry. Me?"

Kat's lip curls with blatant disgust. "*Nooooooo*," she says, forming the long "O" sound like she's falling down a thirty-foot well.

"What the fuck?" I say. I still can't believe I'm hearing her right. "*No*?"

"*No*." She squints her eyes like she's taking aim with a shotgun. "Noooooooooooooooooo," she says again, this time emphasizing the "O" sound like she's falling down a *fifty*-foot well. "Thank you very much for being such a duty-bound gentleman, good sir," she says through gritted teeth. "Believe me, I know you're doing me a *huge* frickin' favor—a *massive fucking favor*—especially since you're a *Faraday* and my family is but an assemblage of lowly commoners without a noble title to our shameful name. Goodness, I really, really appreciate your infinite *generosity* good sir." She rolls her eyes. "But no fucking thank you, Sir J.W. Faraday. This isn't 1815. I'd rather just figure my shit out on my own and roll the dice that even a harlot from a simple family of *serfs* might one day get to marry for *love* instead of motherfucking *obligation*."

I make a face registering my disbelief. "You're kidding, right?"

Kat shakes her head. "No, sir. I am not."

I leap up again, pulling at my hair in frustration, and immediately sit back down. Goddamn, this woman. When that nurse said I couldn't accompany Kat to Colby's room because I'm not fucking *family*, Kat looked at me in that moment like she would have given *anything* in the world to call me her husband—I'm positive I didn't imagine those puppy-dog eyes she flashed at me—and now that I've asked her to marry me only sixty minutes later, she's turning me the fuck down? The woman's deranged. What *sane* woman would ever dream of turning me down?

For fuck's sake, I'm a thirty-year-old with over six hundred million dollars to my personal name—I'm talking *personally* here—and that's not even including unvested shares in Faraday & Sons that will soon be coming my way to the tune of half a billion bucks if we play our cards right—or the eight hundred million bucks my uncle has told Jonas and me he's earmarked for us in his will. And on top of all that, I'm not exactly Quasimodo to look at, either, let's just be real—not to mention the fact that I've got a magic cock and I make the woman come like a fucking freight train every time I fucking *glance* at her. *And she's turning me the fuck down?*

"Kat, don't be a fucking terrorist right now," I say, my voice filled with barely contained rage. "Think about what you're doing."

"Oh, you want me to *think*?" she says. "Am I having trouble *thinking*—perhaps due to the pregnancy hormones, good sir?"

I throw up my hands. "Would you stop calling me 'good sir'? You're annoying the shit out of me. Look, the bottom line is you're having my baby, Kat, and it should have my name."

Kat crosses her arms and leans back in her chair. "Fine. The baby can have your name. Happy?"

I'm stunned. "Well, no. I mean the baby should have my name and so should you—the mother of my child. We should be, you know, a unit—a legal unit."

"Aw, you think so? You think 'the mother' should take your name because that's the way we 'should' do it so we can be a 'legal unit'?" She scoffs. "How sweet."

I nod, not understanding her reaction in the slightest. "That's right."

"You really think so?"

I nod again. Why the fuck is she reacting like this? If anyone should be mad it's *me*. Kat's the one who didn't take her goddamned pill. And now we both have to pay for her mistake for the rest of our lives. Under the circumstances, I think I'm behaving exceedingly well.

"You think we *should,* Josh?" She glares at me like she's laced my iced tea with arsenic and she's waiting for me to keel over. "Golly gosh, Joshua, I truly appreciate your incredible sense of *duty.* You're a man of endless integrity, through and through (and, actually, I'm serious about that, even though I'm pissed at you—you really *are* a man of integrity). But I'm not gonna marry any man out of sheer obligation, not even my filthy-rich-hot-as-fucking-sin-baby-daddy." Her eyes prick with tears. "Not even if he's you."

"Kat," I say, rolling my eyes. "Stop acting like a fucking lunatic. I'm the one who should be pissed, not you."

Kat raises an eyebrow. "Why should you be *pissed?*"

"Because you're the one who fucked up and didn't take your pill."

Kat doesn't speak for a long beat. "I'm really sorry about that," she finally says. "You're right—I totally fucked up." Her eyes catch fire. "But I'm sure as hell not gonna compound one mistake with another. I'll be your baby-momma, Josh, and I'll certainly expect you to step up and be a father to this kid, financially and otherwise (which, by the way, I have no doubt you'll do—again, I know you're a man of integrity). But I'm most certainly not gonna *marry* you for no other reason than I'm gestating your accidental Faraday. Now, if you actually *want* to marry me, that's a different story..." She pauses, her eyebrows raised, obviously expecting me to say something. "If that's something you *want*, regardless of the baby...?"

I stare at her blankly. She's got to be kidding. Why the fuck would I want to get married, other than the fact that she's gestating my accidental Faraday? She knows I have no interest in marriage—I've told her so, as plain as day. There's literally no other circumstance when I'd even *think* of asking Kat, or any woman, to be my wife, sorry-not-sorry. "Kat," I say, emotion suddenly rising up inside me. "You're asking too much of me. Stop being a terrorist and be rational."

Kat's eyes soften with sudden and surprising sympathy. "Josh, I'm not being a terrorist, though if I were, you'd certainly deserve it. I'm being kind to you in the long run, though you obviously can't see it now. This baby was an accident, plain and simple. We both made it, but you're right, I'm the one who flubbed taking my pill. You were relying on me to have my shit together and I blew it—so I hereby release you. You've made it clear how you feel about marriage—you don't see the point in it." She adopts a deep voice obviously intended as an impression of mine: "'If you wanna go, go—if you wanna stay, stay.' I haven't forgotten what you said. Just because I've got an accidental Faraday in my uterus doesn't mean you suddenly want to marry me in your heart. And I deserve to marry a man who loves me—not a guy who's asking me to marry him to appease the ghost of his asshole-father."

A lump rises in my throat. Is Kat right? Is my father *still* controlling me, even after all these years, even from the grave?

There's a long beat, during which Typhoid Joe hacks up his tenth lung of the night.

"Josh," Kat says softly after Typhoid Joe quiets down. She puts her hand on mine in a gesture of tenderness, making my heart pang. "If it weren't for this baby growing inside me, you wouldn't even be *thinking* of asking me to marry you. Today when you introduced me to your friends at flag football was the first time you ever called me your girlfriend—which I really liked, by the way."

"Kat, please just say yes," I whisper, despair overtaking me. She's pregnant and I'm proposing. Why won't she say yes?

"Thank you, Josh. I really appreciate the offer," Kat says, her tone surprisingly sweet. "But how are you gonna vow to be my husband 'til death do us part when you haven't even told me something as simple as 'I love you'?" She looks at me pointedly, like she's willing those three words to come out of my mouth right this very minute.

I run my hand through my hair. Shit. I should say it. I've never felt this way about any woman before. I'm addicted to her in every way. I'm ninety-nine percent sure what I'm feeling for Kat is what normal people call love—which means I should say the goddamned words. I open my mouth and close it again. Fuck.

Kat scoffs. "I know turnabout is fair play and all, but please don't barf on me."

"What?"

"You look like you're about to barf."

I exhale.

Kat waves her hand dismissively, anger once again rising in her face. "Forget it. I'm not gonna be the gold-digging whore who proves your asshole-father right and traps you into marital bondage. I don't want your fucking money or your goddamned name and I certainly don't wanna force you to say something you're not genuinely feeling. Give me whatever to sign and I'll sign it, saying I don't want your freaking money and that you're only obligated to take care of your kid and nothing more." Tears prick her eyes.

"Kat, I don't think you're a gold digger," I say softly. "I've never thought that about you, not for a minute. I know you forgot to take your pill by accident."

"It's okay, Josh. Here's what we're gonna do. We'll keep going the way we are and see where this thing leads—which, if I were placing bets after this conversation, looks to be nowhere—but who knows? And when the baby comes, we'll see where things stand between us—if we're even talking to each other by then—and we'll figure our shit out from there, one day at a time." She glares at me with glistening eyes.

"Kat, listen to me. Just gimme a minute to absorb the situation. Maybe I'm not saying all the right words, but my heart's in the right place."

"No, you're *heart* isn't remotely involved in this conversation— that's the problem."

"Kat," I say softly. If my heart's not involved in this conversation, like she says, then why does it feel like it's shattering?

"It's okay, Josh," Kat says. "I've had a lot more time to process the situation than you have—a full week. Take your time. Think and regroup."

"You've known for a week?" I ask.

"Yeah, I barfed right after I got home from the karaoke bar, so I took a pregnancy test."

"You found out the night of the karaoke bar?"

She nods.

"Shit." I shake my head, remembering myself holding a goddamned boom box over my head in front of her apartment building. "I came over that night—I wanted to apologize to you."

"Yeah. I got your text," Kat says softly. "I couldn't come out. I was too much of a wreck."

My heart is aching. Kat obviously has no idea I stood out in front of her apartment with a boom box, ready to hand her my dick and balls in a baggie.

"Kat," I say. "Fuck what I said about marriage being pointless, okay? All bets are off. You're pregnant with my baby. We should get married. *Please*."

Kat shakes her head.

I throw up my hands, suddenly exasperated with her. "Goddammit. I don't know what you expect from me. You've totally blindsided me here, Kat." I look up at the ceiling, begging God for patience, and then level her with pleading eyes. "Kat, think about what you're doing. You're turning down an offer of marriage from the father of your child—who, lucky for you, happens to be *me*."

Kat scoffs. "Oh, now I'm the 'lucky one'?"

I throw up my hands. What the hell is she holding out for? Some sort of fairytale? Some knight on a white horse, whisking her off into the sunset? "I'm sorry my proposal isn't fulfilling your girlhood fantasies," I say caustically. "But maybe it's time to stop dreaming about being Cinderella and get real. This is as good as it's gonna get under the circumstances."

Kat glares at me for a long beat, her eyes full of homicidal rage. "Fuck you," she finally spits out. "'Get real'? 'As good as it's gonna get'? Fuck you, you arrogant little prick. I deserve the fairytale, whether

I'm knocked up or not, you motherfucking asshole-douche-prick-fuckwad." She glares at me and flips her golden hair behind her shoulder. "I'm Julia Roberts in *Pretty Woman*," she says. "And I'm not gonna settle for, 'Oh, fuck it, we might as well get married,' simply because I *happen* to be a street-walker in thigh-high boots and you *happen* to be Mr. Darcy." She juts her chin at me. "Let me be really clear about something, Josh: I. Don't. Care. About. Your. Freaking. Money."

I blink rapidly, completely floored.

"Yes, I'm impregnated with your mighty Faraday spawn," Kat continues, still seething, "which, according to you, is a huge *win* for me—from an *evolutionary* standpoint, I suppose." She scoffs. "But I'm here to tell you, Joshua, evolution is no reason for me to marry a man who doesn't actually *want* to marry me."

We stare at each other for a long, angry beat. Yet again, she's obviously waiting for me to say something very specific. But she can wait for-fucking-ever as far as I'm concerned. She's crossed a fucking line and I'm fucking done. I ask her to marry me and she calls me a fuckwad? Fuck this shit. She's right. This is a horrible idea. We're obviously fundamentally incompatible. God help me if I were to marry this batshit crazy woman and be stuck with her for eternity—I'd quite literally go insane.

"Well," Kat says primly, filling the excruciating silence. "I just wanted to come out here and tell you about Colby. I didn't intend to tell you about the pregnancy. Sorry. It just slipped out."

I suppress an eye-roll.

Kat narrows her eyes, shooting daggers at me. "Let's just take some time and regroup," she says stiffly. "*Starting right now.*"

I exhale with exasperation. "Have you told your family yet?"

"No. They've got enough to worry about with Colby. Probably won't tell them for a few months—for however long I'm not showing."

"Have you told Sarah?"

"No. She had her finals last week and now she's in Greece, getting engaged to the man of her dreams—a guy who actually *wants* to marry her more than he wants to breathe, by the way." She glares at me like I just flicked her in the forehead.

"Kat, let's play the honesty-game here for one cotton-pickin' minute, okay?" I grit out.

"Yes, please, good sir. I thought that's what we were doing already, but I guess that was just me."

God, she's annoying. "Let's talk about the pink elephant in the room, shall we?" I say.

"I have no idea what the pink elephant in the room is, Josh. I'm pregnant and you're a dick. Those are pretty much the only pink elephants I see, and I just talked about both of them."

I make a noise of frustration.

"But, please, good sir, enlighten me about the pink elephant you see in the room," she continues.

"Would you stop with the 'good sir' crap? I don't even understand the reference."

"Because you're an idiot."

I close my eyes for a moment, once again asking God for patience, and when I feel ready to speak without wringing Kat's pretty little neck, I open my eyes. "The pink elephant is this: my family is worth a shit-ton of money. You don't need to know exactly how much, but trust me, it's more than you think. Now I don't think for one nanosecond you were trying to *intentionally* trick or trap me—okay? But you definitely fucked up here, let's call a spade a spade, and now you're *definitely* coming out on top in The Game of Life. Under the circumstances, it's not outlandish for me to point out that through an honest *mistake* you'll wind up doing quite well for yourself for the rest of your fucking life."

Well, that did it. I just lit the fuse on a gigantic stick of dynamite. She pops up out of her chair and wiggles her body around like she's suddenly possessed by a demon.

I recoil in my seat, genuinely scared of her flailing movement. "Jesus, Kat," I say. "Are you gonna barf on me or dive to the ground and start speaking in tongues?"

Kat abruptly leans into my face. "Go back to L.A. before I do grave bodily harm to you, Josh," she seethes.

"Kat, you're misunderstanding me. What I'm saying to you is that—"

"I know exactly what you're saying to me. And here's what I'm saying to you in reply: Fuck you and the horse you rode in on, you arrogant little rich-boy-prick. My answer to your romantic proposal of marriage is 'no thank you.' And not only that, in the interest of the honesty-game, I should also tell you that I wouldn't marry you if you were the last goddamned man on earth." With that, she turns on her heel and marches away, just like she did after Reed's party—just like she always does.

I follow her, rolling my eyes. Obviously, what I've said came out wrong. Horribly wrong. I just meant that she's pregnant and the best outcome for her would be marriage to the father of her child, especially when he can support her and the baby in ways she's never even dreamed of. She was out of her head about getting a million bucks for taking down The Club? Well, how's she gonna feel about snagging a husband who could buy her a million-dollar diamond necklace on a fucking whim?

"Kat, *wait*," I say.

But Kat keeps stomping away.

I follow her as far as I'm allowed to go, but there's only so far a guy can chase a girl in this particular hospital when he's not a part of her fucking *family*.

Kat bursts through the swinging doors leading into the Hallowed Land of Family Members, leaving me decidedly behind in her pissy, dramatic, tempestuous wake.

"Fine!" I yell toward the doors. "Have yet *another* tantrum, Kat. See if I care."

"Fine! I will!" she shouts, continuing to stomp away.

Goddamn her. Who does Kat think she is, turning me down? Who's she planning to marry, if not me? Cameron Fucking Schulz? Well, I hope she *really* likes Shirley Temples and watching motherfucking *baseball*. I hope when her initials are KUS, she'll appreciate the irony of her name being synonymous with "curse word."

I turn around in a huff and take two angry steps away from her and then abruptly stop dead in my tracks.

Oh shit.

Kat could marry Cameron Schulz—or any other guy in the entire fucking world. Kat could literally have *any* guy she wants—it's the God's truth. All she has to do is crook her index finger at any man, rich or poor, young or old, professional athlete or accountant, and he'd come running, engagement ring in hand—*and she knows it.*

Oh my God. *Kat's gonna give birth to my child and then marry someone else!*

61

"Kat!" I shout, loping back toward the double doors. "*Wait!*"

Kat stops dead in her tracks. She turns around slowly and stares at me with burning eyes.

"Come back," I say. "Please. I have something I need to say to you."

She bites the inside of her cheek for a moment, but then slowly saunters back toward the swinging doors, her eyes as sharp as knives. When she reaches the doors, she pokes her head out, raises her eyebrows and exhales, deigning to give me a moment of her time. "*Yes, Mr. Darcy?*"

I exhale. I have no idea why she keeps calling me that. "Just think about what you're doing," I say. "You're being a suicide-bomber."

Kat squints at me. "*That's* what you called me back here to say?"

I shift my weight. "No. That just slipped out. I called you back to ask you to *please* marry me." I pause. "It's the right thing to do all around. For everyone. And it's... what ... I... want."

"*It's the right thing to do?*" she says slowly. "All around?"

I nod, but I can already tell this isn't going my way.

Kat crosses her arms over her chest, keeping the double-doors open with her shoulder. "*No thank you,*" she says, cold as a fucking sniper.

"Think of the baby," I say earnestly. "Let's not be selfish, either of us. Let's do the right thing. Now's not the time to be a terrorist, Kat."

Without warning, Kat pushes completely through the swinging doors toward me—to the "non-family members" side, as it were—and glowers over me with such ferocity, I leap back, surprised. "I guess you didn't pay very close attention in Las Vegas when I taught Henn how to bag a babe." She leans into my face, her eyes on fire. "Remember what I told him?"

I shake my head.

"Then I'll refresh your memory. 'Every time you're about to say something to a woman, ask yourself: is this more or less likely to get me a blowjob? If the answer is yes, then say it. If the answer is no, then *shut the fuck up!*'"

"What are you talking about? I just asked you to marry me, and you're acting like I spit on you."

"Because you *did,*" she says, her eyes flooding with tears.

I throw up my hands, at a total loss.

"Oh for crying out loud," she says. "Let me spell it out for you, plain and simple." She wipes her eyes and takes a deep breath, gearing up. "Whoever I wind up marrying one day—whether I'm the mother of his accidental spawn *or not*—" She gives that last phrase "or not" exaggerated emphasis. "It'll be for no other reason than he desperately wants *me* and only *me* to be his *wife,* forever and *ever,* as long as we both shall live." She glares at me for a beat, tears streaming down her cheeks. "It'll be because he couldn't stand the thought of living his life without me in it—couldn't stand the thought of me being with any other man—because he loves me more than the air he breathes—more than life itself." She wipes her eyes again. "And it sure as hell won't be because he felt some begrudging sense of obligation toward the unwitting incubator of his accidental spawn." Without letting me respond, she literally harrumphs at me, turns on her heel, and marches down the hallway, her arms swinging wildly with sudden fury.

I watch Kat striding away through the panes of glass in the doors, feeling like I've just been kicked in the balls with a steel boot. When she's gone, I swallow hard and shake my head, the full enormity of the situation descending upon me.

I've got quite the track record with the ladies, don't I? I told Emma I loved her and she said, "Me, too" and promptly ran off with Ascot Man on a polo pony. And now, a year later, I've asked the mother of my impending child to pretty-please marry me, and Kat basically flipped me the bird and told me she wouldn't marry me if I were the last man on earth. Talk about winning in The Game of Life. *Yahtzee.*

I swallow hard again. Fuck this shit. I'm done begging a woman to love me, even if that woman's a unicorn and the most incredible woman I've ever been with. And most of all I'm done handing Katherine Ulla Fucking Morgan my motherfucking dick and balls in a motherfucking Ziploc baggie and letting her throw them into a fucking meat grinder at her bitchy little whim. Clearly, she's always gotten everything she's ever wanted from every other motherfucking man she's ever run across, but not anymore. I'm done.

I wipe my eyes on my sleeve, leaving a surprising streak of wetness on the fabric. And then I flip off the swinging doors with both hands, turn the fuck around, and march out of the hospital without looking the fuck back.

Chapter 11
Kat

"Do you wanna wait for your friend before being seated or go to your table now?" the restaurant hostess asks me.

"I think I'll be seated now. My friend texted she's running a bit late."

"Of course." The woman picks up two menus. "Right this way."

She leads me to a small table in the back and I immediately set down the thick stack of bridal magazines in my arms. "Thank you."

"Can I get you something to drink while you wait?"

"Ginger ale? Extra ice, please," I ask, taking a chair. I pull a Saltine from a baggie in my purse and take a little nibble. Gah. This round-the-clock nausea is getting really old.

A busboy brings a ginger ale to the table along with a basket of bread, and I take a greedy bite of a roll, hoping it'll calm my churning stomach.

My phone buzzes and I glance down, expecting to see a text from Sarah.

"Hello, Stubborn Kat," Josh writes.

My heart instantly leaps at the sight of Josh's name displayed on my screen, just like it always does—but then I remember the current iciness between us, and my heart pangs with an overwhelming sense of hurt and regret. Why'd Josh have to look like his balls were being fed through a wood-chipper when he asked me to marry him at the hospital a week ago? And why'd he have to act like such a spoiled, rich-boy-prick, too? If only he'd looked even the teensiest bit like he actually *wanted* me to be his wife, if only he'd flashed a fraction of his usual down-to-earth, irresistible charm, I surely would have thrown my arms around his neck and screamed, "Yes!" despite myself.

"Hello, Mr. Darcy," I reply to Josh's text.

"Why do you keep calling me that?"

"Google it," I write.

"I did. He's the guy from Pride and Prejudice. But since I haven't seen that movie (a fact I've already mentioned to you, by the way—thanks so much for listening intently to everything I say), I have no idea what you're talking about."

Jeez, I guess being fed a weeklong diet of cold-shoulder by your pregnant girlfriend (or am I his pregnant *ex*-girlfriend?) is enough to make a guy a big ol' grouch.

"Well, Mr. Grouchy Pants," I type, "I'd never dream of spoiling Pride and Prejudice for you by explaining why I keep calling you that name. You'll just have to watch it and find out."

"Go ahead and spoil it," Josh replies. "I'm positive I'll NEVER see that movie."

"Never say never," I write.

"NEVER. Because I don't have a VAGINA."

"You never know."

"I KNOW."

"So is that why you've texted me (in all caps, no less)? To argue about whether you're ever gonna watch Pride and Prejudice?"

"No. Sorry. That just slipped out. I'm texting to ask how Colby's doing and also to find out if you're feeling a bit better today?"

These are the same two questions Josh has politely asked me via text every single day this week. And in return, I've politely responded to him (via text) each and every time, as smoothly and impersonally as Elizabeth Bennett (the well-mannered heroine of *Pride and Prejudice*) would do, assuming she'd lived in the age of smartphones.

I'll admit it's taken quite a bit of willpower on my part not to instigate contact with Josh at all this week. So many times, I've wanted to call him and scream into the phone, "Even if you're an arrogant prick, I still love you! Ask me again!" But I've somehow managed to maintain full control and stuff down the raging, clanging, almost desperate swell of emotion I've felt nearly every moment since I marched away from Josh at the hospital.

And it's not just memories of Josh's so-called marriage proposal that have been plaguing me all week. Even more so, it's the way Josh has been treating me ever since that horrible night—like he's done with me for good. His behavior this past week has been a complete one-eighty compared to the week after the karaoke bar. Back then, there were daily flowers, texts begging for my forgiveness, late-night, drunken voicemails telling me he was hard as a rock and couldn't stop thinking about me. But this week? Nope. There's been none of that. Just polite texts asking after my brother and my health, exactly as the ever-polite Mr. Darcy would do—only signs of his perceived obligation and nothing more. And it's damn-near broken my heart.

Goddammit. I truly thought I was doing the right thing when I turned Josh down at the hospital—I really did—and I guess I still do, intellectually—I mean, jeez, he was such a little prick, oh my God. But, shoot, I just don't know anymore. I can't even think straight these days, I miss him so freaking much. If it weren't for how busy I've been this past week visiting Colby and gathering ideas and information for Sarah's wedding, I'd have hopped a flight to L.A. days ago to fling myself upon Josh's arrogant mercy and beg him to ask me again.

"Colby's doing well," I text to Josh in reply to his polite query. "Thank you for asking." (I refrain from adding, "good sir" to the end of my sentence, though I'm dying to do it.) I tap out a lengthy (and exceedingly polite) status report about Colby, just as I've done every day this past week in reply to Josh's texts. "All in all, great progress," I conclude. "At least regarding Colby's physical healing," I add. "Mentally, Colby's not doing quite as well. When I saw him this morning, he was convinced he'd somehow cost that baby her life. He thinks he should have taken a different route out of the building or something."

"Oh, man. Poor guy. You told him that's crazy, right? He's a hero."

"I told him. But he wouldn't listen."

"Well, he's lucky to have you," Josh writes. "If anyone can put a smile on a man's face, it's you."

My heart leaps. That's the first time Josh has texted anything remotely personal to me in a full week—let alone something so lovely. "Thank you," I write, my heart suddenly gushing with relief and yearning. Oh my effing God, I'm fighting back tears. Oh, how I want to write, "I miss you, Josh! I loooooooooove you. Ask me again and I'll say yes this time, even though I know you don't really want to marry me!" But I can't do that. I know full well Josh doesn't want a wife any more than he wants a baby, and I'll be damned if I'm gonna be the woman who's trapped Josh Faraday into having *two* items of baggage he never bargained for. "It means a lot to me that you'd say that about me," I type, my heart pounding. "Especially now. Just knowing you still feel that way about me is making me want to sob like a baby."

I've no sooner pressed send on my text than my phone rings with an incoming call.

"Hi," I say softly into the phone, holding back tears.

"Hi," Josh says.

Oh God, just hearing his sexy voice for the first time in a week is making my heart explode. "I miss you so much," I blurt. "Josh, I *miss* you."

Josh pauses, just long enough to make my stomach drop into my toes.

"I miss you, too," he finally says, his voice cracking. "So, so much, babe."

"I thought you hated me," I whisper.

"Of course, not. *Never.*" He pauses, apparently collecting himself. "Are you feeling any better today?"

My heart is physically aching. I want to reach through the phone line and kiss him and tell him I love him desperately. "Yeah," I manage to reply. "I figured out Saltines and ice-cold ginger ale take the edge off my nausea a little bit."

"Good." He pauses. "So what are you up to today?" he asks softly.

Oh. We're gonna have a routine conversation? We're not gonna talk about his proposal or this past week? No talking about our feelings? Okay. I can do that. I clear my throat. "Well, I visited Colby in the hospital all morning. And now I'm meeting Sarah for lunch to go over wedding stuff. She and Jonas got back from Greece yesterday—oh, duh—you probably heard that from Jonas. But, anyway, since the wedding's happening so soon—in just twenty-six little days, courtesy of your impatient brother—I pulled together some ideas for Sarah these past few days while she was finishing up her trip."

"Yeah, I heard about that quick turnaround thing. Classic Jonas."

"I guess some people in this world just, you know, really *want* to get married."

Josh exhales.

Shit. I shouldn't have said that. That was a decidedly terroristic thing to say. Shoot. "So, anyway," I continue, trying to deflect attention from my apparently pathological need to strap bombs to my chest. "So now I'm sitting in a restaurant with a stack of bridal magazines, waiting for Sarah to arrive."

"Are you gonna tell her about the pregnancy?"

"No. I think we should wait to tell Jonas and Sarah until after the wedding. They've got plenty to think about 'til then."

"I agree."

"Plus, you never know. It still might not stick. So, anyway, continuing with my exciting agenda for the day, after lunch, I've got a doctor's appointment."

"A doctor's appointment? You mean for the baby?"

"Yeah."

"Why didn't you tell me? I would have flown up for it."

"Flown up for a doctor's appointment?"

"It's my kid, right?"

I bristle.

"Shit. That came out wrong. Kat, please don't freak out. I meant, 'Hey, it's my kid, right?' *Not,* 'It's my kid... *right?*'"

I can't help but smile. "I know exactly what you meant. It's okay. But, bee tee dubs, it's your kid, Josh."

"Yeah, I know that." He pauses. "Well, the point I'm making is that I plan to be there for my kid, right from the start. Doctors appointments and everything. I'm gonna be a real father—not just a wallet. So tell me about appointments, please, and I'll always try to make them."

"Okay. I'm sorry. It didn't occur to me to tell you about today's appointment—we haven't exactly been chatting each other's ears off this week." I clear my throat. "But I'll be sure to tell you next time."

"Please do."

"I will." There's a beat. "So how's your day going, Josh?"

"Fine. I'm just trying to finish this huge report. It's the last thing I've got to do for Faraday & Sons and then I'm free at last, free at last, thank God almighty, I'm free at last. And the other thing I'm doing is sitting here watching moving guys put all my shit into a humongous truck."

"What?"

"Yeah, considering what's going on with you and the baby and everything, I decided to move into my new house a couple weeks early," Josh says.

My heart leaps. "Really? When will you be up here?"

"Really soon. A matter of days. I'll let you know when I get the moving schedule confirmed." He lets out a pained exhale. "Shit. Fuck this, Kat—I can't take it anymore. I've been going out of my head this whole week, dying to tell you—"

"Kitty Kat!" It's Sarah, standing at the edge of the table, holding out her arms for a big hug. "I'm so sorry I'm late."

Chapter 12
Kat

"Hang on, Josh—Sarah's here," I say into the phone, cutting him off. I leap up from the table and give Sarah a huge hug. "Welcome home! Ooooph, I missed you, girl. Let's see it."

Sarah shows me the humongous diamond on her hand.

"Oh my God!" I shriek, ogling Sarah's rock. "It's so huge! And sparkly! Oh, Sarah! That's the most gorgeous ring I've ever seen. To die for! What girl wouldn't kill to get a ring like that?"

We take our seats, both of us giggling and glowing and cooing at each other like we haven't seen each other in twenty years.

"Hello?" a compressed voice says through my phone on the table.

"Oh my God," I gasp, picking up the phone. "I'm so sorry, Josh," I say. "I totally forgot you were there."

"Mmm hmmm. Gosh, it sure sounds like Sarah's ring is big and sparkly, Kat."

I smile demonically to myself. "Oh, you heard all that? I'm sorry. Yeah. It's gorgeous." Sarah smiles at me, oblivious to what's been going on between Josh and me this past week. "You should see Sarah," I say to Josh. "She looks so *happy*. Hang on." I hold the phone out to Sarah. "Say hi to Josh, Sarah—tell him how happy you are."

Sarah giggles and takes the phone from me. "Hi, Joshy Woshy. Thank you.... Hey, that's right, *brother*." She squeals. "Hellz yeah, I will, you silly goose... Yep. Smart thinking... I love you, Joshy Woshy." She giggles again. "I will. Bye." She hands the phone back. "Here you go."

I put the phone to my ear, but Josh is gone. "He hung up," I say, feeling deflated.

"He told me to tell you goodbye. He said he'll talk to you later."

I stare at Sarah, stunned. "You told Josh you love him."

"I sure did, because I do. I loooooove him. Josh is gonna be my *brother*—isn't that awesome? I've always wanted a brother."

"And what did Josh say in reply when you said that?" I ask.

"He said, 'I feel the same way about you, my dearest sister.'" Sarah giggles. "Oh, the Faraday men. Gotta love 'em."

"Yeah. Gotta love 'em."

Oh my God, that should have been *me* saying "I love you" to Josh. I love him more than I knew I could love. I love every part of him, even the douchey parts. *And I'm dying to tell him so.* I already knew it, of course, but this week without him has made me realize I truly can't be happy without him.

"Hello, ladies," the waitress says, standing at the edge of our table. "Can I answer any questions about the menu for you?"

"Oh, gosh. I haven't even looked at the menu yet," Sarah says. "I'm sorry."

"There's no rush. Let me just tell you about our specials today." The waitress rattles off several specials, all of which sound like they'd make me hurl. "What can I get you to drink while you decide?" the waitress asks.

"I'd love a glass of white wine," Sarah says. "Maybe a Pinot Griggio?"

The waitress nods. "And another ginger ale for you, Miss?"

"Thank you."

Sarah looks at me funny. "I've never seen you drink ginger ale before," she says. "Does it have tequila in it?"

I shake my head. "I was feeling a little queasy for some reason—thought ginger ale might help."

"Oh, I'm sorry, Kat. Are you sick?"

"No, I'm fine. Although I must admit I'm totally jealous you just told Josh the exact three words I'm *dying* to say to him."

"You two *still* haven't said 'I love you'?"

I shake my head.

"Why don't you just tell him, Kat?"

"Sarah, please. I'd never say it first in a relationship. Come on. I'm lovesick, but I've still got at least a shred of self-respect."

"Well, *I* just said it first to Josh and he seemed quite receptive."

"Not quite the same thing, honey."

"I know." She giggles. "So you're in luuuurve, huh?"

"Completely-totally-I'm-in-physical-pain-lurve."

"Aw, just tell him. I'm sure he feels the same way. How could he not?"

I sigh loudly. "Things are a bit complicated right now."

"Well, I think everyone should tell everyone else in the whole wide world 'I love you' all the livelong day," Sarah says effusively, glancing down at her huge rock.

"It's like you're high on crystal meth," I say.

"That's how I feel—or so I'd imagine—I've never done crystal meth, of course."

"No offense, but you're the last person's advice I should be following about saying 'I love you' to anyone. You're so high on Jonas-crack right now, you'd swear your undying love to the bag lady on the corner."

Sarah giggles. "As a matter of fact, I believe I did exactly that on my way into the restaurant. I grabbed that bag lady by her *Iron Man* T-shirt and I said, 'I love you, bag lady!' And then I French-kissed her."

I laugh. "You're so freaking weird, Sarah."

"I'm just so happy, I can't contain myself." Sarah giggles for the millionth time since she waltzed into the restaurant. "Once I started saying 'I love you' all the time to Jonas, I can't seem to stop saying it to everyone. I'm addicted. I-love-you-I-love-you-I-love-you. See? I can't stop. I love you, Kat!"

The waitress approaches our table with Sarah's wine and another ginger ale for me. "Are we ready to order?" she asks.

"I love you!" Sarah says to the waitress.

"Oh, wow. Thank you. I love you, too."

"See, Kat?" Sarah says. "Easy peasy."

"Forgive my silly friend," I say to the waitress. "She just got engaged. She's out of her head."

"Oh, congratulations. Did you get a—*whoa*! Oh my god. Look at that ring. *Wow.*"

Sarah giggles and puts her hand down.

"That's quite a ring," the waitress says, her cheeks flushed. "Spectacular."

"Thank you. But it's not nearly as spectacular as the man who gave it to me."

The waitress and I exchange a look like, "Lucky bitch."

Sarah picks up her menu. "I still haven't looked at the menu. I'm sorry. I'm a babbling fool."

The waitress laughs. "Understandable." She flashes me another "lucky bitch" look. "Take your time. Sounds like you've got a lot to celebrate." She walks away.

"So, hey, what did Josh ask you?" I ask.

"When?"

"On the phone just now. When you said, 'Hellz yeah, I will'?"

"Oh. He asked if I'll be taking Jonas' name. He said if I take the Faraday name then I'll 'single-handedly increase the number of Faradays roaming the earth by 33.33 percent.'" She smiles. "So I told him, 'Hellz yeah, I will, you silly goose!'" She squeals with unadulterated joy.

"It's like you've been sucking on nitrous oxide."

Sarah laughs.

"And what did Josh say in response to that?" I ask.

"He said, 'Good. I think it's best for everyone in our family to have the same last name—that way we'll never be turned away when visiting each other in the hospital.'"

My stomach flips over. "So enough about Josh," I say. "I'm dying to hear everything about Greece."

"Oh my God, I can't wait to tell you. But lemme figure out my order first so the waitress doesn't kill me when she comes back."

I watch Sarah study her menu for a moment, my heart going pitter-pat with love for her. She's so damned cute. And so damned *happy.* God, I'm thrilled for her—I really am—but I'd be lying if I didn't say I wish I were in her same shoes, wearing a rock on my finger from Josh. Actually, no, on second thought, I don't even care about the marriage part so much as I just want Josh to *want* me, totally and completely, without reservation, the way Jonas so obviously wants Sarah.

Sarah looks up. "Salmon burger with a spinach salad. *Boom.*"

"Sounds good," I say, even though the thought of anything fishy turns my stomach. "Okay, now *spill,* honey."

Sarah launches into telling me every swoon-inducing detail

about Jonas popping the question, stopping only to chomp on her salmon burger when our food arrives. And when Sarah's done telling me every last thing about Jonas' incredible proposal, we begin poring over the huge stack of bridal magazines I've brought, formulating ideas for the wedding of the century a mere twenty-six days from now (oh my God!).

"Okay," I finally say after almost an hour of brainstorming. I look down at the lengthy list of questions and ideas scrawled on my notepad. "Do you want me to go with you to your meeting with the wedding planner tomorrow?"

"No, I know you're busy getting your new business up and running—I'll handle everything from here on out."

My stomach clenches. God, I hate keeping anything from Sarah. It makes me feel even more like throwing up than I already do. "Sarah, I'm the Party Girl, remember?" I say. "I live for parties—and weddings are just the granddaddy of all parties. Plus, I'm the maid of honor, after all—let me help you pull it all together."

Sarah beams a huge smile at me. "Really?"

"Of course."

"I must admit I'm a bit overwhelmed. Jonas says he'll pay for everything and show up, so I'm kind of on my own here."

"I'm thrilled to do it. Anything you need, whatever it is, I'm your girl."

"Thanks so much, Kat. You're the absolute best," Sarah says. She emphatically closes the bridal magazine in front of her on the table. "So enough about me, me, me. I've talked your ear off this whole lunch. Tell me what's going on with you, you, you? How's Golden Kat PR coming? When's the launch date, you think?"

"Um," I say. I bite my lip. "Hmm."

"I've been thinking," Sarah says. "What do you think about 'Kitty Kat PR'? Too juvenile? It's certainly memorable."

I don't reply.

"Yeah, you're right. Probably too juvenile," Sarah says. "So how's the planning going? Are you having fun?"

I take a small sip of ginger ale, trying to figure out how best to answer Sarah's seemingly innocuous questions without unleashing the kraken on her. Shit. I suppose I should tell Sarah about Colby, but I'm certainly not gonna tell her about my accidental Faraday, not when she's in the throes of planning her dream wedding—plus, the sonogram at my doctor's appointment later today might reveal the accidental spawn is smoking and losing altitude, you never know. And if I'm not gonna tell Sarah about my accidental bun in the oven, then I sure as heck won't be telling her about Josh's so-called marriage proposal, either, or about how I've been crying my eyes out ever since.

"So, come on—tell me everything," Sarah says, sipping her wine.

"Well..." I begin slowly, my stomach in knots. "Um." My lower lip begins to tremble. My eyes water.

Shoot.

I take a deep breath, trying to quell the despair rising up inside me—and then I burst into big, soggy tears.

Chapter 13
Kat

"The doctor will be in shortly," the nurse says, taking the blood-pressure cuff off my arm.

I shift my weight, eliciting a crinkling sound from the wax paper underneath me. "I'm nervous," I say softly.

"About what?" Sarah asks. "A sonogram doesn't hurt, does it?"

"I'm not nervous the sonogram will *hurt*," I say. "I'm nervous about, you know, what it might show—that something might be wrong."

Honestly, I'm shocked at how anxious I am that something might be wrong with my little accidental Faraday. Two weeks ago, when I first peed on those pregnancy tests, the baby going bye-bye on its own was all I kept praying for. But with each passing day since then, I've surprisingly found myself more and more attached to the idea of having a baby of my own—perhaps a little boy who looks just like Josh? Despite myself, I keep imagining a dark-haired boy sitting at the Morgan Family Thanksgiving table in a little blue suit to match his sapphire eyes, or maybe throwing a football in the backyard with Colby, or learning how to play guitar with Dax? Or, craziest of all, I keep finding myself imagining Josh and me cuddled up in a warm bed with our cute little guy, giggling and whispering about how happy we are. It's crazy, I know, but I can't stop thinking about it.

Sarah juts her lip with sympathy as only she can do. "Aw, don't be nervous, honey." She opens my dog-eared copy of *What To Expect When You're Expecting* and flips to a marked page. "I was just reading in your fascinating little book here that being a barf-o-matic is generally regarded as a great sign—that it typically indicates your hormones are at high levels, which is good."

"Thanks, Sarah," I say. "And thanks for coming to this appointment with me. I didn't realize it would be so comforting to have someone here."

"Are you kidding? I wanna come to everything. I wish you'd told me sooner—I would have hopped the next flight home from Greece to hold your hand."

"That's exactly why I didn't tell you," I say. "So, are you gonna tell Jonas?"

Sarah shakes her head. "I think Josh should be the one to tell Jonas he's gonna be an uncle."

"Yeah, probably."

"Just make sure Josh spills the beans really soon, okay? I don't like keeping secrets from Jonas."

I nod.

Sarah buries her nose in my pregnancy book again, but after a moment, lifts her head, smiling. "Hey, you wanna hear something crazy? I think with the time difference, Josh proposed to you *before* Jonas proposed to me." She laughs. "Who would have predicted *that*?"

"Yeah, but Josh's proposal doesn't really count—he was just fulfilling an obligation. It wasn't even in the same universe as what Jonas did for you. That's like comparing a hamster to a racehorse."

Sarah's smile vanishes. "Aw, I'm sorry, Kat."

I rub my face. "I keep thinking maybe I should have said yes—that maybe when I said no I was being selfish and not looking out for the bean."

"What? No frickin' way. You did the right thing—one hundred percent."

"You think?"

"Absolutely. Regardless of marriage, Josh is gonna step up and take care of his kid—there's no doubt about that."

"True."

"And it's not like you need to get married to get onto Josh's medical insurance or something—Josh can well afford to make sure you have the best medical care."

"Also true. In fact, he's already told me he'll pay for all my expenses, medical and otherwise."

"Of course, he will. Which means there were no *practical* decisions to make in response to Josh's proposal—only emotional ones. And in that case, you did exactly the right thing: you followed your heart. Because, Kat, we both know you'd never be happy being married out of obligation. You're a diehard romantic, through and through—and you need the fairytale."

"*Me?*"

Sarah scoffs. "Yes, *you*. You've watched *The Bodyguard* and *Pretty Woman* like ten times each, for Pete's sake."

"Twenty."

Sarah motions like I just proved her case.

"Yeah, you're probably right." I rub my forehead and sigh. "The funny thing is I totally would have said yes if Josh's proposal had been even the slightest bit from his heart—just the teeniest, tiniest bit."

"I gotta be honest, Kat, from what you've told me, I don't really understand what was so horrible about it. I mean, you said he acted like he was doing you a huge favor, but maybe you just misinterpreted him? I'm sure he was just freaking out."

I pause, choosing my words. "Remember Mr. Darcy's first proposal in *Pride and Prejudice?* When he was like, 'Oh, you're so beneath me, Miss Elizabeth and I really shouldn't do this because you're from a disgraceful family and wanting to marry you goes against all reason and logic and will *besmirch* my good name—but, hey, will you marry me?'"

Sarah chuckles. "Yes, I remember it well because you've made me watch that movie, like, three times with you."

"Well, it was just like that. 'Oh, Kat. I have no desire to marry you whatsoever and I'm doing you a *huge* favor and I don't want our child *at all* and you're so *lucky* I'm asking you because I'm *so* rich and amazing, but, hey, will you marry me?'" I wave my hands in the air. "It totally sucked donkey balls."

Sarah nods. "Sounds pretty shitty."

"And not only that, he had the audacity to ask me if the baby is his." My cheeks turn hot at the memory.

Sarah shrugs. "Okay, you just lost me. Why was that such a dastardly thing to ask?"

I'm appalled. "Sarah, he was basically calling me a slut."

"Uh, *no*, he was asking if the baby is his. Not quite the same thing as calling you a slut."

"Josh is the only guy I've been with and he knows it," I say, full of indignation.

"Oh, well, then, you're absolutely right: Josh should never have double-checked the baby he was about to support for the rest of his life, financially and otherwise, is definitely his." Sarah shoots me a scolding look. "Cut him a little slack, honey—I'm sure Josh was just totally blindsided. Plus, you'd be the first to admit you're no virgin. I don't blame Josh for at least asking the question, Kat. I really don't."

I open my mouth to refute her, but then I shut it. God, I hate it when it turns out I've been wrong about something. "Why are you *always* so damned nice, Sarah?" I ask. "It's really annoying."

"I'm not that nice."

"Please don't say that. Because if you're not really, really nice, then that means I'm really, really bitchy."

Sarah laughs. "Okay, I'm really, really nice."

The door opens and my doctor, a slender woman with brown skin and salt and pepper hair, enters the room.

"Hi, Doctor Gupta," I say, shaking her hand. "This is my best friend, Sarah—soon to be Auntie Sarah."

The doctor shakes Sarah's hand and smiles at me. "Are you ready to see your baby, Kat?"

"Heck yeah. How about you Auntie Sarah? You ready to see your niece or nephew?"

Sarah squeals and claps.

After spreading some gel on my stomach, the doctor runs the wand of the sonogram machine over my stomach, and a swirling image of what might as well be outer space comes up onscreen.

"What's that?" I ask, pointing.

"One moment," the doctor says, maneuvering. "Okay. This is your uterus, Kat. And right there? That's your baby."

"Wow," Sarah says, putting her hand to her mouth.

"That's my *baby*?" I ask.

"Yep. He or she is just about the size of a grape."

I look at Sarah. "My baby's a grape."

"Grape Ape," Sarah says.

I bite my lip, too overwhelmed to speak further.

"And do you see that bit of flickering right there?" the doctor continues. "That's the baby's heartbeat. Oh, it's nice and strong—exactly what we like to see."

Sarah makes a sound of wonderment. "Hey, we should take a video of this for Josh."

"Oh, good idea," I say. "My phone's in my purse."

Sarah pulls out my phone and aims it at the screen. "Okay,

79

action. Doctor, will you explain what's onscreen for the baby's father?"

"Of course." The doctor motions to the screen and explains everything, and when she's done, Sarah pans the camera to me.

"Hi, Josh," I say, waving. "Well, it looks like our accidental Faraday is a stubborn little thing—surprise, surprise! I guess he or she's decided they're not going anywhere, after all." I try to smile but tears unexpectedly prick my eyes. Goddammit. Josh must hate me. I'm the one who missed my pill, after all, not him. He trusted me to protect him from the one thing that freaked him out the most and I let him down. I wipe my eyes. "I'm really sorry, Josh," I squeak out.

Sarah turns off the video recorder. "I'm gonna edit that last part out. You have nothing to apologize for, Kat. It takes two to tango."

"No. Leave it in. I forgot to take my pill—and now I've totally ruined his life. I owe him an apology."

"You haven't ruined his life," the doctor interjects, her tone firm. "You've *blessed* it immeasurably. He just doesn't know it yet."

Tears fill my eyes at these unexpectedly kind words from the doctor. "Thank you," I say softly.

Sarah squeezes my hand. "Listen to the doctor. She went to medical school and everything."

Doctor Gupta smiles warmly. "Kat, I've seen many women in your shoes. If you had a crystal ball and could see yourself a year from now, I think you'd be surprised in a good way."

I manage a smile. "Thank you."

The doctor turns back to the machine. "Now. Based on what I'm seeing here, you're about nine weeks along, which makes your due date... December second, give or take two weeks on either side."

"*Oh*," I say, my mood instantly getting a lift. "December second is *Sagittarius*," I say.

"Is that good?" Sarah asks.

I nod. "Same as Henny."

"Oh, that *is* good."

"It's a fire sign. A Sag is adventurous, creative, and passionate. Loves to travel. Makes friends easily. Funny as hell. But also can be bossy and impulsive as hell—especially a female Sagittarius. A female Sag can be hell on wheels."

Sarah raises an eyebrow. "Sounds like the grape isn't gonna fall far from the vine." She addresses the doctor. "Can you tell if the grape is a boy or girl?"

"Not yet. We'll probably be able to determine gender at around twenty weeks."

"Okay, I'm calling it right now," Sarah says, putting up her hand. "You're having a girl."

"You think?"

"I *know*. And do you know *how* I know? Because I believe in God—and if there's one person in this world who karmically deserves to wind up with a hell-on-wheels daughter, it's you, Kat."

"Hey, did you just insult me?" I ask.

Sarah laughs. "Not at all."

The doctor takes the sonogram wand off my belly and cleans up the gel on my skin. "Do you have any questions, Kat?"

"A couple." I take a deep breath, gathering my nerve. "Before I found out I was pregnant, I drank some booze—quite a bit, actually. I was in Las Vegas. When will I know if I gave the baby alcohol-fetus-whatever-whatever?"

"Fetal alcohol syndrome?"

"Yeah, that."

"There's no way to know for sure until later, but the odds are low. In the vast majority of unplanned pregnancies, the mother has consumed alcohol and there's absolutely no ill effect. We'll keep an eye on things, and if there's any sign of a problem, we'll do more testing later."

"Okay," I say, exhaling.

"At this point, I'd put it out of your mind and not worry at all—although, of course, I want you to abstain from alcohol for the remainder of your pregnancy."

"And is it the same answer if I smoked pot once, too?"

Sarah looks surprised.

"Well," the doctor says, doing a much better job of keeping a poker face than Bugs Bunny to my left. "There are no guarantees, yet again, but the chances of a problem are still low. We'll know more at the twenty-week sonogram. Of course, you should swear off all controlled substances for the remainder of your pregnancy."

"Yes, of course." I clear my throat. "It was a one-time thing."

"Any other questions?" the doctor asks.

"Yes. One more. I've had some pretty insane orgasms lately—

like, really, really intense orgasms—some of them while sitting on an orgasm machine with the power of a jet engine, and—"

Sarah gasps. "*What?*"

"Long story," I say. "But, anyway, is it possible I scrambled the baby's brain or, you know, made it implode or something?"

The doctor lets out a surprised chuckle but then quickly pulls herself together. "Generally speaking, sex and orgasms aren't harmful to the fetus during pregnancy—and, in fact, orgasms arguably provide a benefit because they're stress-relieving for the mother."

I shoot Sarah a smart-ass grin. "See? I was just being a selfless mother when I sat on that jet engine and almost passed out from sexual pleasure."

Sarah blushes. "Just as all selfless mothers have done throughout the history of time, Kitty Kat."

The doctor smiles. "At this stage, you need not limit your sexual activity with yourself or a monogamous partner, although I'd definitely advise staying off that jet engine for the remainder of your pregnancy, just to be on the safe side."

"Okay," I say, pouting. "Well, that's a bummer—I like my jet engine."

"Well, then here's some good news to cheer you up," the doctor says. "As soon as your morning sickness subsides, which I predict will happen in the next few weeks, you might very well experience a dramatic increase in your sex drive."

"Whachoo talkin' about, Willis?" I say. "An *increase* in my sex drive?"

"A *dramatic* increase?" Sarah adds, her eyes wide. "Is there a level of sex drive in existence above 'Katherine Morgan'?"

Sarah and I share a laugh and the doctor can't help but giggle with us.

"And here's something else: when you do engage in sexual activity, you might also experience heightened pleasure," Doctor Gupta adds, raising her eyebrow.

I throw my hands up. "Thank you, Baby Jesus in a Wicker Basket," I say. "Finally, some fantastic news in all this. Thank you so much, Doctor."

The doctor chuckles. "So, do you have any other questions?"

"Nope. I'm good. Thank you so much."

The doctor touches my forearm. "You're going to be fine, Kat. You'll see."

Chapter 14
Kat

Sarah and I settle into her car and fasten our seatbelts.

"You wanna swing by Starbucks before I take you back to your car?" Sarah asks, starting her engine.

"Great," I say. I look at my watch. "After that, I think I'll head back to the hospital to check on Colby again."

"Can I join you? " Sarah asks. "I'd love to give Colby a big hug."

"I'm sorry. I think you should visit Colby after he's home. Honestly, he's been pretty depressed lately—he doesn't really wanna see anyone but family."

"Poor Colby," Sarah says. She pulls her car out of the parking lot and heads toward the restaurant where my car is parked. "Hey, don't forget," Sarah says, "before you send that video to Josh, delete your apology at the end."

I don't reply.

"Kat. You don't owe Josh an apology for being pregnant with his child—he made that baby right along with you."

"I know he made the baby with me, but he didn't intend to take the heightened risk he did. If a girl tells a guy, 'Yes, I'm on the pill,' then she'd better be on the frickin' pill to the best of her ability." I shake my head. "Plus, I was pretty harsh with him in the hospital. You know how I get when my panties are in a twist."

Sarah makes a face that tells me she's well aware of how I get when my panties are in a twist.

"But now I realize Josh was just doing his best in a difficult situation," I say. "Oh, Sarah, I want him so much. I don't care about marriage. I don't care about the magic words. I just want Josh to be mine—I want us to love each other completely." I let out a long, tortured exhale and put my face in my hands. "Sarah, I think I might have lost him forever."

Sarah scoffs. "*No.*"

"*Yes.* He's totally pulled away from me this past week. I think he might be done with me for good."

"No, honey. Josh isn't done with you—not even close."

I look at her, tears in my eyes. "I love him, Sarah. I love him like I've never loved anyone before. I'm so scared I've lost him."

"Aw, honey."

"I want to give him everything but he's always holding back. He's always got his guard up. He never lets me in completely."

"Sounds like the Faraday twins are more alike than meets the eye." She smiles sympathetically and touches my hand. "Jonas was the same way and look at him now. He couldn't be more 'all-in.' Just be patient. Josh just needs time."

"I don't know how to be patient."

"I know, honey—but maybe it's time you learned." She purses her lips. "It's really too bad you can't get yourself stabbed by a Ukrainian hitman in a bathroom at U Dub. I really think that would do the trick."

"Damned grape spoils everything," I say. "I'd totally get myself stabbed if it weren't for the damned grape."

Sarah laughs.

"And Josh meeting my family is off the table, too, at least for a while. At this point, that would be a recipe for disaster."

Sarah makes a sympathetic face.

"So other than those two ideas, what other 'external event' could I arrange to make Josh realize he loves me and finally wants to go 'all-in'?" I ask. "Obviously, me being pregnant with his spawn didn't do the trick."

"I dunno," Sarah says. "It's gotta be something that makes Josh realize you love him completely—like, you know, *unconditionally*. If you can convince him he's completely safe with you, no matter what, then maybe he'll feel like he can finally let go and love you the same way in return."

"Good idea in concept," I say. "But I have no idea what that 'something' would be." I bite the inside of my cheek and look out the car window. "Hmm."

"Hmm," Sarah agrees. "Can you think of something that would make him feel—"

"I've got it." I sit up in my seat, adrenaline flooding me. "I know exactly what to do."

"Well, that was fast. What is it?" Sarah asks.

A demonic smile spreads across my face.

"*What*?" Sarah asks. "Oh my God—*what*?"

"I can't tell you," I say. "It's too personal. But trust me, it's something that's gonna make Josh realize I'm one hundred percent all-in—and also that I'm the woman of his dreams."

"You're smiling devilishly," Sarah says.

"Because I'm thinking something *devilish*."

"Gimme a hint," Sarah says.

"Oh, little Miss Sarah Cruz, you couldn't handle it, trust me—your head would explode."

Sarah makes an adorable face. "God, you scare me," she says.

I look out the window of Sarah's car again, my skin sizzling and popping with electricity, a happy smile dancing on my lips for the first time in a week. *Yes.* I know exactly what to do to coax Joshua Faraday to finally let go completely. I've just got to make him see he's absolutely safe with me, in every conceivable way—that I love every little molecule of him, no matter how perverted.

My smile broadens.

They say the way to a man's heart is through his stomach. But in the case of my beloved sick fuck, Joshua William Faraday, I'm quite certain the entry point into his tortured heart is through an organ just a tad bit lower on his anatomy.

85

Chapter 15
Josh

I think Kat was put on this earth to torture me.

Goddammit, I don't just want her. I don't just miss her. I *crave* her like a drug.

I look up from the report I'm writing on my laptop and rub my forehead. Fuck, I can't concentrate worth a shit. I should have finished this stupid report three days ago, but I can't seem to trudge through it. I peer at my screen, just to see if whatever the fuck I've been writing for the past hour makes a lick of sense. For all I know, I've been writing, "Goobledoobledabbah" over and over. Fuck me.

I lean back in my chair.

Why'd I have to give in to my addiction and call Kat two hours ago? I thought hearing her voice would make me feel better, maybe take the edge off the pain I've been feeling all week, but all it did was torture me and make me crave her even more.

I blame 3 Doors Down, the bastards. "Here Without You" came on just as I was texting with Kat about how depressed Colby is, and the next thing I knew, I was texting Kat she could bring a smile to any man's face, and then, right after that, hastily pressing the button to call her, stupidly throwing an entire week's worth of self-imposed Kat-rehab out the fucking window.

"Theresa," I say, looking at my longtime personal assistant across the room. She's standing in my kitchen, cataloging a bunch of stuff that's about to be loaded onto the moving truck out front. "You got any Ibuprofen?"

"Of course." Theresa rummages into her purse and hands me a couple pills and a bottle of water from the fridge.

"Make it four," I say.

86

She hands me two additional pills.

"Thanks." I swallow the pills and look down at my computer.

"You've got a headache?" Theresa asks.

"I'm fine," I say. But I'm a liar. I'm not fine. In fact, I'm a wreck. And I've been a fucking wreck all week long, ever since I dragged my sorry, rejected, confused ass out of the hospital and onto the next flight back to L.A. I was so shattered by Kat's rejection of me that night, so overwhelmed at the bomb she'd dropped on me, I made a decision that very night to quit her once and for all. *If she's my addiction,* I thought, *then I'll just send myself to motherfucking rehab.*

Of course, I knew it'd be hard to quit a fucking unicorn, especially a unicorn tinged with a delicious streak of evil—a unicorn who happens to be the most exciting and incredible woman I've ever been with—a unicorn who sets the gold standard for turning me on— a unicorn who laughs like a dude and thinks like a terrorist and has a sexy little indentation in her chin that drives me wild. But I truly thought I could do it. I'm a fucking Faraday, after all, and, as my dad always used to drill into me, "Faradays never fucking quit." (Other than when they blow their brains out or drive off a bridge, I guess).

"Josh, sorry to bug you," Theresa says. A couple movers walk between us holding one of my black leather couches, and she pauses to let them pass before speaking. "The interior designer asked if we could move our consultation at the new house from Wednesday to the following Monday? She's got a family emergency."

After six years of running my life, Theresa surely must know what I'm going to say in response to her question. But, okay, I'll say it anyway. "If I happen to be in town on Monday, I'll be there," I reply. "If not, handle it for me. Just make the house look the way I like it—masculine, sleek, expensive, and in good taste—like it popped out of a glossy magazine."

"Okeedoke," Theresa says. "Gotcha."

I look down at my laptop again.

"Just one more thing," Theresa says.

I look up, annoyed.

"Your cars won't arrive at the new house until Tuesday at the earliest. So I went ahead and rented you a Ferrari 458 until then. It'll be sitting in your garage when you arrive in Seattle. Keys on your kitchen counter. I've arranged a limo to pick you up from the airport."

I nod and look back down at my laptop. I have no idea what Theresa just said. I think she said she rented me a Ferrari, but I'm not sure. I can't think. I can't track. Shit. I can't eat or sleep or breathe. I'm losing my fucking mind. *Kat, Kat, Kat.* She's all I can think about. I'm drowning in an all-consuming ache. I need to see her. Touch her. Fuck her. Smell her. Bite her. Spank her. I'm dying. I actually think I might literally be dying. This week has been goddamned fucking hell.

"Hey, Miss Rodriguez?" one of the moving guys asks. "Sorry to bug ya, but is this painting—"

"Yes, that's one of the items that was purchased by the new owner and will stay with the house," Theresa says, hopping up from her stool with obvious exasperation. "Put that painting down and come with me. I'm gonna show you which artwork stays and which goes *again.*"

My phone buzzes with an incoming text and I look down.

Kat.

My heart leaps. This is the first time all week Kat's instigated contact with me.

"Hi, Josh," Kat writes. "Just finished my doctor's appointment. Attaching a video of the sonogram. XOXO Kat. P.S. I told Sarah about the baby at lunch and she went to the appointment with me. Sorry. It just slipped out." She attaches a blushing-face emoji. "P.P.S. I'd strongly advise you NEVER send me into war with any classified information. Oh, and Sarah says she won't tell Jonas about the baby—she'll leave that to you. But she says you better tell your brother he's going to be an uncle soon—because even though Sarah's not nearly as big a blabbermouth as me (but who is?), she's still only human."

I shake my head. It's so *Kat* to insist we hold off telling Jonas and Sarah about the pregnancy until after their wedding and then go right ahead and blab about it to Sarah not five minutes later. I press play on the video, still shaking my head, completely annoyed.

"Doctor," Sarah's voice says, "will you explain what's onscreen for the baby's father?"

My entire body jolts at Sarah's use of the word "father." Holy fuck. Sarah's referring to *me.*

The doctor explains what's onscreen, including pointing out a flicker she says is the baby's heartbeat—what the fuck?—the baby's got a *heartbeat* already?—and when the doctor's finished talking, the camera pans to Kat.

Kat.

Oh my God.

My heart wrenches at the sight of her. She's lying on an examination table, her blouse pulled up, her golden hair splayed around her head—and her eyes looking as sad and lackluster as I've ever seen them. Oh my God. My heart's absolutely breaking at the pitiful, lonely, *tortured* look in Kat's beautiful blue eyes.

Instantly, all the anger I've been feeling toward Kat this week evaporates into thin air. I can't get over how unhappy my gorgeous Party Girl looks—and utterly exhausted, too. Clearly, she's not well. She's still hot as hell, of course—she's Katherine Ulla Morgan, after all—but I've never seen Kat look quite so ragged. So *vulnerable.* So fucking *miserable.* Even when she was hung-over and functioning on three hours of sleep in Vegas, even when she was scared to death to walk into a bank and impersonate a Ukrainian pimpstress, *even when she found out I didn't tell her about my move to Seattle*, Kat never looked quite the way she does in this video.

"Hi, Josh," Kat says toward the camera, waving half-heartedly. "Well, it looks like our accidental Faraday is a stubborn little thing—surprise, surprise! I guess he or she's decided they're not going anywhere, after all." Emotion overwhelms her all of a sudden. She wipes her eyes. "I'm really sorry, Josh," Kat says, her voice wobbling.

The video abruptly ends.

I lean back in my chair, my heart exploding with yearning and regret and sympathy. Oh my God. *Kat.* My Party Girl with a Hyphen. My beautiful unicorn.

The woman I love.

Oh my God, yes. It's suddenly as obvious to me as the nose on my face: *I love Kat.* I don't know why it's taken me so long to realize it. I love Katherine Ulla Morgan and I can't live another day without her. I can't fucking *breathe* without her. Jesus Fucking Christ. What the fuck have I been doing this whole past week, staying away from the woman I love? I should have been comforting her—taking care of her—telling her we're in this cluster-fuck of a situation together. I should have been strong enough—compassionate enough—*man* enough—to tell the voices in my head to shut the fuck up.

I feel like the earth has suddenly broken off its axis and hurtled uncontrollably into space. Oh my God. *I love Kat*—and I should have been there for her this whole past week while she was dealing with Colby's injuries and the shit-storm her life's become, rather than sitting around moping and wallowing in self-pity and fear. Oh my God. I'm such a prick. An immature, self-involved, pussy-ass of a little prick.

I pick up my phone, adrenaline coursing through my body.

"Hi," Kat says softly, answering after one ring.

"Hi," I reply. "I got your video, Kat—I saw the grape."

Kat exhales. "I'm so sorry, Josh." She lets out a little yelp.

My heart squeezes. "You have nothing to apologize for," I say, emotion overwhelming me. "I'm the one who's sorry."

"You? But I'm the one who forgot to take my pill."

"Kat, so what? Birth control pills aren't one hundred percent effective in the best-case scenario. So we took a *slightly* higher risk than I'd originally realized. It was a fucking *accident*."

"But you trusted me and I screwed up."

I scoff. "Who could remember to take a pill with the schedule we were keeping in Vegas? Seriously, Kat, if the situation were reversed, I would have missed a whole *week's* worth of pills, I guarantee it."

Kat lets out a little whimper.

"Whatever the increased odds were after missing one pill, I'm sure I would have taken them in advance, I just wanted to fuck you so goddamned much."

Kat laughs through tears.

"I'm sorry I've been a prick this week—I guess I had some shit to work out."

"You haven't been a prick—you've just been extremely *polite.*"

"I made you feel like you're alone in this, and you're not."

Kat sniffles loudly but doesn't say anything for a long beat. "I thought maybe you were done with me, Josh. I was scared you didn't want me anymore."

"Done with you? Are you mad? No fucking way."

Kat breathes a huge sigh of relief.

"Are you done with *me*?" I ask, holding my breath.

"No fucking way," she says. "I'll never be done with you, Josh. *Never*."

My heart lurches like a guard dog on a leash. "So, hey, how 'bout that grape," I say. "Pretty crazy, huh?"

"Crazy corn chowder," Kat replies.

"That's a total Henn-ism, you know."

"I think that's where I got it." She sniffles again.

"Seeing the baby's heartbeat made everything seem so *real*," I say softly.

"Totally," she agrees. "This shit is real, man."

"Crazy."

"You know, it's so weird," she says quietly, "but when I saw the heartbeat, I started feeling protective about the grape—like I don't want anything to happen to it, after all."

"Immortality through reproduction, remember? It's evolution, baby."

"But I've never wanted a baby. I don't even think babies are cute. They just look like tiny old men."

"Your heart's answering the call of the wild, babe."

"But it's so unlike me."

"Yeah, I guess we're both doing things we never thought we'd do, huh?" I pause, hoping Kat will address her soul-crushing rejection of me in the hospital, but she doesn't. "So, hey, PG," I say, clearing my throat. "It turns out I'm moving on Wednesday."

"Yay," she says.

"I've got to see you," I say, my heart racing. Fuck me. That's the understatement of the century.

"Shoot," Kat says. "Wednesday's not good for me. Colby's getting out of the hospital and my entire family's gonna hang out with him. Can we do Thursday?"

"Thursday it is. I'll text you my new address. Seven o'clock?"

"Great. I can't wait to see your new house." She pauses. "I can't wait to see *you*."

"Same here. I've missed you," I say. I clutch my chest. Jesus, I can barely breathe.

"Josh, I've missed you so much," she whispers. "I've been feeling like I'm *dying*."

"Me, too, babe. Exactly. I've been in physical pain without you. You have no idea."

I can hear her smiling over the phone line, even as she sniffles. "Really?"

"Hell yes. I've been miserable."

"Me, too," she says softly. She sniffles again. "I'll be counting the minutes until Thursday. And maybe Friday, too? Because... you'll be living here, so . . ?"

"Yep. Absolutely," I say, breathing a sigh of relief. "You'll be seeing me so much, you'll get sick of me. I promise."

Kat sniffles again. "Impossible. I could never get sick of you. *Ever.*"

My heart squeezes.

"Okay. Well. I gotta go," Kat says. "I'm gonna hang up and sob my eyes out now."

"Okay, babe. Have fun. Call me later."

"I will," Kat says. "I can't wait to see you."

"I can't wait to see you, too. I miss you so much, babe."

"I miss you, too—so, so, so, so much."

"Don't be sad anymore, Kat. I'm here now—and I'm not going anywhere."

She starts bawling on the other end of the line and my heart shatters at the sound of her wails.

"It's okay, baby," I coo. "I'm right here. Don't cry, beautiful. I'll see you really soon."

"Okay. I gotta go," she murmurs, obviously still crying. "I'll call you later after I pull myself together."

"Wait, baby. Don't go," I say. "Don't leave like this. You're crying."

"No, I'm okay. I gotta go. I wanna have an ugly cry on my own."

"Okay, baby," I say. "But call me again soon."

We hang up and I sit, staring at my phone for a long moment. Oh my fucking God. I love her. I love Kat with all my heart and soul. And I'm gonna tell her so on Thursday—the way I should have told her at the hospital if I'd had an ounce of sense.

Kat was absolutely right to turn me down at the hospital. Actually, I never should have proposed in the first place—I know that now. I have no genuine desire to get married—I was just trying to appease the ghost of my father—get his absolution from the grave. But fuck that. My father's not here to disown me anymore, and even if he were, I'd tell him to fuck off. Okay, fine, I've got a hot baby-momma-girlfriend. So fucking what? It's not the end of the world. We'll figure it out. The most important thing is that I love her—I know that now. *I love Kat.* And when I see her on Thursday, I'm gonna tell her exactly how I feel, no holds barred—and I don't need a fucking ring and the promise of a stupid piece of paper from the government to do it. I'll tell her straight from my heart and soul. Oh shit. I've suddenly got a brilliant idea. Oh my God, I'm a fucking genius. I close my laptop and leap up from the table, a surge of adrenaline flooding me. "I'm going out, T-Rod!" I call to Theresa in the back of the house.

"Hang on," Theresa's voice calls from another room.

"Gotta go!" I yell, bounding toward the front door. "I've got something important to do!"

"Hang on a sec," Theresa says, entering the room breathlessly. She's holding a cardboard box.

"Sorry, T-Rod," I say, striding toward the front door. "I've got something I've got to do."

"Just take a quick peek at this stuff, Josh." She holds up the box. "The movers were about to load this stuff onto the truck and I thought you might want to pull a few things out to take with you on Wednesday."

"No. Whatever that stuff is, they can load it onto the truck."

"But the truck's gonna take four or five days to get to Seattle. Is there anything here you want to have with you the first night in your new house—you know, something to make it feel like home on your first night there?"

I'm exasperated. A house is just a house, for fuck's sake—there's no such thing as a home. But, fine. Anything to make Theresa happy. I peek inside the box and half-heartedly rummage through its contents for half a second. "Nope. Nothing I care—" I shut my mouth. Oh. Yep. There's one thing I care about. A whole lot, in fact. I pull it out reverently. "Just this," I say. I run my fingertip over the three smiling faces gazing back at me from the framed photo. "Don't let them load this onto the truck—I'll take it with me in my bag."

Theresa nods. "I'll put it into your carry-on—inside pocket. Don't forget it's there, okay? You don't want it to break."

"Thanks."

"Of course."

I turn toward the front door again. "Hey, T-Rod," I say, turning back around to face her. Why don't you give yourself a raise? Maybe, I dunno, twenty-five percent?"

Theresa smiles. "Thank you. Very generous of you."

"And, hey, can you do something for me?"

"It's my reason for living, Josh."

"Arrange a romantic dinner-for-two at my new place in Seattle for Thursday night. Seven o'clock. I'm talking a top-rated chef, a waiter in a tux, flowers everywhere, candles all over the place—the whole nine yards. You know, a five-star-dining experience, but right in my own dining room."

"No problem. But the truck won't be there with your furniture until Saturday. I'll have to rent some furniture for the night—at least a table and chairs."

"Great. And as long as you're renting stuff, would you rent me a pool table for a couple nights? I might wanna play pool before my table arrives—it always helps me relax."

"Sure."

"Oh, and rent me a really comfortable bed for Thursday night—a *really* nice one. Pillow-top mattress. Silk sheets. You know, the whole nine yards."

"Josh, just a little tip: you never need to say the phrase 'the whole nine yards' to me. I know when it comes to you there are only two gears in everything you do: zero and 'the whole nine yards.'"

I laugh.

"Speaking of which, what do you think about a violinist to play during dinner?"

"Ooh. I like that. Do it."

"I'll set it up," Theresa says.

"Just do whatever you have to do to make me look really good, T."

"Don't I always, Josh? Speaking of which, I just bought you three new Anthony Franco suits from his new collection, already tailored to fit you to a tee. Do you want them loaded onto the truck or sent in a garment bag with you on the plane?"

"Is one of them blue, by any chance?"

She grins. "Of course. Sapphire blue to match your eyes."

"Garment bag for the blue one, truck for the others. I'll wear the blue one Thursday night." I wink. "Gotta look sharp for my big night."

"Oh, it's a big night?"

"It sure is. I'm finally gonna talk about my fucking feelings—to a *girl*."

"To a *girl*? Ooooh. Wow. That *is* big." She beams a huge smile at me. "Lucky girl."

"That's what I told her."

Theresa laughs.

"I'm not kidding, unfortunately. That's exactly what I told her."

Theresa grimaces.

"Yeah. So now I've got my work cut out for me to get myself out of the doghouse."

"Ooph. I think we'd better add a cellist. Sounds like an emergency."

My smile broadens. "Thanks, T."

"You're very welcome, Josh."

"I mean, you know, thanks for everything."

"Just doing my job."

"Hey, how about we make that raise thirty percent? Sound good?"

Theresa makes a "meh" face. "Well, thirty percent is certainly *good*. Nothing to sneeze at—believe me, I'm grateful for your generosity. But you only live once, right? Why not 'go big or go home,' I always say?"

"Ah, you want 'the whole nine yards,' huh, T?"

Theresa laughs. "You've rubbed off on me, I guess."

"Okay. Forty percent. But that's my final offer."

Theresa nods. "I think that sounds about right." She winks.

I laugh. "Okay. Forty it is—until the next time you squeeze me, that is." With that, I turn around and waltz out my front door, a spring in my step and a gleam in my eye for the first time in an entire fucking week.

Chapter 16
Josh

"Six-ball in the side pocket," I say. I bend over the pool table and sink my shot with a loud clack.

"Kat turned you *down*?" Jonas says, incredulous.

"Third worst day of my entire life," I say. "She hit me with a mean left cross followed by a crushing right hook. *Bam!* Right on the chin."

"I can only imagine. Sounds horrible, Josh."

"Four-ball off the bumper, ricochet off the seven-ball into the corner pocket," I say. I line up my shot carefully, whack the white cue ball with confidence, and sink the four, exactly as described. "Damn, I'm good," I say.

"Pretty impressive."

"My life may be falling down around my ears, but I can still sink a goddamned billiard ball, motherfucker."

"Sorry I wasn't here for you when all this shit was happening. Sounds like you took it pretty hard."

"No worries, bro. 'Twas merely a flesh wound. I'm over it now—back in the saddle. Two-ball in the far corner—straight shot." I bend down over the table and take my shot, but I've miscalculated the angle by a hair and the ball rebounds off the bumper. "Shit," I say. "Goddammit. I always miss the easy ones." I motion to Jonas. "Okay, go ahead and run the table now, bro. I'll just sit down for the rest of the game."

"You never know," Jonas says, rubbing chalk on the end of his stick. "I haven't played in months—I might be rusty."

"Mmm hmm," I say, leaning against the wall. "You've never been rusty at anything in your life."

Jonas walks around the table, surveying his first shot. "I'm thinking the seven-ball off the bumper right here and then off your two-ball into the side pocket," Jonas says.

"Pfft. Good luck with that—tough angle, bro. Just do the three. The three's a clean shot."

"No, the three's a red herring. If I sink the seven first, then I'll have my whole table set up for me like clockwork."

"If you say so."

"Oh, I do." Jonas bends over, takes his complicated shot, and sinks it with ease.

"Goddamn, you." I roll my eyes. "I hate playing against you. Against everyone else, I'm a fucking beast."

"I'm sure you are. So how far along is she?"

"Almost ten weeks."

Jonas whistles. "Wow."

"Last week, the baby was the size of a grape. This week, it's already the size of a kumquat." I can't help smiling to myself. *The Kumquat's carrying a kumquat.*

"Good to see you smiling about it."

I pause, surprised. "It's actually kind of amazing how fast a guy can adjust to a new reality when there's no other option," I say.

"'Happiness depends upon ourselves,'" Jonas says.

"Gosh, thanks, Plato."

"Aristotle. You want Plato?"

"No," I say.

"'There are two things a person should never be angry at: what they can help, and what they cannot.'"

"Incredibly profound," I say. "I feel magically better now. Hey, you wanna see something wild?" I pull out my phone and show Jonas the sonogram video Kat sent me the other day.

"Sarah was there?" Jonas asks at the sound of Sarah's voice asking the doctor to explain the image on the sonogram screen.

"Yeah. Kat blabbed to her at lunch right before her doctor's appointment. I guess Sarah didn't wanna steal my thunder by telling you—she thought I should break the news to you." I put my hands out like ta-da! "'Hey, Jonas—you're gonna be an uncle!'" I say with faux excitement. "There, I told you."

Jonas shakes his head. "I'm impressed Sarah was able to keep such a big secret."

"Kat couldn't keep a secret to save her life," I say, rolling my eyes. "Actually, I wouldn't have minded Sarah telling you. I wish I could crawl under a rock and not have to tell anyone, to be honest."

"You're not jumping for joy about your impending fatherhood, I take it?"

"Pretty much shitting a brick."

"So when's the baby due?" Jonas asks. He calls another shot and sinks it with ease, yet again, and I place my stick on a rack in the corner in utter resignation.

"December second," I reply. "Sagittarius."

"Sagittarius?"

"Just like Henn."

Jonas laughs. "Oh, shit. That'd be funny if you had a kid just like Henn."

I can't help but join Jonas laughing. That really would be funny.

"So do you believe all that astrology stuff?" Jonas asks.

I shrug. "Sort of. Kat's kind of made a believer out of me, actually."

Jonas surveys the table, lining up his next shot. "I can't believe you're gonna be a father, Josh."

"So I'm told."

Jonas stands upright from the table and assesses me for a long beat. "You're gonna be a fantastic father."

My cheeks feel hot all of a sudden. "You really think so?"

"I *know* so. You were born to be a father, Josh—more than anyone I know. It's in your DNA—you got it from Mom. You take care of people—it's who you are—who you've always been."

"Wow. Thank you."

"It's the God's truth. That's one lucky kid."

I bite my lip. "Thanks, Jonas."

Jonas leans over the pool table again, assessing his next shot. "Can you even imagine what Dad would be saying right now? 'I'll disown you faster than that gold-digger can demand a paternity test!'"

"Dude, stop, please. I don't have to imagine it—I've been hearing Dad's voice screaming in my ear since Kat dropped the baby-bomb on me."

Jonas calls his next shot and sinks it with ease.

98

"Mr. Faraday?"

I look toward the door. It's the violinist Theresa hired for me, a petite Asian woman in a black dress.

"The cellist and I are all set up in the dining room," the woman says. "Do you want us to stay hidden in the kitchen until your signal, or... how do you wanna play this?"

I look at my watch. Kat should be here in just under thirty minutes. "I think you should start playing the minute my girlfriend walks through the front door—you know, set the mood right away that this is gonna be a magical night for her."

"Okay, great," the violinist says. "We'll just stand in position and wait for your signal, then."

"Why don't you start playing the minute the doorbell rings? That can be your signal."

"Perfect. Oh, and the chef wanted me to tell you he's all ready, too. He has a few questions."

"Great. Will you tell him I'll be right out? I'm about to get my ass whooped. Shouldn't take too long."

She chuckles and leaves.

"Wow, you're really going balls to the wall here," Jonas says. "Flowers. Candles. Chef. Violin. Cello. I gotta get everyone's contact info from you—Sarah would go nuts for something like this."

"Email T-Rod and ask her for the info—she set everything up for me."

Jonas leans down and lines up his next shot. "Well, yeah, I figured."

"She just gouged me for a forty percent raise, by the way. The woman's a shark."

"She deserves every penny."

I laugh. "True."

"Oh, which reminds me—thanks for the bottle of champagne and fruit basket you sent to Sarah and me in Mykonos to congratulate us on our engagement. So thoughtful of you."

We both burst out laughing.

"You're so welcome," I say. "It was the least I could do."

"I ought to chip in for half of Theresa's raise. Half the shit you do for me is probably her."

"I'm not gonna dignify that with a response," I say, though he's one hundred percent right.

"One-ball in the side pocket," Jonas says, just before sinking the shot. "So did Theresa help you pick out Kat's ring, too? Something that'll 'sear her corneas'—I believe was the phrase you used when you nagged me about it?"

"Oh, no," I say, scoffing. "I'm not *proposing* to Kat tonight. I'm not a fucking masochist. I already asked her once and she practically flipped me the bird. Getting disemboweled once by Kat was plenty, thank you very much."

"What the fuck did you say to Kat when you asked her? I don't understand why she said no."

"Actually, I think her exact words were, 'I wouldn't marry you if you were the last goddamned man on earth.'"

Jonas grimaces. "Wow, that's pretty harsh."

"That's Kat for you—you never wonder where you stand with her."

"Josh, seriously. Why'd she turn you down? I don't understand. You love each other, right? And she's carrying your baby. So it should be a no-brainer—you two should get married."

I shrug. "I pissed her off. It's not hard to do—trust me. And now she doesn't wanna marry me. Which is fine because I don't wanna get married." I motion to the pool table. "Take your shot, bro. Kat will be here soon."

"But if you're not gonna ask Kat to marry you tonight, then what the fuck are you doing with the violin and the chef?"

I grin. "Tonight's gonna be even better than a marriage proposal. I'm giving Kat a once-in-a-lifetime gift—and then I'm finally gonna tell her the three little words."

Jonas raises his eyebrows, clearly surprised. "You haven't already told her you love her?"

My stomach clenches. He's making me feel insecure. "No. I'm gonna tell her tonight. Plus, like I said, I'm gonna give her a gift she'll never forget."

"But you already asked her to marry you."

"Correct."

"I'm totally confused. You proposed *marriage* to Kat without telling her you *love* her?"

I nod, suddenly feeling sick to my stomach. It sounds so wrong when he says it in that holier-than-thou tone of voice.

Jonas scowls at me. "You said 'Will you marry me, Kat?' but you didn't also say 'I love you more than the air I breathe, Kat'?"

I nod. I wish he'd drop it already.

"Josh, what the fuck did you say to Kat when you asked her to marry you? I can't for the life of me fathom what you said if it didn't include the words 'I love you more than life itself and I can't live without you.'"

I shift my weight. I feel my cheeks flushing. "I just told her, you know..."

Jonas waits for me to finish my sentence, and when I don't, he shakes his head at me, bends over the table, and lines up his next shot. "Nine-ball off the ten, then off the side, and then into the side pocket." He sinks his shot in one fluid, confident motion.

"Why do I even bother playing pool with you?" I say. "If I don't run the table out of the gate, I might as well just sit the fuck down. It's pointless."

"Three in the far corner." He bends over and sinks his shot. "How could you possibly propose marriage to a woman and *not* tell her you love her in the same breath?"

I roll my eyes. "Jonas, come on. I'd just found out Kat's pregnant with my accidental spawn. I was a deer in headlights. Love was the furthest thing from my mind. I was just trying to do the right thing."

Jonas grimaces. "Well, shit. No wonder Kat turned you down—rightfully so, you dumbshit." He calls his next shot and sinks it with startling ease.

"Yeah, fuck it—it doesn't matter. It all worked out for the best," I say, feeling defensive. "Kat really did me a big favor by saying no. I didn't know it then, of course—at the time, it felt like Kat was kicking me in the teeth—but now I see she was the only one thinking clearly. Holy shit, I can't believe I just said that about *Kat*."

Jonas stands completely upright and rests his hands on the end of his pool cue, staring at me intensely. "Do you love her?" he asks.

"Yeah. I do. Without a doubt."

"And she's carrying your baby?"

I nod. "Yeah, we've already established that fact. I showed you the video, remember?"

"Then *marry* the girl, for fuck's sake, Josh. It's not that complicated."

I exhale in exasperation.

"Josh, Kat obviously turned you down because you were asking her out of obligation, not love. If you ask her again, but this time tell her you love her, she'll say yes—I guarantee it."

I wave Jonas off. "I'm not gonna ask Kat again. Once was enough. The truth is I have no interest in getting married, not even to Kat. If I wanna be with someone, I'll be with them. And if I wanna go, then I'll go. And it's the same for her. I think it's more satisfying to know the other person's there because they *want* to be—not because they *have* to be based on some stupid piece of paper from the government."

Jonas shakes his head but he doesn't speak. After a moment, he surveys the table again. "Eight-ball, rebounding off your two, and then into the far right corner." He sinks his shot and wins the game.

"Goddammit, Jonas. I hate playing against you."

Jonas puts his stick on the rack, his jaw muscles tight.

"What?" I ask.

"Nothing."

"Dude, I can tell you've got something to say. Just say it."

"Nope. I've got nothing to say. Congratulations on telling Kat you love her tonight. Big step. I'm sure she'll be thrilled to hear it."

"Jonas," I say, exhaling. "You don't understand. I'm gonna support my kid, okay? I'm gonna be the best father I can be. That's a given. And I'm hopefully gonna raise the kid with Kat because I love her and wanna be with her. She's the most incredible woman I've ever been with and I can't imagine finding anyone better, ever. But I'm not the marrying kind of guy. I don't need a piece of paper *forcing* me to be with Kat—I'm gonna be with her because I *want* to be."

There's a long beat.

"Cool," Jonas says, clearly brushing me off. "Congrats. Come on. The chef wanted to talk to you, remember?"

"Yeah, and you gotta get the fuck out before Kat gets here." I look at my watch. "Kat's supposed to be here in ten minutes—which means she'll be here in thirty."

We start walking toward the dining area.

I keep expecting Jonas to say something, but he doesn't.

"What?" I finally say. "Just say it."

Jonas presses his lips together.

"Fuck, Jonas. I know what you're thinking."

"You do? What am I thinking?"

"You're thinking I should propose to Kat again. And, yeah, I know that's the way we were raised—you get a girl pregnant, you marry her. No other option. I know that's what Dad would demand of me. But I'm not beholden to Dad anymore. He's gone—he made his choice—and I'm a grown-ass man. I've decided I'm not gonna ask Kat to marry me and that's final. It's my choice. I love her, I really do, and that's enough. I've decided I'm gonna love Kat with all my heart and be committed to her and help her raise our baby and we'll just see what happens between her and me. If she wants to go, she can. Same for me." I'm breathing heavily. My chest is tight. *"What?* Stop looking at me like that."

"Mr. Faraday?" It's the chef, accompanied by a guy in a tux. "How are you this evening, sir? This is Gregory. He'll be serving you tonight."

The four of us shake hands.

"Is this your guest for the evening?" The chef asks, motioning to Jonas.

Jonas and I look at each other and laugh.

"No. This is my brother. He's just leaving. My guest will be arriving in a few minutes."

"But I'd love to get your card," Jonas says. "I'm thinking about hiring you guys as a surprise for my fiancée."

I smile at the exuberant tone of Jonas' voice when he says the word "fiancée."

"When's the wedding?" the chef asks.

"Exactly three weeks from today."

"Oh. Congratulations."

"World's shortest engagement," Jonas says, laughing. "And she's not even pregnant."

I glare at him. Low blow.

Jonas winks at me.

"So, Mr. Faraday," the chef says, addressing me. "I just had a few questions..." He runs through his menu items, making sure I'm happy with each course as he plans to prepare it, and I give him approval on everything.

"Wonderful. We'll start with a light appetizer and drink pairing when she arrives."

"Oh, I should have told you: my girlfriend's pregnant," I say. "No alcohol this evening for either of us."

"Oh. No problem. Thanks for letting me know. Congratulations."

The chef and waiter head back into the kitchen.

"Well, have fun," Jonas says, slapping my back. "I'd better get home. Sarah just sent me a text saying she misses me—always a good sign." He snickers.

"Hang on a second," I say. "We're not done." I motion to a loveseat (rented for me by Theresa), and we sit.

"What?" Jonas asks, obviously anxious to leave.

"I just... " I exhale. "I need you to understand something."

Jonas waits.

"I have no desire to get married, not even to Kat. From here on out, just don't give me a hard time about it, okay? It is what it is. I know Kat's pregnant and I know we were raised to—"

"I don't think you should ask Kat to marry you," Jonas says, interrupting me. He levels me with his startling blue eyes.

"You don't?"

"No."

"But *you're* getting married."

"Yeah, and that's exactly why I don't think you should marry Kat."

"I'm confused."

Jonas sighs. "Josh, I'm marrying Sarah in twenty-one days because I can't wait a day longer than necessary to call her my wife. I'm marrying Sarah because I can't wait to declare my undying love for her in front of God and everyone we know. I'm marrying Sarah because she's the air I breathe, the embodiment of my hopes and dreams and my every drop of happiness. Because I want Sarah to be mine, all mine, in every possible way 'til the end of time. Because I never want another man to touch her, ever again—because even the *thought* of another man touching her makes me homicidal. Because I want to be there for her, for better or worse, for richer or poorer, in sickness and in health, until death do us part—and I want to promise that to her in the most sacred way possible. I'm marrying Sarah

104

because I don't want there to be any doubt in her mind how I feel about her, not even for a moment, for the rest of her life." He scowls at me. *"And not because I think I need a motherfucking piece of paper to tell me my love is real or official."*

I swallow hard, rendered completely speechless.

"So if you don't feel exactly the same way about Kat," Jonas continues, his eyes burning like hot coals, "if you don't want to make that woman your wife for all the reasons I just described, then she didn't just do *you* a favor by turning down your proposal—she did *herself* a favor, too."

Chapter 17
Josh

My heart is pulsing in my ears. I open my mouth and close it, but Jonas has stunned me into complete silence.

The doorbell rings and, instantly, the violin and cello begin playing.

"Oh shit," I say. "You're not supposed to be here, Jonas. You gotta get the fuck out."

"I'll go in the kitchen and slip out when you and Kat head into the dining room."

"No. That's stupid." I sigh. "Why don't you just say hi to her—you can congratulate her on the kumquat."

We move to the front door together, my head spinning. I've never been kicked so fucking hard in the teeth by Jonas in my entire life. What the fuck just happened? I feel like I'm walking through molasses with cement blocks strapped to my ankles as I trudge to the front door. I smile at the violinist and cellist as I pass them on my way to the front door, but my smile is a façade. I seriously can't breathe.

When I reach the door with Jonas a few feet behind me, I take a deep breath, gathering myself. I'm gonna give Kat an amazing gift tonight—a truly once-in-a-lifetime gift—and then I'm gonna tell her I love her. And that's a pretty big fucking deal. I just need to shake off what Jonas said—the man's clearly pussy-whipped beyond anything I could have fathomed. I just need to shake it off.

I exhale and open my front door, my heart pounding at the thought of seeing Kat after this past long, torturous week apart. This is gonna be an epic night for both of us. A new beginning. But when I swing open the door, it's not Kat—it's the male version of her,

106

holding a motorcycle helmet in his arm and dressed in a black leather jacket, a pair of dark jeans, and an *Rx Bandits* T-shirt.

The male version of Kat puts out his hand. "Sir J.W. Faraday, I presume?"

I shake the guy's hand.

"Hey, Josh." The guy smiles. "I'm Dax, Kat's brother?"

"Oh." I clear my throat. "Yeah. Hey, Dax. Kat's told me a lot about you. Glad to finally meet you."

Dax peeks behind me into the house. "Wow. Violin and cello. Oh, hey, do you mind if I get the musicians' contact info? I'm recording an album next week and I could totally use violin and cello on a couple of my songs."

"Uh. Sure. Yeah. Come on in." I open the door wide and Dax bounds into my house like he owns the place. "So where's Kat?" I ask.

"Oh." Dax turns around. "Sorry. I got so excited about the violin and cello, I forgot why I'm here. Kat asked me to give you this."

He hands me a sealed envelope and my heart instantly drops into my toes.

Shit.

Kat's not coming.

I look at Jonas and he looks as crestfallen as I feel.

Kat sent her baby brother to hand me a "Dear John" letter? Is she really *that* heartless? Yes, she is, unfortunately, and I've always known it—deep down inside, I've always known this day was coming. Maybe that's why I've been holding back all this time with Kat—because I knew deep down in my bones this thing with her was just too good to last—that she'd eventually slip past my borders with a bomb strapped to her chest and blow me to fucking bits.

"Uh. This is my brother, Jonas," I manage to say, my cheeks hot.

"Hey, Dax," Jonas says, shaking Dax's hand. "Nice T-shirt. Rx Bandits is my all-time favorite band."

"Hey, mine, too. Ever seen 'em live?"

"Yup. Lots of times. Best live band ever."

I'm literally shaking. I feel like crying like a pussy-ass little bitch, but I swallow it down.

"So it's okay if I talk to your musicians real quick?" Dax says.

"Go ahead," I say, my throat tight. I call over to the violinist and cellist. "Hey, ladies, you can stop playing. It's not my girlfriend."

The music ceases.

"Well, are you gonna open the card?" Jonas asks.

I swallow hard. Part of me doesn't want to open the envelope. If Kat's decided she's done with me—*even though she's carrying my goddamned kid*—I'm not gonna bounce back any time soon. In fact, I'm gonna be in a world of fucking hurt for the rest of my fucking life, to be honest. Visions of Kat dragging my kid to baseball games with her new boyfriend flood me—images of Kat fucking another man while my baby's fast asleep in a crib in the other room. Fuck me. Based on the way I handled the whole thing with Emma, I can't even begin to imagine the human pile of rubble I'm about to become after I read this note. I absent-mindedly touch my left bicep and instantly feel an avalanche of anticipatory regret. Oh my God. I can't believe I got a fucking girlfriend tattoo mere days before my girlfriend decided to break up with me. Oh, irony of ironies—please, God, no. I shake my head at my own stupidity. Kat warned me, didn't she? "Johnny Depp had to change 'Winona Forever' to 'Wino Forever,'" Kat told me way back when. "*Don't do it.*" But did I listen to her? Fuck no—of course, not. *Dumbshit.*

"Josh," Jonas says emphatically, drawing me out of my rambling thoughts. "Open the fucking envelope."

I stare at Jonas dumbly.

"Open it, for fuck's sake."

I open the envelope slowly and pull out the card—and as I do, something falls onto the floor.

Jonas bends down and picks it up—and when he straightens up, glory be, he's holding a poker chip in his palm, his eyebrow raised.

Relief and excitement flood me. Thank you, God. Kat's not a heartless terrorist—well, yeah, she is—*but she's also the woman of my dreams*!

I hastily open the notecard and read, my heart racing, my dick tingling.

"Hello there, my darling, beloved Playboy," the card reads. "The doctor said my sex drive might increase *dramatically* due to pregnancy hormones. Well, guess what? *She was right*! I'm excited to see your new house one of these days, I really am, and I sure hope you didn't go to too much trouble with dinner tonight—because there's been a change of plans, baby! Tonight, my beloved, sexy, beautiful Playboy, we're going to fulfill one of your all-time sick-fuck fantasies. That's right, honey—I hope you like windows—*wink!*—because you're about to fuck one any which way you please." Kat writes the name and address of a nearby five-star luxury hotel plus a room number. "Hurry up, my gorgeous, well-hung Playboy. Your window's waiting for you—along with her selected window dressing (*another wink!*). I guarantee you're gonna *love* how dripping wet this window is you when you get here, baby. XOXO Kat."

I look up from the note, my eyes bugging out. I'm rock hard. Oh my God.

"Good news?" Jonas asks.

"Call Sarah," I say abruptly. I grab my suit jacket off the back of the loveseat. "A romantic dinner for two just fell into your lap, bro. Enjoy." I call out to Dax over by the musicians. "Hey, Dax. Nice to meet you, man. I've gotta go—I've got an unexpected dinner date with your diabolical sister. Hopefully, we'll have a chance to talk another time."

Dax waves. "Oh, I'm sure we'll have a chance to talk one of these days, Josh—maybe at the hospital when Kat gives birth to your baby?"

I stop dead in my tracks and turn around to face him, my cheeks instantly burning.

Dax shoots me an evil smile that reminds me so much of his heinous sister, it freaks me the fuck out. "Don't worry, Sir Faraday," Dax says, still smiling. "Kat didn't tell anyone else in our family about your little 'oops'—it's just impossible for her to keep a secret from me." He winks.

I swallow hard, words failing me.

"I won't say a word to anyone," Dax adds. "I promise."

"Thanks," I manage to say.

"I'm actually gonna enjoy watching you guys tell the fam." He chuckles. "Ought to be extremely entertaining."

My stomach flips over. "Yeah. Should be a real blast."

"So, yeah, looks like we'll be seeing a lot of each other in the future, huh? Assuming, of course, you're planning to do more than write checks and attend your kid's birthday parties once a year?"

"Hey, Dax," Jonas says stepping forward, his muscles visibly tensing. "Josh would never—"

"I got this, bro," I say, putting up my hand. "Dax, I'm gonna do a whole lot more for this kid than write checks and attend birthday parties. I'm gonna be this baby's father in every sense of the word—every single day for the rest of my life. You can count on it."

Dax's face softens. "Good." He shifts his weight. "Sorry. Just looking out for my sister."

"Understandably," I say. "I'd do the same."

Dax beams me a genuine smile this time, without even a hint of evil. "You better go, man," he says. "My sister's not exactly patient."

I chuckle. "That's an understatement. She's hell on wheels, bro. But I wouldn't have her any other way."

Dax nods, seemingly pleased with that answer. "You better go."

I hug my brother goodbye—nice to know he was ready to beat the shit out of Kat's little brother for me, if necessary—gotta love Jonas—and stride into the kitchen.

"Change of plans," I say to the chef. "My brother and his fiancée will be dining tonight—so let the booze flow, after all."

The chef says something but I don't catch it. I'm too busy grabbing the keys to my rented Ferrari off the counter and racing out of the kitchen.

"Wait, Josh," Jonas yells at my back, just before I make my escape through the front door of my house. "Hang on just a sec."

I stop, though it pains me to do it.

I turn around to face my brother. "Jonas, please, I gotta go. Kat's waiting, man."

"Hang the fuck on," Jonas says. He saunters up to me slowly, clearly enjoying torturing me, and when he finally reaches me, he opens my palm and lays the poker chip inside it. "You can't meet Kat without your ticket to ride."

"Oh yeah. Thanks." I turn on my heel.

"Wait," Jonas says.

I exhale and turn around to face him again. "*What?*"

Jonas leans in and lowers his voice. "I don't know what this poker chip buys you this time, Josh, but, whatever it is, don't even *think* about calling me and asking me to play Boring Blane ever again."

110

Chapter 18
Kat

Always the hooker, never the john? Is that how that old saying goes? Or maybe that's bridesmaids? Well, whatever. Either way, I just paid a woman for sex—and when I did, my clit buzzed like a bumblebee trapped inside a windowsill.

"Thank you," Bridgette says, stuffing the wad of bills I just handed her into her Fendi bag. "I sure hope this means you're gonna follow through this time."

"I already told you, Bridgette, last time Josh and I were just too early in our relationship—honestly, I was just too insecure. I gave Josh mixed signals and I think he felt the need to reassure me. But this time, I'm rarin' to go. And if *I'm* rarin' to go, Josh will be, too."

Bridgette sniffs, apparently not completely convinced.

"I wouldn't have flown you all the way up to Seattle and paid you a shitload of cash if we weren't gonna do it this time."

Bridgette narrows her eyes. "My time is valuable, you know. I'm giving you the benefit of the doubt only because you're so damned fuckable." She runs her fingertip up my arm. "Otherwise, I wouldn't have bothered."

"I give you my word. Now, stop stressing me out, Bridgette. I've never done this before and I need to relax. "

Bridgette's eyes flicker. "I thought you said you'd done this once before in college?"

"Well, yeah, sort of, but it was amateur-hour. Second base only and I didn't even have an orgasm."

Bridgette's aghast. "No *orgasm*? Aw, poor little pussycat. Don't worry, I'll be sure to get you off this time." She bites her lower lip. "How about a drink to calm your nerves?"

I shake my head. "No, thanks. I'm good." I look at my watch. "Will you do me a favor and take off your clothes? Josh will be here any minute and I want to give him an insta-boner when I open the door."

Apparently, I don't have to ask Bridgette twice. I've barely gotten the words out and she's already peeling off her clothes, revealing her world-famous body underneath. "You want my bra and panties off, too, *häschen*?"

"Not yet. I'll take them off you later. We'll make a show of it."

"Ooh. Fun." She tosses her clothes on a chair and stands before me, her hands on her hips. "How's this?" She poses like the supermodel she is, jutting her hip and pushing out her breasts, and, instantly, every hair on my body stands on end.

Holy crap, Bridgette's incredible. I can't imagine any human, man or woman, straight or gay or otherwise, who wouldn't feel insanely turned-on by the sight of her almost-naked body, especially when she's posing like the superstar she is.

Bridgette tosses her blonde hair behind her shoulder. "And you?" she asks. "Let's see what you're hiding under that dress, shall we?"

"Um." I slide my hands down the front of my dress nervously. "I think I'll wait until Josh gets here to—"

There's a loud knock at the door.

"Eep!" I say, clamping my hand to my mouth.

Bridgette chuckles.

I sprint to the door and look through the peephole. "Holy shitballs, it's Josh."

"Were you expecting someone else?"

"Oh my God," I say, nervously shaking out my hands.

"What's gotten into you? You had ice in your veins last time and now you're acting like a mouse."

I take a deep breath, trying to calm myself. "Well, yeah. This time, I'm actually gonna do it. Plus, I haven't seen Josh all week— it's been a bit of a rough week. He's somehow gotten hotter since I last saw him, if that's possible." I peep through the door again. "Oh my god, he looks amazing. He's wearing this incredible blue suit that fits him perfectly. Really brings out his eyes. Gah."

Bridgette laughs. "Pull yourself together, Kat. I think I liked you better when you were Heidi Kumquat."

Josh bangs on the door. "Kat?"

"Hang on!" I call through the door. "I'll be right there!"

"Take off your clothes," Bridgette says. "We're gonna give him a show, remember?"

"Oh yeah. I almost forgot." I peel off my clothes, revealing a hot pink lace bra and G-string underneath.

"Very nice," Bridgette says, blatantly ogling me.

Josh knocks again.

"Hang on!" I call through the door.

Shit. I'm suddenly wracked with nerves. I've arranged this threesome to prove to Josh I'm the anti-Emma—that I truly love him—*all of him*—even the parts that make him a sick fuck. But what if he unexpectedly pulls some caveman shit on me and declares, "Nobody touches my Party Girl with a Hyphen but me!"? A counter-move like that would undeniably stroke my ego (just like it did last time), but it certainly wouldn't get me any closer to my mission of *owning* Josh in a way no other woman ever has. By God, if it's the last thing I do, I'm gonna worm my way into Josh's damaged heart—even if I have to sneak in through a hidden trap door marked "Sick Fuck."

Josh knocks again. "Kat?" he yells through the door.

"Hang on!" I yell. "Don't forget," I say to Bridgette. "You're only allowed to touch yourself and me, but—"

"Not Josh," Bridgette interrupts. "Yes, yes, you've made that perfectly clear. I'm a hooker, you're my client, and Josh is *your* client—you've already told me all that. Trust me, I have no desire to touch that asshole ever again. I'm here for no other reason than I want to fuck you, plain and simple—so let that kinky bastard in so I can finally get my hands on you."

"Before I let him in the room, I'm gonna talk to him at the door for a minute, just me and him."

Bridgette looks at me suspiciously.

"We're not gonna ditch you, I promise."

"I'll give you five minutes, and if you don't come back into the room by then, I'm outta here."

I open the door and quickly slip my body in front of it, keeping it open just a tad with my backside.

Josh's eyes instantly blaze at the sight of me. "Please answer the door dressed like this every fucking time." He sweeps me into his arms and devours me with a passionate kiss. "Oh God, I've missed you. I was such a prick to you this week—forgive me." He takes my face in his palms and kisses me again. "I felt like I was dying without you all week long."

Oh God, I wanna tell him I love him. I'm aching to say the words, physically aching. "I've been in pain without you," I mumble into his lips, my heart racing.

"I can't live without you, baby," he replies, kissing me furiously. "I..." He pauses and every hair on my body stands on end. "I..."

I hold my breath. This is it. I can *feel* it.

"I can't live without you," he finally says.

Oh, well, not what I was hoping for, but I can't complain. I run my hands through his hair and kiss him passionately, pushing my pelvis into his hard-on.

Josh breaks away from kissing me and cranes his neck, obviously trying to look through the small gap in the door. "Why are we standing at the door?" he asks.

Oh yeah. *Bridgette.* When all the blood in my brain whooshed into my crotch, I instantly forgot all about the supermodel on the other side of the door.

"We're standing at the door because I have a surprise for you," I reply.

Josh cranes his neck to look past me again, but the crack in the door is too narrow for him to see inside. "I got your note," he breathes, his voice brimming with excitement. "You said you're gonna be my *window* tonight?" Josh looks like he's literally holding his breath.

"Yeah," I say. "I'm your window—and I've invited someone quite lovely to be our window dressing."

Josh's eyes blaze.

Oh, wow. The look of arousal on his face is making my clit zing.

"Tonight's all about you, babe," I purr, pulling away from him and stroking the hard bulge in his pants. "You've delivered all my fantasies to me, one after another on a silver platter, and now it's time for me to return the favor." Josh's erection jolts under the fabric of his pants. "Tonight, I'm gonna give you what turns you on the most, baby—no holds barred."

"*You're* what turns me on the most," he says softly, kissing my neck.

Damn, he's good. "Well, then," I say, "I'm gonna give you what turns you on the *second* most." I press the entire length of my body against his. "I wanna do it this time, babe—I really do. This isn't reverse psychology, I promise. All I wanna do is turn you on and let your sick fuck run amok."

Josh eyes me, obviously not completely convinced of my sincerity.

"I'm serious, babe. I want you to enjoy this without reservation— and so will I. Whatever gets you off, whatever it is, you can always tell me and show me and do it to me or with me, and I promise I'll never ride off on a polo pony with a guy wearing an ascot."

The look on Josh's face is priceless. I can't imagine he'd look any more touched if I'd just said, "I love you."

"As long as you don't touch her—same as before," I caution. "That's the only rule."

Josh nods, his eyes smoldering.

"So is that a yes? Are you in, my beautiful sick fuck?" I ask.

Josh nods. "I'm in."

"Excellent." I grab Josh's hand and begin pulling him through the door.

"Wait a sec," he says, dropping my hand.

I stop and stare at him, but he doesn't speak further. "What?" I finally ask.

"I... " he begins.

Oh my God, my Scooby Doo senses tell me he's about to tell me he loves me. It's on the tip of his luscious tongue—I know it. I can practically hear the words rattling around in his head like gumballs in a chute.

"What?" I whisper fiercely. "Whatever it is, just say it." I pinch the width of Josh's face between my fingers and thumb and squeeze, making his lips pucker like he's a blowfish. "Say it," I say, squeezing Josh's cheeks, trying to physically coax the words out of him.

Josh bats my hand away, chuckling. "What the fuck are you doing?"

But I'm not laughing. I feel like a woman possessed. "Say it," I coax. "*Please,* Josh."

115

Josh's eyes drift to the gap in the door. "Now's not the time for chitchat." He kisses me, pressing his hard bulge into me again. "I can't think straight right now, babe—you've got me too wound up, talking about windows and shit." He grins. "All I wanna do is fuck my beautiful window and make her come."

"Well, who doesn't?" I say. "The line forms behind the hot blonde inside the suite."

Josh's eyes flicker. "Is she a hooker?"

I bite my lower lip. "It's Bridgette again."

"*What*? Bridgette? Fuck, Kat. *No.*"

"Yeah, she graciously flew up to Seattle to fuck me for your viewing pleasure."

"Are you fucking kidding me? Come on, Kat."

I shrug.

"Kat, not *Bridgette*." Josh takes a step back. "How the fuck did you even convince her to—"

"I paid her."

"*What?*"

"A shitload of money, too. But it's okay because I'm a mill-i-on-aire, so I can afford it—money well spent."

"You're joking, right?"

"No."

"*Bridgette?*" He scowls. "Kat, she's not human. She's got no heart."

"Which makes her perfect for the job of being our window dressing. I'm not gonna bring some wonderful woman with a heart of gold into our bed who's gonna make you fall head over heels in love with her."

Josh rolls his eyes in complete exasperation. "There's no danger of me falling in love with anyone else, Kat." He opens and closes his mouth in rapid succession, apparently contemplating saying more, but nothing comes out.

Oh my effing God. *Because I'm in love with you.* That's what Josh was about to say—there's no doubt in my mind. *Come on, Josh,* I think. *Just say it.*

But Josh remains mute.

I exhale, resigned. I'm obviously gonna need a lot of lube to extract those damned words from Josh's vocal cords—lube in the form of a certain lesbo-fantasy. "So you wanna watch me get it on with Bridgette or not?" I ask. "Should I ask the poor girl to leave?"

"You sure about this?" Josh asks.

"I'm positive. *YOLO.*" I wink.

Josh grins. "You're seriously the perfect woman."

"Yeah, I know." I look at my watch. "Well, if we're gonna do this, then we'd better get in there. Bridgette said if we don't come back within five minutes, she's leaving and it's already been six minutes."

"You're not actually trying to manipulate me into 'absconding' with you, are you?"

"No, I told you—I'm being sincere. I want you to let your inner sick fuck out—no holds barred."

"And you're feeling up to it?" He gently touches my stomach, making my entire body twitch with excitement.

"Yeah. I'm feeling much better these days. Still sick now and again, but a lot better."

"And it's safe?"

I nod. "The doctor said sex is just fine." I press myself into him. "So, it's decision time. Are you in or out, Playboy?"

Josh touches the indentation in my chin with his fingertip and then licks it with a sensuous flicker of his tongue. "I'm all-in, Party Girl. Let's do it."

Chapter 19
Josh

"Here you go," Bridgette says, handing me a glass filled with tequila and an opened bottle of Patron.

"Thanks," I say. I put the bottle on a little table next to me, lean back in my armchair, and shift my dick in my pants, my eyes fixed on Kat. She's sitting on the edge of the bed in her bra and panties, her body visibly trembling, her skin covered in goose bumps.

"Can I put some music on?" Bridgette asks.

I nod and Bridgette leaves the room, striding away confidently on her impossibly long legs.

Kat and I stare at each other, both our chests heaving.

Have Kat's tits always been this perfect? And that belly ring of hers—damn, it slays me. The way her blonde hair falls around her shoulders... I can't get enough of her. I swig the tequila in my glass and shift my dick in my pants again.

"Sugar" by Maroon Five begins blaring—not at all what I would have picked—this song's the musical equivalent of a fucking chick flick. But Kat's exuberant face makes it clear she's thrilled with the song choice and that's good enough for me.

Bridgette re-enters the room, shaking her ass to the song.

"I love this song," Kat says.

Bridgette joins Kat on the end of the bed. "Me, too, pussycat." She places her hand on Kat's knee and Kat jolts at Bridgette's touch.

My cock twitches at the sight of them sitting together, both of them barely clothed. Oh shit. This is really happening. I've done this multiple times, of course, *but never like this*. Never with a woman I love—wait, no—not *a* woman I love—*the* woman I love—the *only* one. Oh my God, it's true. Kat's the only woman I've ever truly loved, heart and soul—and, holy fuck, she's really doing this for me.

118

Or so she says. God help me, if this is a test—if Kat's actually hoping I'll stop everything, the same way she expected me to stop her from kissing Henn in Vegas, the same way she expected me to whisk her away from Bridgette the last time. Because, if so, she's gonna be sorely disappointed—I'm not stopping shit this time around.

I take another swig of my drink.

Bridgette runs her hand up and down Kat's arm. "Relax," she coos. "Ssh, pussycat—just relax." She strokes the full length of Kat's thigh. "Take a deep breath."

I smirk. This is so fucking awesome.

Kat takes a deep breath and her breasts visibly strain in her pink pushup bra.

Oh my God, I feel like my dick's gonna explode, this is so fucking hot. Is this normal? Shouldn't I be sweeping Kat into my arms and making love to her, showing her my new tattoo and saying the magic words? Because that's exactly what I'm gonna do—I swear to God—*right after this*.

Bridgette leans in and whispers something into Kat's ear, and Kat nods and whispers something back.

"Could you ladies speak up, please?" I say.

Both women turn their heads and look at me.

"I'd like to hear what you say to each other," I say. "Please."

Kat's blue eyes are trained on me like lasers. "Your wish is my command," she says, one side of her mouth hitching up. "Bridgette said she had a sex dream about me the night we first met."

"I did," Bridgette says. "It made me come in my sleep."

My cock jolts.

"And what I said to Bridgette in reply was, 'That makes me so wet, honey—my clit is throbbing.'"

My chest constricts. Jesus Christ. I gulp down the rest of my tequila and put the glass down on the table.

"Enough talking, pussycat," Bridgette says. She leans in slowly and lays a soft, closed-mouth kiss on Kat's lips.

"Hang on," Kat says softly. She turns her head and gazes at me, clearly asking for permission to continue.

I nod. Fuck yeah, I do.

Kat's eyes darken and burn. She turns her face toward Bridgette again. "I'm ready, baby."

I can barely breathe.

Bridgette cups Kat's face in her hands, leans in, and kisses her lips gently, and, much to my shock, Kat leans into Bridgette, slides her palm onto Bridgette's smooth cheek, cupping her jawline, and shoots her glistening tongue straight into Bridgette's gorgeous mouth.

Oh my fuck.

I quickly unzip the front of my pants and pull down my briefs, freeing my hard-on from its bondage, breathing like I'm on a fucking treadmill. Oh my fuck. Well, it's official. Emma was right—I really am a sick fuck. I'm supposed to be at my new house right now, telling Kat I love her for the first time to the dulcet sounds of fucking Mozart, but instead, I'm watching the woman I love play tonsil-hockey with an almost-nude bisexual supermodel, my hand stroking my hard dick. Am I really this depraved? Well, apparently so, because I'm finding this hot as fuck.

The two women are kissing passionately now—and, from Kat's body language, it's clear to me she's not pretending to be turned on. Holy fuck, she's genuinely on fire. She's so fucking sexy, it's like she's another species of woman altogether. I've never seen anything like her, paid or otherwise.

I grasp my shaft and work myself with more urgency. Every little arch of Kat's back, every shudder of her tight little body, every soft lapping noise of her tongue and lips is making my cock jolt and throb in my hand. Oh, fuck, I love this woman. I thought I knew what love was with Emma, but I was an idiot. This is love. Right here. *This.* There's no one else like Kat Morgan in the world. She's perfect.

Kat reaches behind Bridgette's back and unclasps her bra, and Bridgette's bountiful breasts bounce free. Bridgette quickly finishes the job and tosses her bra off and then returns the favor, unclasping Kat's bra and practically ripping it off her body.

Both women are topless now. Their nipples are erect, straining toward the other's. They're moaning softly, breathing hard—both of them obviously turned-on.

And so am I. Oh my fuck, so am I.

Bridgette stands and pulls off her undies, revealing her fully waxed pussy underneath, and even from here, I can see goose bumps rise up on Kat's skin at the sight of her naked body.

Bridgette pulls Kat to standing, whispering something into her ear again. Motherfucker, I wanna tell Bridgette to speak the fuck up, but I couldn't talk right now if the hotel were burning down around us.

The women are standing nose to nose. Breast to breast. Nipple to nipple. Bridgette leans forward and her nipples brush gently against Kat's.

An involuntary groan escapes me. Oh, shit.

Bridgette kneels and begins pulling Kat's G-string down slowly—kissing her hipbone as she does it.

My cock lurches. I can't breathe. I feel dizzy.

As Kat's panties reach her knees, she turns her head and looks straight at me, her eyes drunk with arousal, her chest rising and falling visibly. Her eyes drift down to my hand pumping up and down my hard shaft, and then back up to my face. She licks her lips. "Yes?" she asks, her breathing ragged.

I nod, incapable of speaking.

Bridgette lays a kiss on the inside of Kat's thigh, drawing Kat's attention away from me. She reaches between her legs and runs her fingers over the top of Bridgette's blonde head, and then rakes her fingers passionately through Bridgette's thick, shiny hair.

Bridgette lets out a low moan of excitement and Kat replies with a moan of her own.

Holy fuck, I'm gonna blow.

Kat's undies are completely off. She's nude with a head of long, blonde hair bobbing and moving between her legs—a blonde head attached to perfect fucking tits and an un-fucking-believable ass and perfectly curved hips and toned thighs, and oh my fucking God I'm about to fucking blow.

Bridgette's lips trail up from Kat's thigh toward her pussy. She's an inch away from the money and obviously going in for the kill.

"Wait," I choke out, shocking myself. "Stop."

Both women freeze and look at me. They're panting, heaving, trembling with arousal—and so am I.

"Don't touch her pussy," I say. "Her pussy's all mine."

Bridgette looks up at Kat, incredulous, but Kat's looking at me, her mouth hanging open in shock.

"Kat's pussy's all mine," I murmur, gaining my equilibrium. "She's got a magic pussy and it's all mine."

"Are you fucking kidding me?" Bridgette bellows, clearly on the verge of losing her shit.

"Ssh." Kat puts her slender hand on Bridgette's head, signaling her to stay put and cool her jets. Kat begins stroking Bridgette's hair like she's a kitten. "My pussy's all yours, baby," Kat coos to me, still stroking Bridgette's hair. "But *just this once* Bridgette's gonna lick my pussy and make me come really, really hard, solely for your pleasure." Her eyes flicker. "She's our Mickey Mouse roller coaster, babe—just this once. And then never again."

Kat brushes her fingertips against her own erect nipples and bites her lower lip and it's suddenly crystal clear to me Kat's not doing this for me at all. Maybe it started out that way for her—in fact, I'm sure it did—but now, in an unexpected turn of events, doing this is getting Kat off more than she ever expected. I thought I'd caught a tiger tonight, but I'm suddenly realizing I'm the asshole gripping the tiger by its fucking tail. And for some reason, this realization turns me the fuck on.

I nod slowly, my pulse pounding in my ears.

Kat smiles devilishly and looks down at Bridgette kneeling on the floor. "Eat me like you're a world class whore who charges a million bucks a night and your only job is to give me my money's worth. Can you do that for me?"

Bridgette shoots me a steely look that quite clearly says, "Fuck you, asshole," and then she leans with exaggerated flourish into Kat's waxed pussy and begins lapping at her clit with outrageously enthusiastic swirls of her glistening tongue.

At the touch of Bridgette's effusive tongue, Kat throws her head back, grips Bridgette's hair, and releases a guttural growl.

And what am I doing? Oh, nothing much. Just jolting in my chair like I'm being electrocuted by a thousand electric eels. Oh my fucking shit. With each and every energetic swipe of Bridgette's glistening, wet tongue against Kat's beautiful pussy, every movement of Bridgette's jaws, every bob of Bridgette's head, my dick twitches like Bridgette's sucking my tip. Or would that be punching me in the balls? Oh my fuck. I'm turned on and jealous as hell all at the same time. Oh God, that should be *me* and my flickering tongue tasting Kat's slippery sweetness. That's *my* magic pussy and no one else's, goddammit—my juices to lap up. But oh my holy fuck—this is the hottest thing I've ever seen in my fucking life by a long mile. I love it. I hate it. I'm dying. I'm in pain. *I'm gonna come so fucking hard.*

I stand, rip my pants and briefs completely off, and begin quickly unbuttoning my shirt—but just as I'm about to pull my shirt off my shoulders, I remember my new girlfriend-tattoo on my left bicep, and I stop. There's no way I'm giving Kat her first ever glimpse of my once-in-a-lifetime gift to her while she's fucking Bridgette.

I leave my unbuttoned shirt on and move behind Kat, pressing my hard-on into her ass and kissing her smooth shoulder as Bridgette continues lapping at her pussy from her knees.

The instant my lips touch Kat's skin, goose bumps visibly erupt on her skin. She lets out a low moan and begins jerking her hips in a phantom humping movement, obviously so overwhelmed with arousal at my unexpected touch, her body's going suddenly haywire.

I reach around Kat's torso and stroke her erect nipples as my mouth trails the length of her shoulder to her neck and then to her jawline.

Kat lets out a loud groan of pleasure and gyrates her pelvis back and forth from Bridgette's mouth in the front of her to my erection poking her in her ass.

I swipe Kat's blonde hair off the back of her neck and kiss her hidden Scorpio tattoo and she reaches up and grips my hair, her entire body jolting.

I press my lips against her ear and pinch her nipples, grinding my hard-on into her with urgency. "Let your inner sick fuck out to play, Party Girl," I coo into Kat's ear, my voice low and intense. My palms explore the smooth skin of Kat's belly, and when my fingertips unexpectedly brush the soft hair atop Bridgette's bobbing head, my cock jolts. "Enjoy every minute, baby," I growl, letting my fingertips float back up to Kat's breasts. "Because after tonight, no one but me is gonna touch your magic pussy again."

Kat inhales sharply and her body stiffens. A guttural roar emerges from her throat, followed by a string of expletives, followed by a pained wail. I slide my finger between her ass cheeks and press my fingertip against her anus just in time to feel her orgasm ripple against my finger, and my cock throbs at the delicious sensation.

Even before Kat's orgasm is over, Bridgette leaps to standing and clutches Kat's shoulders like she's going to kiss her full on the mouth, but I rip Kat's shuddering body away from Bridgette's grasp and drag her to the bed. In one fell swoop, I push Kat down forcefully onto her hands and knees on the bed, grip her hips from behind, and enter her, letting her feel every inch of me as I slide my cock into her tight wetness. "Tell me you were aching for my cock when she was licking you," I command, pumping in and out of her all the way, pulling her hips into me.

"*Yes.*"

Bridgette crawls slowly onto the bed like a cat, her ass in the air, and positions herself shoulder to shoulder with Kat like the two of them are the bottoms in a naked-cheerleader pyramid. As I continue fucking Kat, Bridgette spreads her legs slightly, her ass in the air, giving me an unimpeded view of every inch of her ass crack and pussy all at once, gyrating her hips like she's inviting me to fuck her in any hole.

Bridgette's hot, I'll give her that, but I force myself to look away and focus on Kat. "You have a magic pussy," I growl to Kat—but it's actually a message for Bridgette. She can shove her pussy and asshole at me all night long, but I'll never take the bait. I've got my unicorn right here and she's all I need.

I rub Kat's smooth back with my palms and shift the angle of my entry on my next thrust, trying to find the exact spot inside Kat that's gonna push her into ecstasy, and at the shift of my body, Kat inhales sharply—always a good sign—and suddenly begins gyrating her body in synchronicity with my thrusts.

"Get it, baby," I say. "Let's make it rain."

As I continue sliding in and out of Kat's sweet pussy with strong, deliberate strokes, Bridgette runs her fingertips down the length of Kat's back and licks at her shoulder. In reply, Kat turns her head and kisses Bridgette, lapping at her with languid swirls of her tongue.

Bridgette reaches out and runs her hand down the full length of Kat's back, continuing to kiss her as she does, and Kat lets out a loud moan that makes me physically shudder with excitement. Thank you, God. If I ever doubted your existence, I take it all back.

I change the angle of my dick yet again, and, holy shit, that's the magic bullet. Instantly, Kat breaks away from her kiss with Bridgette, gasping and whimpering.

"Oh my God," she growls. "Oh, *fuck.* That's it. *Yes.*"

I grip Kat's hair and pull her head back forcefully and that's all she needs: her pussy begins clenching around my cock in rolling ripples.

Bridgette exhales—perhaps realizing she's not getting fucked tonight—and flips onto her back next to Kat. "You're so sexy, honey," Bridgette purrs. She reaches out and fondles Kat's dangling, swinging breast. "I love watching you get fucked, pussycat."

At Bridgette's touch, Kat arches her back like a cat on a hot tin roof and then forcefully slams her spine down in the opposite direction, over and over, like her body's trying to expel a demon.

"Kiss me, pussycat," Bridgette purrs. "Come down here."

Bridgette grabs Kat's face with her slender hands and gently pulls on her head, coaxing Kat to lie with her on the bed, and, in response, Kat slowly lowers herself, taking me and my thrusting cock with her, until Kat's lying on her right side, kissing Bridgette passionately, while I'm spooning Kat and fucking her from behind.

Holy fuck, this is literally the hottest thing I've ever experienced—way hotter than anything I did in The Club by a long mile. I'm fucking the woman I love—the woman who gets me off like no one ever has—while watching her French kiss one of the most beautiful females on the planet.

I let my eyes drift down the length of Bridgette's long, ridiculous body. She's lying on her back, her legs spread, her fingers working her own clit.

"Touch her, Kat," I whisper into her ear. "Make her come for me."

I reach around and massage Kat's clit and she moans into Bridgette's mouth.

"Touch her and make her come," I command, working Kat's clit with authority.

Kat's jerking with pleasure at my touch, but she nonetheless follows orders. Her hand trails down Bridgette's torso slowly and slides straight into her pussy, taking over the job from Bridgette's fingers. Oh my God, I'm right on the edge. I bite Kat's shoulder and increase the speed and depth of my thrusts, groaning loudly. Oh yeah, I'm about to boil over.

I press my lips against Kat's ear. "You're a sick fuck, baby," I whisper.

Kat moans. "*Yes.*"

"Lick her tits for me," I say. "Make her come."

Without hesitation, Kat bends over Bridgette and begins sucking and licking her erect nipples, all the while continuing to stroke Bridgette's pussy—and all while getting fucked by me—and within thirty seconds, Bridgette arches her back, blurts something in German, and comes completely undone.

It's quite plain to see Bridgette's orgasm is doing wonders for Kat—she's clearly on the very brink of an epic climax herself.

I press my lips against Kat's ear. "Enjoy this, baby, because after tonight, your pussy's all mine."

Kat lets out a pained wail, arches her back, and squirts, gushing warm liquid all over my dick and balls in a torrent.

I jerk out of Kat, my hard-on straining, guide her quivering body onto her hands and knees, and enthusiastically suckle her pussy from behind, sucking and lapping up every drop of sweet cum off her lips like I'm licking the cream filling out of an Oreo. By the time I've got Kat's pussy all cleaned up, I'm in a frenzy—completely out of my mind. I flip Kat onto her back, rest her calves on my shoulders and plunge myself balls-deep into her wetness.

Holy fuck, I'm enraptured. Kat's never felt *this* good, has she? It's like we were designed for each other, like we're the last two pieces of a celestial jigsaw puzzle, just now snapped into place. Oh my fucking God, Kat's the answer to every question I didn't even know I had.

Kat lets out a mangled cry and I join her, groaning and growling like a man possessed as I continue fucking her with all my might.

Bridgette, apparently recovered from her orgasm, reaches out and runs her slender fingers over the smooth skin of Kat's thigh, even as Kat's legs are wrapped around me.

"No," I bark at Bridgette, slapping at her hand. "She's mine. Fuck off."

"Josh," Kat breathes, her blue eyes blazing. "*Yes.*" She runs her hands into my hair and yanks on it roughly. "*Yes.*"

I can't breathe. The room is warping and spinning. Kat's as hot as sin and as depraved as fucking hell. She's an angel and the devil all rolled into one. *And I love her more than life itself.* I lean my face into Kat's, intending to kiss her passionately, but Madame Terrorist has her own ideas. Even as I'm pumping in and out of her, Kat turns her head and levels her foe with an icy glare.

"He's mine," Kat hisses, her beautiful face an inch away from Bridgette's.

Bridgette chuckles. "Oh, go fuck yourself, bitch—I don't even want him."

"Good, because you can't have him," Kat spits out.

I grab Kat's face roughly, wrenching her attention away from Bridgette. "This isn't about her," I growl. I pull Kat's arms above her head and pin her wrists together. "This is about you and me."

Kat's eyes ignite at my rough touch. "*Yes*," she purrs.

"Just you and me, baby," I say, thrusting with all my might. "No one else."

Kat's eyes are absolutely blazing with rabid excitement. She lifts her pelvis to receive me even more deeply, her breathing ragged, and I respond by slamming her even harder with my full length.

I lace my fingers tightly into Kat's. "You're all mine," I growl, my body on the brink of release.

"Yes," Kat breathes. "*Harder.*"

My thrusts are becoming savage. I'm on the very cusp of losing myself completely. I grip Kat's hands in mine and stare into her blue eyes, willing myself to hang on as long as possible. Oh my God, this feels so good, I want it to last forever.

"Yes," Kat groans, her blue eyes leveling me, her fingers entwined in mine, her heart beating wildly against my chest.

"You feel so good, baby," I growl. "You always feel so fucking good."

Kat's eyelids flutter. Her eyes roll back into her head. And she's gone. Her muscles surrounding my cock begin clenching and rippling fiercely, sending shockwaves of pleasure throughout my entire body.

"Get it, baby," I choke out. "Get it."

As I thrust into her, I kiss Kat voraciously and she returns my hungry kiss, enthusiastically swirling her tongue inside my mouth and devouring my lips.

Out of nowhere, I feel fingers grip my swinging balls... followed by a wet, warm tongue lapping at them furiously... and then, holy fuck, a warm, wet mouth envelops my entire ball sack. With a loud growl, my body hurtles into a brutal release that leaves me gasping for air and certain I'm dying an extremely pleasurable death.

Several moments later, when Kat and I have both stopped

quaking, I lie on top of Kat, the most sexual and sensual and beautiful creature I've ever encountered—sweat pouring out every inch of my flesh, my breathing ragged, my hands still clasped tightly in hers— and I try my mighty fucking best to understand what the *fuck* just happened to me.

I realize my brain is likely short-circuiting right now and my thought processes probably aren't particularly trustworthy, but the more I ponder the situation, the more I think I know exactly what happened. In fact, yep, there's only one *sane* conclusion to be reached: my magical, mystical unicorn *momentarily* transformed into a magical, mystical *octopus* with a supernatural mouth. Yep, that's got to be it—or, at least, that's my story and I'm sticking to it.

Because when a guy's got a smokin' hot baby-momma-girlfriend with a white-hot temper, a woman undoubtedly capable of committing double-murder if properly provoked (and that was before pregnancy hormones began coursing through her blood stream, making her even crazier)—and when the guy's absolutely certain his smokin' hot future-murderess of a baby-momma-girlfriend would, indeed, feel provoked to kill if she were to believe her firm "no touch" rule had been violated by a certain bisexual supermodel (through no fault of the boyfriend, mind you)—well, then the boyfriend can't help but conclude it's most prudent for everyone involved if he conjures a paranormal unicorn-turned-octopus rather than try too hard to come up with any other plausible explanation.

But, hey, the magical-unicorn-turned-octopus theory isn't really *that* far-fetched, is it? No, I really don't think so. Because if there's one woman in the entire world who could pull off grabbing and licking a man's balls, and then tea-bagging his entire ball sack like a fucking champ, all while simultaneously getting plowed with her hands firmly pinned above her head and her mouth otherwise engaged in a passionate kiss, then that woman would have to be the one and only magical, mystical unicorn, Katherine Ulla Morgan.

Chapter 20
Josh

"God, I thought she'd never leave," I say, pulling Kat away from the door and onto my lap on a nearby couch.

"You were pretty rude to her just now," Kat says, throwing her arms around my neck and pressing her forehead against mine.

"Fuck Bridgette. I couldn't wait to be alone with you." I press my nose against Kat's until she appears to have one big, blue eye. "Mike Wazowski," I say.

Kat giggles.

"I can't believe you *paid* her to fuck you," I say. "You're a savage beast, Kat."

"She said I had to pay her money as 'collateral' to ensure I'd actually go through with it."

"How much did you pay her?" I ask.

Kat tells me the number with wide eyes like it's some astronomical sum, and I can barely keep from laughing.

"Babe, Bridgette earns that amount of money per *minute* as a model."

"Oh."

"Clearly, she didn't come here for the money. In fact, I'm one hundred percent sure she would have paid *you* for the pleasure of fucking you. Anyone would. Just look at you. You're a fucking unicorn." I stroke her hair. "A kinky little unicorn." I bite her naked shoulder and she squeals.

"I didn't even know I was *that* kinky, to be honest," Kat says. "I thought I'd chicken out after second base, just like I did in college."

"Well, hot damn, you certainly didn't chicken out tonight, baby. You rounded third like a pro and slid headfirst right into home."

129

Kat giggles. "I guess you bring out the sick fuck in me, Playboy."

"Oh no, don't you dare pin your sick-fuckeduppedness on me. You out sick-fucked me by a long mile tonight, baby. I'm the one who said 'no pussy' and you *begged* me to let her keep eating you."

Kat grins gleefully. "Oh, yeah. I did, didn't I?"

"You sure did."

We share a smile.

"I almost passed out at one point. I was seeing pink and yellow flashes of light."

The hairs on the back of my neck stand up. "Do you think it's safe for the kumquat for you to come that hard? Maybe we should be taking it easy?"

"No, the doctor said sex and orgasms are fine. I'm just not allowed to sit on a jet engine, that's the only limitation."

"You asked the doctor if you could ride your Sybian?" I chuckle. "Oh, Jesus. I can only imagine the dinner conversation your poor doctor had that night with her husband when he asked about her day."

We both laugh.

"You know she was Googling that shit the minute you left her office," I add.

"Probably."

I roll my eyes. "Oh, Kat."

"Oh, Kat," she agrees.

"Sorry you can't ride your toy for a while."

"Just one of the many sacrifices we mothers make for our children," she says piously.

I grin. She's so damned cute. If I didn't already love this woman, I would have just fallen in love with her.

"Actually, I don't even need my Sybian anymore," Kat says matter-of-factly. "Now that you and I finally live in the same city, you'll be my one-and-only orgasm machine every single night."

"Amen," I say. I stroke her golden hair. "Hey, you think when I was fucking you really deep at the end the kumquat was like, 'Eek! An anaconda!'?"

Kat giggles. "Or maybe the kumquat was like, 'A little to the left. *Lower*. Aaaah."

I grimace. "Ew, Kat. *No*. That's disgusting. Don't say that."

Kat looks stricken. "No, I meant like a baby-back-scratcher—you know, like your dick was scratching an itch on the kumquat's back." She makes a face. "I didn't mean anything *sexual*, for cryin' out loud."

I put my hands over my ears. "Stop. Please. Either way, I don't want to think about my *dick* touching our baby. You're totally traumatizing me."

"Oh. I'm sorry. I just meant—"

"*Stop*. Please. I might never be able to get a hard-on again if I'm thinking about my dick scratching our baby's back."

Kat's face bursts into a huge smile.

"You're charmed by the thought of me becoming impotent?" I ask.

"You just said 'our baby.'"

I look at her blankly.

"'Our baby's back,'" she says. "That's what you said."

"Yeah. Because I don't want my dick to become a baby-back-scratcher. Duh."

"*Our baby*," she says reverently. "You called the kumquat our baby." She grins.

"I did, didn't I?" I tilt my head, trying to figure out what I'm feeling right now—and, honestly, I'm feeling *happy* and nothing else. "Our baby," I repeat.

Kat visibly swoons.

"Our wee little baaaaaybaaaaaaaaaaaaaay," I say.

Kat giggles.

"You know what?" I say. "I just realized I'm not freaked out anymore."

"Me, either."

"Well, actually, I'm still a little freaked out, don't get me wrong, but not nearly like I was when you first told me."

Kat smiles. "Onward and upward."

"Indubitably."

"Hey, bee tee dubs, it's anatomically impossible for anyone's dick to become a baby-back-scratcher, even a dick as huge as yours."

"Really?" I ask.

Kat nods. "I researched it. The cervix is in the way. Impossible, no matter how big the donkey-dick."

131

"You're *sure*?"

"Look it up for yourself, Anaconda-boy. Literally impossible."

"When did you look that up?"

"A couple days ago."

"Why?"

She shrugs. "You're huge—I was worried about the wee little baaaybaaay."

"Aw. Check out the momma-Kumquat looking out for the baby-kumquat. That was a very motherly thing for you to do. Well, I assume it was motherly. I haven't seen an actual mother in the wild any more than I've seen an actual wife. But I *think* you're having what the anthropologists call 'maternal instincts.'"

The look on Kat's face is utterly adorable. It's the same look I'd expect from her if I'd just asked her to go steady.

"So, hey, hot momma," I say, pulling her close. "Are you hungry?"

"*Famished*," Kat says.

"Room service or dine out?"

"Room service."

"Burgers and fries or five-star?"

"Burgers and fries," Kat says. "And milkshakes. Oh, and will you see if they have split pea soup? I have a weird craving for split pea soup—oh, and cantaloupe—or any kind of melon, really, except honeydew—oh, and maybe some blueberry yogurt?"

"Wow, I guess that whole pregnancy-cravings thing is real, huh?"

Kat pats her belly. "The kumquat wants what the kumquat wants. I guess the little guy (or gal) burned lots of calories dodging that big ol' anaconda who's been trying to scratch his back all night long."

"Well, then, by all means, let's feed the kumquat—not to mention get it a therapist. Lemme up, babe. I'll make the call." I pat her thigh and she hops off my lap. I stride across the room and pick up the hotel phone. "Room service, please."

"Yes, sir. One moment, please."

While I'm waiting for the call to connect, Kat grabs her purse and pulls out a package of crackers.

"You feeling sick?" I ask, still holding the phone to my ear.

Kat nods. "It mostly hits me these days when I'm hungry. Or

tired. And late at night, too—and early morning. Oh, and in the car."
She rolls her eyes. "It still hits me a lot, I guess."

I make a sad face.

"Thank you for waiting," a male voice says into my ear. "What
would you like to order, Mr. Faraday?"

I place our ridiculously bizarre order. "How long will it take?" I
ask. "I've got a pregnant woman here who needs to eat right away."

"About forty-five minutes."

"They say about forty-five minutes, hot momma," I say to Kat.
"Are you gonna be okay for that long?"

"Yeah, I'll be okay," Kat says, holding up her Saltines. "I'll just
go lie down until the food arrives."

"Yeah, go rest, Party Girl. I'll let you know when the food is
here."

She disappears into the bedroom.

"Okay, let me make sure I've got your order right, Mr.
Faraday..." the voice on the phone says.

But I'm not listening. I can't concentrate. Kat only left me to go
into the next room and my heart's suddenly yearning for her like
she's a thousand miles away.

"Is that correct?" the guy asks.

"Yes. Thanks," I reply.

After I hang up the phone, I stand for a moment, looking around
like a lost puppy, not sure what to do with myself. I'm physically
aching for her *and she's only in the next fucking room.* What's
happening to me? Who am I? I lived across the country from Emma
for three fucking years and that was just fine by me. And now I can't
stand to be more than fifty feet away from Kat?

There's a mirror hanging on the wall a few feet away, and I stare
at my reflection for a moment, marveling that I still look like me on
the outside, despite the fact that I've apparently turned into my pussy-
whipped brother on the inside. That's my Anthony Franco suit on my
body. That's my dark hair. And those are my blue eyes. Ah, but my
eyes. They look slightly deranged, don't they? They give me away.
I'm definitely a man possessed—a man who's head-over-heels in
love with the perfect woman. Or, perhaps, more accurately, a *sick
fuck* who's head-over-heels in love with the perfect *sick fuck*. I smirk.
Damn, I'm a lucky bastard.

133

I stride toward the bedroom, my heartbeat pulsing in my ears. *It's time.* I'm gonna tell Kat I love her right now. It's not perfect timing, I know—she's not feeling well, plus our food's on the way—and it'd probably be best for me to wait for a time when I can tell her while making love to her, slowly and gently. But fuck it. I can't wait another minute to tell that woman how I feel about her.

I burst through the door of the bedroom, my heart bursting... and... *Oh.*

My heart wilts.

Kat's fast asleep in the bed, a half-eaten package of Saltines lying in her opened palm.

I smile wistfully to myself.

Now there's a woman I wouldn't kick out of bed for eating crackers.

I shake my head—oh, life—and head back into the main room.

"Yes, Mr. Faraday?" the front-desk guy asks when he picks up my call.

"I just ordered a bunch of food from room service and I need to change my order," I say into the phone.

"Of course. One moment, please." There's a long pause while the call connects. "Yes, Mr. Faraday? How can I help you?"

"On that room service I just ordered, cancel everything except the melon and yogurt, plus add a couple cold turkey sandwiches and maybe five or six other cold-food items to choose from—stuff that'll keep for hours. My girlfriend's the one who wanted all that stuff I ordered earlier and now she's fallen asleep. The new plan is for there to be a bunch of food ready for her whenever she wakes up."

"Yes, sir. Not a problem."

"And do me a favor, don't knock when you bring the food. Enter the main room of the suite and load everything into the refrigerator behind the bar. We'll be in the bedroom with the door closed. And please be extra quiet. My girlfriend's pregnant and needs her rest—she hasn't been feeling all that well." Why is my heart racing like this? My entire body is buzzing and I don't understand why.

"Yes, sir. We'll be very quiet. Any requests on the food items for the new order?"

"Nope. Surprise me. Just give her lots of options. She eats like a truck driver these days. Go crazy."

The guy laughs. "Yes, sir."

"Thanks."

I hang up the phone and lay my palm on my chest. My heart's racing a mile a minute and I don't understand why. All I did was order food for Kat—so why is my skin suddenly feeling electrified? I take a deep breath, trying to calm myself. Wow, I feel like I just ran a hundred-yard dash. Why is my heart thumping like this?

I grab a cold water bottle from the refrigerator behind the bar, creep into the bedroom, and close the door behind me. Gently, I lift the package of Saltines out of Kat's open palm and place the crackers on the nightstand along with the bottle of water—and then I stand over Kat's sleeping body, transfixed by her beautiful face.

I've never felt the way I do, standing here right now. Not once in my whole goddamned life. Something new is coursing through my veins—something that wasn't there when I first knocked on the door to the suite tonight. What Kat did for me tonight—and how she so obviously got turned on doing it—was the final piece of a puzzle I didn't even know I was trying to solve. Kat didn't just *participate* in tonight's depraved little fuck-fest, and she didn't need to be *coaxed* into doing it with me, either—she *arranged* it and then *begged* me to keep going when I tried to throw on the brakes midway through— proving once and for all she's an even bigger sick fuck than I am.

Which makes me love this woman more than I ever thought possible.

And, now, out of nowhere, I suddenly feel a primal desire to take care of Kat's every need, to make sure her every desire, big or small, is fulfilled—and not just sexually. In every conceivable way, top to bottom.

I gaze in wonder at Kat's sleeping face, my heart straining for her. God, even without animation, Kat's features are spectacular. Her lips slay me. Her high cheekbones. Her bold eyebrows. That little cleft in her chin. If the kumquat-inside-the-Kumquat pops out looking anything at all like its freakishly beautiful mother, the kid's gonna fucking rule the world.

I pull off all my clothes, flip off the lamp next to Kat, and quietly slide underneath the sheet behind her.

Her breathing is rhythmic and slow. Her hair is soft against my nose.

I scoot right up against Kat's naked backside and wrap my arm around her—and then I lay my palm flush against her flat belly and cradle our little baby-to-be, the kumquat I didn't even know I wanted until this very moment.

I lie still for a long time, breathing in her scent, pressing my hand against her flat stomach as it moves with her breathing—thinking about the words I'm gonna say to her when she wakes up. After a while, I hear the main door to the suite open, followed by a soft clatter—and then the sound of the main door opening and closing again. Silence. Nothing but the sound of Kat breathing and the beating of my heart against her back.

"I love you, Kat," I whisper softly. I shift my palm on Kat's belly, spreading my fingers out, trying to cradle every inch of it. "And I love you, too," I say softly.

And that's the last thing I do before surrendering to serene and blissful sleep.

Chapter 21
Kat

I wake up with a start. Josh's arm is around me.

I'm in a warm bed.

I glance around the moonlit room, momentarily confused about my whereabouts.

Oh, yeah—now I remember. The hotel room where Josh and I let our sick fucks run amok with Bridgette.

Delicious.

But I've no sooner had that highly pleasant thought than bile rises in my throat and my mouth waters. Shit.

In a flash, I disentangle myself from Josh's muscular arm and bolt out of bed, straight into the bathroom—where I proceed to hurl every Saltines cracker and drop of fluid out of my body with loud, ghastly heaves. Oh, God. I'm so gross. Gah.

I flush the toilet and whimper. I feel like I'm made of cardboard, not flesh and blood. *I need to eat something right now or else I'm gonna die.*

I wash out my mouth, rinse my face, and hobble back into the bedroom, expecting to find Josh sitting up in bed and staring at me, aghast at the horrendous noises I just made in the bathroom. But, somehow, Josh is still fast asleep, completely oblivious to the T-Rex I just wrestled in the toilet.

I stand over Josh's beautiful sleeping body for a moment, looking at his peaceful face in the moonlight. Normally, when I think of Josh, the first word that pops into my mind is *sexy*. Typically followed by *funny*. And *generous* soon thereafter. But right now, standing over his striking features in the moonlight, the only word coming to my mind is *beautiful*.

137

I sigh.

I love him.

With all my heart and soul.

More than I ever thought possible.

And I'm aching to exchange the words with him—to finally give full voice to my overwhelming feelings for him.

My stomach clenches hungrily, drawing me out of my Josh-induced stupor, so I pad carefully out of the darkened room to the main room of the suite, desperate to find something to eat.

I flip on a lamp and instantly spot a room-service tray on a table, so I head over there like a starving hyena looking for a carcass.

Along with utensils and tiny salt-and-pepper shakers, there's a handwritten note on the tray: "Mr. Faraday, per your request, an assortment of cold-food selections are in the refrigerator. Please let us know if you require anything further."

I make a "yay" face to myself and happily beeline over to the refrigerator.

Sweet Baby Jesus, I've hit the mother lode. If I didn't already love Josh, I would have just fallen in love with him. How'd he know to have food waiting for me when I woke up? Is he some sort of pregnant-woman whisperer?

For a solid fifteen minutes, I'm a ravenous animal, stuffing food into my mouth with both fists and making "nom nom nom" sounds in the quiet room like Homer Simpson at a doughnut shop—and when I'm done eating and feeling fan-fucking-tastic again, a steely determination suddenly washes over me: *It's time to get my man.*

I head back into the dark bedroom and fumble around in the moonlight until I find my laptop. I scroll into my music and stop when I see Audra Mae, my new obsession. "Addicted to You" with Aviici leaps out at me from my song list. Oh, how I want to make love to Josh to this redonkulously awesome song—but I'll just have to wait. Josh and I have already confessed we're *addicted* to each other—now it's time for us to take our words to the next level. But to get Josh over the line, I'm thinking I'm gonna need a song that'll beat Josh over the head with an "I love you" sledge hammer—a song that leaves absolutely no room for misunderstanding.

As I scroll through my music, I realize I've got lots of options—the lyrics "I love you" aren't exactly a rare commodity when it comes to pop music—but I stop scrolling when I see "1234" by the Plain White T's. I absolutely love this sweet little song—and the lyrics are so literal, Josh would have to be a pill bug not to catch their meaning.

I set the song to play on a loop, tiptoe slowly to the bed, and, as the song begins, slip naked under the covers onto my left side, facing Josh.

When I slide my arm over Josh's sleeping body, his skin is warm and smooth. Delectable. I nuzzle Josh's nose with mine and kiss his soft lips and run my fingertips over the ridges in his abs. Gently, ever so gently, I stroke his dick from his balls to his tip, and then stroke his shaft with the barest of touches, and the sensation of him hardening in my hand, even before he's fully awakened, ignites me.

I throw my leg over Josh's hip and slip his full length inside me and ride him slowly, reaching between my legs to feel him slipping in and out of me as I do, and in no time at all, Josh's lips find my neck, his warm hands find my breasts and belly and hips and clit, his tongue slips inside my moaning mouth, and his movement inside me deepens and intensifies. And all the while, the Plain White T's sing those three little words repeatedly, telling Josh exactly how I feel— and more importantly, instructing him there's only one thing to do: say "I love you."

"Kat," Josh breathes. "I missed you."

Not the words I'm hoping for, but this feels so damned good, I don't even care. I gyrate my hips passionately, coaxing Josh to his release, but, much to my surprise, Josh pulls out of me, pushes me onto my back, and begins pleasuring me in every conceivable way. He kisses my breasts and neck and face and runs his hands over my thighs and sucks on my fingers and toes and kisses my inner thighs, and, finally, laps at me with his warm, wet tongue, licking my clit with particular fervor. A warm and delicious orgasm rolls through me, almost lazily, like it's taking its time on a quiet Sunday afternoon. Finally, Josh slips inside me again and gyrates on top of me until he comes, too, just as the Plain White T's are telling him, as explicitly as song lyrics can possibly do, it's time for him to freaking tell me he loves me already.

When we're done, we lie nose to nose for a long moment, stroking each other's warm skin in the dark.

"Did you choose this song or was it the next song on your playlist?" he asks.

"I chose it. Because of its lyrics. Specifically. For you."

There's a beat.

Josh takes a deep breath. "I love you, Kat."

Every hair on my body stands on end. Thank you, Baby Jesus in the Manger.

"I love you more than the air I breathe," Josh continues. "More than life itself. I love you so, so much, Kat." He lets out a shaky breath. "I love you, I love you, I love you."

Thank you, God. I throw my arms around Josh's neck and kiss the hell out of him. "I love you, too," I blurt. "I love you, Josh. Oh my God. I love you, I love you, I love you."

Josh clutches me fiercely. "I love you with all my heart and soul, Kat."

"I love you to the moon and back again," I say.

Josh is trembling, covering my face and neck with kisses. "I love you more than I knew was even possible," he says.

"I love you, I love you, I love you," I reply.

"No one's ever said those words to me before," he whispers. "Thank you. Oh my God, thank you."

"What?" I say, but my words are muffled by his furious lips.

"I love you," he says, over and over, kissing me without reprieve.

I laugh and cry at the same time, I'm so completely flooded with joy. "I can't live without you," I murmur into his lips. "I can't breathe without you. I can't—"

Josh pulls away from kissing me. "Move in with me, Kat," he blurts.

My heart leaps. I don't even need to think about it. "Yes."

"Yes?"

"*Yes.*"

He kisses me voraciously, yet again.

Damn, I wish I could see Josh's beautiful blue eyes right now, but the room is too dark. "Are you sure?" I ask, and immediately regret it. Why am I giving Josh a chance to worm out of his offer? Stupid Kat!

But my worry is for nothing—Josh thrills me with his immediate and confident reply: "I'm sure," he says. "I can't live without you. I love you more than life itself."

I exhale and hug him fervently. "I love you," I gasp. "I love you, I love you, I love you."

"I can't stand being away from you," he says. "I want to sleep with you every night. I want to wake up to the sight of you every morning. I want to take care of you—to make all your dreams come true."

"Oh my God. I'm gonna explode," I say, tears rising in my eyes.

"When can you move in?"

"Right away."

"Oh my God," he says. He's panting. "This is gonna be awesome."

He's shaking like a leaf. Is that anxiety or joy coursing through his veins? I wish I could see his face.

"I haven't even met with the interior designer for my house yet," Josh says breathlessly. "We'll decorate the place together. It'll be *our* house, Kat—with *our* baby—yeah, and we'll make one of the rooms a nursery, and you can decorate it however you like and we'll live together and raise our kid and we'll be *happy*." He's rambling maniacally, practically gasping for air, stroking my face feverishly. It's like the Hoover Dam has broken inside him and a pent-up reservoir of words and feelings is gushing out of him all at once. "We'll be together because we *want* to be," Josh continues, his words pouring out of him like a torrent. "Because we *love* each other. We won't need a piece of paper to make our commitment official." He abruptly stops talking. His voice quavers. "Right? We love each other and that's all we need?" He swallows audibly. "Right?"

"I don't need a piece of paper," I say soothingly. "All I need is you, Josh. If you promise to love me and our baby the best way you know how, that's enough for me."

He exhales a huge breath. "I promise. I'll love you and our baby. That's what I can give you."

"Then that's enough."

He's panting now. "I want you to live with me, babe—I want you to be all mine."

"I will be. I am."

"Promise?" He's trembling against me.

"I promise."

His chest is heaving against mine. He's literally twitching and jerking next to me. I touch his face. His cheeks are wet.

I'm flabbergasted. "Josh? Oh my God. Are you okay?"

Josh grips me to him. "I love you more than I ever thought possible. I didn't know I could love like this. I didn't know I was *capable*."

Wetness is streaming across my fingertips.

"I love you, too," I say, trying to calm him. "More than I thought possible. Baby, what's wrong?"

Josh takes a shuddering breath, obviously trying to collect himself.

"Josh, honey, calm down. *Breathe*. You're going off the deep end all of a sudden. This is a happy thing—nothing to cry about."

Josh suddenly sits up in the bed, shaking, and I rub his back, trying to soothe him. This isn't how I expected this to go. I thought I'd coax the magic words out of him and we'd hug and kiss and make love and then nuzzle noses. I don't understand. It's almost like he's having some sort of panic attack. What the hell is happening to him?

"When I asked you to marry me at the hospital, you were right to say no," he says, panting. "I was just doing the right thing. I was acting out of obligation—trying to appease my father's ghost—or maybe flip him the bird, I dunno. But I shouldn't have asked that—I realize now I can't deliver on that."

The hairs on the arms are standing up. "Sssh," I soothe. "I don't care about getting married. I just want *you*. We're having a baby together—that's plenty for us to deal with. Our love is enough."

There's a very long silence between us. I have no idea what to say or do, so I continue rubbing his back. He's quiet for so long, I'm beginning to feel like maybe he's regretting telling me he loves me.

"Josh?" I ask, my stomach clenching. "I don't understand why you're freaking out."

Josh pauses. "My dad blew his brains out onto her wedding dress, Kat," he says softly, barely above a whisper.

My heart is pulsing in my ears. I wait but he doesn't elaborate. "I don't understand," I finally say.

"If you were my wife," he continues, "and if I lost you, I'm scared I'd do the same fucking thing. He always said I'm just like him."

My heart lurches into my throat. "Josh," I whisper. "Why are you... ? I don't understand." I sit up next to him and put my cheek on his shoulder, still rubbing his back. "Please explain what you're feeling right now."

"I've lost everyone I love, my whole life," he says, barely above a whisper. "Every single time I love someone, they wind up leaving me—or trying their damnedest to leave me. That's what I'm always trying to 'overcome.' And now that I love you, now that I'm not holding anything back... Kat, I couldn't overcome it if I lost you."

"Well, then, that's easy. You won't lose me. Simple."

Josh scoffs. "No, you don't understand."

I wait.

"What if it's not your choice?" he finally says. "It wasn't my mother's choice."

I take a deep breath. "Well, sorry to be blunt about it," I say, "but that's just the gamble of life, honey. Life can be a bitch and a half and there's nothing we can do about it. Look what just happened to Colby. But I'm telling you I'm not going anywhere, if I can help it. Wild horses couldn't drag me away and that's all I can promise you. And that's got to be enough, babe—I'm only human."

Josh makes a sound I can't interpret.

"What?" I ask.

"What if I fuck up? What then? Will you leave me then?"

"Just don't fuck up."

Josh scoffs. "*Kat.*"

I smile in the dark. "What?"

"I'm serious."

"So am I."

"Kat, I'm gonna fuck up—we both know that. How could I not? I told you—I don't know what love looks like up close. I'm a blind man feeling my way in the dark with my hands tied behind my back. I'll fuck it up and then you'll leave me and then my brains will be splattered on the ceiling."

"Well, first off, that's just dumb," I say. "You're not giving yourself enough credit for your awesomeness. You're covered in Teflon, baby, remember? But second off, I've got an easy fix for the whole situation." I touch his face and I'm shocked to find his cheeks are still wet. "Oh, Josh," I breathe.

Josh abruptly turns his face away from my touch. "What's your easy fix?"

Lauren Rowe

I kiss his broad shoulder and turn his face toward mine in the dark. "I'll teach you what to do, honey. Problem solved. Slowly but surely, I'll teach you how to do this love-thing. And so will my family. And so will our baby. And whenever you fuck up, I'll forgive you and you'll get better and better at it until you hardly fuck up at all."

He doesn't reply. And in the silence, I suddenly realize the Plain White T's song on constant repeat is starting to annoy the shit out of me. I reach over to my laptop and flip my playlist onto shuffle, and "Mirrors" by Justin Timberlake randomly begins to play.

I scoot back to Josh in bed, smashing my breasts against his broad back. "Babe," I say. "Listen to me. You can totally do this. Remember when you started the L.A. branch of Faraday & Sons? You didn't know a goddamned thing about running a business, but you learned on the job and kicked ass and now you're a freaking beast. Well, same thing here."

Josh lets out a long exhale.

"Plus, it won't even be possible for you to blow your brains out onto my wedding dress because there won't *be* a wedding dress. Ever. Easy peasy pumpkin squeezy. Problem solved."

Josh doesn't reply.

Shit, this man is a tough nut to crack.

"Hello?" I say. "You've gone completely mute on me, boy. At least gimme a hint about what you're thinking."

"I'll give you more than a hint," he says, his voice soft but intense. "I'm thinking I love you. I'm thinking I'm so lucky I found you. And I'm thinking I hate myself for crying like a little bitch right now."

"I love you, too," I say, sighing with relief. "And you're not crying like a little bitch. You're crying like a normal human. *Finally.*"

Josh kisses me passionately. He's obviously calmed down and returned to his usual form. His panic attack, or whatever the heck it was, seems to be over.

"Okay?" I ask, stroking his hair. "All better?"

"Yeah," he says, sounding like the weight of the world has just been lifted off him. "I'm good."

"Honey, slowly but surely, you'll learn how to do the love-thing and you'll become wise and powerful and unstoppable. Okay?"

144

"Well, I'm already wise and powerful. I've told you that a hundred times. Damn, you're a horrible listener."

"Oh, yeah," I coo. I touch his cheeks in the dark. They're dry now. Sticky with his dried tears, but dry. "I know you're wise and powerful," I whisper. "I was just seeing if you were listening."

"I love you, Kat," Josh whispers.

"I love you, too—I love you, I love you, I love you."

Josh's breathing hitches. "Thank you for saying 'I love you' and not 'me, too.' I had no idea how awesome it would feel to hear you say those *actual* words to me."

"I love you, I love you, I love you," I say. "*Forever.*"

Josh kisses me—but he doesn't say that last word back to me, I notice.

Well, damn. I knew I was pushing my luck hoping for a promise of "forever" from Josh Faraday, but, hey, it didn't hurt to try. Really, I should have known "forever" simply isn't in the man's vocabulary. It's okay, though—I'm content. Josh has promised to be mine—to love me and make a home with me and to be a father for our child. Considering what he's been through in his life, and how fucked up he is underneath all that glitter, I'm pretty sure that's the most I could ever hope to squeeze out of this particular turnip.

I pull on his shoulder and guide him to lie back down in the bed with me, nose to nose, just as the song on my laptop flips to the next random song on my computer: "The Distance" by Cake.

"Oh, God, I love Cake," Josh says.

"Me, too. I saw them last year. They were fantastic."

"You did? In Seattle?"

"Yeah."

"I saw them in L.A. last year," Josh says.

"Oh my God, the dude with the trumpet—"

"I know," Josh says cutting me off enthusiastically. "I couldn't take my eyes off him the whole time. He was singing backup-vocals and playing keys and trumpet, all at the same time. Incredible."

"Incredible," I agree. I sing the chorus to "Sheep Go To Heaven, Goats Go To Hell," one of my favorite Cake songs, and Josh laughs.

"I love that song," he says, nuzzling his nose into mine in the dark.

"Well, I love you," I reply.

He presses his body against mine. "That Plain White T's song was a stroke of genius—utterly diabolical," Josh says. "Thank you for that."

"I've been dying to tell you," I say. "I thought I was gonna explode if I didn't finally tell you. I figured if that song plus the thing with Bridgette didn't finally make you break down and say the magic words to me, then nothing ever would."

"What do you mean the thing with Bridgette?"

"Yeah. The thing with Bridgette. You know. I figured the way to unlock your tortured heart once and for all was through a trap door marked 'Sick Fuck.'" I smile smugly in the dark. "And I was right, of course."

Josh laughs. "Oh my God. You think you *manipulated* me into saying 'I love you' tonight?"

"No. Not *manipulated* you—more like made a *safe place* for you to say it. I'd say I 'set the stage' for you to say it."

"Well, guess what, Madame Terrorist? I was gonna say it tonight no matter what. So there."

I scoff.

"It's true. I had everything planned. I had a romantic dinner lined up at my house and I was gonna tell you tonight."

"Mmm hmm. Sure thing, Playboy."

"Babe. I had a violinist and a cellist—a chef and waiter. Five-star meal. *Candles.* I was gonna do this whole romantic thing."

"Oh, that's so sweet. I had no idea. Thank you. But you wouldn't have said it unless I masterfully *unlocked* you—I guarantee it."

Josh chuckles. "Nope. I was already gonna say it."

"Hmmph," I say, completely unconvinced.

"Hmmph?"

"Yes. Hmmph."

"You don't believe me?"

"Nope."

"You wanna bet?"

"We can't *bet* because there's no way to objectively prove it."

"Oh, yes, there is."

"Prove it, then."

"What do I get when I do?"

"I dunno. If you prove it, then I'll decide after the fact what you win. You'll just have to take a leap of faith." I roll my eyes, even in the dark. "But just because you had a violinist doesn't *prove* you would have taken the next step and told me you love me. In fact, I think it's highly unlikely you would have said it with a violinist standing there breathing down your neck."

Josh pauses. "Hmm. You might be right about that part. But I still would have said it—maybe after dinner, when we were alone in bed."

"I highly doubt that," I say. "You needed an expert push from a woman who knows you better than you know yourself."

"No, I didn't—I was gonna do it all by myself."

"Nope," I say.

"Ha!" he says. "Get ready to eat crow, Madame Terrorist." Josh sits up, turns on the lamp next to him, and lies back down next to me on his side, smiling devilishly.

"Well?" I ask. "Why are you smiling like that? All you've proved is that you know how to turn on a lamp. That proves absolutely nothing."

"Look at my arm," he whispers softly.

"Hmm?"

"Look at my arm, babe."

I sit up and peer at Josh's muscled arm in the dim light and instantly gasp.

Holy shitballs. Josh has a brand new tattoo on the outside of his left bicep—a golden cat with big blue eyes, long lashes, and a mischievous feline-smile on her sleek face. Wow. She looks just like me if I were reincarnated as a cartoon cat.

For a long moment, I study Josh's tattoo in detail, marveling at it's amazingness. The cartoon-cat version of me is wearing a pink collar adorned with a dangling "PG" charm at its center and she's holding a martini glass filled with two olives in her slender paw. And, best of all, her bottom legs are entangled in a swirl of barbed wire that trails from her tail and wraps clear around Josh's bicep.

"Josh," I gasp. "You got a girlfriend-barbed-wire-double-social-suicide-tattoo!"

"Yep," Josh says, his face bursting with excitement.

I laugh gleefully.

Josh puts his finger under my chin, his eyes smoldering. "I know I've gotten some questionable tattoos in my life, babe, but do you really think I'd have committed *double social suicide* if I wasn't planning to tell you I love you?"

I can't speak. It's taking all my energy not to pass out, cry, or climax. This is the most incredible gift Josh could have given me—way better than a big, fat diamond any day. (Well, okay, not way better than a big, fat diamond, let's not get too carried away here—but pretty damned close.) Certainly, in the land of Joshua William Faraday, this barbed-wire-girlfriend tattoo is the closest thing to a promise of forever I could ever hope to receive. And that's good enough for me.

I nuzzle my nose into Josh's. "You do realize you're gonna have this thing *florebblaaaaaah*?" I say.

"That's the idea, baby. I'm gonna love you *florebblaaaah*." He laughs. "I promise."

I laugh with him. "I was wondering why you didn't take your shirt off during the Bridgette thing—I just thought you were being extra careful not to piss me off."

Josh laughs. "Well, yeah, that, too."

"Thank you so much," I say, running my fingers through Josh's hair. "The tattoo is incredible. I love it."

"My supreme pleasure." He kisses me.

Damn, my clit is throbbing like crazy. I do believe this man's about to get lucky again.

"So, Madame Terrorist," Josh says, pulling away from our kiss. "Do you concede?"

I raise an eyebrow. "*Concede?*"

"Yeah. Do you admit my tattoo empirically proves I was gonna tell you I love you, whether or not you arranged the Bridgette thing?"

I squint at him.

"Well?" he asks, a smug smile dancing on his lips.

My nostrils involuntarily flare.

"You're seriously gonna be Stubborn Kat about this?" he asks.

I smash my lips together and narrow my eyes further.

Josh shakes his head. "You're such a little terrorist. You know full well this tattoo proves I would have—"

I place my fingertip on Josh's lips, shushing him. "*Josh,*" I whisper seductively.

148

He abruptly stops talking.

"In the big picture, it really doesn't matter who's right and who's wrong, now does it?"

"*It doesn't matter*? Ha! I've finally got Stubborn Kat dead to rights for once in my life."

"*Josh*," I coo quietly, shushing him again.

He shoots me a wicked smirk. "*What*?"

I lick my lips. "What's the cardinal rule for bagging a babe?" I ask, reaching underneath the sheet and sliding my fingers down his abs to his penis. "What's the most important thing I taught you and Henn about bagging a babe?"

Josh's cock instantly responds to my touch. A lascivious smile spreads across his gorgeous face. "*Oh*," he says.

"What's the rule, Playboy?" I whisper, skimming my lips against his, sliding my hand up and down his thickening shaft.

Josh smiles into my lips. "Ask yourself, 'Is what I'm about to say more or less likely to get me a blowjob?'" He presses his pelvis forward and his hard-on presses emphatically into my palm. "'If the answer's yes, then proceed—and if not, then shut the fuck up.'"

I nod slowly. "So, based on that one simple rule, what do you think you should do right now?"

Josh smiles. "Shut the fuck up."

"Give that man a salami," I say. I touch the tip of his erection and swirl my finger around and around. "And to answer your question," I whisper. "Yes, I'm gonna be Stubborn Kat about this. Surprise, surprise." I shoot him a naughty smile. "But I truly don't think you'll mind."

Josh nods, but, smartly, doesn't say a word.

"Congratulations, baby," I whisper, biting my lip. "I do believe you just bagged yourself a babe."

Josh's hard-on twitches in my hand.

With a happy giggle, I lift the sheet and begin kissing my way from Josh's muscled chest all the way down to his massive hard-on. After sucking on his tip like a lollipop for a brief moment, the anticipation is too much for me to bear—I gotta have him. I slide his full length into my mouth, all the frickin' way—eliciting an excited sound from the other side of the sheet—and then I proceed to give the love of my life the most enthusiastic and heartfelt Katherine Ulla Morgan Ultimate Blowjob Experience the world has ever seen.

Chapter 22
Kat

"Wow, it's nice," Josh says, pulling his Lamborghini to a stop in front of my parents' house.

I've always been proud of my childhood home—it's the place everyone always wanted to hang out when I was growing up—but now that I'm looking at it through Josh's eyes, I'm realizing the entire house probably would fit inside the *garage* of Josh's childhood home.

"This house is right out of a movie," Josh says.

"What movie would that be, babe?" I ask.

"You know, every movie where a suburban high-schooler throws a raging kegger when his parents go out of town."

"Oh, I think I've seen that one," I say. "Does everyone get trashed and start jumping into the pool, fully clothed?"

"Yeah. And then hijinks ensues."

I giggle. "That's right. I'm pretty sure Ryan was in that movie at least ten times in high school, always playing the guy throwing the party."

"I think I'm gonna love Ryan."

"Oh, you will—he's your spirit animal."

Josh chuckles. "Ryan Morgan's my spirit animal?"

I laugh. "Yes."

"Is he gonna be here tonight?"

"Yep. Everyone but Keane—he had to work. Oh, and by the way, don't mention the whole male-stripper thing to my parents. They have no idea Keane's become Seattle's answer to *Magic Mike*."

"Would they care if they knew?"

I shrug. "Keane seems to think my dad would be really disappointed in him. But I told him, 'No, Peen, Dad would have to

150

have actual *expectations* in the first place in order to be *disappointed.*'" I snort.

"Well, that wasn't a very nice thing to say."

I chuckle. "When you meet Keane, you'll understand. He's just... *Keane.*" I touch Josh's arm. "So are you ready to go in and face the firing squad?"

"Why you gotta say that?" Josh asks. "I'm nervous enough, babe."

"Aw, I'm sorry. Just teasing. They're gonna love you."

"Just do me a favor. Don't let it slip about the baby tonight, okay? Just like we agreed. First time out, I want your family to get to know me as Josh, not as The Guy Who Knocked Up Their Precious Baby Girl."

"Babe, we already agreed to keep mum—my lips are sealed."

"Kat, your lips are never sealed—you're the biggest blabbermouth I know, bar none."

I'm genuinely aghast at Josh's characterization of me. "No, I'm not—I'm a steel safe."

Josh hoots with laughter. "Kat, you blabbed to Sarah not five minutes after you said we should wait 'til after the wedding to say anything, and then you told Dax right after you said we were gonna wait to tell your family until after you're showing."

"Well, yeah, but Sarah doesn't count as *blabbing*—telling Sarah's the same thing as telling myself. And Dax doesn't count as telling my *family*—because he's *Dax.*" I roll my eyes. "Trust me, I'm a steel safe, babe—a locked vault."

"Oh really? Well, guess who called me this afternoon out of the blue to congratulate me on our 'little Cinnabon in the oven'?"

I bite my lip, too afraid to give myself away by venturing a guess—but I'm pretty sure there's only one person in the world who'd ever refer to a baby as a "little Cinnabon in the oven."

"*Henn,*" Josh says, confirming what I'm thinking. "He called to congratulate me and ask why the hell I didn't tell him myself."

I make a face that says, "Oops."

"When did you tell Hannah?" Josh asks, scowling at me.

I flash Josh my most charming smile. "Okay, now, see, telling Hannah wasn't my fault. Hannah and I went to lunch today and she was asking me about Golden Kat PR, hinting about how much she wants to be a part of it, and I didn't want to string her along into thinking I was gonna be starting my company any time soon as originally planned. So I told her, 'Hey, I can only handle birthing one baby at a time—and this year, my one-and-only baby's gonna be the accidental Faraday that's currently growing inside my uterus.'"

Josh shakes his head. I can't read his expression well enough to gauge if he's genuinely upset with me.

"Was Henny pissed he heard the news from Hannah and not you?" I ask.

"No, you know Henn. He's always chill. I told him I didn't tell him about the baby because you and I had solemnly agreed to keep it quiet until you're showing." He glares at me, but his eyes are sparkling. "Little did I know the 'steel safe' was out blabbing to everyone and their uncle about our little 'Cinnabon in the oven.'"

"Oh, speaking of which, have you told your uncle?"

"Uh, *no.* Because we'd agreed to keep things quiet, you blabbermouth."

I laugh. "So what did Henn say?"

"He said every time he sees our kid he's gonna wonder if he personally witnessed it being conceived."

I groan. "God, that was so embarrassing."

Josh laughs. "He also said he predicts an entire minivan filled with screaming kids in my near future."

My entire body jolts at the thought. "Slow down, High Speed," I say, my heart in my throat.

"Oh, and he said I'm the luckiest bastard in the whole wide world." He touches the cleft in my chin. "Which is the truth."

I blush like a schoolgirl on a first date.

"And, hey, Miss Steel Safe, guess who called me right after Henn?" Josh asks, mock-glaring at me.

I hold my breath, trying to remember if there's anyone else I've blabbed to besides Sarah, Dax, and Hannah. Nope. Not a soul. Only the girls at my yoga class, but they don't really count. Oh, and the UPS guy—but only because I'd ordered a bunch of maternity leggings and he mentioned his wife is pregnant—so what was I supposed to do—*not* tell him? Oh, and the barista at my favorite Starbucks, of course—but that was only because I'm no longer drinking caffeine and my usual barista noticed I'd ordered a decaf, so that one's not my fault, either. Oh, and Sarah's mom. But that was only because I went to see the new additions she's making to Gloria's House (thanks to the finder's fee money she received after we took down The Club), and Gloria said I looked "awfully pretty"—so what was I supposed to do then—*not* tell her I'm pregnant? I scour my memory, trying to think if I've told anyone else—but, nope, I think that's it.

Oh, Josh is staring at me, apparently expecting me to guess who called him after Henn.

I shrug. "I have no idea who called you," I say. "I haven't told anyone else."

"*Reed*," Josh says. "Because, apparently, Henn called Reed right after Hannah told him the news."

"He did? Oh."

"Yeah, he did. Which is so unlike Henn, I was shocked—if you wanna see what a *real* steel safe looks like, look no further than Peter Hennessey—so I asked Reed what Henn had said to him, *and do you know what Reed said*?"

I shake my head.

"He told me that when you told Hannah our baby news, Hannah asked if you were keeping things on the down-low for a while—*because she was fully prepared to keep our secret and respect our privacy*—but *you* said, and I quote, 'Not at all! I don't care who knows about it! Blab away, Hannah Banana Montana Milliken! I'm bursting at the seams for the whole world to know!'"

I bite my lip. "I said that? I don't think I said *that*."

"Well, either you said it or Hannah's lying. Which is it?"

"Hannah's lying. Definitely. She's a big, fat liar. Actually, there's something you should know about Hannah: she's a pathological liar. Poor thing truly can't discern the difference between truth and fiction. It's such a shame. She's a really sweet girl otherwise."

Josh is clearly suppressing a smile. "Huh. Pretty weird you set Henn up with a known pathological liar. That wasn't very nice of you."

I shrug, trying to suppress my smirk.

"And even weirder you wanted her to be your right-hand-woman at Golden Kat PR. That sounds like horrible judgment on your part, PG."

"Well, you know, I was hoping to rehabilitate her—kill her with kindness until she saw the error of her ways."

Josh chuckles.

"So you're not mad at me for being a blabbermouth?" I ask.

"No, if you wanna blab, go ahead. All I ask is that you *tell* me first so my best friends aren't calling me up, congratulating me on my forthcoming *child*, and I'm sitting there like a flop-dick with my thumb up my ass."

"I'm sorry. I just couldn't keep it to myself. Now that I'm finally through the first trimester and feeling so much better, I'm bursting to tell people."

Josh grabs my hand. "You're so fucking adorable, Kat."

I grin. "So what did Reed say? Was he shocked?"

"To put it mildly," Josh says. "But when I told him I'm starting to get sort of excited about our little kumquat, he was really happy for me—for us."

"*Lime.*"

"Huh?"

"The baby's the size of a *lime* now." I pat my stomach. "No longer a kumquat."

Josh makes a face that melts me. He touches my stomach. "No matter how big the baby gets, it will always be the-kumquat-inside-the-Kumquat to me."

My heart leaps. "You told Reed you're getting sort of excited about the kumquat?"

Josh beams a beautiful smile at me. "Yeah."

"And are you?"

"Babe, what the hell have I been doing this whole past week with you, shopping for cribs and diaper changing tables and fucking onesies and maternity leggings if I'm not starting to get at least a little bit excited about the-kumquat-inside-the-Kumquat?"

I shrug. "It still feels nice to hear you say it."

Josh grabs my hand, his eyes sparkling. "Well that settles it, babe—you've definitely got a vagina."

"I sure hope so," I say. "Because pushing a baby out my peen would *really* hurt."

"Oh my God. Gah." He shudders with phantom pain and puts his forehead on his steering wheel. "Don't say that. Just the thought."

I giggle. "Okay, Playboy. You ready to go into Morgan Manor now?" I look at my watch. "Oh, we're still a bit early—it's ten to seven. My mom said to come between seven and seven-thirty."

Josh takes a deep breath. "Good. That gives me a little more time to prepare mentally."

"Prepare mentally? To meet my family? Babe, they're gonna love you. Don't worry, they're predisposed to love you because *I* love you and I told them so. I told them I love you, I love you, I love you—and I do."

"But you said the same thing about Garrett-Asswipe-Bennett and Colby hated that fucker."

I roll my eyes. "No, Colby hated Garrett-Asswipe-Bennett because he was an asswipe, and you're not. Plus, I didn't actually love Garrett—I just *thought* I did because I was young and stupid and blinded by hormones. And, anyway, regardless, I never told Garrett I loved him and I certainly never, ever told my family 'I love him, I love him, I love him,' the way I've told them about you." I touch Josh's thigh. "Because I've never love, love, *loved* anyone before you—and my family will easily be able to see that."

Josh's smile could light the night sky. "I love you, Kat."

I sigh happily. "It'll never get old hearing you say that."

"Hey, you know what I just realized?" Josh says. "After all your blabbing, I bet someone's gonna say something about the baby to your parents at Jonas and Sarah's wedding—definitely not the way we'd want them to find out."

"Oh, shit," I say. "Good point." I twist my mouth. "Shoot. I guess that means I'd better tell them before the wedding." I grimace. "Which means I gotta tell them this week." My stomach flips over at the thought.

"Yeah, but just don't do it tonight, okay?" Josh says. "And let's not tell them you've moved in with me, either. After they get to know me a bit, that's when we'll hit them with all our fantastic news. No sense making them hate me the first time they meet me."

"They're not gonna hate you when they find out we're shacking up—and they're not gonna hate you when they find out you knocked me up, either. They'll handle all of it with grace."

Intellectually, I know I'm telling Josh the truth and not just placating him—my parents will most certainly deal with whatever I throw at them, like they always do. But that doesn't mean my stomach's not clenched tightly right now, imagining myself telling them I'm pregnant. The truth is, no matter how much my family has always treated me like one of the guys in some ways, I'm still my parents' baby girl and my brothers' Kum Shot—and there's no doubt me becoming an unintentional mother isn't the future my family members envisioned for me.

I look out the window of the Lamborghini for a moment, gazing at my parents' house, lost in my thoughts.

"Hey," Josh says softly, touching my arm. "You want me to be there when you tell your parents about the baby this week?"

"Nope. It should be just me and them." I let out a slow exhale, suddenly wracked with anxiety. "It'll be fine."

Josh takes a deep breath and mimics my slow and anxious exhale.

"Wow, the two of us are really not living up to our nicknames right now," I say. "Come on. Let's pull ourselves together, Playboy—time to get this party started."

Josh lets out a loud puff of air. "Maybe I should have driven the Beemer instead of the Lamborghini? You know, gone for something a little less ostentatious?"

"Babe, first of all, your Beemer's not exactly a low-key car. I didn't even know they made Beemers that fancy. Second, Ryan would have *killed* me if he found out you drive a Lamborghini and he didn't get to see it."

"Oh yeah? Well, Ryan can do more than see it—he can test drive it tonight if he wants. Shit, I'll let him borrow the damned thing for a week."

I grimace. "Josh. Pull yourself together."

Josh makes a face. "Too much? Douchey?"

"Not douchey, honey—sweet. But a tad bit *desperate*. Next thing you know, you'll be standing with a boom box over your head on my parents' front lawn." I snort, but Josh grimaces. "What?" I ask.

Josh shakes his head. "Nothing."

"I was just kidding, babe. I know you'd never do something that 'desperate.'" I wink.

"So, okay," Josh says, rolling his eyes. "I shouldn't hand my Lamborghini keys over to Ryan. Any other tips for tonight?"

"Yes. Madame Professor says: 'The best way to bag a family is to be your awesome self—and the rest will take care of itself.'"

"Excellent advice. Thank you, Madame Professor."

"You're so cute," I say. "I've never seen you nervous like this."

"I've never tried to bag a family before. Babes, I can bag by the dozens in my sleep—families not so much."

"Haven't you ever met a girl's family before?"

Josh shakes his head. "Not really. I've met parents before—lots of times—but only incidentally. That tends to happen in the circles I move in—lots of black-tie galas and bumping into people on the slopes or at birthday parties—or maybe I was fucking some girl at her parents' vacation house in wherever and her parents unexpectedly dropped by to say hi." He laughs. "But I've never been invited for 'next level' spaghetti with a girl's parents and brothers on a quiet suburban street in Seattle. And I've certainly never brought *pie.*" He motions to the pie box sitting on his lap. "I feel like I'm in a movie."

"Babe, you've got it backwards. Going to black-tie galas or staying at Gabrielle LeMonde's vacation home in Aspen is the thing that's like a movie. Pie is real life."

"Not to me. This is amazing. I don't wanna fuck it up." He looks down at his black button-down shirt and jeans. "I'm so damned glad I dressed like Jonas tonight. Thanks for the heads up about that."

"You look great."

Josh nods decisively. "Okay. Let's do this, Party Girl." He grabs the bouquet of flowers off my lap and the pie off his. "Can you hand me the wine and Scotch?"

I grab the booze bottles down by my feet. "You can't carry everything plus the pie," I say. "Let me carry something."

"Okay. You take the Scotch," Josh says. "I can handle everything else." He reaches for his door handle. "Stay put, babe. I'll let you out."

I sit primly with my hands in my lap as Josh moves around the back of the car and opens my door.

"Thank you, sir," I say as Josh helps me out of the car and escorts me toward my parents' front door. "Glenfarclas 1955," I say, reading the label on the box of Scotch in my hand. "I know nothing about Scotch. Is that a good one? "

Josh lets out a little puff of air. "Yeah."

I stop short. That little air-puff raised the hair on the nape of my neck. "Hang on," I say.

Josh stops. "What?"

"How good?" I ask.

"How good what?"

"How good a bottle of Scotch is this?"

"Good. You said your dad loves Scotch, so I got him something I was sure he'd really like."

"Oh, jeez."

"What?"

"Josh. *Honey*. Your idea of a 'good' Scotch is gonna be different than the average person's."

Josh looks at me blankly.

"Josh, how much did this bottle of Scotch cost?"

He opens his mouth and closes it.

"Josh?"

"It cost me nothing. My uncle gave it to me from his private collection."

"Your uncle . . ? Oh, shit. Josh, what's it *worth*?"

Josh winces. "Well, okay, it's a *little* on the extravagant side, I'll admit that—but not too bad. Not, like, *crazy*. I just wanted to be sure it'd be something your dad would really like."

"How much is a *little* extravagant, honey? Gimme a number."

"Don't forget this is a special occasion. I'll never again meet your parents for the first time. I just wanted to make a good impression."

My heart's racing. "Josh, you're freaking me out. How much is it worth?"

"Eight."

I inhale sharply. "Eight hundred dollars?"

Josh looks as guilty as sin.

"Eight *hundred* bucks for a bottle of Scotch?" I ask again slowly, incredulous.

Josh doesn't reply, but he looks like he just confessed to murder.

"Josh, you can't give my father an eight-hundred-dollar bottle of Scotch—especially not the first time you meet him."

Josh grimaces.

"It was such a sweet thought, honey, but you're gonna freak him out and make him think you're some sort of eccentric tycoon or something—like, who's that hermit-guy with airplanes?"

"Howard Hughes."

"*Yes*. My dad's gonna think you're Howard Hughes—or, worse, he's gonna think you're trying to buy his affection."

Josh winces like I've punched him in the stomach. "Shit. I just wanted to give your dad something he'd really, really like."

"I know, babe, but it's too extravagant. I'm sorry."

Josh exhales. "Well, shit." He looks crestfallen. "If an eight-*hundred*-dollar bottle of Scotch is too extravagant to give your dad, then I *really* screwed the pooch here."

I pause, processing what Josh is trying to say. "It's not an eight-hundred-dollar bottle?" I ask.

Josh shakes his head.

"Oh, Josh," I say gasping. "Eight *thousand*?"

He nods. "I called my uncle to ask for a recommendation and he insisted on sending me a bottle of the good stuff from his private collection."

"Oh my God. *Josh*. If my dad knew how much that bottle was worth, he'd never open it. He'd sell it and finally take my mom to Hawaii, instead."

Josh's face lights up. "Your parents have never been to Hawaii? What about your brothers? Do you think they'd like to go, too?"

"Josh, focus. You're not taking the entire Morgan clan to Hawaii. We're talking about Scotch."

Josh laughs. "You read my mind."

"I know I did."

"It'd be fun, though, wouldn't it?"

I laugh. "You're crazy."

"I know I am. But that doesn't mean it wouldn't be fun."

"Oh, it'd definitely be fun," I say.

"Maybe after Colby's feeling better and the baby's born we could take a big family trip to celebrate both?"

I smile. This is the first time I've heard Josh make future plans. "Maybe." I bite my lip, my heart bursting. "That would be incredible."

"Then we'll do it. It's a plan."

"I love you, Josh."

I've never seen Josh smile quite so big. "God, I love it when you say that," he says. "I love you, too."

My entire body's tingling. "Well, you've artfully distracted me, my darling Playboy. I was telling you to put the Scotch in the car."

Josh's facial expression morphs from elation to disappointment. "I'd hate to meet your dad empty-handed."

"You're not empty-handed, babe—you've got pie and wine and flowers. That's plenty. Maybe you can give my Dad an eight-thousand-dollar bottle of Scotch to celebrate him becoming a grandfather when the baby comes. You know, once he already loves you and knows you're not a hermit-tycoon-weirdo."

Josh's shoulders droop. "Okay."

I hand Josh the Scotch and he hands me the wine bottle to hold in return. "I'll be right back," he says, turning around and heading toward the car.

"Hang on," I say, the hair on my neck standing up again.

Josh stops and looks at me expectantly.

"What about this, Playboy?" I ask, holding up the wine bottle.

Josh waves me off. "Oh, that's just, you know, a Cabernet."

"Mmm hmm. Just a Cabernet?"

"Yep."

He's not fooling me for a minute—he looks guilty as hell. "Like, you mean the kind of Cabernet someone could pick up at Whole Foods for twenty bucks?" I ask. "Or, maybe if they *really* wanna splurge, for like, fifty?"

Josh looks like I've just tweaked his nipple. Hard.

"Joshua?" I coax. "What kind of Cabernet are we talking about here, babe?"

Josh purses his lips. "Goddammit, Kat. I can't be expected to follow your stupid rules. I am what I am."

I laugh. "Did you buy it or get it from your uncle?"

"I bought it. And it didn't cost even *close* to eight thousand bucks, I promise. We're good."

"If it's more than a hundred bucks, it's too much, baby. I'm sorry."

Josh makes a face but doesn't speak.

"It's more than a hundred bucks, isn't it?"

He nods. "But only slightly. How 'bout we give it to her and not mention its pedigree? We'll just let her think it's some Australian red I got at Whole Foods on the way here."

"How much, Josh?"

He shrugs. "Four."

I squint. "*Hundred*?"

He shakes his head.

"Josh!"

Josh makes an absolutely adorable face.

I point at his car. "Put it in the Lamborghini with the Scotch," I say. "Jesus God, man. Have you no common sense?" But even as the words come out of my mouth, I glance at his ridiculous car that probably cost as much as a condo and feel like I just answered my own question.

Josh laughs. "Babe, but this particular Cabernet's a *really* great vintage."

I shake my head. "Oh my God, you're so out of touch, it's scary. You can't give my mom a four-thousand-dollar bottle of wine, honey. I'm sorry. You're a sweetheart, you really are, but you're insane."

"Shit," Josh says, looking bummed. "Fine." He grabs the wine from me and hands me the pie, and then traipses to his car, exhaling in resignation as he goes. "Sorry," he says when he returns to me on the walkway again. "I was just trying to..." He trails off and doesn't finish his sentence. He shrugs.

"I know what you were trying to do," I say. "But it's too much."

Josh twists his mouth. "Douchey?"

I kiss him. "Not at all. *Sweet*." I kiss him again. "God, I love you."

Josh grins into my lips. "Say that again."

"I love you," I whisper.

Josh nuzzles my nose. "One more time."

"I love you," I coo. "I love you, I love you, I love you. Infinity."

"I love you, too," he says. He takes a deep breath. "Okay. I'm good now. Momentary blip. I'm ready to get in there and give 'em the Playboy Razzle-Dazzle."

"They won't know what hit 'em, baby," I whisper.

"That's right," he says. He glances toward the house, unmistakable anxiety flickering across his face. "The Josh Faraday charm-bomb's about to go off all over your family's unsuspecting asses." He swallows hard. "*Ka-boom*, baby. Let's do this shit."

Chapter 23
Kat

I was wrong. Ryan's not Josh's spirit animal—he's his soul mate. Watching them meet was like watching one of those movies where the hero and heroine see each other across a crowded room and everyone else instantly fades away. It was insta-love of the highest order. But, just in case anyone hadn't caught on to the immediate connection, there was no missing it when, not twenty minutes after Josh and I had entered the house, Ryan invited Josh to play foosball in the garage.

The way it went down was like this: We were all gabbing amiably in the family room, talking about I don't know what. And even Colby, laid out with his leg in a cast and his arm in a sling and his dog Ralph by his side, was chatting Josh up. And that's when my Dad asked Josh how a Seattle boy wound up living in L.A.

"I went to UCLA and wound up staying down there after graduation to open a satellite branch of my family's business," Josh answered.

"Were you in a fraternity at UCLA?" Ryan asked.

"Yeah," Josh answered. "I lived in the house my first two years. I didn't get a whole lot of studying done, but I got *really* good at foosball."

And that was it. Cupid's arrow had struck. Ryan lifted his head like a meerkat on the African plains, little red and pink hearts twinkling where his pupils should have been.

"Oh-no-he-di'n't," I said.

"Here we go," Dad said.

"Oh, it's on," Dax agreed.

Poor Josh looked perplexed, clearly not aware of the Pandora's Box he'd just opened.

162

"We have a foosball table in our garage," I explained. "It was a Christmas gift from Ryan to my parents years ago—"

"Which was actually a present to *himself*," Dax added.

"And now our family's sort of obsessed with it," I said. "It's kind of our family's *thing.*"

"*Oh,*" Josh said. "Well, I haven't actually played foosball in forever."

"No excuses," Ryan said, leaping up from the couch. "You and me, Josh." He motioned to Dax and me. "We're gonna kick the Wonder Twins' asses."

"Aw, come on," Dax said. "Don't make me play with Jizz."

"Hey now," I said. But that's all I could muster. I'm the worst foosball player in our family (other than Mom, of course), and everyone knows it, including me.

"Don't worry, we'll play a second game and switch up the teams," Ryan assured Dax. "If need be, I'll get stuck with Jizz the second game."

"*Hey,*" I said again.

But Ryan just laughed.

"You need help, Mom?" Dax called to Mom in the kitchen.

"Nope! Dinner will be on the table in thirty!" Mom called back, prompting the four of us to grab our drinks and barrel into the garage, leaving Dad and Colby on the couch, semi-watching a baseball game.

As it turned out, Ryan and Josh soundly kicked the Wonder Twins' asses in the first game, and, in the second game, after poor Josh was saddled with me (because Dax shoved me at him and screamed "You take her, for the love of God!"), my team lost *again.*

"Are you starting to see a pattern here, Kum Shot?" Ryan teased after my second loss. "Now let's think. Who was the common player on *both* losing teams?"

"Hardy har," I replied, feigning annoyance. But I wasn't annoyed. Not even a little bit. In fact, I was walking on air, despite my two foosball losses. Because despite how much I typically abhor losing at anything, I felt like I'd just gained something a whole lot better than a couple of stinkin' foosball victories: I'd gained my brothers' approval of the man I love.

Holy shitballs, Ryan must have slapped Josh on the back at least *five* times during our first game and high-fived him another *ten.* And in the second game, when Ryan and Josh were on opposing teams, Ryan floored me by doing the one thing that conveys matriculation into the Morgan clan more than anything else: he christened Josh with a stupid nickname.

"Aw, come on, *Lambo*," Ryan teased when Josh failed to guard against one of Ryan's many goals. "You can do better than *that.*"

"Eh, you got lucky, Captain," Josh shot back easily.

My heart stopped. I looked at Dax, ready to share a look of pure elation, but Dax's gaze was fixed squarely on Josh.

"I thought you said you actually knew how to *play* this game, Hollywood," Dax zinged at Josh. "Pfft."

Josh laughed. "You best not be talking any smack, Whippersnapper—or else it's gonna come back to bite you in your rock-star ass."

And that was that. My brothers had made their feelings about Josh crystal clear—and Josh had returned their affection in no uncertain terms. Just like that, it was two Morgans down, four to go (or, rather, two Morgans down, *three* to go, since we all know Keane's vote doesn't matter).

And now, having finished our two foosball games, the four of us are walking into the family room, laughing and teasing each other as we go, joining Dad and Colby (and Colby's boxer Ralph) on seats around the TV.

"Oh, yeah!" Colby shouts at the television. "Come on, baby! Come on!"

I settle myself onto Josh's lap in a big armchair and glance at the TV, just in time to see the center fielder for the Twins run back, back, back—and then watch helplessly as a long-ball disappears over the center-field fence.

"*And that ball is gone, baby,*" Ryan says.

Colby and Dad shout with glee and the camera cuts to... *Cameron Schulz*, the All-Star shortstop for the Mariners, rounding second-base and fist-pumping the air.

At the sight of Cameron, I stiffen on Josh's lap and look down, hoping against hope he's somehow, through the grace of God, not looking at the TV right now.

"And *Cameron Schulz* smashes a three-run homer to put the Mariners ahead of the Twins three-two in the bottom of the third," the

TV announcer says, just in case Josh isn't paying attention to what's happening onscreen. "That was *Cameron Schulz's* twelfth homer of the season after a ten-game drought."

At the mention of Cameron's name on the TV, I glance at Josh to find him shooting me a look that can only be described as *homicidal*.

I bite my lip.

"Schulz is sucking ass this season," Dax says. He flashes me a snarky look, clearly reminding me he knows Cameron's penis was once lodged deep inside me.

I shoot Dax a look in reply that unequivocally warns him not to say or do a goddamned thing to give my secret away or else I will cut him.

"Yeah," Ryan says. "The guy's having a shitty-ass year. Glad he finally did *something* to earn his big, fat paycheck."

Dax opens his mouth to say something but I shoot him daggers again, and he shuts it—for a nanosecond, that is—and then he opens it again. "I heard the guy's juiced up," Dax says, smirking at me. "I bet he's got a tiny little peepee."

I squint at him.

"Well, if that guy's on 'roids, he should fire his dealer," Ryan says, swigging his beer. "Because they're definitely not working."

Josh laughs.

"Totally," Dax says. "The Mariners should trade him."

"They're not gonna *trade* Cameron Schulz," Colby says. "He's a franchise player."

"Poor guy's just having a bad year," Dad pipes in. "It happens to the best of 'em. Give him a break."

Josh's face is mere inches from mine. His eyes are smoldering. He touches the cleft in my chin, a gesture I interpret to mean I'm his and only his (and definitely not that asswipe Cameron Schulz's)—and goose bumps erupt all over my body.

Josh licks his lips and I know he wants to kiss me, but he doesn't—a show of restraint around my family, I suppose. Instead, he leans back in his armchair, his eyes burning holes into my face, wraps his arms around me, and pulls me into him.

"So how's the album coming, Dax?" Josh asks, stroking my hair. "You were about to start recording when we first met at my house."

"Oh, it's going great," Dax says. "We've already got three songs in the can."

"You've got three songs finished?" Dad says. "Wow, that was fast."

"Yeah, we still might tweak the mixes, I'm not sure," Dax clarifies. "But, yeah, all the instrumentation is recorded."

"Did you wind up using the violinist and cellist you met at my house?" Josh asks.

"Yeah, and they slayed it. Total game-changers on the songs."

"Well, let's hear what you've got," Dad says.

Dax looks at me for nonverbal guidance.

Normally, Dax would reply to Dad's question by saying, "Not 'til the songs are one hundred percent finished, Dad"—because that's just the way Dax is. I'm the only one Dax ever lets hear his works in progress (and, in fact, he emailed me MP3s of his three new songs last night, swearing me to secrecy). But Dax refusing to play his new songs right now with Josh sitting right here would be a felony-stupid thing for my brother to do. What if Josh loves the songs (and there's no doubt in my mind he will)? Josh might very well offer to forward them to his best friend Reed, without me ever saying a word about it.

I nod encouragingly at Dax, telling him he should play the songs.

"You can listen to 'em right now, Dad," Dax says. "I've got 'em on my laptop in the back room." He hops up and disappears into the hallway.

"Louise!" Dad calls excitedly to Mom in the kitchen. "Get in here! Daxy's gonna play three songs from his new album."

There's a clatter in the kitchen. "Oh my gosh! I'm coming!" Mom calls—and in a heartbeat, she appears in the family room, her eyes sparkling, her cheeks flushed, a glass of red wine in her hand. "I'm so excited." She plops herself down on the couch next to Dad and puts her head on his shoulder (her patented move), and Dad clasps her free hand in his.

I glance at Josh and I'm not surprised to observe he's absolutely transfixed by my parents and their easy show of affection. *That's right, Playboy,* I think, warmth gurgling at my core like molten lava. *Watch and learn how it's done.*

Dax returns with his laptop and hooks it up to the sound system and a few seconds later, his first song fills the room.

"Oh, your voice is gorgeous, honey," Mom coos. "Smooth as silk." She pauses, listening. "Oh, and that guitar—I *love* it." She pauses again. "Oh my gosh, those lyrics—so clever. Beautiful. Oh, Daxy."

"Ssh, honey," Dad says gently, stroking Mom's arm. "*Listen.*"

I glance at Josh again to find him still mesmerized by my parents. Damn, I wish I could read his thoughts.

The song ends and everyone enthusiastically praises it.

"How do you record a full song like that with all those instruments?" Colby asks, scratching his beloved dog's head. "Did everyone in the band stand in a room and play the song together?"

"No, recording a song's not like playing it live," Dax says, and then he goes on to explain in detail how songs are recorded in a studio, each instrument and vocal methodically recorded one at a time onto separate tracks, and then layered, one on top of the other. "It's like putting together a giant Jenga tower," Dax explains.

"That's so cool," Colby says. "Well, however you did it, the song turned out great."

I shoot Mom a relieved look about Colby and she returns it. Colby's been staying at my parents' house to recuperate, and this is by far the most engaged and upbeat I've seen him in all the times I've come over to hang out with him.

Dax plays his second song, and when it's over, we all agree it's a great song, no doubt about it. But when Dax plays his third song, the room catches fire. And I'm not surprised. When I heard Dax's third song on my computer last night, I instantly became obsessed with it. And hearing it today over a nice sound system has only heightened my love affair with it. The song is ear candy and soul candy all rolled into one, one of those songs you hear to the end and immediately play again.

After everyone in the room has praised the song up and down, Dax tells Josh that all those stringed instruments we just heard on the track were nothing more than those two musicians Dax met at Josh's house, each woman playing on about ten separate tracks to simulate an orchestra.

"Oh my gosh, those violins absolutely make the song," Mom gushes. "I was mesmerized."

"I guess it was kismet I met those ladies at Josh's house when I did," Dax says. He looks at Mom and Dad. "Kat asked me to deliver a dinner invitation to Josh at his house—she'd planned a surprise dinner for him at a restaurant, even though, unbeknownst to her, Josh had planned a romantic dinner for *her* at his house on the same night. When I got there, Josh had a violinist and cellist all set up to play for them during dinner, so I got the musicians' phone numbers."

I shoot a grateful smile at my baby brother, nonverbally thanking him for calling my note to Josh a "dinner invitation" in front of our parents.

"Well, that was sweet of you, Josh," Mom says, putting her hand over her heart. "What a shame you put in all that effort and Kat never saw any of it." She shoots me a scolding look like I somehow *purposefully* fucked up Josh's big plans.

"How was I supposed to know he'd planned a romantic dinner?" I ask.

Josh laughs. "It's okay. My brother Jonas and Sarah wound up enjoying the dinner I'd arranged, and Kat and I had a lovely meal elsewhere."

I force myself not to snicker at Josh's use of the phrase "lovely meal" to describe what we wound up doing with Bridgette that night.

"And, anyway," Josh continues, his eyes shifting to me, "I'd only planned all of that stuff so I could tell Kat I love her for the first time—which I did that night, regardless."

My heart stops. *Oh my God.*

"Because I realized," Josh continues, his eyes darkening, "'Hey, I don't need violins and a private chef to tell Kat I love her—I can do that anywhere, anytime.' So that's exactly what I did."

Oh my effing God. I just had an orgasm, right here in front of my parents. And, apparently, so did my mother—she literally just made an unmistakable "O" sound, God bless her.

For a brief moment, there's an awkward pause in the conversation as Mom and I flutter and twitch and coo and then giggle uproariously at how much we're completely embarrassing ourselves—all while the male members of my family exchange looks that say, *They've definitely got vaginas.*

In the midst of my momentary meltdown, I glance at Dad. He's smiling at me—a full smile that reaches his eyes.

I glance quickly at Colby and he's looking at me with twinkling eyes—the first time I've seen light dance in his eyes since the accident.

And then I look into Josh's beautiful eyes mere inches from mine—the eyes of the man who just declared his love for me in front of my entire family (minus Keane, but he doesn't count), and I'm instantly home—even more so than inside the physical walls of my beloved childhood house. This beautiful man is my safe place. He's where I belong. Always.

"I love you," I whisper.

"I love you, too," Josh whispers back, almost inaudibly.

I kiss him on the cheek, my crotch burning, my heart fluttering, my very soul soaring around the room.

Mom clears her throat. "Well, that was very sweet of you, Josh." Oh, man, her cheeks are flushed. Get that woman a cigarette. "Very, very sweet."

There's another awkward silence, which Colby rescues by redirecting the conversation back to Dax. "That third song blew me away, Dax. By the end, it sounded like you had an entire orchestra playing behind you."

"That third song's my favorite of anything you've ever done," Mom says.

"Mine, too," I say. "And you know how much I love everything you've ever done."

"Hey, I don't know if Kat's mentioned it to you," Josh says to Dax, "but my best friend from college owns an independent record label. I'd be happy to forward your songs to him if you'd like. He's always scouting new talent."

Holy fuckburgers. *Jackpot.*

Dax's eyes immediately dart to mine, and there's no mistaking the elation in them. And I'm right there with him. I'm literally jiggling on top of Josh's lap, unable to contain my excitement. Not only will Dax's songs find their way to Reed, exactly as we'd hoped and schemed, but *Josh*, not me, is gonna give them to him. *And,* best of all, it was completely Josh's idea, with no prompting by me. This is truly the absolute best-case scenario.

"Wow," Dax says, somehow managing to keep his composure (sort of). "That'd be amazing, Josh. Thank you." Oh my God, he's practically hyperventilating. "You think I should wait 'til I have all ten songs recorded on the album or send these three now?"

Oh God, I can see Dax's chest constricting from here.

169

"It's up to you," Josh says calmly. "I'll forward whatever you want, whenever. Just lemme know."

Dax looks at me, obviously trying to keep his eyes from bugging out. "What do you think, sis?"

"Send these three now," I say definitively. "Reed won't need ten songs to know you're amazing. Strike while the iron is hot."

Dax's face lights up. "Awesome. Thanks, Josh. I'll send you all three MP3s now. What's your email address?"

Josh gives Dax his email address, just as a timer goes off in the kitchen.

"Oh," Mom says, hopping up. "Everyone up, up, up. It's time to eat!"

Chapter 24
Kat

"Kat didn't exaggerate, Mrs. Morgan," Josh says. "This is the best spaghetti sauce I've ever had."

Mom's face bursts with joy. "Thank you, Josh. I simmer for ten hours and put red wine in the sauce—oh, and a little dash of nutmeg, that's the secret. And, please, call me Louise."

Josh's smile is absolutely adorable.

"Mom, Josh has been to Italy, so if he says it's the best sauce ever, that's a huge compliment," I say.

Mom is positively beaming. "Well, thank you. Where in Italy have you been?"

Josh shifts in his chair. "Pretty much all over."

"Oh, how nice. I've always wanted to go to Italy. I think I was Italian in a past life." She grins. "So Kat tells us you've just moved back home to Seattle?"

Josh has just taken a huge bite of spaghetti, so he simply nods in reply.

"Josh came home to start a new company with his brother Jonas," I say. "Rock climbing gyms."

"Wow, cool," Ryan says. He asks Josh several questions about Climb & Conquer, which prompts Dad and Colby to chime in and ask a few, too, and Josh answers every question with obvious enthusiasm.

"How wonderful to start a business with your brother," Mom says. "Is Jonas older or younger?"

But, once again, Josh is scarfing down a big bite of spaghetti just as Mom asks her question.

"Jonas and Josh are twins," I say. "Fraternal."

"Oh. Sorry, Josh. I keep asking you questions right after you've taken a bite."

Josh swallows his food. "No, I'm sorry. I'm acting like a caveman. I can't control myself. This is the best spaghetti I've ever had."

Ryan chuckles. "Oh, man, Josh. You just bumped Keane out of the number one spot."

"I don't have a number one spot," Mom says defensively. "You're all in the number one spot—except for you, Ryan, for saying that." She scowls at him.

"And if she did have a number one spot, it certainly wouldn't be occupied by *Keane,* for crying out loud," Dad adds.

We all burst out laughing—Dad never joins in on razzing Keane.

"Nice one, Dad," Ryan says.

Mom wags her finger at Dad. "That's not funny, Thomas. Don't encourage them." She addresses all of us kids. "You guys stop picking on Keane all the time. He's more sensitive than he lets on."

We kids all roll our eyes.

"He *is,*" Mom insists. "He used to write me poetry when he was little."

Ryan laughs. "What was it? 'Roses are red, violets are blue, but enough about flowers and shit, Mommy, let's talk about me?'"

Everyone laughs, including Mom.

"'And, by the way, can I borrow twenty bucks?'" Dax adds to the poem.

Everyone laughs again.

"Mom, Peen asks for it and you know it," Ryan says. "A guy can't act like he does and not expect to get razzed for it. He's made his choice."

Mom's expression is noncommittal, which is tantamount to admitting Keane deserves every bit of razzing he gets.

"Mom," Dax says, "I love our penile brother more than anyone in this family, probably, and I still think he's an idiot."

Oh, now he's crossed a line—but not because he called Keane an idiot. "You don't love Keane more than anyone," Mom says, scowling. "I'm his *mother*—which means *I* love him more than anyone. That's the very definition of 'mother.' 'She who loves the most.'"

I put my hand on Josh's thigh under the table.

"Really?" Ryan asks. "That's what 'mother' means? You mean, like, in Latin or something?"

"No. That's *my* definition—I made it up." Mom sighs reverently. "She who loves the most."

Ryan chuckles.

"And just to be clear, I love *all* my kids the most, not just your penile brother."

Everyone laughs, even Dad. Mom's never called Keane a penis before. Could it be my darling mother's already well into her third glass of wine?

Mom shoots Ryan a scolding look. "See what you did? You dragged me into the muck with you. No more referring to penises at the dinner table for anyone—and that includes me. It's just not nice."

We all laugh again.

"So anyway, Josh," Mom says, pushing a lock of her blonde hair away from her face like she's just kicked someone's ass in a street fight. "Sorry about that. We're a bunch of hoodlums in this family— completely out of control." She takes a sip of her wine. "So Kat says you're originally from Seattle?"

Josh is smiling from ear to ear. "Yes."

"What part?"

Josh's smile vanishes. He clears his throat. "Medina," he says evenly, apparently trying to make that word sound as ho-hum as humanly possible.

I glance around, gauging everyone's reactions to the revelation of Josh's hometown—and it's immediately clear everyone fully understands the implication: it means Josh Faraday could use hundred-dollar bills to wipe his ass every day for the rest of his life and still afford to buy himself mansions all over the world. Surely, my family must have at least suspected Josh has cash to burn when he drove up in a freaking Lamborghini—but now they know Josh could buy an entire *fleet* of Lamborghinis if he wanted.

"Oh, Medina's very nice," Mom says politely, but it's plain to see she's flustered. "Some of the homes there are spectacular."

"Was Bill Gates your next-door neighbor growing up?" Dax asks, going straight for the jugular as only my baby brother can do.

My stomach clenches. Shoot. It didn't even occur to me to tell everyone to refrain from asking Josh questions about his childhood.

"No. Bill Gates lives about three miles from where I grew up," Josh says.

Lauren Rowe

"Where did you go to school?" Mom asks.

"St. Francis Academy."

"Oh," Mom says, obviously surprised. "Catholic school?"

Josh nods. "Yeah. I went there from grade school all the way through high school. Sixty-two people in my entire graduating class. After that, I couldn't wait to get to UCLA. A student population of thirty-five-thousand sounded awfully good to me."

"Oh, I bet," Ryan says.

"I had total anonymity for the first time in my life—I absolutely loved it."

Of course, I know Josh landed at UCLA immediately after the death of his father and institutionalization of his brother—which means it might not have been the best of times for him, despite the way he's portraying it right now. But my family certainly doesn't need to know about any of that.

"Are you a practicing Catholic?" Mom asks.

Josh smiles from ear-to-ear like Mom's said something highly amusing. "No," he says simply without elaboration. He takes a huge bite of his food. "This is so good, Mrs. Morgan."

"Louise."

"Louise. Thank you. This is delicious."

Mom beams a huge smile at him. "Thank you. Actually, feel free to call me *Lou*."

My heart stops. Only family and very close friends call my mom Lou. I rub Josh's thigh under the table. *Three down, two to go*, I think.

"So before you decided to open rock-climbing gyms with your brother, what did you do for work?" Dad asks.

Josh proceeds to politely tell everyone about Faraday & Sons—a topic I'm sure he has no interest in, since he's never once talked about it with me. As I listen to him, I learn a lot I didn't know, actually—and also realize, hey, Josh is pretty damned smart. But my attention span quickly evaporates and, while Josh is explaining something horrendously boring, no offense, I steal a glance at Colby. He's studying Josh intently, listening to every word he says, nodding occasionally. There's color in Colby's cheeks, I notice—a sparkle in his eyes. In fact, Colby looks remarkably close to his former self—as good as he's looked since the roof so horribly caved in on him, literally and figuratively, four weeks ago.

174

"So your father started the business, then?" Mom asks. "He's the 'Faraday' in 'Faraday & Sons'?"

Josh's thigh tenses under my palm. "That's right."

"And do your parents still live in Medina?" Mom asks.

Josh's thigh twitches under the table and I squeeze it.

"Mom, Josh doesn't wanna talk about that," I intervene.

"No, it's fine," Josh says, patting my hand under the table. He clears his throat. "My parents have both passed away."

There's a palpable shift of energy in the room. Instantly, the air is thicker—heavier—and every member of my family, without exception, suddenly looks some variation of ashen, somber, or flat-out devastated.

"I'm so sorry," Mom says.

Everyone follows Mom's lead and mumbles some form of condolence.

"It's okay," Josh says. "It's been a long time."

"How old were you?" Mom asks. "Did they die together in some sort of accident?"

"Uh, no, not together. My mom died when I was seven. She was murdered in our home by an intruder. And my dad died when I was seventeen."

Josh's last sentence hangs in the air. Clearly, everyone is waiting for Josh to identify the cause of his father's death the way he identified his mother's—but Josh doesn't say another word.

"What happened to your father?" Dax asks after a moment.

Mom puts her hand on Dax's shoulder as if to quiet him. "Unless you don't want to talk about it, honey," she says, her voice awash in tenderness. "We totally understand."

"No, it's fine," Josh says. "Uh. My father suffered from severe depression after the death of my mother." Josh bites his lip. "He never got over losing her." He presses his lips together and leaves it at that.

For the first time, I'm seeing exactly why Josh once told me he hates telling people his life's story. *Everyone suddenly looks at me funny when I tell them,* he said. *Like they think I'm "laughing through the pain."*

And now I see exactly what Josh meant. Of course, I know my family members are looking at Josh with nothing but deep sympathy, but I'd shut the hell up over time, too, if people constantly looked at me the way my family's looking at Josh right now.

"Well," Mom says definitively. "I'm very sorry for your losses, Josh."

"Thank you," Josh says. "Like I said, it's been a long time."

"Please know you're always welcome here. Any time."

"Thank you," Josh says. His cheeks are red.

There's an awkward silence. Mom looks like she's gonna cry.

Josh shifts in his chair and then, almost like a turtle burrowing himself into his shell, he takes a huge, conversation-ending bite of spaghetti. "This really is the best sauce I've ever had," he mumbles between chews, filling the awkward silence.

Mom's face is bursting with compassion. "I'm glad you like it— especially since it's your turn for extras."

We all exchange looks, nonverbally acknowledging our shock.

From the look on his face, it's clear Josh doesn't understand the gift Mom's just bestowed upon him.

"Whenever Mom makes her spaghetti sauce or chili or lasagna," I explain, "two or three of us get to take home a huge portion of leftovers to put in our freezer. We call it getting extras."

"It's always Keane plus someone else," Ryan adds.

"It's not *always* Keane and someone else," Mom says defensively. "Sometimes, I don't give extras to Keane."

"Mom, it's always Keane and someone else," Dax says.

Mom looks to Colby for support, but Colby nods in solidarity with Dax.

"Well, Keane's not here tonight, is he?" Mom sniffs. "So that means he doesn't get extras this time." She pauses, smirking. "If your penile brother would rather dance in his underwear for a bunch of screaming women at a bachelorette party than eat dinner with his dear mother, well, then, that's his choice, isn't it?"

Every single person at the table, including Mom and Dad, simultaneously lose their shit.

"You think I don't know what Keane's been up to?" Mom says, laughing hysterically.

But Colby, Ryan, Dax, and I can't compose ourselves enough to reply to her. We're like flopping fish on a riverbank, incapacitated by our laughter.

Mom shrugs and takes a long sip of her wine, her eyes full of pure evil. "Let this be a lesson to all of you kids: in the age of smartphones, don't even try to get away with something devious—your mother will always find out."

My brothers and I can't stop screaming with laughter.

"Who ratted him out?" Ryan finally asks, clutching his stomach.

"One of my friends from Bunco. Her daughter Deanna went to a bachelorette party the other night, and apparently a certain male stripper showed up to entertain the ladies with some gyrating dance moves." Mom rolls her eyes. "I must say the photo I've got of Keane dancing around in his underwear is definitely one for my memory book—I'm gonna put it right next to the one I have of Keane dancing around in his diapers."

Everyone laughs again.

"Oh my God," Dax says, holding his sides. "Best day ever."

"So, anyway," Mom continues, "the point is you guys gotta actually show up for dinner in order to get extras—it's how I bribe you to come home occasionally. Which means Keane's extras are now Josh's." She smiles sweetly at Josh and takes a long sip of her wine.

"Oh, no, I couldn't take Keane's extras," Josh says politely, but even I can hear how much he's hoping she'll insist.

"I *insist*," Mom says, right on cue, much to my joy and relief.

Josh's thigh jiggles under my palm.

"I coddle Keaney way too much, anyway," Mom continues. "It's time for that boy to get off the teat."

We all burst out laughing, yet again. Oh my God, when Mom gets a little tipsy, she's truly hysterical.

Mom leans toward Josh, her eyes sparkling. "You're in the line-up now, honey, whether you like it or not. Ask the other kids—when it comes to extras, what I say goes."

"Yup," Ryan says. "And not just about extras. Mom runs a tight ship all around. Don't let that pretty face fool you—she's a barracuda." He winks at Mom.

Josh beams a huge smile at Mom. "I think I see where Kat gets her backbone."

Dad and all three of my brothers simultaneously express agreement with that statement.

"Thank you very much," Josh says. "I'm thrilled and honored to be in the extras line-up."

"We're thrilled to have you," Mom says—and my heart skips a beat at the smile she flashes him.

Oh my God, this night is going better than I could have dreamed. I rub Josh's thigh under the table and I swear I can feel an electric current buzzing just underneath the denim of his jeans.

Mom turns her iron-butterfly gaze on Ryan. "You get extras tonight, too, Rum Cake."

"Yesssss," Ryan says, fist-pumping the air. "Thank you, dearest Mother."

"Enjoy, honey. Thank you for coming to dinner—I know you're busy." She takes a deep breath and wipes her eyes, betraying the emotion she's actually feeling, despite her outward swagger. "So, it's settled: Josh and Ryan get extras; Josh is welcome here any time; and Keaney's a male stripper. New topic. How's the planning for Sarah's wedding coming along, Kitty? Seems like you've been running all over town like a chicken with your head cut off."

It takes a moment for me to regroup—I kinda feel like Mom just gave me mental whiplash—but I somehow manage to reply coherently—sort of—about everything I've been doing to help Sarah pull off the wedding of the century in such a short amount of time. But, honestly, though I'm speaking coherently—sort of—my mind is engaged elsewhere—namely, with Josh and his beautiful, damaged heart. Not to mention the palpable electricity I feel buzzing underneath my fingertips as my hand rests on his muscular thigh.

"Well, it sounds like you've been an exceptional maid of honor," Mom says. "Sarah's lucky to have you."

"You've been doing all that stuff for Sarah and still coming to help me every day, too?" Colby asks. "I had no idea, Kat. I'm sorry."

"Colby," I say. "I've *wanted* to help you. I wouldn't have had it any other way."

"Thank you—I just didn't realize you were so busy."

"It's no big deal. I'm unemployed, remember? I've had all the time in the world to help my two favorite people."

"Hey," Dax says. "I thought *I* was your favorite person."

"Ssh," I say. "Let Colby feel special just this once—the dude's got broken bones, after all."

"No need to make me feel special," Colby says. "I've been feeling a lot better."

"Yeah, but you're still on the mend, Colby," I say. "It's a slow climb—you can't overdo."

"How much longer 'til the wedding?" Colby asks.

"Six days," I say.

"Okay, then, in six days, you're officially gonna be done with *both* your maid-of-honor *and* Florence-Nightingale duties. Starting a new company's hard work, Kumquat. If you're gonna get your PR company off the ground, you're gonna need to focus all your time and energy on that. I'll be fine."

My stomach somersaults. Ooph. I feel sick all of a sudden. I hate letting Colby (and my entire family) think I'm still chomping at the bit to start my own PR company when, in actuality, I put that sucker on the backburner the minute I saw those two little pink lines.

Now don't get me wrong, I'm no stranger to lying to my family—I've told them plenty of whoppers throughout the years. But telling lies to my family about how many martinis I've had or whether I've studied for an Algebra test or saying I spent a hundred bucks on a pair fringed boots when I actually paid two isn't quite the same thing as sitting here impliedly telling every member of my family (except Keane, of course, but he doesn't count) that I'm planning to launch a new PR company when in fact I've got *What To Expect When You're Expecting* sitting on my nightstand at home—oh, and, by the way—fun fact!—my "home" these days is actually Josh's gorgeous new house.

"Just go on your trip with Josh and have fun," Colby continues, "and when you get back home, start focusing on your own life for a while."

"You and Josh are taking a trip?" Mom asks. "Where to? You haven't told me about any trip."

"Oh, I didn't tell you about that?" I ask.

"No," Mom says. "Where are you going?"

Josh's palm lands firmly on my thigh under the table and I place my hand on top of his.

"Oh. I thought I told you. Yeah, Sarah's gonna surprise Jonas during their honeymoon by taking a short detour to Venezuela to see Jonas and Josh's childhood nanny, Mariela. Josh and I are gonna meet them there."

"In *Venezuela?*" Mom says. "Wow. I've never even thought of going there. How exciting. Is it safe?"

"Yes, Mom." I look at Josh. "Josh and Jonas haven't seen their nanny since they were seven, since right after their mother died. This is gonna be a really special reunion for them both."

Color rises in Josh's cheeks. He nods.

"Wow," Dad says. "Where in Venezuela?"

Josh clears his throat. "Just outside Caracas. Mariela just bought a new house there, and I figured as long as Kat and I are gonna be in South America, I might as well take Kat to Brazil and Argentina, too."

Mom and Dad look at each other, their faces bursting with excitement.

"That sounds fantastic," Dad says. "Wow, guys. How fun."

"How come Colby knew about this trip and Daddy and I didn't?" Mom asks, pouting.

"Because, Mom," Colby says, "you two were at work when Kat was here, yacking my ear off about it." Colby shoots me a smile that melts me. "I'd gladly switch places with either of you, trust me— these days, the girl never stops talking to me and I can't get up and walk away."

Mom and I share yet another elated look. Yep. It truly seems our beloved Colby is back (or, at least, well on his way)—which means the rest of us Morgans can finally exhale the anxious breath we've been holding for four long weeks.

Everyone at the table peppers Josh and me with questions about our itinerary for the trip, as well as about Mariela, and Josh answers each and every question smoothly.

"Jonas and I decided to launch Climb & Conquer right after Jonas gets back from his honeymoon," Josh says, "so I thought I might as well travel at the same time. I figure this trip with Kat will be a nice little vacation before I start putting in eighteen-hour days."

"Well, it sounds like perfect timing," Dad says. "Because Kat will be putting in long hours when she gets home, too, launching her new company." He shoots me a proud smile that makes my stomach twist.

"You know, Kitty Kat, that reminds me," Mom says. "I just got some new billing software that's super easy to use on a Mac. When you come to walk Ralph tomorrow morning, I'll sit you down and show you how it works. I think it would work well for you, at least to start with. And don't worry—it's not complicated. If *I* can figure it out, *you* certainly can."

I can't reply. My tongue feels thick in my mouth.

"And if you'd like to talk to the guy at my bank about setting up a commercial account—you know, so your business can take credit card payments—I can take you over there and introduce you."

I nod. Sort of. Oh, God, I feel like I'm gonna barf.

"Kitty, what's wrong?" Mom asks.

I look at Josh, swallowing hard. Oh my God. I gotta tell my family about the-kumquat-inside-the-Kumquat. I can't lie like this anymore. It's time to come clean.

Josh squeezes my thigh under the table and I look at him, pleading with him to let me spill the beans. Josh's jaw muscles pulse for a moment, and then he nods.

I shift my gaze to my parents, my breathing shallow.

"What is it?" Mom asks, her face awash in anxiety. "Is everything okay, honey?"

I scan the faces at the table. Dax's eyes are full of sympathy—he knows what's coming and, clearly, he's taking no pleasure in what I'm about to do. Ryan looks mildly concerned. But Colby's blue eyes are killing me—he's genuinely worried.

I look at Mom and Dad again. "Mom. Dad," I begin. I take a huge breath and squeeze Josh's hand under the table. "I'm pregnant with Josh's baby."

Chapter 25
Josh

There's a pause, like that moment just before a tidal wave crashes onto the shore. Kat's parents inhale sharply—and then nothing. No exhale. No words. No sounds. Just silence for what feels like forever, though it's probably only a nanosecond.

Kat squeezes my leg under the table.

"Oh, Kat," her mom says. "*Honey.*"

I look around the table at Kat's brothers and their facial expressions all convey the same exact sentiment: *Holy fucking shit.*

"It's okay, Mom," Kat says, coming off as much more composed than I'd be able to manage. "It was definitely an accident, that's for sure—and I totally freaked out when I first found out—but Josh and I are both starting to adjust to the idea pretty well. In fact, I think we're both starting to get kind of excited." She looks at me and half-smiles and I nod in solidarity.

I steal a quick glance at Kat's parents and my cheeks blaze. The way they're looking at me, I'm positive they're both imagining me boning their daughter right this very minute. I clear my throat. "Please be assured I'm fully committed to Kat and our baby. I'm gonna take care of them both."

Kat's mom breathes a visible sigh of relief. "How far along are you?" she asks.

"Twelve weeks."

"Oh my gosh."

"I know—end of the first trimester. The baby's the size of a lime."

"A lime? Ohmigosh."

Kat's father clears his throat but doesn't speak.

"Yeah, but no matter how big the baby gets, Josh says it's still the-kumquat-inside-the-Kumquat. Isn't that cute?"

Colby can't keep himself from smiling at that and Kat's mom shoots me an adoring look—but Ryan and Kat's dad both still seem to be processing things.

"Oh, honey," Kat's mom says. She rubs her forehead. "How are you feeling? Have you been to the doctor? Is the baby healthy?"

"I'm good, Mom. Yes, I went to the doctor—I saw the baby's heartbeat. So far, so good—knock on wood." Kat shoots me an anxious look, and I'm pretty sure she's thinking about the booze and weed she ingested before we knew—something I've thought a lot about, too. "I was throwing up nonstop for a while," Kat continues, "but that's tapered off a bit. Now it's mostly late at night and early morning." Kat squeezes my hand again. "I'm good, Mom. The baby's good. Josh is good."

Kat's mom sighs with relief, yet again. Wow. If I'm not mistaken, I'm beginning to see a glimmer of excitement in Louise's eyes—just that fast.

"So what are your plans?" Kat's father asks evenly, breaking his silence. My eyes shift away from Louise's beautiful face—damn, that woman looks so much like her gorgeous daughter it's truly freaky—and I'm met with two blue chips of steel. Oh, boy. There's not a hint of excitement on Kat's father's face. It's all fierce protectiveness.

My stomach clenches.

Kat squeezes my hand under the table. "The plan?" she says, replying to her father. "The plan is I'm gonna move in with Josh—er, actually, okay, to be honest, I already did. Got the last of my stuff moved in yesterday."

Kat's father glances at his wife and his face quite clearly conveys deep concern.

"So, you know, we're gonna live together," Kat continues. "And have a little tiny human that's made up of both our DNA. And we'll raise it together. And be happy. The End."

"I meant what are your *plans*? For the child? For the future?" He motions to Kat and me. "For the two of you?"

"*Oh*," Kat says, like she totally understands—but then after a beat she cocks her head to the side, apparently perplexed. "What do you mean? I just told you. We're gonna live together and raise our kid. The End."

I gently extricate my hand from Kat's steel claw and wrap my arm around her shoulders. "Mr. Morgan, as far as I'm concerned, the

183

plan is for me to take care of your daughter and our baby in every conceivable way," I say evenly. "You don't have to worry about either of them, I promise. They'll want for nothing. I give you my word on that. I'll always take care of my baby and the mother of my child, no matter what happens." I clear my throat. "And not just out of obligation. Because I love Kat, Mr. Morgan. I love your daughter with all my heart and soul."

Kat twitches against me and I squeeze tighter.

There's a brief beat of silence during which Kat's mom visibly swoons and then bursts into tears.

"Mom," Kat says, holding up her arms.

Kat's mom leaps out of her chair and lopes around the table to her daughter, sounds of femaleness gurgling out of her as she goes.

"Everything's gonna be okay, Mom," Kat says into her mom's blonde bob.

Kat's mom sniffles. "*I* should be reassuring *you*, honey. I'll help you—you know that, right? We'll do this together." She kisses Kat's cheek twenty times, making Kat giggle through her tears.

"Come here, Josh," Kat's mom says, breaking away from her daughter and reaching for me. She hugs me. "Welcome to the family, honey," she murmurs into my chest, squeezing me tight.

"Thank you," I say, my heart racing.

When Kat's mom pulls away from our hug, Ryan and Dax are standing behind her, offering handshakes and hugs—but Kat's father is still sitting in his chair, his face unreadable to me.

"Daddy?" Kat says when it's clear he doesn't plan to get up and join the hug-fest.

The look on the man's face makes my hair stand on end.

"So you're not planning to marry Kat?" he asks me evenly.

"*Thomas,*" Kat's mom says, obviously mortified. "They're adults. It's none of our business."

Kat's father steeples his fingers under his chin and exhales. "Josh, I really appreciate everything you just said, believe me—it's good to hear. And I'm glad you two are in love. That's great. But what about ten years from now? Are you gonna draft some sort of support agreement, in case things don't work out between the two of you—or is this just, you know, we'll see how it goes and *whatever?*"

I feel like he just punched me in the balls.

"*Dad*," Kat says, sounding exactly like her mother did a moment ago.

Kat's father shrugs. "It has to be said, honey. If no one else is gonna say it on your behalf, then I sure will. You need some form of commitment about the future, one way or another."

I swallow hard. "I'd be happy to sign a support agreement," I say, my blood whooshing into my ears. "I'll have my lawyer draft it up. As I say, I'm making a commitment to be a father in every way. My word is my bond, every bit as binding as any written agreement. I have no qualms about memorializing my verbal promise in writing."

Kat looks utterly appalled. "Jeez, this isn't some kind of corporate acquisition, Dad. I'm not *chattel*." She turns her gaze on me, her eyes blazing. "You don't need to call your *lawyer*, Josh—our relationship is between you and me. We don't need legal documentation."

"I'm not talking about your *relationship*—I'm talking about the child," Kat's dad says. "I'm talking about securing my grandchild's future and therefore yours."

Kat shoots an icy glare at her father. "With all due respect, it's none of your business, Dad. Josh has promised to take care of the baby and that's his only obligation as far as I'm concerned. He owes me absolutely nothing. Our relationship will rise or fall, just like anyone else's, whether we have a piece of paper making us official in the eyes of the government or not." Oh man, she's ramping up into full terrorist-mode. "You and mom don't realize how unique you are. Saying marriage vows doesn't guarantee anyone a happily ever after, Dad. Fifty percent of marriages end in divorce—did you know that? The piece of paper doesn't guarantee a damned thing. In fact, the divorce rate's the highest among couples who married for no other reason than an accidental pregnancy." She sniffs. "So no thanks to that."

"Kat, don't get all riled up—" Kat's father begins. But, surely, he must know his words are pointless. Kat's already riled up and she's not even close to coming down.

"Josh and I have talked about it, Dad. We don't believe in marriage for the sake of marriage. All that matters is that Josh is gonna be a father to this baby—which he's promised to be," she continues, her head held high. "The rest will take care of itself. We'll just live in the moment and do our best, which is all anyone can do, anyway, whether they've got a piece of paper or not. I don't even want to get married, to tell you the truth. The idea of it freaks me out. I'd much rather stay because I want to stay and go if I want to go." She's practically panting. Damn, apparently her father hit a nerve. Jesus. The lady doth protest too much, methinks.

"Kat, you're flying off the handle. I was just—"

"No, I'm not. You're butting in where you don't belong, Dad. I'm twenty-four. And Josh is *thirty*."

I don't particularly like the way Kat just said my age. She said it like I'm older than the hills.

"And we've decided, after discussing it like reasonable adults, that we don't want to get married. It's just not for us. In fact, I wouldn't even say yes if Josh proposed this very minute at this table—I really wouldn't."

I make a face of surprise. Is she serious?

"And do you know why?" Kat asks, forging right ahead, breathing hard. "Because I don't want to get married for the sake of a kid and nothing more. That's just a recipe for unhappiness and I'm not about to—"

"*Kitty*," Kat's mom says sharply, shutting Kat up. "Honey, you need to stop now. *Please*."

Kat's mouth is hanging open. Her chest is heaving. Her eyes are bugging out.

Kat's mom strokes Kat's cheek, obviously trying to calm her batshit crazy daughter down. "Honey, your father and I support you, one hundred percent. Don't we, Thomas?"

"Of course."

"Now see?" Louise exhales loudly. "Good lord, Kat."

Kat takes a seat and so do I.

"Goodness gracious," Louise says, moving back to her chair on the other side of the table. "You get so riled up sometimes, honey."

Ryan chuckles.

"I'm sorry," Kat's dad says. "You're right. You're both adults. It's none of my business. I was just looking out for you. But it's your life. I'm sorry." He sighs and puts his hand on his forehead. "I was just trying to help."

Kat lurches around the table and into her father's arms and he hugs her.

"You're sure you're okay, honey?" he whispers.

Kat nods into his chest. "I was scared at first but now I'm happy and excited. And Josh is amazing, Dad. You'll see. I love him so much, Dad."

"I was just looking out for you because I love you so much."

"I know, Daddy. I know."

I clutch my chest. I've never seen a father behave like this with his kid. This is straight out of a movie. He told her he loves her—even after she told him she royally fucked up. And now he's hugging her and kissing her cheek, showering her with fatherly affection? Wow. *This is the kind of father I'm gonna be,* I think. *Just like this.*

"Okay," Kat's father says. He kisses his daughter's cheek again. "I'm glad you're happy. Just wait. You're gonna love this baby more than you ever thought possible—and so will we." He looks at me. "I'm sorry, Josh. I didn't mean to butt in where I'm not wanted and I certainly didn't mean to imply you were gonna shirk your obligations as a father. I'm just not used to this new way of doing things, I guess." He smiles ruefully at his wife and she flashes him a sympathetic face. "I'm too old-fashioned for my own good sometimes."

"You don't have to worry about Josh's intentions," Kat says. "Babe, show my dad your arm." She addresses her dad. "Josh got a girlfriend-tattoo in my honor."

I know Kat means well, but, at this particular moment, hearing Kat call my permanent declaration of love for her a "girlfriend-tattoo" feels like she just called me a flop-dick.

"Show 'em," Kat says. "Wait 'til you see this, Dad—then you'll understand how much Josh loves me."

I have zero desire to bare my Kat-inspired tattoo to her family, but I obviously can't leave her hanging. Begrudgingly, I roll up my sleeve to display the full expanse of my bicep—and everyone instantly expresses amazement and amusement all at once.

"What's 'PG' on her collar?" Ryan asks, leaning in to get a closer look.

"Party Girl," I say. "The first night I met Kat, I asked her how a magazine article would label her if they were writing an oversimplified article about her, and she said, 'They'd call me a Party Girl with a Heart of Gold.'"

Kat's entire family expresses agreement with that assessment.

"I wanted to put K-U-M on the collar, but I figured Kat would kill me if I told the entire world her initials."

"Ha!" Ryan says, looking at Kat. "You don't want the world to know you're name is semen, Jizz? You see what you did to your poor daughter, Mom? You've scarred her for life. She'd rather be known as a party girl than get called Kum Shot everywhere she goes."

Kat's mom rolls her eyes. "Only you guys would even *think* to call her that. Katherine Ulla is a beautiful name."

"Sure it is, Mom," Ryan retorts. "That wasn't a cruel thing to do to your one and only daughter at all—was it Kum Shot?"

"Stop it," Kat's mom snaps. "You won't be able to say that in front of your niece or nephew, you know, so you'd better start cleaning up your act now."

"Not gonna happen, Mom," Ryan says breezily. "That baby will think Kum Shot is Mommy's given name."

Kat's mom covers her face with her hands.

"I like the two olives in the martini glass," Dax says, scrutinizing my arm. "Nice touch."

Kat kisses her dad on his cheek. "See, Dad? A man doesn't get a tattoo for his girlfriend lightly." She smiles broadly. "I'd say it's pretty serious."

Shit. Yet again, I know Kat means well, but every time she uses the word "girlfriend" I feel like she's calling me flop-dick.

"Hey, Kumquat," Colby says, breaking his silence. "What's a guy with a broken leg gotta do around here to get a hug from his pregnant sister?"

Kat breaks away from her dad and bounds to the end of the table where Colby's marooned with his leg in a cast. Gingerly, Kat takes Colby's face in her hands and kisses him on the cheek and the two of them hug for a long minute.

"What the hell is 'chattel,' by the way?" Colby asks softly into Kat's hair. "And why the hell do you know that word?"

Kat laughs. "Sarah always says it. I think it just means, you know, like when a woman used to be a man's property?"

"Ah. I see." Colby locks eyes with me. "Welcome to the family, Josh," he says. "I think you'll find it's a pretty fucking awesome family—excuse my language, Mom."

"Oh, well, shit, that's okay," Kat's mom says. "If ever there was an appropriate time to drop an f-bomb, this is it. Speaking of which— holy fuck—I'm gonna be a grandma."

Everyone laughs.

"Welcome to our fucking awesome family, Josh," Kat's mom continues. "I for one already love you."

My heart explodes in my chest. "Thank you, Lou."

"So what do you say we dig into that pie you brought, huh?" Louise says. "I feel the sudden need to eat a very big slice."

Chapter 26
Josh

I peek through a crack in the door and peer out into the courtyard, scanning the faces of Jonas and Sarah's wedding guests, all of them seated and patiently awaiting the start of the ceremony. Obviously, ninety percent of the attendees at this wedding are Sarah's friends and family—which doesn't surprise me. Jonas and I have no family other than Uncle William—and if Jonas has made any close friends over the years, he's certainly never introduced them to me.

"Wow, those flowers are incredible," I say, surveying the virtual explosion of flowers in the courtyard. "I've never seen anything like that. It's like a gingerbread house made of flowers."

"Sarah saw this 'wall of flowers' in some celebrity magazine and lost her shit," Jonas says behind my back. "So I told her to do whatever her little heart desired."

"It's amazing. Hey, are those the violinist and cellist from my house the other night?" I ask, spotting the two women playing a symphonic piece, along with a third woman playing a large harp.

"Yeah," Jonas says from behind me. "Sarah had originally planned to have just the harpist, but when she heard the violin and cello at your house during our 'romantic dinner for two'—thanks again for that, by the way—she flipped out and hired them for the ceremony on the spot."

I chuckle. "Those ladies ought to give me a commission for all the work I've indirectly sent their way. Kat's brother Dax hired them to play on his album, too."

"Yeah, I know. I met Dax, remember?"

"Oh yeah. I forgot."

"Have you heard his album?" Jonas asks.

"Just the first three songs. They're really good—I sent them to Reed and he absolutely loved them. He's probably gonna sign Dax's band. He just wants to watch them play live first."

"Awesome," Jonas says. "I'd love to hear them."

"Stay still, Jonas," Uncle William says from behind me. "Joshua says I have to retie the knot to make it *perfect*. Stand still, Jonas, for the love of God."

"Sorry. I'm bouncing off the walls."

"Really? I hadn't noticed," Uncle William says, chuckling.

I continue scanning the faces of the guests, looking for anyone I recognize.

Well, I see Henn and Hannah in the third row, sitting with their hands clasped tightly together. And there's Uncle William's longtime housekeeper (and longtime lover?), Katya, sitting next to my uncle's vacant chair. I see a handful of familiar faces from Faraday & Sons—the CFO, Jonas' assistant and her husband, a few people on Jonas' team. There's Sarah's mom Gloria in the front row wearing a corsage and Jonas' friend Georgia with her boyfriend and son Trey, all of whom I met last night at the rehearsal dinner.

My eyes lock onto T-Rod in the back, standing in front of a mammoth wall of white flowers, talking to a woman in black holding a clipboard. I smile to myself. Six years ago, when I decided to dive headfirst into launching the L.A. branch of Faraday & Sons, I hired Theresa through a temp agency, thinking I was gonna need someone a few hours a week (at most) to organize my life and possibly run a few errands for me. I never in a million years thought, six years later, Theresa would be my faithful 'woman behind the curtain' for the Wise and Powerful Oz.

Holy shit. There's Miss Westbrook—Mrs. Santorini now—sitting with three kids, including a teenage boy who must be her son Jonas, the one she named after my brother. I smile to myself. Sarah Fucking Cruz is a force to be reckoned with, I swear to God. Apparently, she's hell-bent on "healing" my brother's tattered soul, through any means (and people) necessary, God love her.

My eyes continue drifting over the faces in the crowd and finally lock onto Kat's parents, seated in the farthest row. Kat's mom is in the process of whispering something into her husband's ear and he's smiling and nodding. Man, they're a handsome couple. Especially

Kat's mom. Damn. She's a knockout, even at fifty-something, especially in that sparkling gold dress. Holy shit, it blows me away how much Kat looks like her mother. It's like Louise is a crystal ball, showing me exactly what her hot twenty-something-year-old daughter's gonna look like thirty years from now: a hot fifty-something-year-old.

As I'm spying on her, Louise rests her cheek lovingly on her husband's shoulder—the exact same move Kat always uses on me—and all of a sudden, I feel the world warp and buckle around me, like I've slipped through a gap in the space-time-continuum. Suddenly, I'm no longer looking at Kat's parents awaiting Jonas and Sarah's wedding, I'm seeing Kat and me, awaiting our son or daughter's wedding, thirty years from now.

Whoa.

I quickly shut the door, my heart pounding in my ears, and turn around.

Uncle William's just finishing tying the knot on Jonas' tie.

"There we go," he says, patting Jonas' chest. He grabs Jonas' shoulders and turns him toward me like he's a preschooler on picture day. "I used a Windsor knot the second time. Does that meet with your approval, Master Joshua?"

I survey my brother from head to toe. "Yeah, he looks absolutely perfect now. Good job."

Jonas beams a huge smile at me. "I'm right here—you can compliment me directly."

"You look absolutely perfect, Jonas."

"Thank you."

"I'm gonna take my seat now," Uncle William says. He hugs Jonas and pats him on the cheek. "I'm happy for you, son. Sarah's a great girl. Be good to her."

"I will. Always."

"I know you will. You're an exceptionally kind-hearted person, Jonas. Always have been." He pats the side of Jonas' neck. "She's a lucky girl."

"I'm the lucky one."

"Be happy, Jonas," Uncle William says softly, emotion warping his voice. "That's all I've ever wished for you, son." His voice cracks.

Jonas swallows hard. "I will be. I already am."

The emotion on Uncle William's face is making my eyes water—I've never seen him look quite like this before.

Uncle William turns to go.

"Hey, Uncle William?" Jonas says.

Uncle William stops and turns around.

"Thank you for letting Sarah wear Sadie's necklace. It means a lot to me that you did that for her. Sarah was absolutely thrilled. Thank you."

"Oh, I'm glad you mentioned that," Uncle William says. "When I gave the necklace to Sarah last night, she seemed so excited to make it *both* her 'something old' *and* her 'something borrowed' for the big day, I didn't have the heart to tell her I was *giving* her the necklace and not just loaning it to her." He chuckles. "I figured I'd tell her after the ceremony. So when I drink way too much Scotch at the reception and forget to tell Sarah the necklace is hers, will you make sure to tell her for me?"

"Oh, wow," Jonas says. He looks at me, astonished—but since I've never seen the necklace they're talking about, I can't return his expression. "Sarah's gonna be shocked as hell. Are you sure? She's not expecting that *at all.*"

"Of course. It's my wedding gift to Sarah—my way of welcoming her into our family." He looks wistful. "Sarah reminds me of Sadie, you know. Same spirit. Sadie would have been thrilled to know her favorite necklace will be worn again, especially by someone as beautiful as Sarah, rather than sitting and collecting dust in a vault for another thirty years."

"Thank you so much. Sarah will be thrilled. I'll be sure to tell her."

Uncle William grins. "Now go get married to your dream girl, son."

"Yes, sir. With pleasure."

When Uncle William is gone, I take a good, long look at my brother from head to toe and marvel at the joy wafting off him. I've never seen him look so damned *happy* before. Hell, I don't know if I've ever seen Jonas look happy at all before Sarah came along. Maybe every smile and laugh before Sarah was nothing but a dress rehearsal, a dry run preparing him for true happiness.

"You ready?" I ask my brother.

"I've never been more ready for anything in my entire life," Jonas replies.

I hug Jonas and kiss his cheek, and as I do, my eyes tear up. I pull back from our embrace, wiping my eyes, intending to turn my back on him, but Jonas grabs my neck and forces me to stay put.

"Josh," Jonas says softly, his palm on my neck, his forehead against mine. "You're the best brother a guy could ask for. I thank God for you every single day."

My body twitches with the emotion I'm stuffing down. What the fuck is happening to me? I'm a fucking wreck. I swallow hard, successfully forcing down the huge lump in my throat.

A woman with a clipboard pokes her head into the room and saves me from myself. "You gentlemen ready?" she asks.

Jonas nods. "Just give us a minute."

"Okay. Take your positions in the courtyard whenever you're ready. We'll cue off you."

"Thanks." Jonas takes a deep breath and smiles at me. "You need a minute?"

I nod.

"Take your time, Josh," my brother says, grinning. "They can't start this shindig without me."

I look up at the ceiling for a moment, and once I've got complete control of my emotions again, I fix my eyes on Jonas' face. "Jonas, I'd be lost without you," I say quietly. I rest my palm on his broad shoulder and take a big gulp of air. "Seeing you happy is the best thing that's ever happened to me." I swallow hard. "I love you."

Jonas' lip trembles and his face contorts like he's trying to keep himself from crying. But it's no use. His eyes fill with water. "Fuck, Josh," Jonas says, sounding pissed. He wipes his eyes. "What are you trying to do to me, motherfucker?"

"Sorry."

"I was fully prepared to cry like a baby at the sight of Sarah walking down the aisle—that's to be expected—but I wasn't prepared to cry with *you*, just standing here, talking about our fucking feelings, for Chrissakes. Come on, man, leave me a shred of dignity on my wedding day, would you?"

"Sorry, bro. How's this? 'Hey, fucker. Congrats on bagging an awesome babe. Hope you have a fucking awesome life, you cocksucker—now fuck off.'"

"That's much better. Jesus. You scared me. For a minute there, I thought you were going soft on me."

"No chance of that," I say. "I'm the emotionally stunted asshole of the two of us—you know that."

Jonas grins, his eyes sparkling.

"Okay, motherfucker," I say warmly. "Time to bag yourself a wife and me a sister."

"Fuck yeah, it is."

"Fuck yeah."

We smile at each other.

"I'm so happy for you, Jonas," I say softly.

"I'm so happy for me, too," he says. He takes a deep breath. "Okay. Enough yapping—it's time for me to get married to the divine original form of woman-ness, the goddess and the muse, the magnificent Sarah Cruz."

Chapter 27
Josh

Jonas and I take our positions in front of the audience, standing to the left of the wedding officiant. The distinctive scent of gardenias—my mom's favorite flower—blasts me all of a sudden. I turn around to glance at the spectacular wall of white flowers towering behind us—and, yes, although there are certainly roses and lilies and all sorts of other unidentifiable white flowers comprising the blooming wall, gardenias are by far the most prominent. Did Sarah do that on purpose? Did Jonas tell her how Dad always said Mom loved gardenias?

I look at Jonas and he's gazing anxiously toward the back of the room, his cheeks flushed, his breathing labored. I can almost hear his heart beating from here. Or maybe that's my own heartbeat pounding forcefully in my ears. Why the fuck am I nervous? I'm not the one getting married.

The music shifts to a Mozart-Beethoven-type thing, a pleasant piece of elegant music I've heard a thousand times at various black-tie events, and Kat appears at the back of the center aisle.

My heart skips a beat at the sight of her. Holy fuck, she's absolutely stunning.

"I'm getting fat," Kat said yesterday when she tried on her bridesmaid dress to make sure it still fit. "I should have had the tailor leave a little extra room through the midsection—my belly's totally pooching out."

I laughed. There was literally no hint of a pooch in the dress—which makes sense because, despite our kumquat in the oven, there still hasn't been even the slightest change in Kat's figure since the day I first laid eyes on her in Jonas' living room.

"Babe," I said to her yesterday. "You're not showing at all. Like, literally, not at all."

"You're blind, babe," Kat said. "*Look.*" She pointed at the perfectly smooth midsection of her dress. "It's like I'm hiding a volleyball under there."

"Do you have body dysmorphic disorder?" I asked.

I grabbed her shoulders and moved her in front of the full-length mirror on the other side of our bedroom, and then I stood behind her, staring at both our reflections in the mirror, my palms resting on her smooth, bare shoulders.

And that's when I completely forgot whatever the fuck I was gonna say. I'd meant to drag Kat in front of the mirror to prove my point she's not showing yet (and that she's batshit crazy, too, which certainly isn't news to me), but for some reason, staring at us together in the mirror, looking at her in that blue dress—even with her hair in a ponytail and her face completely bare of makeup—she took my breath away.

So, of course, I proceeded to get my Party Girl with a Hyphen the fuck out of that dress and myself inside of her.

But that was yesterday.

Today, Kat in that same blue dress isn't merely taking my breath away—she's stopping my heart, too. The dress fits Kat the same way it did yesterday, of course—like a glove. But, today, she's not just *wearing* her bridesmaid dress as she glides down the aisle, she's *strutting* in it like a peacock—or, rather, I suppose, like a pea*hen* graced with a pea*cock*'s tail. (Thank you, Jonas.) And Kat has every reason to strut like she's on a catwalk—lord almighty, does she ever. Her golden hair is falling around her shoulders in perfectly formed tendrils. Her skin peeking out of her sweetheart neckline is glowing. Her sky-high heels accentuate the glorious length of her lithe frame. And, oh my God, Kat's gorgeous face, always radiant, always mesmerizing, is downright spectacular today. It's the face that could launch a thousand ships, bring a grown man to his knees, make a man believe in God. And at this moment, lucky me, the blazing eyes lighting up that supernaturally beautiful face are trained on *me*.

By the time Kat reaches the end of the aisle and takes her position to the officiant's right, my heart's bursting, my cock is tingling, and my brain is utterly scrambled. I beam a huge smile at Kat and she winks.

197

The musical selection changes and everyone in the audience stands.

For a moment, I can't identify the song the musicians are playing. I know the melody, but it's not a song normally played by a harp, cello, and violin, so I'm having a hard time placing it. Oh, wait. I've got it. It's "Melt With You" by Modern English. Great song— cool arrangement. I glance at my brother. He's about to burst into a trillion tiny molecules and scatter into the sky.

I fix my gaze at the end of the aisle, my heart in my throat, and there she is—our beautiful bride for the occasion. Our George Clooney. Jonas' handler. My brand new little sister. The great love of my brother's life. *Sarah Fucking Cruz.*

I glance at Kat to find her lower lip trembling and her eyes filled with tears. I look at my brother again and my breathing hitches at the unabashed demonstration of joy and love on his face. Oh my God, Jonas is clearly on the verge of crying.

Keep it together, man, I think.

But, really, I should be using all my keep-it-together mojo on myself. For fuck's sake, I'm shaking like a leaf as I try to contain the emotion welling up inside me.

I take a deep breath and successfully force it down.

Sarah glides down the aisle slowly, her eyes fixed on Jonas, her smile as wide as I've ever seen it. Wow, she's beautiful. Simply stunning. Glowing from the inside-out. And not only that, she's a sexy little thing, isn't she? Hot damn. I knew my brand new sister was a hot tamale and all, but Jesus Fucking Christ—she's scorching hot. Are brides supposed to be this *sexy*? Good lord. Sarah's strapless, white gown hugs every curve of her body leaving absolutely nothing to the imagination, and then fans out mid-thigh, accentuating her hips to full effect. Holy hot damn, that's quite a dress. I'm guessing Sarah picked it especially for Jonas—my brother always has been an ass-man.

For a fleeting moment, my deranged brain actually forms the thought: *I wonder what kind of wedding dress Kat would wear for me?*

My heart squeezes. What the fuck am I thinking? Have I gone insane?

A loud sob lurches from the front of the audience, grabbing my attention. It's Sarah's mother, crying her eyes out at the sight of her beautiful daughter. I can't help but smile. I only met Gloria last night and I already love her—it seems Jonas definitely lucked out there.

I steal another look at Kat, thinking I'll catch her giggling about Gloria's meltdown, but, nope—Kat's crying her eyes out every bit as much as Gloria, completely lost in her own Cinderella-fied world. Wow. Is Kat crying like that because she's so happy for Sarah—or because she's despairing she'll never get to be the one wearing the white dress?

I peel my eyes off Kat and gaze at Sarah Fucking Cruz walking toward us. She's almost at the end of the aisle—and now that she's closer, I can plainly see why Jonas shot me that look of astonishment about Uncle William's gift. Holy shit, the necklace encircling Sarah's elegant neck is fit for a queen. I mean, I'm no expert on diamonds, but that's got to be half a million bucks worth of them, if not more.

It makes no sense, and I know I should be ashamed of myself for thinking it, but for a fleeting moment, jealousy rises up inside me that Uncle William gave that thing to Sarah, and not to Kat. Kat deserves to have the crown jewels around her neck, too.

Wait. What the fuck am I thinking? If it wouldn't be a totally weird thing to do in front of all these people, I'd slap the shit out of myself right now for my rambling and bizarre thoughts.

Sarah glides up to the officiant and Jonas lurches over to her. He grabs both her hands and leans in to whisper something into her ear. Sarah nods and smiles and Jonas kisses Sarah full on the mouth like they've just been pronounced husband and wife.

"Not quite yet, Jonas," the officiant says, and everyone laughs.

Jonas laughs and pulls away, but then quickly leans in and pecks Sarah's lips one more time, like he's literally stealing a kiss.

Everyone laughs again.

"Oh, Jonas," Sarah says, beaming at him.

"You look beautiful," Jonas says softly.

"So do you, love. You've got *happy* eyes."

"Very happy eyes," Jonas whispers. "I love you, Sarah."

"I love you, too, *mi amor. Te amo.*"

"I can't wait to call you my wife."

The officiant clears his throat comically. "Excuse me," he says. "Would you two lovebirds mind if I cut in?"

Everyone in the audience laughs, yet again.

"Would you two like to get married, or . . ?"

"Yes, please," Sarah says.

"As quickly as humanly possible," Jonas adds.

Again, the entire place collectively chuckles.

I steal a look at Kat and she beams at me through her tears.

"I'm thrilled to welcome everyone to this happy occasion—the marriage of Jonas Faraday and Sarah Cruz," the officiant begins. "Both Jonas and Sarah have told me, separately, that they believe finding the other was their life's sacred destiny, their soul's mission—that the other is the missing piece to their soul's sacred puzzle."

Normally, this kind of you-complete-me marriage-speak at weddings doesn't affect me any more than a speech about global warming, but this time, for the first time ever, the officiant's words are making my heart palpitate and the hair on my neck stand up.

After a few opening remarks and a prayer, the officiant reads from Corinthians about the nature of love. "Love is kind and not jealous," he says—and when he says the word "jealous," I can't help but shoot a pointed look at Kat. She flares her nostrils and narrows her eyes in reply, making me smile. I love it when Kat gives me her dragon-lady look.

"Love doesn't brag and is not arrogant," the officiant continues solemnly—and at the word "arrogant," Kat shoots me a snarky look that tells me in no uncertain terms the guy's talking about *me*.

I bite my lip and look away from Kat so I won't burst out laughing at her expression.

"But love rejoices with the *truth*," the officiant concludes—a statement prompting Kat and me to simultaneously grin at each other.

"Honesty-game," Kat mouths to me, making me bite my lip. The woman just read my mind.

"For love bears all things, believes all things, hopes all things, and endures all things, but above all, love never fails."

The snarky smile dancing on my lips a moment ago vanishes. I look at Kat and the earnest expression of love and tenderness on her beautiful face is like a mirror reflecting my own feelings back to me.

"And now, Jonas and Sarah have prepared vows they wish to say to each other under God, to be witnessed by you, their dearest family and friends," the officiant says. He turns to Sarah. "Sarah?"

Sarah grabs both of Jonas' hands and looks deeply into his eyes. She smiles a truly lovely smile. "Jonas," she says softly. "My sweet Jonas—*mi amor*. When I look into your beautiful, kind eyes, I see the man of my dreams—my destiny. With you, I'm completely safe for the first time in my life. With you, I know who I am and who I hope to become. With you, I'm finally *me*. Thank you for showing me what true love is, my sweet Jonas—for teaching me how to love with all my heart and soul. And, even more, for teaching me how to be loved. I love you, my beautiful, sweet, generous, devoted Jonas, and I promise to be your loving and loyal wife from this day forward, forever and ever, 'til the day I die and long after that when I hold you in my arms in heaven."

The courtyard is filled with nothing but muffled sniffles and sighs as everyone, especially Jonas, processes everything Sarah's just said. After a beat, Jonas takes Sarah's face into his palms and kisses her so fervently, the entire audience collectively sighs. And even though Jonas is obviously jumping the gun by planting that kiss on Sarah at this point in the proceedings, the officiant apparently doesn't have the heart to stop him.

As Jonas kisses Sarah, my eyes drift to Kat, my heart clanging wildly in my chest. What would Kat vow to me before God, in front of all our family and friends? And what would I say to her in return?

Kat's eyes are glistening as she returns my gaze. Oh my God. She's looking at me the exact same way Sarah always looks at Jonas—like I'm the answer to her prayers. My skin prickles with goose bumps.

A titter rustles through the crowd and I peel my eyes off Kat. Jonas and Sarah's kiss is finished.

"Thank you, Sarah," the officiant says. "Jonas?"

Jonas sheepishly takes a folded piece paper out of his pocket.

I look at Kat again, my pulse raging in my ears. Oh my God. She's still doing it—looking at me the way no one's ever looked at me before.

"Sarah," Jonas begins, drawing my attention away from Kat. He looks down at his paper, his hands visibly shaking. "My Magnificent, Beautiful, Loving Sarah. My precious baby. My life. Plato says at the touch of love, every man becomes a poet. So I sat down and tried to write you an epic poem rivaling *The Odyssey* that would adequately convey how I feel about you, baby—but, unfortunately, when I tried to rhyme about my feelings for you, I sounded like Dr. Seuss."

Everyone chuckles.

Wow, I think. *Intentional humor by Jonas Patrick Faraday.*

"So I've decided to speak to you from the depths of my heart and soul, instead." Jonas takes a deep breath. "Sarah Cruz, you're the goddess and the muse. You're The One, my love—the heart that sings my heart's song back to me. I was lost and you led me to the light outside the dark cave—to my destiny." Jonas shifts his weight, his chest heaving. "Sarah, our love is the wonder of the wise, the joy of the good, the amazement of the gods. We're the greatest love story ever told, baby—the divine original form of love. You're the air I breathe—the blood coursing through my veins—my very heart and soul. And I vow from this moment forward to dedicate my life to your eternal happiness—to love and protect you always and forever, to the very best of my ability—to strive every day to lead you to the top of your personal mountaintop and rejoice with you when you get there." Jonas takes a deep breath, puts his paper away, and cups Sarah's face in his palms. "Sarah, my beloved, the greatest joy in this life will always be the honor and privilege of calling you my wife."

"Oh, Jonas," Sarah breathes, clearly overcome with emotion. "That was beautiful."

Jonas kisses Sarah, yet again—I guess normal marriage-ceremony rules don't apply to him?—and everyone watching laughs.

Everyone, that is, except for me.

I can't laugh.

I can't move.

Jesus Fucking Christ, I can't breathe.

I feel like I've suddenly been struck by a lightning bolt. *My greatest joy in this life will always be the honor and privilege of calling you my wife.* Oh my God. I've got goose bumps. My chest is tight. My heart is pounding in my ears. *My greatest joy in this life will always be the honor and privilege of calling you my wife.*

I look at Kat, every hair on my body standing up. She's staring at Jonas and Sarah, a look of unadulterated love on her face.

Holy shit.

Kat's The One.

Of course, she is. I don't just *love* Kat. I don't just *want* her. *I want the honor and privilege of calling Kat my wife.*

She's the air I breathe.

The blood coursing through my veins.

My very heart and soul.

I can't live without her. I *need* her like a plant needs water and sunshine and soil. Oh my God. I love Kat and I always will, forever and ever, 'til the day I die—and, holy fuck, Kat deserves to hear me say it in front of God and everyone we love. *Yes.* Kat deserves to be the one gliding down the center aisle wearing a white dress—not to mention a shit-ton of diamonds, too.

I want Kat to be my bride.

Fuck my father.

Fuck the past.

Fuck being scared of what tragedy tomorrow might bring.

Whatever might happen tomorrow—*whatever it is*—I want Kat by my side to experience it with me, good or bad.

"Repeat after me, Sarah," the officiant is saying.

I steal another look at Kat. She's still watching Jonas and Sarah, completely unaware that my head and heart and body and soul are all exploding simultaneously like fireworks on the Fourth of July.

"Jonas, with this ring, I promise to be your faithful and loving wife..." Sarah is saying.

Yes, I want to declare my eternal love to Kat in front of our family and friends and God and I want her to take my name. I want to make a life with that demonic-devil-woman. I want to be her husband—her *family*. "This is my beautiful wife," I want to say when I'm introducing Kat at a party. "Oh, you haven't met my wife yet? Well, here she is—Katherine Faraday."

Sarah slips a ring onto Jonas' finger and he exhales a loud, shaky breath.

"And now it's your turn, Jonas," the officiant says. "Repeat after me."

I look at Kat again to find her blue eyes trained on me.

"Sarah, with this ring, I promise to be your faithful and loving husband..." Jonas is saying.

My eyes are locked with Kat's.

My chest is tight.

Jonas slides a sparkling ring onto Sarah's shaking hand and she squeals with glee, making everyone in the audience chuckle, yet again.

"And now, by the authority of the state of Washington, I pronounce you husband and wife," the officiant declares. "Jonas, you can now *officially* kiss your lovely bride."

Jonas swoops Sarah into his arms and plants a passionate kiss on her lips to raucous applause.

"Ladies and gentlemen, may I present to you—for the very first time—Mr. and Mrs. Jonas Faraday."

The place erupts with cheers.

I clap and cheer, too—of course—but I'm distracted.

My eyes are still locked onto Kat's.

My heart is pounding in my ears.

There's no doubt in my mind—I want to make that beautiful terrorist my wife.

Jonas and Sarah link arms and bound happily down the aisle together, waving and fist-pumping as they go, and Kat and I link arms and follow them, exactly as we were instructed to do during last night's rehearsal. But tonight's walk down the aisle with Kat feels completely different than last night's dry run. Because tonight, for the first time in my entire life, I finally know what I need to be truly happy in this one and only life: I need to make Katherine Ulla Morgan mine, all mine. *Forever.*

Chapter 28
Josh

"Go Henny! Go Henny!" Kat shouts, and the crowd around Henn on the dance floor joins in on the chant, goading him on.

How much has Henn had to drink tonight? He's always entertaining, but this right here is a gift from the comedy gods. I can't tell if he's trying to break dance or if he's going into cardiac arrest; but either way, I'll never forget the sight of him as long as I live.

I look up at the band as I dance with Kat. The horns players are swiveling in synch as they play. Two women in fringed dresses and go-go boots are shaking their asses and singing their hearts out at center stage. And the guitarist is totally laying it down. I don't know who was responsible for finding this awesome band, whether it was Jonas or Sarah or Kat—but whoever it was, they deserve a medal. I've never had so much fun dancing in all my life. Even Jonas has been dancing all night long.

The band begins playing a new song—"Uptown Funk" by Bruno Mars—what else would a wedding band play these days?—and Uncle William grabs Kat's hand and steals her away from me, twirling her around.

Kat doesn't know this, but during dinner, while Kat was chatting with Sarah, I pulled my uncle aside and told him the news about my impending fatherhood—and also about my nascent plan to ask Kat to marry me. It was the first time I'd told anyone my intention to make Kat my wife, having only formed the idea two hours earlier—and my uncle's reaction was better than I could have imagined.

"Hallelujah! The Faradays are multiplying!" Uncle William exclaimed, hugging me enthusiastically and patting me on the back. "This is the second best day of my life." And then he poured me a tall glass of fifty-year-old Scotch from the bottle he'd brought with him from New York—a bottle of Glenfarclas 1955, exactly like the one he'd given me for Kat's dad—and we clinked glasses.

"You got yourself a knockout with that one," Uncle William said, looking at Kat across the room. "She looks just like your mother."

I swigged my Scotch rather than reply.

"And don't you worry, Joshua," Uncle William continued, taking a long sip of his pricey liquor. "I'll make sure Kat's dripping in diamonds for you every bit as much as Sarah was for Jonas today—you can be sure of that." He winked and leaned into me like he was telling me something confidential. "Like I *always* say, we Faraday men *always* keep our women dripping in diamonds."

It was a truly bizarre statement, given that, one, I'd never heard Uncle William say a damned thing about women and/or diamonds before, and, two, I have no idea who "our women" would be in relation to "we Faraday men." But, still, the fact that my uncle was so effusive about my news and immediately wanted to spoil my future bride every bit as much as he'd spoiled Sarah today sent electricity shooting through my every nerve ending.

"Fuck yeah, Uncle William," I said, clinking his glass. "Cheers to that. That's how we Faraday men keep our women—*dripping* in the biggest fucking diamonds the world has ever seen."

"Fuck yeah," Uncle William replied, making me laugh.

It was an unexpected (and supremely ridiculous) conversation, to say the least, and so fucking awesome, I'll never forget it as long as I live. And now, on top of all that awesomeness, Uncle William's dancing with Kat like a madman, laughing with her and throwing his hands up every time the singer in the band commands everyone to "hit their hallelujah." Best night ever.

I look to my left on the dance floor, and there's Jonas, sweating like a pig, smiling from ear to ear, dancing with Sarah like he doesn't have a care in the world. I'm not sure I've ever seen Jonas dance before tonight—but if I have, I've certainly never seen him dance like *this*. He's the epitome of that old saying, "Dance like no one's watching."

Through the dancing bodies on the dance floor, I glimpse Kat's parents at the back of the restaurant, sitting all alone at an otherwise empty table, and I realize now's my chance to steal a private moment with them. I glance over my shoulder at Kat, and she's still happily cutting a rug with Uncle William, so I move quickly off the dance floor toward the back of the restaurant, taking a brief detour at my uncle's table to pour two tall glasses of his rare Scotch.

"Hey, Mr. and Mrs. Morgan," I say, sauntering up to their table. "Can I hang out with you for a bit?"

"Thomas and Lou, remember?" Kat's mom says warmly. "And, *of course.*"

Louise pats the chair next to her and I take a seat.

"I brought you a present, Thomas," I say, putting one of the glasses of Scotch in front of him. "It's a Glenfarclas 1955 from my uncle's private collection. Fifty years old."

"Oh my God," Thomas says. "Really?"

"You want to try it, Lou?" I hold up the second glass to her.

Louise crinkles her nose. "No, thank you. I'm not a big Scotch drinker. I'll just take a little sip of Thomas'."

"How about some more champagne, then?"

Louise's face lights up. "Ah, now *that* I'll happily accept. We're staying at the hotel across the street, so I'm really letting loose tonight."

I flag down one of the roving waiters and grab Louise a flute of champagne and she takes a greedy sip.

"Okay, Thomas. Ready to have your taste buds ruined for any other Scotch?"

Thomas lifts his Scotch in reply and we both take sips at the same time.

"Oh my God," Thomas says, his eyes bugging out.

"Amazing, right?" I say.

"*Damn.* That stuff should be illegal."

"My uncle's somewhat of a connoisseur," I say. "He's got an amazing collection."

Thomas takes another sip. "Wow. So smooth."

I'm about to tell Thomas I've actually got a bottle of this exact stuff for him at my house—the bottle Kat wouldn't let me give to him a week ago—but in light of what I'm about to ask the guy, I refrain. Now's definitely not the time to make Kat's father think I'm trying to buy his affection.

I take a deep breath. "I wanted to talk to you both privately," I say. I look over my shoulder to make sure Kat's not nearby and quickly spot her on the dance floor, still whooping it up. "I want you to know I love your daughter—she's the best thing that's ever happened to me."

Louise makes an adorable face.

"And now that I've met the two of you and your incredible family, I'm realizing what marriage and family can be." I take a deep breath. "So, what I'm trying to say is I'm planning to ask Kat to marry me and I'm hoping you'll give me your blessing."

Kat's mom throws her arms around my neck, exactly the way Kat always does, and kisses me on the cheek. "*Of course*, you have our blessing, Josh. Oh my gosh, we're thrilled. Absolutely *thrilled.*"

When she pulls away from me, she's got tears in her eyes.

I look at Thomas, hoping for a similar reaction, but he's stoic.

There's a short beat that feels like an eternity.

Finally, Thomas lifts his Scotch in the air, inviting me to clink his glass, which I gratefully do. "Welcome to the Morgan family, Josh," he says calmly. "We're thrilled to have you."

I let out a huge sigh of relief. "Oh, thank God," I say, laughing.

Kat's mom giggles—and, suddenly, it's clear to me she's pretty damned tipsy.

"So when are you gonna ask her?" Louise asks, leaning into my face and batting her eyelashes. "And *how* are you gonna ask her, hmm? What you got up your sleeve, Joshy-baby?"

I chuckle. "Um. I don't know yet. I've got to get a ring first, make a plan. I'll do it as soon as possible after we get back from our trip—I won't have time to get a ring before we leave."

"When do you leave?"

"Tomorrow night."

"Oh. Well, if you need help shopping for a ring when you get back, I'd be happy to go with you," Louise says. "I know Kat's taste like the back of my hand."

"Thank you, Lou. I'll definitely take you up on that. We can make a day of it. I'll take you to a nice lunch, too." I motion to her champagne flute. "With plenty of champagne."

Louise squeals—oh yeah, she's definitely looped—and leans forward excitedly. "From now on, you can call me Mom if you want, honey. I mean you don't have to, of course, but you can. Or Momma? Or, hey, maybe Momma Lou?" She giggles again.

"*Momma Lou*?" Thomas asks, incredulous. "Louise, Josh isn't gonna call you *Momma Lou.* Do you think you run a soup kitchen in the South, for cryin' out loud?"

Kat's Mom throws her head back and laughs like a dude. "Sorry. I was thinking about what I want the baby to call me and I thought maybe Gramma Lou? Wouldn't that be *adorable*? So then I guess my mind just wandered to Momma Lou." She takes a swig of her champagne, giggling happily to herself. "Gramma Lou—isn't that darling? Or maybe Grammy Lou?" She sighs. "Gah. I can't wait."

"Slow down, Gramma Lou," Thomas says, rolling his eyes. "You're spinning out of control, honey. First things first—let the boy ask her."

Louise laughs heartily. "Well, anyway," she says, poking her fingertip into the top of my hand. "The point is, Josh, as far as I'm concerned, I just now birthed my fifth son." She guzzles down the rest of her champagne.

"*Louise.*"

Louise giggles. "Oh, Josh knows what I mean. All I'm saying is Josh is now one of my sons, every bit as much as the others. That's all I meant. What's your full name, honey?"

"Joshua William Faraday."

"*Joshua William,*" Louise says reverently. She makes a trumpet sound. "Doo doo doo doo! Birth announcement! The Morgan Family has just adopted a fifth son. There's Colby Edwin, Ryan Ulysses, Keane Elijah, David Jackson, and now *Joshua William.* You're now officially a member of the Morgan family, honey. Welcome."

Thomas rolls his eyes. "Maybe slow down on the champagne, honey."

Louise giggles and waves him off. "Oh, you'll benefit later, old man, so hush up." She puts her hand on my forearm. "We couldn't be more thrilled, Josh."

"Thank you," I manage to say, my heart leaping.

Louise flashes me a truly lovely smile. "No, thank *you.* You obviously make our Kitty Kat *very* happy."

Speak of the she-devil, Kat sidles up to our table, a bottle of water in her hand, her face covered in a light sheen of perspiration. "You guys look like you're plotting the invasion of a small country," she says. "What's shakin', bacon?"

I leap up and give Kat a kiss on her rosy cheek and guide her to the seat next to mine. "Hey, babe. I was just giving your dad a taste of my uncle's Glenfarclas 1955."

Kat shoots me a look of chastisement. "You just couldn't resist, could you, Playboy?" She looks at her parents. "Josh always says *I'm* the blabbermouth who can't keep a secret but look who's the blabbermouth now. Ha!" She snorts and swigs her water. "I told him it was too extravagant, but I guess the Playboy just couldn't control himself."

Kat's mom and dad look utterly confused.

"What are you talking about?" Thomas asks.

There's a beat as Kat realizes she's just blabbed yet another secret. "Oh. You... didn't give my dad the bottle?" she asks.

I shake my head.

"Damn," Kat says. "Whoops." She grins sheepishly. "Well, Dad, surprise! Josh is *giving* you that bottle of that Glenfarkity-fuckity-fuck-whatever. Do you like it?"

I shake my head again. "Kat, no. My uncle brought his *own* bottle of Glenfarclas tonight—he has several bottles of it in his collection. I just brought your dad a *glass* to *taste* from my *uncle's* bottle. I've still got your dad's bottle—*which I didn't tell him about and was still planning to give him later as a surprise.*"

Kat's face turns bright red. "Oh. Well, oops again." She snorts. "Well, Dad, Josh got a bottle of the stuff for you but I wouldn't let him give it to you because I said it was too extravagant a gift."

"Oh, wow," Thomas says. "Really? Thank you, Josh. But Kat's right, that really is too extravagant."

"Can I get all the single ladies onto the dance floor?" the lead singer of the band calls over the microphone on the far side of the restaurant. "It's time for the bouquet toss!"

"No, Thomas, I insist," I say. "I'll have the bottle delivered to your house this week." I shoot Kat a scolding look. "There's no sense in waiting now, is there?"

Thomas looks elated, but he nonetheless says the polite thing. "No, I really can't accept."

"Too late. It's yours. If you feel too weird about it, then open it for a special occasion—maybe when the baby's born?"

Thomas beams a wide smile at me. "All right. Thank you. I

accept, but only if we're gonna open it together to celebrate the birth of my grandbaby."

"Deal," I say.

"And, Mom, don't feel left out," Kat says. "Josh got some fancy Cabernet for you, too. Some hoity-toity vintage."

"Oh, Josh. You're so sweet," Louise says. "But I really wouldn't know the difference. I'm happy with a twelve-dollar bottle of merlot."

Beyoncé's "Single Ladies" starts blaring over the sound system.

"Last call for all the single ladies to try to catch Sarah's bouquet!" the bandleader calls out.

"Too late," I say. "I already got it for you, Lou. I guess you'll have to grin and bear it."

"Well, thank you, Josh. You're so sweet." Louise glances at the commotion happening on the dance floor. "Honey, aren't you gonna get over there?" she says to Kat.

Thomas touches Louise's forearm, obviously signaling his wife to shut the fuck up and she clamps her lips together, apparently realizing she's treading into dangerous territory.

"Mom, *please*," Kat says, her tone suddenly indignant. "Like I told you guys last week, Josh and I aren't gonna get married. Deal with it. We've talked about it like adults and made our decision. Please respect that."

"Oh, we do, honey," Thomas says, pacifying his little stick of dynamite. "We completely respect that."

"Here we go!" the bandleader says behind us on the dance floor. "Are you ready, Sarah?"

Kat looks longingly toward the dance floor for a beat and then back at us, setting her jaw. "I can understand how being at this wedding has probably made you guys dream about watching me walk down the aisle in a white dress. Dad, seeing as how I'm your only daughter, I'm sure you can't help imagining yourself walking me down the aisle on your arm. But it's just not gonna happen, okay? You've got to let it go. I certainly have. One hundred percent."

Thomas, Louise, and I trade a long, skeptical look, all of us nonverbally acknowledging this girl's full of shit.

Louise throws up her hands. "Well, jeez. I'm sorry I mentioned it. I certainly didn't know I was opening a big ol' bottle of whoop-ass on myself."

Kat laughs. "It's a big ol' *can* of whoop-ass, Mom—not a bottle."

"Well, you know what I meant—I'm just saying I didn't mean to make you mad. Your father and I will never bring up the topic of marriage ever again. I swear. You two kids do whatever's right for you and we'll support you. Our lips are sealed. In fact, please don't get married. Blech. Marriage. Ew. Horrible idea." She mock-shudders.

Thomas touches his wife's arm again, glaring at her.

"Sorry," Lou says, giggling. "I've had a little bit to drink. I won't bring up marriage again—that's all I'm saying." She locks her mouth and throws away the key.

Thomas glares at his wife for a long beat. "As your mother said, we support you kids, whatever you decide."

Kat nods. "Thank you. Josh and I really appreciate that." Kat smiles at me and my heart aches at the blatant expression of longing reflected in her eyes.

How, before tonight, did I not understand how much Kat wants the fairytale? And how the fuck did I not want to give it to her?

There's a loud cheer from the dance floor.

"Let's hear it for *Hannah*!" the bandleader shouts into her microphone, and everyone on the dance floor cheers.

Kat glances over her shoulder toward the commotion behind us, and when she sees Hannah triumphantly holding up Sarah's bouquet, her face falls for the briefest moment. "Like I said, all this hoopla just isn't for us," she says, her jaw setting with resignation.

Kat's parents and I share another look.

"We completely understand," Thomas says evenly.

Louise nods like a bobble head doll. "We sure do. We all know how much you hate *hoopla*, Kitty Kat." She snorts.

"*Louise.*"

Kat's mom laughs like a dude and clamps her hand over her mouth again. "Sorry."

I put my arm around Kat's shoulder, demonstrating my faux solidarity with her. "Thanks for understanding," I say to Kat's parents. "As Kat said, we've talked about it and marriage just isn't for us."

"We understand," Thomas says.

"Good," Kat says, jutting her chin. "Now enough about that. Let's celebrate Jonas and Sarah's happy day—and never speak of the whole marriage-thing again."

Chapter 29
Josh

"Looks really good," Jonas says, looking at the spreadsheet displayed on my laptop screen. "I'd like to get our costs down by two percent over the course of the first year, ideally—especially as we start funding our designated charities—but as initial operating costs, I think these numbers crunch pretty well."

Sarah and Kat burst into a collective sob in the other room and Jonas and I exchange a smile. Just over an hour ago, the girls went into one of the bedrooms of our shared hotel suite to watch a chick flick on my iPad while Jonas and I got a little work done in the main room, and it seems the walls of this Venezuelan hotel are paper-thin.

"Anything else you need me to look at?" Jonas asks.

"No, I think Kelly and Colten have things well under control until we get back," I say, referring to the two regional managers we've hired to manage day-to-day operations of our initial twenty gyms. "I'll send them your notes and set up a meeting for the week we get back."

"Good. Thank you. And how about the grand opening?"

"I've got T-Rod overseeing the final details with an event planner. We were originally gonna have a DJ, but the band at your wedding was so awesome, I hired them to play the event. Go big or go home, right?"

"Well, cost-wise, I'm not sure if we really need to—"

"Jonas, I'll cover the band personally if you think the cost is excessive. I wanna kick things off with a bang—you know how much I love a good bang."

Jonas smirks. "Yeah, I'm well aware, Josh. Okay, thanks. Now what about the conference call with the sales team? We should get their numbers in advance of the call so we can—"

I shut my laptop with gusto. "Nope. No more work allowed for you for the rest of your trip."

213

Jonas opens his mouth to protest.

"If anything else comes up this week, I'll handle it. You're on your honeymoon, bro—erase work from your mind."

"Well, yeah, but you're on vacation, too."

"A honeymoon trumps a pre-baby vacation every time. Besides, Kat's been sleeping a ton lately—she gets pretty wiped out these days—so I'll have plenty of downtime in Argentina whenever she's napping to address anything that might come up."

Jonas exhales with relief. "Okay, cool. Thanks, Josh."

"Just enjoy your honeymoon, man."

"I plan to. We're going to Belize next."

"Ah, back to the scene of the original crime, huh?"

Jonas' face lights up. "Yup. A tree house in the middle of the jungle, surrounded by howler monkeys—my idea of heaven on earth."

"Sounds awesome."

"So how's Kat doing? Is she still puking?"

"Yeah, but not as much. She's mostly just really tired. Apparently, it takes a lot of energy to incubate a mighty Faraday spawn. The good news for me is that, when Kat's not sleeping or puking, her pregnancy hormones are through the roof." I snicker. "It's like my unicorn permanently strapped a jet engine between her legs."

Jonas laughs. "Excellent."

"Oh, yeah. I highly recommend pregnancy hormones." I kiss the tips of my fingers like a French chef blessing his masterpiece.

"Good to know. Hopefully, Sarah will have the same experience when it's her turn to incubate a mighty Faraday spawn."

"Oh, you and Sarah are thinking about having kids?"

"Definitely. Not any time soon—but yeah."

"Well, don't wait too long," I say. "My mighty Faraday spawn's gonna need another mighty Faraday spawn to boss around sooner rather than later."

"Oh, please. Your spawn's gonna be my spawn's little bitch," Jonas says.

I laugh. "Bullshit, motherfucker. My spawn's gonna kick your spawn's tiny ass."

"Ha! My spawn's gonna make your spawn cry like a little baby."

We both laugh.

"So how was New Zealand?" I ask.

"Fucking amazing," Jonas says, leaning back in his chair. He gives me a summary of his and Sarah's exciting Kiwi-adventures over the past week. "We stayed at the coolest place," he says. "I'll get you the info so you can take Kat."

I scoff. "I think it'll be a while before I take Kat rappelling down cliffs and bungee jumping off bridges."

"Oh yeah." Jonas grins. "I guess you'll be laying low for a while on stuff like that, huh? How far along is she?"

"Fourteen weeks."

"When the fuck will she actually look pregnant, by the way? She looks exactly the same as she always has."

I shrug. "Hell if I know. I've never done this before."

The girls let out a tortured wail in the other room—and then immediately giggle together—and Jonas and I laugh.

"I think there's a good chance the two humans in that bedroom have vaginas," I say.

Jonas nods his agreement. "God, I hope so, or else I've been seriously duped. So how was Brazil?" he asks.

"Un-fucking-believable." I give him a brief synopsis of Kat's and my travels through Brazil and show him a few photos on my phone. "In Rio, we stayed at this bungalow right on the beach. This is the view from the deck out front."

"Whoa," Jonas says, looking at my photo. "Send me the info on that place, would you? Maybe I'll take Sarah to Rio later this year."

"Oh, you should take Sarah for *Carnival*," I say.

"Oh, good idea," Jonas says. "Yeah, I'll do that."

I tap out a quick text to Theresa on my phone. "I'm texting T-Rod to send you the info on where we stayed in Rio. She'll hook you right up."

"Thanks," Jonas says. He gets up and ambles to the bar in the corner of the suite. "You wanna beer?"

"Yeah. Hit me with some Venezuelan *cerveza* I've never heard of before, bro."

Jonas opens the fridge. "Hmm. Looks like we've got something called *Cardenal*?"

"*Perfecto, mi hermano.*"

Jonas hands me an opened beer and sits back down.

"*Gracias,*" I say.

"*De nada,*" Jonas says, swigging his beer. "*Con mucho gusto, mi hermano estupido.*"

"You did really well talking to Mariela today," I say. "I was impressed."

"Yeah, Sarah speaks Spanish to me all the time," Jonas says, grinning. "She's so fucking sexy." He sighs happily. "But my Spanish was already pretty good before Sarah came along. I guess it's just burned into the deep recesses of my brain from when Mariela used to talk to us as kids."

"Well, maybe it's burned into the deep recesses of your brain, but it's certainly not burned into mine. I couldn't understand a fucking word Mariela was saying all day besides *gracias* and *mi hijo* and *amor.*"

Jonas chuckles. "You didn't need to understand Mariela's words—I think she made herself pretty damned clear with her body language."

"Definitely," I agree. "It was pretty hard to misunderstand all that hugging and kissing and crying."

The girls squeal loudly in the other room and Jonas glances toward the source of the sound.

"Damn, these walls are thin," Jonas says. "Maybe I should have gotten a separate suite for Sarah and me?"

"Meh, it's fine," I say. "It's only for two nights. Plus, the four of us will be out all day tomorrow exploring Caracas—we'll hardly be in the suite together except to sleep at night."

"Well, maybe you and Kat plan to *sleep.* But I'm on my honeymoon, man—sleeping's not on the agenda." Jonas snickers. "And Sarah's a *screamer.*"

"Dude, why you always gotta go there? I know you love screwing your beautiful wife, okay? I got it." I roll my eyes. "I don't need that visual of you."

"What the fuck?" Jonas says, laughing. "You just told me your unicorn has a jet engine permanently strapped between her legs, and I'm not allowed to—"

"Blah, blah, blah," I say, cutting Jonas off, making him laugh again. "All I'm saying is if you've got a problem with all of us sharing a suite, then you'll have to be the one to move, not me. Theresa said this is the only hotel in Caracas that's up to my standards—and there's only one penthouse suite in the whole goddamned hotel. So if you wanna move to a ghetto room on a lower floor be my guest, motherfucker, but I'm staying right here where the streets are paved with gold."

"You're such a snob, you know that?"

I shrug and take a sip of my beer. "I make no apologies—I like what I like."

"Eh, Sarah won't want to switch rooms, anyway," Jonas says. "She insisted on staying with Kat our two nights here. She's been going through some sort of Kat withdrawal this past week."

I laugh. "Same with Kat. Every little thing we did in Brazil, Kat was like, 'Oh my God, Sarah would love this.'"

We grin at each other for a long beat.

"How'd we get so fucking lucky?" I ask.

Jonas shrugs. "I have no idea. A broken clock is right twice a day, I guess."

"Sarah's really sweet," I say. "I can't believe she even *thought* to arrange a reunion with Mariela, let alone pull it all together on the sly like that."

"That's Sarah," Jonas says. "She's the sweetest person I've ever met. Just genuinely *kind.*"

"She's the sweetest person I've ever met, too," I agree.

"What about Kat? She's not the sweetest person you've ever met?"

I snort. "Hell no."

Jonas laughs. "Well, that's not a very nice thing to say."

"Aw, come on," I say. "Kat's *sweet*—really sweet. Heart of gold. But it's buried underneath a thick outer shell of evil. The woman's a demon spawn of the highest order." Once again, I kiss my fingertips like a chef.

Jonas chuckles. "You always did like 'em evil."

I mock-shudder like the very mention of evil excites me. "And, even better, *crazy*-evil."

"Well, Sarah doesn't have an evil bone in her body," Jonas says. "Does she have a crazy-bone? Hell yes. A bossy-bone? Fuck yes. But an evil-bone? Not even in her little toe."

"Like I said, Sarah's the sweetest person I know," I say, swigging my beer. "Which is perfect for you—you've always liked 'em sweet."

Jonas shrugs. "I don't think that's a particularly weird thing to like, Josh."

"Bah," I say. "Gotta have a little evil to brighten your day, I always say."

Jonas chuckles. "Sicko."

"I am what I am. So were you shocked when you got off the plane and saw Kat and me standing there—or did you already have a hunch?"

"I was completely shocked—and then I was even more shocked when we drove up to that big ol' house and Mariela came out. I couldn't believe my eyes."

"Dude, me, too—I thought I was gonna keel over in shock."

"For so long, I always thought, 'If Mariela passed me on the street, would I recognize her?'" Jonas says. "All through the years, whenever I'd see a Latina woman of the right age walking by, I'd think, 'Could that be Mariela?' But then, the minute I actually saw the real thing, there was no doubt it was her—a thousand memories instantly came rushing back to me."

"I didn't recognize her *physically* so much as I recognized her..." I trail off, searching for the right word. "Her *soul*? Is that a totally Jonas Faraday thing to say?"

Jonas chuckles. "I hate to break it to you, but you're actually referencing Plato's theory of forms without realizing it. Plato said when we see something in the physical realm with our eyes, we're seeing the imperfect form of it—because nothing's perfect in the physical world—but your *soul* is nonetheless able to recognize it, despite its imperfections, because it innately knows the thing's divine original form from the *ideal* realm." He pauses briefly. "I think for both of us, Mariela was our divine original form of nurturing—an ideal form of safety and affection and love—and our souls recognized her instantly, even if our eyes didn't."

I smile at Jonas. There's just no one like my brother. "Makes perfect sense to me," I say.

Jonas smiles.

"Hey, did you catch her *scent*?" I say, taking in a deep breath through my nose. "I didn't even know I remembered that scent, but the minute Mariela hugged me, I instantly remembered how she used to rock us to sleep in that big rocking chair—remember that?—and I'd nuzzle my nose into her neck and breathe in that flowery scent."

Jonas shakes his head in apparent awe. "It's amazing what the brain retains that we don't even realize on a conscious level." He drinks his beer. "When Mariela hugged me and called me Jonasito today, I felt like I'd traveled back in a time machine to when I was seven years old."

I sip my beer and consider that concept for a minute. "Dude," I say. "I'm thinking deep thoughts about the illusion of time and the infinite nature of love. Make it stop, Jonas. Please. My head hurts."

"Jesus, Josh. You can't be thinking deep thoughts like that— you'll fuck up the entire world order."

I smirk. "Okay. Phew. I'm thinking about motorboating pretty titties now. I'm good."

Jonas laughs. "That was a close call. God help us if you created some sort of butterfly effect and fucked us all."

"Seriously. That was truly scary."

"Don't do anything like that again," Jonas warns. "You've still got five days in Argentina with your pregnant girlfriend after this— for fuck's sake, don't injure yourself, man, especially if your unicorn's on a hot streak."

"Hey, that reminds me," I say. I peek toward the bedroom. This is the first time I've been alone with Jonas since the wedding—and his use of the word "girlfriend" just reminded me I haven't told him about my plan to ask Kat to marry me. I glance toward the bedroom again to make sure Kat's not coming out. "Hey, at your wedding, I had this epiphany that slammed me like a ton of bricks, man," I begin.

The girls let out a collective sigh followed by a cheer in the other room and I glance at the door again.

"When we get home," I say, "I'm gonna ask Kat to—"

Sarah and Kat burst out of the bedroom, both of them sobbing, and I abruptly shut my mouth.

"Oh my gawd," Sarah bawls, wiping her eyes. "Best movie *ever.*"

"Ever, ever, ever!" Kat agrees, tears streaming down her beautiful face. She hands my iPad to me. "Thank you, babe. Oh my gawd. I *loved* it."

"One of my all-time faves," Sarah says.

"Me, too. Top ten for sure. Maybe even top five."

"Fo shizzle pops." Sarah plops herself onto Jonas' lap. "Hello, hunky monkey husband."

"Hello, wife."

Kat follows suit and plops herself down onto my lap, too. "Hey, PB," she says

"Hey, PG," I reply, my heart panging. Shit. If ever there was a time when our Playboy-Party-Girl nicknames felt woefully insufficient, it's right now. Ever since Jonas and Sarah's wedding, I've been chomping at the bit to call Kat my wife, and with each passing day, my desire becomes more and more urgent. "What movie were you two watching in there?" I ask. "It sounded like you were watching *Schindler's List*."

"Oh, no, it was a romantic comedy."

Jonas and I share a chuckle.

"*About Time*," Sarah says reverently. "Oh my *gawd*. Have you seen it?"

"Never heard of it," I say.

"You gotta see it," Kat says. "The girl from *The Notebook* is in it. Have you seen *The Notebook*?"

I shake my head.

"Oh. Well, did you see *Love Actually*? You know the rock-star-British guy in that one?"

"Dude, unless Seth Rogan or Will Ferrell or Adam Sandler is in a movie, it's a good bet I haven't seen it."

Kat rolls her eyes. "Do you know the red-haired guy from the *Harry Potter* movies?" Kat asks.

"Well, of course," I say. "Now you're speaking my language."

"But not the one who played Ron Weasley," Sarah interjects. "The redheaded guy who played his older brother."

Kat swats my arm. "The guy in *Ex Machina*."

"Oh," I say. "Yeah?"

"He's the main guy in this one and he's so cute—"

"*So* cute," Sarah agrees.

"And he figures out he can time-travel by going into a closet and then he meets *The Notebook* girl and—what's her name, Sarah?"

"Rachel McAdams. She's so cute."

"*So* cute. So, anyway, I won't spoil it for you, in case you ever wanna watch it but it's *so* good." Kat lets out a long, swooning sigh.

Sarah mimics Kat's swooning sigh. "So good," she agrees.

Jonas and I exchange a look. Honestly, I don't know what the fuck either of these two women have said for the past three minutes—I pretty much tuned out after Kat said the words *The Notebook*—but, damn, both of these girls are fucking adorable.

Clearly, Jonas agrees with my assessment because he's begun nuzzling Sarah's neck and whispering to her.

Sarah makes a sound of sheer happiness. "Oh, how I love you, hubster," she breathes.

"Oh, how I love you, *Mrs. Faraday,*" Jonas replies.

Sarah runs her hand through Jonas' hair. "I'll never forget the look on your face when you saw Mariela today. You were beautiful, love."

"Thank you for arranging that for me. I'll never forget it."

"Yeah, thank you, Sarah Cruz," I say. "I'll never forget today as long as I live. It was amazing."

"It was my pleasure. It warmed my heart to see the Faraday boys looking so happy."

"Mariela had quite a house, didn't she?" Kat says. "I'd say Mariela's livin' large in the ol' Vee-Zee, baby."

"Half a million bucks goes a really long way here," Jonas says, referring to the finder's fee money we secured for Mariela (along with equal shares for Sarah's mom, Jonas' friend Georgia, and Miss Westbrook).

Sarah whispers something into Jonas' ear and he kisses her tenderly.

I look away from them and I'm met with Kat's intense gaze. *Oh.* I know that look—it means my unicorn's feeling frisky.

Kat runs her fingertip over my bottom lip. "Are you all done with your work, honey pot pie?" she whispers.

I chuckle. "Someone's been hanging out with Sarah Weirdo Cruz today."

Kat giggles. "Yeah, that was extremely Sarah-Cruz-ish, wasn't it?"

"Yes, it was. And, yes, I'm all done with my work." I stick out my tongue and lick the tip of Kat's finger. "I'm all yours for the rest of the night, hot momma."

Kat presses her forehead against mine. "Mike Wazowski," she whispers.

I grin.

Kat presses her lips against my ear and whispers softly, "I'm so frickin' horny, I'm gonna blow."

"God, I love pregnancy hormones," I whisper back.

Kat smiles.

Out of nowhere, Jonas makes a kind of growling noise and abruptly stands with Sarah in his arms, lifting her like a rag doll. "Good night, guys," he says. "It seems Mrs. Faraday and I have a date with a Venezuelan mattress. Come on, wife." Without waiting for our reply, Jonas barrels away like the gorilla he is, happily carrying his love-monkey-bride in his protective arms.

"Good night, guys!" Sarah calls to us, just before their bedroom door closes with an emphatic thud.

"Those two are so freaking cute," Kat says.

My stomach clenches with envy. Fuck me. I want to say, "Come on, wife!" to Kat, exactly the way Jonas just said that to Sarah. And, fuck me, I want to say "Mrs. Faraday and I have a date with a Venezuelan mattress!" too, even if, yes, that's a supremely cheesy thing to say. Shit. At least fifty times this past week in Brazil, I almost blurted, "Will you marry me, Kat?" But I refrained every time—of course, I did—because the sane part of my brain knows I've already asked Kat to marry me without a ring or ironclad plan in place and that she replied, "I wouldn't marry you if you were the last man on earth." So, obviously, another spontaneous (flop-dick) proposal ain't gonna cut it a second time around.

Kat skims her lips against mine, yanking me out of my thoughts, and I slip my tongue eagerly into her mouth. In reply, she presses herself into my hard-on.

"How are you feeling, beautiful?" I ask, kissing her softly.

"Good," she says. "I didn't barf *once* today."

"Wow," I whisper. "Sexy. You know I can't resist a woman who doesn't barf."

"One might even say it's your Achilles' heel, although I seem to recall you're also quite willing to fuck a woman who barfs on your shoes."

"Not 'a woman' who barfs on my shoes," I say. "Only *you*."

"Sweet-talker."

"Okay. Enough chitty-chat," I declare suddenly. I stand and swoop Kat into my arms, and Kat practically growls with excitement. "It's time to put those pregnancy hormones of yours to maximum use, Party Girl."

Chapter 30
Kat

"I've got a present for you," I coo as Josh lays me down on the bed.

"Oh yeah?" Josh pulls off his shirt, revealing his gloriously muscled and tattooed torso.

"Oh my God," I say, ogling him.

Josh pulls down his pants and briefs, letting his straining donkey-dick spring free.

"Sweet Baby Jesus," I blurt. "I feel like my clit's a lawnmower and you just yanked its starter-cord."

Josh smiles wickedly. "Oh, the things I'm gonna do to you, hot momma." He advances on me like a panther.

"Wait. Close your eyes."

Josh exhales like I've asked him to stop and change the oil in my car. "You're killing me, Smalls," he says.

"Close 'em, Playboy. I've got a surprise for you. It'll take five seconds and then you can do whatever you please to me."

Josh settles onto his knees next to me, his naked body taut, his erection massive. "You've got twenty seconds and then I can't be held responsible for what this dick might do to you."

I pull my sundress off, revealing my leopard-print-electric-blue bra and undies underneath, and carefully cover my hipbone with my palm.

"Okay," I say. "Open."

Josh opens his eyes. "Great surprise. You're gorgeous. Now lie back." He pushes me back gently.

"No, you fool," I say. "I haven't shown you the surprise yet."

Josh exhales again.

"You ready?" I ask.

Josh motions to his straining dick in reply.

I bite my lip and remove my hand, revealing the temporary "tattoo" Sarah drew on my hip with a Sharpie pen while we watched *About Time* in the other room. "For you, Playboy," I say, unveiling the famous Playboy-rabbit-head-logo drawn onto my hip. "I can't get a tattoo while pregnant—apparently, there's a risk of infection or whatever—but I finally figured out what I'm gonna do for my second tattoo after the baby's born."

Josh's hard-on visibly twitches. "Aw, you're gonna get a *boyfriend* tattoo?"

I nod.

Josh's sapphire eyes smolder. "Sounds pretty serious, babe."

"Oh, it is—as serious as it can be."

Josh advances on me slowly, his taut muscles flexing, his hard-on huge, and slowly pushes me onto my back. He deftly removes my bra and, the minute my breasts bounce free, he buries his face into my cleavage and motorboats my boobs, making me giggle.

"I'll be damned, your pretty titties might actually be getting a little bit bigger, babe," he says.

I look down at myself. "Really?"

"Maybe. Lemme double check." He takes my left nipple into his mouth, swirling his tongue around and around.

I let out a soft moan.

"Yeah, definitely," he says. He runs his palm over my belly. "And you're a tiny bit rounder here, too, I think."

My heart lurches into my mouth with excitement. "You really think so?" I sit up, completely distracted from our imminent fuckery. "Do you think I'm finally pooching?" I look down and poke myself with my fingertip.

"Lie back down, babe," Josh says, pushing me back. "I'll examine you and let you know for sure."

I stare down at myself. "I think you might be right. *Look.*" I poke my belly again and there's definitely a little pooch under my fingertip. "I put on my favorite skirt this morning and it didn't fit quite right but I thought I was imagining it."

Josh pushes gently on my shoulders again. "Lie back, beautiful."

"By the end of this trip, nothing I packed is gonna fit right," I say, my skin buzzing. "I'm probably gonna need maternity clothes any day now, babe, and I didn't pack any."

"Lie back, hot momma," Josh persists. "We'll go shopping in Buenos Aires if we need to—surely, there are pregnant women there, too. *Relax.*" He peels off my undies while licking my neck and firmly pushes me back onto the bed.

"Do you really think I'm showing?" I breathe.

"Oh yeah." He licks my ear and slides his fingers between my legs. "Definitely. What fruit is the baby now?"

"A lemon."

"A *lemon*?" He shudders like I just said a dirty word. "God-*damn*, I've got a pregnant-woman fetish these days." His fingers are massaging me. His lips are on mine. His tongue is in my mouth. "My sexy little baby-momma," he whispers.

He begins trailing kisses down my body, heading slowly toward my bull's-eye—and when his warm, wet tongue finally reaches my clit, I arch my back and exhale, settling in for what's surely going to be a delicious ride. But just as Josh's mouth begins devouring me in earnest, the unmistakable sound of Sarah having an orgasm in the other bedroom wafts into our room. The sound is muffled, and oddly restrained, like Sarah's trying her damnedest to be quiet but utterly failing.

Josh lifts his head and looks at me, a smirk on his gorgeous face, and we both giggle. "Sounds like they're having fun."

I snort.

Josh sits up, his eyes dark with desire. "You wanna play a game, Party Girl?"

I bite my lip. "What kind of game?"

Josh lies alongside me, grabs a pillow, and places it under his head. He licks his lips. "Have a seat, babe." He waggles his tongue at me, making my clit flutter.

"That's the game?" I ask. "I sit on your face?"

"No, the game is you sit on my face and try not to scream the way Sarah just did. If you scream, I win—if you don't, you win."

I smirk. "Am I trying not to *come*—or trying not to *scream* when I do?"

"Oh, you're gonna come—there's no doubt about that." He licks his lips with an exaggerated motion. "In fact, I'm gonna eat your

225

pussy 'til I make it rain." He snickers. "And good fucking luck not screaming through *that*."

"Babe, the walls are so thin. I have no desire for Jonas and Sarah to hear me climaxing."

Josh shrugs. "So does that mean you accept my challenge?"

"Of course. And I assure you, I'm gonna win. I'm a sniper, baby—total control."

"We'll see about that."

"What do I get when I win?"

"If you can squirt without waking half of Caracas, then I'll be your sex slave for the rest of the night. Command me as you please, hot momma." He begins stroking his erection, a pervy gleam in his eye. "But if I make you scream louder than Sarah just did, then you're all mine, every fucking inch of you, for the rest of the trip."

I giggle. "Sounds like I'm gonna come out a winner in this game either way."

Josh adjusts the angle of the pillow under his head and makes a loud smacking sound like he's calling a horse. "Come on, m'lady—hop aboard your valiant steed. I'm thirsty for some lemonade."

"Oh my God, Josh. That's disgusting."

He laughs and continues stroking his hard-on.

"You really are a sick fuck, you know that?" I say, crawling over his face.

"Yes, I am."

After positioning myself carefully over Josh's beautiful mouth, I lower myself onto his lips and immediately sigh with pleasure at the sensation of his warm tongue penetrating me. "Oh, God," I say. "That's so good, babe."

Josh growls underneath me and slides his finger into my ass and I jerk my pelvis against him like I'm slowly fucking his face. Within minutes, my skin pricks with goose bumps and my toes curl—and it's quite clear to me I'm gonna lose this goddamned bet. Oh, God, yes, I'm gonna lose this motherfucking bet by a landslide—*which means, of course, I'm gonna win.*

"I love you," I breathe, my pleasure ramping up. "Oh my God, yes, babe—oh, my fucking-motherfucker-fuck. *Yes*." I bite the tip of my finger, trying to relieve the pressure rising inside me, but it's no use. This is just too freaking good. Oh my God, *yes*.

Josh growls underneath me again and slips his finger right up my ass and the wall of my vagina contracts sharply. Josh's lips and tongue continue voraciously eating me and my body tightens again, and then again, ratcheting itself up for what promises to be an outrageous release.

"*I love you so much,*" I choke out, fondling my breasts. "Oh, God, I love you." But those are the last coherent words I utter before letting out a scream that's not only sure to be heard by Jonas and Sarah in the next room, it's no doubt going to awaken the entire continent of South America, too.

Chapter 31
Josh

I've been lying here in the dark, spooning Kat's sleeping body, for over an hour—but sleep won't come, no matter how many Venezuelan sheep I try to count.

Fuck.

I carefully extricate myself from Kat's long limbs, slip quietly out of the bed, and pad into the moonlit suite. After grabbing a water bottle from the fridge, I head out to a large balcony overlooking pre-dawn Caracas, expecting to grab a few minutes of insomnia-laden solitude. But I'm surprised to find I'm not alone out on the balcony.

"Jonas?"

My brother turns around in his chair. "Hey," he says softly.

"What are you doing out here, bro?"

"Same as you, I'm sure," he says. "I can't sleep."

"You want something from the fridge?" I ask, holding up my water bottle.

Jonas holds up a glass in his hand.

I sit in a wicker chair next to my brother and look out at the skyline. "Why can't you sleep?" I ask.

Jonas shrugs. "I've had chronic insomnia my whole life. This time, luckily, I've got *happy* insomnia—I can't stop thinking about how *happy* I am." He smiles. "You?"

I run my hand through my hair and exhale. "I've been wanting to tell you about this, actually. I've decided to pop the question to Kat—and I can't figure out how the fuck to do it."

"Really? Congrats. That's great. When are you gonna do it?"

"As soon as I can get a ring and figure out how the fuck to do it right this time. There's no margin for error—failure isn't an option."

228

Jonas looks genuinely elated. "Well, do you have any ideas? Bounce 'em off me—I'll help you figure it out."

"Dude, I have no idea how to do it—that's why I've got insomnia. I can't just, you know, take her to dinner and pull out a ring or take her to a basketball game and ask her on the fucking Jumbotron. Whatever I do, it's gotta be *big*." My stomach clenches. "Honestly, I'm kind of freaking out about it, bro. I asked Kat once and totally fucked it up. I gotta do it right this time or I dunno if she'll give me a third bite at the apple." I rub my forehead. "Kat didn't just turn me down the first time—she got *pissed*. And even worse than that, she got her feelings hurt. I'm the first man in the history of the world to ask a woman to marry him and make her feel *shitty* about it."

Jonas grimaces. "How'd you manage that?"

I shrug. "I have no fucking idea."

"Come on. You must have an idea what you did wrong. How'd you ask her? You never told me any details. All I know is your proposal *didn't* include the words 'I love you.'"

I shake my head, not wanting to relive it.

"Tell me, Josh. We gotta figure this out."

I begrudgingly tell Jonas every detail of how that night at the hospital went down. "And then the whole next week, I felt so rejected and bummed and confused, I actually told myself I was done with her," I say, rolling my eyes at the absurd thought. "And the most aggravating part was she kept calling me 'Mr. Darcy,' and I have no idea why."

"You mean from *Pride and Prejudice*?" Jonas asks.

"Why the fuck do you know that? I had to Google that shit to figure it out."

Jonas shrugs.

"You amaze and appall me," I say. "But we're off track here. The point is, I fucked it up and Kat said no and I've never felt so rejected in all my life. For both our sakes, I couldn't handle a repeat performance. I have to do it right this time."

"Yeah, well, proposing in a hospital waiting room when the girl's sitting vigil for her brother definitely doesn't sound like a story Kat would wanna 'tell her grandchildren one day'—unless, of course, you want her to tell her future grandchildren 'The Story of How Grandpa was a Dumbshit.'"

"The scary thing is I truly didn't realize I was fucking up at the time—I thought I deserved a fucking medal for being so honorable."

"Well, that's the problem right there. Women don't want honorable—they want love."

"Yeah, I know that now. Duh. *Now* I realize Kat just wanted to hear me say 'I love you' and 'you're the woman of my dreams' and all that—okay, I get it—but at the time I was too freaked out to say any of that. But still, I'm not sure why she punched me so fucking hard in the balls. She could have just said 'no thanks'—that would have been sufficient, thank you very much. But not Kat. Of course, not. She was *livid*, man—and, honestly, I still don't fully understand why. Which means I could totally piss her off again and fuck it up completely and not even realize I'm doing it."

"Well, duh, Josh. You seriously don't know why?"

I shrug.

"Josh, you made Kat feel like you were doing her a fucking favor by marrying her—like *she* was the lucky one. No woman wants to feel like that, especially when a man's proposing to her—she wants to feel like a princess out of a fairytale. She wants to feel like the grand prize."

"Holy fuck, Jonas. That's exactly what she said. *Exactly*." I close my eyes, chastising myself. "How is it possible you know more about this than I do?"

"Because I've watched *Pride and Prejudice* and *Fools Rush In* and a bunch of other chick flicks—and those movies tell a guy everything he needs to know about the female psychology, you dumbshit."

"Well, I fully realize I'm the lucky one now, believe me—I'd be the luckiest bastard in the world to call Kat Morgan my wife."

"Well, just tell her that, then. Perfect."

"No, that ship has sailed man," I say. "I've gotta bring out the big guns now—this is round two, bro. I need a whole lot more than a good proposal—I need a shit-ton more than 'I love you'—I need *redemption*."

"Yeah, I guess you're right," Jonas says. He squints, clearly thinking hard about something. I've seen this look on my brother's face a thousand times when he's poring over an acquisition report and crunching numbers in his head. "Okay. If you wanna crack Kat's secret code, you gotta figure out what makes her tick. For Sarah, it was overcoming her lifelong fears and finally letting go completely. That was the key with her—making her *surrender* and let go. So, first off, I took Sarah to the top of a thirty-foot, underground waterfall in Belize and made her jump off. That was stage one. And, then, when I finally proposed to her, I took her to the highest mountaintop in Greece and made her jump off and paraglide down to the beach." He chuckles, apparently at some memory. "I made Sarah face her fears and let go and, man, it was fucking epic. You've just gotta figure out how to do the same for Kat. Unlock her. Figure out her secret code and crack her. And that's how you'll deliver her unto pure *ecstasy* in the way the ancient Greeks defined that word—'the culmination of human possibility.'"

I roll my eyes. My brother is such a fucking freak. "Well, Kat's not afraid of a goddamned thing," I say. "I could take her to the top of a waterfall and she'd cannonball off it, honking her boobs as she plummeted down."

Jonas laughs. "Well, then, fine—overcoming fear clearly isn't the ticket with Kat. But there's got to be *something* that will unlock Kat's deepest desires—something her soul is desperately yearning for."

I'm silent.

"Well?" Jonas says.

"I'm thinking," I say.

"Don't strain yourself."

I laugh.

"Hey, you're wise and powerful, remember?" Jonas says. "Even if Kat's not scared of a damned thing, she's gotta be *scarred* by something—or maybe secretly *yearning* for something. *Think.* What's buried deep, deep, deep inside that woman's heart and soul? Figure it out, unlock it, and deliver it to her on a silver platter—bigger and better than she'd ever imagine—and that's how you'll give her a proposal she'll 'tell her grandchildren about.'"

I wince. "When I said that to you at Uncle William's house, I never thought in a million years it would come back to bite me in the ass."

"Well, it has. So take your own advice. Your exact words were, 'If you're gonna surprise the girl, then make sure you blow her socks off. This is the story she's gonna be telling her grandkids one day. So don't fuck it up,'" Jonas says. "That's *exactly* what you said to me." He brings his glass to his lips and surveys the twinkling Caracas skyline. "So now it's time to walk the walk, motherfucker."

I lean back in my chair, my mind reeling. "Shit," I say. "I seriously have no idea what to do."

"Well, whatever it is, you've got to pull out all the stops."

"Fuck," I say, feeling suddenly panicked. "Kat said she wouldn't marry me if I were the last man on earth, Jonas. Help me, man. I need to trick that demon-woman into saying yes."

Jonas laughs. "You've tricked her pretty well so far."

I scowl at him.

"Don't worry, Josh," Jonas says soothingly. "We'll figure this out. She's but a mortal woman and you're a wise and powerful demigod. We'll topple her."

"Thank you, Jonas," I say, feeling mildly comforted. "So where do I start?"

"Well, let's start with the basics," Jonas says. "You gotta tell her you love her this time."

"Thank you, Einstein."

"And you gotta get her a ring so big it sears her fucking corneas."

I nod. "Yet again, not rocket science."

"You say that but you weren't already planning to do that, were you?" Jonas says.

"Yes, I was. *Duh*. I'm gonna get Kat a ring so big, she's gonna need a fucking *crane* to carry it around."

Jonas laughs. "Good boy."

I swig my water, my mind reeling. Fuck me. I've got to get this exactly right.

"So what else are you thinking?" Jonas says. "'Whatever you do, it's gotta be rock solid, man—it's got to be a homerun. There's absolutely no room for failure.'"

Obviously, he's quoting me from Uncle William's dining room. Who knew my own words would come back to put the fear of God into me a mere two months later? Back then, I truly thought I'd never get married—a thought that's absolutely laughable to me now.

"Okay, okay," I say. "I get it. I talk a good game when it's not me stepping up to home plate." I swig my water again. "Stop razzing me and help me, Jonas. Please. I'm desperate."

Jonas chuckles. "Finally, the Kung Fu master begs Grasshopper for help."

"Jesus, are you gonna berate me or help me? I need your help, Jonas. I already asked her once and she said no. If she turns me down again, especially now that I love her like I do, I'd seriously never recover, man. I'm not exaggerating. I'd be a broken man, forever." I clutch my stomach, suddenly feeling ill.

Jonas looks sympathetic. "Aw, Josh. She won't say no. She loves you."

"You don't know Kat," I say. "She's capable of anything. She's a demon spawn, like I said. She'd cut off my balls and make s'mores out of 'em without batting an eyelash."

Jonas grimaces. "Jesus."

"Welcome to my world."

"Well, she won't say no—because you won't fuck it up this time."

"But what if I can't help myself? What if I'm just so clueless I'm incapable of getting it right?"

"You can't fuck it up, Josh."

"Well, that's obviously not true."

"No, I mean, you can't fuck it up this time. All you have to do is follow Kat's own advice."

I look at my brother blankly.

"When I was Boring Blane for you—which by the way gave me a mild case of post-traumatic stress disorder—thanks so much for that—I asked Kat's advice about proposing to Sarah. And you wanna know what she told me?"

"No, Jonas. Please keep that little nugget to yourself."

"She told me to keep it simple. She said as long as I spoke from my heart, whatever I said would be grandchildren-worthy."

I sigh. "Kinda vague to be helpful, bro."

"Not really. Just speak from your heart. Tell her you love her. Tell her all the reasons *why* you love her. That right there will be epic enough."

"Says the guy who shoved his fiancée off Mount Olympus and made her paraglide to the Aegean before he'd kneel and give her the ring."

Jonas laughs.

I look out at the city. The sky behind the faraway buildings is beginning to lighten with the faintest glow of orange.

"Jonas, I need something more concrete than 'speak from your heart,'" I say. "*Please.*"

"Well, I don't know, man. I don't know Kat like you do. You just gotta think about what makes her tick and deliver it to her."

I think about that for a minute. "Fantasies. Mini pornos," I say. "She's got the most active imagination of anyone I've ever met."

"Okay. Good start," Jonas says.

"She loves shit like *The Bodyguard* and *Pretty Woman,*" I continue. "She's seen her favorite movies like twenty times each."

Jonas laughs. "Well, there you go."

"In the beginning I thought Kat was a total dude—I kept asking her if she was hiding a dick and balls under her dress—but now that I know her really well, it turns out she's a chick through and through. A diehard romantic."

"Well, you just answered your own question. Make Kat feel like *Pretty Woman.* Give Kat the modern-day fairytale she obviously yearns for."

I swig my water, thinking about that. It makes perfect sense, actually. "I've never seen *Pretty Woman,*" I confess.

"What? Are you kidding me?"

"You've seen it?"

"Of course."

I shake my head. "Jesus, Jonas. Have some pride, man."

"Josh, you're an idiot. Why do you think romantic comedies are so successful? *Because women absolutely love them.* So why the *fuck* wouldn't you want to know *why?*" He shakes his head at me like he's explaining something ridiculously basic to me. "If you know *why* women love that stuff, then you gain invaluable insight into what makes them tick—which you can then use to your benefit in countless glorious ways."

I must admit, he's got my attention. "I'm listening," I say.

"God, it always freaks me out when you're the dumb one," Jonas says. He shakes his head at me again. "Josh, the movies Kat watches over and over, the movies she so obviously loves, are the most obvious roadmap to her deepest desires. If she loves *Pretty Woman,* then watch it and give it to her."

My pulse is pounding in my ears. "You know what, bro? You're absolutely right. *The Bodyguard, Pretty Woman, Say Anything, Magic Mike*. She loves 'em all."

"There you go. Whatever floats her boat and gets her going, watch it, learn it, and deliver it to her. She's telling you as plain as day how to hack her. So do it—*hack the shit out of her.*"

"Oh my fuck, yes," I say. I'm suddenly so excited, I can barely sit still. "This is brilliant, bro. I'm gonna hack the fuck into Katherine Ulla Morgan and give her what she's always wanted."

"There you go." Jonas takes a sip of his drink. "Sounds like you've got some research to do."

"Fuck yeah, I do. I'll watch all her stupid movies on the sly whenever she's asleep—which is a lot these days."

"Hey, you should watch that movie the girls watched tonight, too," Jonas says. He snaps his fingers like he's trying to come up with the title.

"Shit. You're right," I say. "What was that thing called? I was only half listening."

"I dunno. I was only half-listening, too," Jonas says. "*The Notebook?*"

"No, that wasn't it—but I'd better watch that one, too."

"Yeah, good idea. That one's pretty sappy. Have a barf bag ready when you watch that one."

I laugh. "You've seen that one, too?"

"Of course."

I shake my head. "You're better at this woman-thing than I gave you credit for, Jonas."

"Thank you. Finally, you understand my brilliance."

"Okay, so back to the task at hand. What the fuck was the movie the girls watched tonight? Kat said the woman from *The Notebook* was in it. That's when I tuned out."

Jonas pulls out his phone. "The girls said a red-haired guy's in it, too, right?"

"Yeah. That's right. The guy from *Harry Potter* and *Ex Machina.*"

"Boom," Jonas says, looking at his phone. "*About Time.*"

"That doesn't even remotely ring a bell," I say.

"Well, not for me, either. I must have tuned out, too. But it's gotta be it. It's Rachel McAdams and some redheaded guy." He shows me his phone, upon which a decidedly vaginal movie poster is being displayed.

"Yep. That's definitely it. Can't get much more chick-flick than that. Hey, I just thought of another movie I gotta watch," I say. "*Pride and Prejudice*."

"Oh, definitely. She's been calling you Mr. Darcy, you better figure out why."

"I can't believe you've seen that one," I say. "Have you no pride?"

"No, I don't—but you obviously do—hence the reason Kat kept calling you Mr. Darcy." He rolls his eyes. "I can't believe Kat called you that and you didn't even bother to watch the movie and find out why. Clearly, she was giving you a coded message."

"It didn't even occur to me."

"Well, watch it, you dumbshit. Mr. Darcy proposes twice in that movie and the heroine turns him down the first time." A light bulb clearly goes off in Jonas head. "Oh shit," he says, sitting up in his chair. "And do you know what the woman says when she turns Mr. Darcy down the first time?"

I shrug. "Fucketh you-eth?"

"Holy shit, Josh. *No.* She says, 'I wouldn't marry you if you were the last man on earth.'"

"Oh my fuck." I slap my forehead. "Kat's diabolical."

"No, you're just a dumbshit of epic proportions."

"Apparently," I agree.

"Watch it and pay careful attention to the difference between the first and second proposals. That'll tell you everything you need to know about what she wants the second time around."

I exhale. "Shit. I'm an idiot."

"You really are."

"Damn. I've got a lot of homework to do."

"I'll grab my hotspot out of my room so you can download all the movies onto your iPad. The hotel Wi-Fi is for shit."

"Thanks, bro."

Jonas gets up and moves toward the French doors.

"Hey, Jonas?"

Jonas stops and turns around, his eyebrows raised.

"I don't know what I would have done without your help on this. I was really stressed out and now I feel like I've got a plan of attack. Thank you."

"No thanks required," Jonas says. "I'm not doing this for you— I'm doing it for me."

"Oh, really?"

"Yes. If you marry Kat, then Sarah will be insanely happy, which will make *me* insanely happy. Happy wife, happy life." He smiles from ear to ear. "Very, very happy life."

"Ah. Well, you're a selfish bastard, then."

Jonas laughs and turns toward the French doors, but before he leaves, he turns back around. "Hey, by the way. What the fuck did you do to poor Kat earlier? I thought *Sarah* was a screamer. Holy fuck, Josh."

I grin and take a long sip of my water—I'm a gentleman, after all.

"So I take it you found the books I sent you helpful?" Jonas asks.

My smile broadens. "Yeah. Definitely. Although what I did to Kat earlier was all me—no research required." I snicker.

Jonas' white teeth are glowing in the pre-dawn light. "Hey, whatever works—just as long as you keep your unicorn well fed, right?"

"Fuck yeah," I say.

"Fuck yeah," Jonas replies. He pauses. "Hey, if I didn't happen to be out here on the balcony when you had insomnia, would you have asked me for help?"

I don't reply.

"You can lean on me, Josh," Jonas says earnestly. "It doesn't always have to be you carrying me on your back all the time. I'm right here. I can help you sometimes, too."

"Dude, are you on crack? I lean on you all the time," I say. "You're the man, Jonas—a fucking beast."

Jonas flashes me a look of such unadulterated love and kindness, my heart squeezes in my chest.

"Now go get me that hotspot, cocksucker," I say. "Or any second now you're gonna make me wanna slap my own fucking face—I can feel it coming on now—and it's way too early in the morning for me to be doing that shit."

Chapter 32
Josh

The band onstage behind Jonas and me finishes playing a cover of Pharrell William's "Happy" and the partygoers packed into Climb & Conquer's flagship Seattle gym applaud uproariously.

"Welcome to our grand opening," I say to the crowd, speaking into the microphone in my hand. "I know you're all chomping at the bit to keep climbing and conquering our rock walls for the first time ever today—so we're gonna keep the talking to a minimum. We just wanted to thank you all for coming out to the gym today to celebrate the birth of our baby."

Everyone claps and cheers.

"For those of you who don't already know," I continue, "I'm Josh Faraday and this is my brother, Jonas—and we're the founders of Climb & Conquer." The band behind us breaks into a spontaneous riff of "For He's the Jolly Good Fellow" and everyone laughs. "Wow, could you guys follow me around wherever I go?" I say.

Everyone in the room chuckles.

"Although, if you're gonna follow me around playing my own personal theme music, I think it'd have to be 'The Joker.'"

The band instantly breaks into a few bars of that song, and everyone in the entire building, including me, bursts out laughing.

"Wow, you're good," I say, pointing at the bandleader, and she points back at me, a huge smile on her face. I address the crowd again. "Jonas and I have worked hard to bring Climb & Conquer to life—but it's really Jonas who first had the vision—so I'm gonna turn the microphone over to my brother and let him tell you what Climb & Conquer is all about. Jonas?"

Everyone applauds and I hand the microphone to my brother.

"Hi, everyone. Thanks, Josh." Jonas flashes his most charming smile and begins telling the rapt audience about what climbing has meant to him personally during his life and how he's always dreamed of sharing his passion with the world.

Wow. For a guy who despises public speaking as much as Jonas does, I'm duly impressed with how well Jonas is pulling this off—especially since, when we were planning our speeches for this event a few days ago, Jonas practically begged me to do all the speaking. "How about I stand onstage next to you and nod while you talk?" he said. "I'll be the 'something shiny'—remember that?"

"Sorry, bro," I told him, much to his obvious chagrin. "Your 'something shiny' days are officially over—you're our frontman now, baby. And, anyway, C&C has been your dream from day one—you gotta be the one to explain it."

He looked totally bummed.

"Plus, as a practical matter," I continued, "a bunch of local news stations are gonna be covering the grand opening. If one of our faces is gonna be plastered all over the news talking about our company's mission, it's gotta be yours, Pretty Boy."

Jonas groaned.

"Oh, just nut up, Jonas. It's not my fault you're the pretty one."

"But that's the thing, Josh," Jonas replied. "You always say I'm the pretty one—that I've got the looks and you've got the personality—but in all seriousness—and believe me, I hate to stroke your ego about this—I truly think you're better looking than I am."

"Well, yeah, *duh*, I'm better looking than you are, numnuts—of course, I am," I said. "It's just that, for some reason, no one else seems to recognize that obvious fact."

Jonas laughed.

"It is what it is, bro—embrace it. You're the pretty one, which means you've got to do the pretty-brother-speech." I patted him on his pretty cheek. "Just pretend everyone in the audience is naked. Isn't that what they always say you should do for public speaking?"

"Yeah," Jonas sighed, resigned to his fate.

"Except for Kat—don't pretend Kat's naked or I'll have to punch you in your pretty face."

"Isn't Henn gonna be there?" Jonas asked.

"Good point." I grimaced. "Don't picture Henn naked, either, or you might give yourself an aneurysm."

"And Sarah's mom? And Kat's parents? Because I'd rather cut off my arm than imagine any of them naked," Jonas said.

"Okay, fine. Shit," I replied. "I wasn't being literal. I was just saying don't stress about the speech—you'll be great."

Jonas laughed. "Don't worry—I'll be fine. I'll *hate* to do it, but I'll manage it. I'll just look at Sarah the whole time and I'll be fine."

The audience in front of me laughs at something Jonas is saying and my brain tunes back into the present moment.

".... . our initial twenty gyms in five states," Jonas is saying into the microphone, "and we're just getting started."

My eyes scan the crowd and land on Kat's gorgeous face—and then immediately drift down to the adorable baby bump that's only recently popped out of her slender frame. Damn, Kat's hot as hell. I can't get enough of that terrorist under normal circumstances, but nowadays, with her cute little belly and blossoming tits and raging pregnancy hormones, my Kat-addiction is now officially completely out of control. If Kat were a drug, there'd be no choice but for my loved ones to stage an intervention.

"How's our avocado today?" I asked Kat just this morning in our bed, running my hands over her naked belly, pressing my hard-on into her side, licking her nipple, inhaling her scent.

"Oh, no, babe," she said, sighing with pleasure when my fingertips migrated south and began gently stroking her tip. "The kumquat was an avocado a couple weeks ago—the kumquat's a freaking bell pepper now."

"A bell pepper?" I said, running my fingertips lightly over her slick tip, coaxing her into delicious hardness. "Whoa, this kid's unstoppable."

Kat shuddered with pleasure and arched her back as my fingers began massaging her in earnest, and that was all the dangling carrot I needed to stop talking and get serious about pleasuring her. With a loud growl, I opened her thighs, burrowed my head between them, and begin licking my hot little momma into a delicious frenzy.

"... and that's why the Climb & Conquer brand embodies adventure, fitness, and, most of all, the pursuit of excellence," Jonas is saying. "Each person's individual but universal quest to find the *ideal* version of himself."

I smile to myself. Jonas had originally planned to say "each person's individual quest to find the *divine original* form of himself," but I told him no fucking way. "Mark my words, the news stations will run that one sound-bite out of context, and all anyone will remember is the word 'divine,'" I said.

"And what's wrong with that?" Jonas asked.

"Dude, they'll think we're some sort of religious cult, not a rock-climbing gym. It's off-brand. Tell Plato he's gotta stay the fuck away from my grand opening. He's cramping my style."

"Fine," Jonas said begrudgingly. "I'll kick Plato to the curb just this once and dumb it down, Josh Faraday style. Happy?"

"Yes. Happy as a clam," I said.

"So what should I say if not 'divine original'?"

"I dunno. What would Josh Faraday say? That ought to lead you to the right level of dumb."

"... all about reaching higher than you ever thought you could reach—literally and metaphorically..." Jonas is saying—and I have to force myself not to roll my eyes at that last bit. *That's* Jonas' idea of pretending he's a dumbshit like me—saying our company's all about reaching one's highest peak 'literally and metaphorically'? It's true, of course—that's what we're all about—but Josh Faraday would never say that particular phrase in a million fucking years.

"... and becoming better than you ever thought you could be," Jonas says.

Everyone claps enthusiastically.

"And as part of our genuine commitment to extraordinary aspiration," Jonas says, yet again making me want to roll my eyes at his word choice, "Climb & Conquer has identified certain designated charities we'll be supporting with a portion of our proceeds."

I look at Sarah in the crowd. She's standing next to Kat and Henn and Hannah, staring up at her new husband like he's a golden god. Just as I'm about to look away from Sarah, she pushes a lock of dark hair away from her face and her rock sparkles at me all the way up onstage. Shit. I hate seeing Sarah's big-ass diamond—no offense to her. As happy as I am for Mr. and Mrs. Jonas Faraday, that goddamned ring only serves to remind me how much I'm physically *aching* to slip a big-ass ring onto Kat's finger, too.

The good news is that, last night, after watching *Pride and Prejudice*, the last of the movies on my "Kat's all-time favorites" list,

Lauren Rowe

I *finally* figured out exactly how to propose to Kat. Actually, the gist of my plan came to me weeks ago in Argentina while watching *Pretty Woman*—specifically, the scene where Julia Roberts goes into that ritzy store in Beverly Hills, all dressed up in her brand new clothes, and tells the bitchy store clerk she made a "huge" mistake the prior day by refusing to help her—but, last night, every last detail of my entire plan finally came together in my mind.

Everyone claps at something Jonas has said, so I clap, too, not wanting to look like I'm not listening (which I'm not).

"So, without further ado," Jonas says, "let's let the band play while you guys climb and conquer our rock walls and have a great time."

Everyone claps and cheers.

I grab the microphone from Jonas. "Thanks for coming, everyone—Happy Birthday, Climb & Conquer!"

Everyone cheers again.

I motion to the band and they launch into a rousing rendition of "Shout" that has everyone instantly throwing up their hands and singing along.

Jonas and I stand for a moment, smiling together in front of a "Climb & Conquer Grand Opening!" banner as a photographer takes a hundred shots. When we finally make our way offstage, Sarah and Kat greet us, both of them sporting huge smiles.

"I'm so proud of you," Kat coos into my ear, throwing her arms around my neck. "Watching you up there made me wanna attack you, babe—you're a freakin' rock star. Gorgeous. Funny. Charismatic. The sexiest man alive." She literally growls and presses her body into mine, making my dick open its single eye and say, "Did I just hear a cock-a-doodle-doo?" "Oh my God, you make me horny," Kat whispers, pressing her body into mine. "I feel like I've got a vibrator permanently pressed against my clit these days."

"Babe," I whisper. "You can't say that to me right now. You're making me rock hard."

"Oh my God. Press it against me."

I do.

"Ooph. I can't resist you," Kat says. "I wanna give you a blowjob right now."

I don't hesitate. "Bathroom in my office in twenty," I whisper.

242

"It's a date." She makes a sexual sound. "God *damn* you turn me on, Joshua."

"You're killing me, Katherine," I whisper. "I still gotta say hi to your fucking parents, for Chrissakes."

"Sucks to be you, I guess," she says. "Except that it's about to be freaking *awesome* to be you, baby." She winks.

"You're killing me," I whisper.

"What a way to go," she whispers back.

"Come on, Kitty Kat," Sarah says. "Dance with me."

"Great," Kat says, letting Sarah pull her to the dance floor. But just before she disappears into the crowd, Kat flashes me a look that's so naughty, I have to put my hands in front of my crotch to hide my arousal.

Damn. Who knew pregnancy could be this fucking awesome? It started out rough, I'll admit that, but these days, it's nothing but fun. The woman's been on fire lately, even for her.

"Can I ask you a few questions?" a female reporter asks Jonas to my left, her cameraman in tow—and for a split second, I'm reminded of Heidi Kumquat, who I seem to recall asked the Super Bowl MVP that very question. *Kat.* There's never a dull moment with her. I'm so fucking head over heels in love with that girl, so obsessed with the idea of making her my wife, so *addicted* to her, mind, body, and soul, I can barely function these days. I can't even remember how it felt not to love her and sleep with her every night and fuck her at every opportunity. I truly never knew I could love someone this way—so completely. So *honestly.* It's like Kat's unlocked something that was hidden deep inside me, and every day I become more and more fully *me,* as ridiculous as that sounds.

"Sure," Jonas says to the reporter, but then he looks at me with desperation in his eyes, clearly hoping for some backup.

But he's shit out of luck. For once, Jonas' ever-reliable brother is going rogue.

I smile and wave at Jonas and, much to his obvious shock and annoyance, quickly slip into the crowd. Deserting him is a chicken-shit thing to do, probably, especially today—but I've got some important personal business to take care of before my bathroom date and only a limited opportunity while Kat's distracted on the dance floor. Plus, there's no doubt Jonas can handle that reporter on his own—she's a woman, after all—which means all he needs to do is smile at her and she'll throw her panties at him and offer him the lead-off spot on the six o'clock news.

I scan the crowd looking for Louise, and quickly locate her standing next to Thomas, Ryan and Colby (who's leaning on crutches), all of them watching the band and looking festive.

"Hey, everyone," I say when I reach the group. "Thanks for coming."

"Lambo!" Ryan says. He bro-hugs me. "Congrats. This is awesome."

"Thank you."

"Congratulations, Josh," Colby adds, shaking my hand. "Really impressive."

"Thanks. You've all got lifetime memberships, if you want 'em," I say. I motion to Colby's leg. "Standing offer for you, Colby, whenever you're up to it."

"Thanks," Colby says. "Gimme three more months and I'll definitely take you up on that."

"Fantastic. I'll personally climb with you whenever you want."

"I'll join you guys," Ryan says. "Best work-out, ever. Hey, Dad, you should try it with us. I think you'd like it."

"Maybe I will."

"You've never climbed a rock wall?" I ask Thomas.

Thomas shakes his head.

"Gimme a call. I'll give you a private lesson."

"Thanks. That sounds fun," Thomas says.

"Sure thing." I glance across the room, making sure Kat is still dancing. "Hey, Louise, can I talk to you for a second?"

Louise's face lights up. "You bet, honey. Excuse us, fellas."

Kat's mom and I move several yards away from the group, both of us looking furtively toward Kat on the other side of the large room. The band is playing "Brown Eyed Girl" and Kat's twirling Sarah around and singing the song to her.

"Did you get it?" I whisper. "Hey, that just sounded like we're doing a drug deal, huh?"

Louise giggles and looks covertly across the room at her daughter. "It came in yesterday—and it's *gorgeous*." She fishes into her purse and pulls out a ring box and then palms it to me like she's handing me a kilo of hashish. "It's sized and polished and ready to go."

"Thanks for picking it up for me. I've been crazy-busy this past week."

"Oh, honey, it was my pleasure. Plus, it was safer this way—it would have been terrible if Miss Busy-Body somehow intercepted the delivery at your house." Louise glances at Kat across the room again. "Just a little warning for you—Kat's peeked at every single Christmas present I've ever gotten for her. She unwraps the gift and then rewraps it and puts it back under the tree." Louise rolls her eyes. "Kat doesn't know I know she does that, by the way, so don't tell her I know. This year, I'm gonna beat her at her own game and put a wrapped box of hemorrhoid cream under the tree for her to peek at— that ought to teach her a lesson about peeking."

I chuckle. "Now I see where she gets that little dash of evil I love so much." I slip the box into my pocket. "Thank you again."

"Aren't you gonna look at it? It's beautiful, Josh. Gives me chills every time I look at it."

Carefully, taking great care not to let anyone around me see what I'm doing, I open the box a tiny crack, just enough to confirm it contains the engagement ring Louise and I picked out for Kat on our highly enjoyable shopping trip together last week.

"Wow," I say. "It's incredible."

"Just be prepared—Kat's gonna lose her mind when you give this to her. Like, seriously, honey, she's going to go completely ballistic on you. Just be ready to scrape her off the floor."

"Oh, God, I pray you're right," I say. "If Kat says anything but hell yes, you'll have to scrape *me* off the floor, and not in a good way."

Louise touches my forearm. "Why on earth would Kat say no? She loves you."

I shrug. "Unexpected things have happened to me before, Lou. Bad things. I'm kind of used to getting blindsided by life."

Louise's face melts. "Oh, honey. No. Kat loves you. She's having your baby. For God's sake, she'll say yes."

"But you heard her: 'Marriage just isn't in the cards for us.'"

Louise snorts. "Oh, please. Kat's full of it and we both know it."

I grin. "I sure hope so."

"Josh, I know so. I'm her mother. Trust me."

I give Louise a quick hug. "Thank you again." I pause. "*Momma Lou*."

Louise blushes. "Oh my gosh, I *love* the sound of that!" She giggles. "Although, I must admit, Thomas is right—it does sound a bit like I run a soup kitchen in the South, doesn't it?" She giggles again, reminding me of Kat for the millionth time. "Don't tell Thomas I said he's right, by the way—I wouldn't want him to get a big head."

"I'll never tell."

"Josh."

I turn around. It's Theresa.

"Jonas asked me to come get you. He wants you to join the interview. He says *please*." She motions across the room to where Jonas is still talking to that same reporter. He's feigning comfort quite well from the looks of him, but I know him well enough to know he's dying on the inside.

I chuckle. "Okay. Josh to the rescue. Bye, Louise. Thanks again."

"My pleasure. Keep us posted."

"Will do."

I cross the room quickly and help Jonas finish up his interview, much to his obvious relief, and when that's over, Jonas disappears into the crowd to find Sarah.

I scan the room looking for Kat and spot her talking to her family—looks like I've still got some time—so I survey the place, searching for Henn. *Boom.* He's talking with Hannah and Sarah, and when I catch his eye, I motion for him to meet me in a quiet corner behind one of the rock walls.

"Hey, man," I say, bro-hugging Henn when he reaches me. "Thanks for coming today. You didn't have to do that."

"I wouldn't have missed it," Henn says. "Plus, it gave me an excuse to come see Hannah."

"So, hey, man, do you think you could do me a favor? I need to find someone—get me dialed in."

"Sure. Who is it this time, boss?"

I tell him the name of the person I want him to locate and everything I know, which isn't much.

"Okay. Shouldn't be hard. I'll see what I can find out."

"Thanks, man. As soon as possible, please."

"Yeah, I figured. When have you ever asked me to find someone 'whenever it's convenient for you, Henn'?"

I chuckle. "Sorry."

"No worries. Whatever you need. Always."

"Thanks, bro. So what's been shaking with you?" I ask. "Work good?"

"Yeah, finally finished working with the feds on our sitch. They've got enough to put the pimpstress extraordinaire into an orange jumpsuit forever, probably. Bye-bye, Oksana. Nice knowing you."

"That's a relief. Any sense there's anyone else left in The Club organization we should be keeping an eye on?"

"There are definitely some heavy hitters in Russia and Ukraine who ran a big part of the show from there, but no one stateside with any real power—and certainly nobody who'd know about us."

"Keep an eye on things, though, would you? Just so we know if there's ever something we should be concerned about. Jonas is already starting to doubt his decision to leave Oksana standing—we should probably give him periodic assurances that everything's still quiet."

"No problem."

"So what are you working on now that The Club stuff is all done?" I ask.

"Oh, I just did a really fun job." He tells me about a large department store chain that recently hired Henn to try his mighty best to breach their own computer system for the purpose of testing their security. "It was awesome," Henn says. "They truly believed they were impervious to hacking. They'd supposedly hired 'the best cyber-security team money could buy' to protect their data, but I dug around and broke 'em wide open in less than a day. I waltzed into my first meeting with their supposedly 'expert cyber-security team—'" He snorts loudly with glee. "And I was like, 'So, hey, folks, great to meetcha. Oh, by the way, I got into your piddly-diddly system four different ways from Sunday in about six hours—here, here, here, and here,' and they totally shit their Depends." He sighs happily. "God, I love my life."

247

Lauren Rowe

I chuckle. "And how's everything else? Things with Hannah good?"

"Better than good. *Awesome.* She's moving to L.A. next month."

"Really? Wow. That's fantastic."

"Yeah, the long distance thing is killing us, man. And since Kat's decided to put her PR company on the back burner for a while to become a mommy, Hannah's decided to look for a PR job in the entertainment industry."

"Awesome. Hey, you should ask Reed if he knows someone who might be able to help her with her job search. Reed knows everyone."

"Yeah, I already talked to him. He's on it."

"Good."

"So how are things with Kat? Have you two been nesting, getting ready for baby?"

I glance at Kat across the room. She's dancing with Sarah again, wiggling like she's got ants in her pants, throwing her tiny belly around with abandon. "I'm gonna ask Kat to marry me." I pat my pocket. "Got the ring right here."

"No shit?" Henn hugs me. "Awesome. When are you gonna do it?"

"As soon as you get me that info."

"Ah. Interesting. What does one thing have to do with the other?"

I briefly explain how I'm planning to propose to Kat, using the information Henn's gonna get for me.

"Very cool," Henn says. "Okay. I'll put a rush on it, boss." He grins. "Wow. I never thought I'd see the day Josh 'YOLO' Faraday would get married and settle down."

"I never thought I'd see the day, either. And now it's all I want." I bite my lip. "Let's just hope Kat says yes."

Henn waves his hand dismissively at me. "Bah. Just dick it up and she won't be able to resist you."

I laugh. "Yeah, well, I've recently learned the whole dick-it-up-strategy might not be *quite* as effective as I originally thought." I steal another look at Kat. "At least not with Madame Terrorist."

"I'm really happy for you, Josh," Henn says.

"Thanks, man."

"You've definitely come a long way from the dude who got YOLO inked onto his ass-cheek over a quote from *Happy Gilmore*."

"God, I hope so. Hey, what was that quote we were arguing about, by the way? I can never remember what it was."

"Oh, it was really deep and profound. Grandma in the nursing home asks Ben Stiller if she can trouble him for a warm glass of milk because it helps her sleep. And he goes, 'You could trouble me for a warm glass of shut the hell up!'"

I laugh. "Oh, shit. Really? No."

"Yes."

"Really?" I ask.

"Yes."

"I got YOLO stamped on my ass over *that*?"

Henn nods, laughing. "You were *positive* Ben Stiller says, 'You could trouble me for a *tall* glass of shut the *fuck* up.'"

I shake my head. "God, I was such a little punk. Please tell me I'm not that big a tool anymore."

Henn puts his hand on my shoulder. "You were never a tool, Josh—you've always been the greatest guy ever, right from day one. And you've only gotten better with age. You're a fine wine, man."

My heart pangs. "Thanks, Henn. Back at you."

He smiles.

"Okay, well, this fine wine had better get back to his adoring public," I say. "Thanks again for coming—and thanks for the favor."

"Any time," Henn replies.

We bro-hug again and then Henn slips into the crowd, saluting me as he goes.

My eyes drift to where Kat was dancing with Sarah a moment ago—but she's not there. I reflexively look at my watch. Oh shit—it's been way longer than twenty minutes since Kat and I made our "date."

I practically sprint toward my office in the back of the gym, getting stopped at least ten times along the way by well-wishers, and finally manage to slip unnoticed through a door marked "Authorized Personnel Only." Once inside my darkened office, I beeline to the bathroom in the back and rap softly on the door. "Kat?" I whisper.

The door opens a crack and in one fluid movement, Kat grabs a fistful of my shirt and yanks me forcefully into the bathroom.

"I just made myself come while waiting on you, Playboy," she whispers, furiously unbuckling my belt, her eyes on fire. "You're such a naughty boy for making me wait."

"Oh, yeah?" I ask, my dick throbbing with anticipation. "My pregnant whore is feeling horny, huh?'

She reaches into my pants and strokes my hard-on furiously. "Oh, yeah," she says. "Heidi Kumquat's on fire. She's aching to give you your money's worth, baby."

"God, I love you," I growl, my body jerking as she works me with her hands.

"I love you, too," Kat says. "I love you, I love you, I love you." She fondles my balls. "*And I love your dick.*"

Without further ado, Kat kneels down and swirls her tongue on the tip of my cock—right into my little hole—making me jolt. "Oh my fuck, Kat."

She looks up at me from under my straining cock and smiles. "I never knew I could love someone the way I love you, Joshua William Faraday," she purrs—and then she takes the full length of my cock into her mouth and proceeds to deliver a blowjob so intense, it makes me grip the sink ledge to keep from falling to my knees.

"Oh, God, I love you," I growl, trying to hang on. I grip her hair and press myself farther into her open throat. "You're worth every fucking penny, baby," I choke out, my passion reaching its boiling point. But even as I'm saying those words—because, of course, those are the magic words Kat loves best when she's giving me head—what I'm actually thinking is something new for me while in the midst of receiving a mind-blowing blowjob: *If a guy needs more than this to be eternally happy with one woman, then he's either crazy or just a greedy-ass motherfucker.*

Chapter 33
Kat

"Blood pressure looks good," the nurse says, removing the cuff from my arm. "Sit tight for a bit and Dr. Gupta will be right in."

"Thank you," I say. I exhale and squeeze Josh's hand. "I'm nervous."

Josh kisses my forehead. "The kumquat's gonna be fine," he says softly. "Hey, Sarah Cruz. Hit us with some 'Would You Rather?' questions. Kat's nervous—we gotta distract her."

"Okay, Josh Faraday," Sarah says. "But under the circumstances, I'm gonna keep it family-friendly."

"Boo!" I shout.

"Yes, Kat," Sarah says sternly. "Playing X-rated 'Would You Rather?' in this crowd would hurtle us into TMI territory on a bullet train."

I laugh. "Probably true."

"Okay, then," Sarah says. "Would you rather be hideously ugly but extremely wealthy, or spectacularly good looking but dirt poor?"

We all ponder that for a moment.

"Jonas?" Sarah asks. "What say you, love?'

"In which of these scenarios do I have a better shot at snagging you?" Jonas asks.

"Doesn't matter. I'd love you rich or poor, gorgeous or hideous."

Jonas shrugs. "Then I don't care. You pick. As long as I have you, I'm good."

Josh shoots me an annoyed expression, and, in reply, I pretend to stick my finger down my throat.

"Is it your life's mission to make me look like a prick?" Josh asks Jonas. "Because I was about to say rich and ugly."

251

"Aw, come on, babe," I say. "Good looking and poor, all the way."

"No, babe. If I'm rich and ugly, I can wine and dine you, which means I'd still bag you. Best of both worlds—I'd still be rich *and* I'd still have you."

"You'd bag me even more if you were dirt poor but looked the way you do, I assure you." I wink. " If you wanna wine me and dine me when you're dirt poor, just make me one of your orgasm-inducing PB&Js."

"*Kat*," Sarah chastises, putting her hands over her ears. "Family friendly, remember?"

"Okay, okay," I say. "Ask another one, Sarah."

"But this time don't lob a softball at your husband that makes me look like a total prick, Sarah Cruz," Josh adds.

"I don't think it was Sarah's question that made you look like a total prick," Jonas says.

I look at my watch and shift on the examination table, making the wax paper crinkle underneath me. "Where's the doctor?"

"Okay, Kat. Listen up," Sarah says. "Would you rather have balls hanging from your chin or a two foot tail that wags every time you feel excited?"

We all laugh at the ridiculousness of the question.

"Hey, I thought these were supposed to be *hypothetical*," Josh says, and we all laugh again.

"Okay, okay," Sarah says. "That was a dumb one. Here's a good one: would you rather be a wildly successful artist who makes totally uninspired crap you abhor creating, or a starving but brilliant artist who makes art that feeds your soul?"

"Wildly successful artist who makes total crap," Josh says without hesitation.

"Yeah, baby!" I shout, high-fiving Josh. "Me, too. Totally."

Sarah and Jonas look at each other, absolutely dumbfounded.

"Are you joking?" Jonas asks. "You've only got one *soul*, for fuck's sake."

Sarah high-fives Jonas. "You tell 'em, baby."

"There you go again, making me look like a prick," Josh says.

"Aw, screw them," I say. "Let Jonas and Sarah be soulful *arteests* while you and I make oodles of cash off our bottle-cap-pipe-cleaner sculptures. And while they're eating Kraft Macaroni & Cheese in their rat-infested hovel in SoHo, surrounded by their frickin' *art*, we'll head to Cabo on our private jet and 'feed our souls' while making love on a white-sand beach."

"You're a fucking genius, babe," Josh says.

"You truly can't keep it family-friendly if your life depended on it, can you, Kat?" Sarah says.

"Oh, come on, Cruz. That was PG-rated at worst," I say. I look toward the door. "Where the heck is Dr. Gupta? She doesn't normally take this long."

"Okay, listen up, Party Girl," Josh says. "Would you rather be the star player on a football team that loses every game of the season or warm the bench on a team that wins the Super Bowl?"

"Hmm," Sarah says. "Play on the losing team, I think. What do you think, my love?"

"I think I'd rather sit the bench on the winning team," Jonas says. "Because, ultimately, I'd aspire to become the head coach—so this way, I'd have the opportunity to watch and learn from the best."

We all burst out laughing.

"What?" Jonas asks. "That's my honest answer."

"Oh, Jonas," Sarah says. She touches his cheek tenderly and her diamond rings sparkle under the lights of the examination room. "I love you."

"Okay, I've got one," I say. "Would you rather be stuck on a desert island for the rest of your life all alone or with someone who talks incessantly?"

"I'd rather be stuck on a desert island with *you*, babe," Josh says sweetly.

"Aw, that's lovely, honey—but you gotta pick one of the choices."

Josh raises an eyebrow. "Oh, I *did* pick one of the choices."

Everyone bursts out laughing, even me, just as the door to the examination room opens.

"Oh, wow," Dr. Gupta says. "There's a party going on in here."

"Hi, Doctor," I say. "You remember Josh—my baby-daddy?"

Josh blanches. He hates it when I call him that, which is why I keep doing it.

"And this is my best friend, Auntie Sarah, whom you've met

Lauren Rowe

before," I continue. "And Sarah's husband, Uncle Jonas, who also happens to be Josh's brother."

Dr. Gupta shakes everyone's hand and introduces us to the technician who'll be conducting the sonogram. "So are you ready to see your baby?" Dr. Gupta asks.

We all respond enthusiastically.

I lie back on the examination table and the technician spreads some gel on my baby bump. "My heart is racing," I say, putting my hand on my heart. "I'm really nervous."

Josh leans down and kisses my forehead. "The kumquat's gonna be fine."

The tech puts the wand on my belly and moves it around and, suddenly, we're met with the unmistakable image of an actual *baby*.

"Holy crap," I say. "That's a *baybay*!"

"Oh my God," Josh says. "Definitely not a kumquat."

"Quite different than the first sonogram, isn't it?" the doctor says. She begins pointing out various body parts, all of which, she says, look perfectly formed and right on track.

"Oh, thank God," I say, sighing with relief. "I was really worried I'd hurt the poor thing with too much partying before I knew."

"Well, this should put you at ease, then," the doctor says, patting my hand. "So, do you want to know the baby's gender?"

"Heck yeah," Josh says. "That's the dangling carrot we used to lure Uncle Jo Jo and Auntie Sarah to this shindig."

"Do you already know?" I ask.

"I sure do. The baby's legs are spread wide and I've got an unimpeded view." The doctor pauses for effect. "Any guesses?"

"Girl," Sarah says calmly.

The doctor nods. "Yep. Congratulations. You're having a baby girl."

Tears spring into my eyes.

"Oh my God," Josh breathes. He leans down and kisses me. "I love you, Kat."

"I love you, too," I whisper into his lips.

"I was hoping for a girl so much," Josh says.

I'm shocked to hear Josh say that—don't all big, athletic men secretly hope for a boy who'll grow up to play on the Seahawks one day? But when I look at Josh and see the moment he's sharing with

254

Jonas, I suddenly understand completely—this baby's a tribute to their late mother in heaven, a baby girl to keep their mother's memory alive.

Josh and I haven't discussed baby names yet—in fact, several times I've told Josh I was too freaked out about the booze and pot thing to think about baby names until I was sure everything was okay—but now that I've seen our baby girl growing inside me—and especially now that I'm witnessing the expressions of emotion on both Josh and Jonas' faces, there's only one name I'd even consider.

"Grace," I blurt.

Josh's face lights up. "Grace," Josh repeats reverently, nodding. He bends down to kiss me. "Thank you."

I mumble "of course" into Josh's lips, but my words are incomprehensible.

"Grace Louise?" Josh asks, pulling away suddenly from my mouth.

"Perfect," I say, smiling.

"Aw," Sarah says. "That's so sweet. Gracie Louise Faraday."

"Hey, Doctor," Jonas says, putting his arm around Sarah. "Are you sure? I've heard stories of people painting a room pink based on the sonogram and then giving birth to a boy."

"Oh, I'm positive," Dr. Gupta says. She points to the sonogram screen. "See between her legs there? Definitely no penis. The baby's made it really easy for us by spreading her legs wide."

Josh snickers.

"*Don't say it*," I warn sharply, slapping his arm.

"Don't say what?" Josh says, grinning.

"You know what."

Josh chuckles and kisses me tenderly. "Babe," he says. "I would never make a crass joke about my baby girl making it easy just like her hot momma does for me every night—because that would be rude and inappropriate. But, just so you know, if I ever do compare our beautiful daughter to her gorgeous mommy in any way, shape or form, I'll *always* mean it as the highest compliment, no matter what."

255

Chapter 34
Kat

"So where do you guys want to go for lunch?" I ask, floating happily through the parking lot outside my doctor's office, my hand caressing my baby bump. But when I realize nobody's walking alongside me, I stop and turn around. "Guys?" I ask. "Any ideas on where we should go for lunch to celebrate little Gracie Louise?"

"I'm sorry, honey," Sarah says. "I can't do lunch. I promised to help my mom today."

"Oh," I say, deflated.

"There's only two more weeks before school starts back up, so I promised I'd help down at Gloria's House every day 'til then."

"Oh, no problem," I say, trying my best to sound sincere. Of course, I know intellectually that helping victims of domestic abuse is far more important than celebrating my baby's gender—and, of course, I know we can celebrate any time, not just today—but I still can't help feeling disappointed, nonetheless.

"No worries," Josh says breezily. "The four of us will go out another time. How about a celebratory dinner later this week?"

"Great," Sarah says. She gives me an enthusiastic hug. "Bye, sweetie. Congratulations again." She pats my bump. "Bye-bye, Gracie Louise. I can't wait to meet you, boo."

Jonas hugs me goodbye and then shocks the hell out of me by tenderly placing his palm on my belly—a move so full of affection—and so unlike him—it catches me off guard. "I can't wait to meet you, Gracie Faraday," Jonas whispers.

I exchange a swooning look with Sarah.

Josh follows suit, putting his hand on my belly when Jonas pulls his hand away.

"I can already tell you're gonna own me, Gracie Louise," Josh says. He bends down and kisses my belly, making me swoon. "I already love you, Little G," he whispers.

Oh my God, I can barely stand, I'm so overcome by this beautiful moment. "Josh," I say, barely above a whisper.

Josh stands. "Good God, I'm gonna be surrounded by a shit-ton of estrogen in my own house," he blurts, completely shattering the fairytale-nature of the moment. "I'm officially fucked."

We all laugh.

"Yep. You're definitely gonna hone your *listening* skills," Jonas says.

"Oh, you know you'll love it," I say. I look at Jonas and Sarah. "Okay, guys, I love you truly, madly, deeply, but the kumquat's hangry—so if you're not coming with us to eat, then you best get out of my freakin' way so I don't start barfing all over you."

"You're *still* barfing?" Sarah asks.

"Not nearly as much, but, yeah, on occasion, especially when I get really hungry."

Sarah grimaces. "You poor thing."

I pat my belly. "It's okay. Seeing Gracie today made it all worth it."

Josh and I wave to Jonas and Sarah as they drive off in their car, and then, since we'd hitched a ride with Jonas and Sarah to get here in the first place, we grab a taxi.

"Hotel 1000," Josh instructs the driver as we settle into the backseat of the cab. "Okay with you, babe? There's a new restaurant in the hotel I wanna try."

"Great," I say. "What kind of food do they—*Oh.*" I abruptly stop talking, my hand on my belly.

"What?" Josh asks, his eyes wide.

I hold up a finger, holding my breath—and there it is again: a teeny-tiny jabbing sensation in my lower abdomen, poking me from the *inside*. "Oh my gosh," I say. "I think I just felt the baby *move*."

"Really?" Josh asks, his eyes lighting up.

I place Josh's hand on my bump, right where I just felt movement, and it happens again. "Did you feel that?" I ask.

Josh shakes his head, his eyes on fire. "What did it feel like?"

"It felt like someone poking me—like *this*." I touch the top of Josh's hand with my fingertip. "Only imagine feeling that little jab from *inside* your body—like a little alien wanting to get out."

"That's so cool," Josh says. He places both palms on my bump, squinting like he's concentrating on complex calculus—and for the rest of the taxi ride, he forbids me to speak while he silently touches every inch of my tiny bump, trying with all his might to feel movement. But it's no use. Every time I feel a little jab, Josh can't feel it with me.

"I guess the kumquat's just too small for you to feel her yet," I finally conclude. "I'm sorry, babe."

"Damn. Tell me every time you feel her move, okay? I'm dying to give her a high-five with my fingertip."

I swoon for the twentieth time today. Who is this adorable man sitting next to me in this taxi? I can't believe the man touching my baby bump with such tenderness and enthusiasm is the same commitment-phobic playboy who not too long ago said he planned to wait until eighty to have a baby so he could simultaneously have the kid and forget he was ever born.

"I love you so much, Josh," I say softly, touching his cheek.

"I love you, I love you, I love you, Kat—more than I ever thought possible," Josh replies, just before planting a kiss on me that makes me forget where I am.

After a moment, the driver clears his throat. "Um. Excuse me. We're here," he says.

Josh brushes my cheek with his thumb, and then touches my chin with the tip of his finger, and finally, slowly, tears himself away from me to pay the man.

We float inside the hotel together, Josh's arm around my shoulders, but, much to my surprise, Josh steers us away from the restaurant in the lobby and toward the elevator bank.

"Hey, isn't that the restaurant?" I ask, pointing behind me.

Josh stops walking and pulls me into him, a huge smile on his face. "We're not going to the restaurant, my love—I only told you that to lure you here."

My love? Did Josh just call me "my love"? He's never called me that before.

"Why aren't we going to the restaurant?" I manage to ask.

"Because we're going to our room," Josh replies simply—and before I can say another word, he fishes into his pocket, pulls out a poker chip, and places it in my palm, a wicked smile dancing on his lips. "Let the mini-porno begin, baby."

"Ooh!" I squeal. "Yay! Which fantasy are we doing, babe?"

"Actually, today we're doing one of *my* fantasies—a fantasy I've never told anyone about, not even you." Josh wraps me into his arms and smashes his hard body into mine. "It's my top fantasy, actually—something I've only recently discovered I want to do."

"You didn't write about it in your application?"

"Nope. I've never told a single soul about this particular fantasy—didn't even know I had it until recently. But today, for the first and only time, I wanna do it with you, Party Girl." A huge smile spreads across his face. "*My love.*"

Chapter 35
Kat

"Oh, that was good—the artichoke was hangry as hell," I say, putting my napkin onto the table and patting my belly. I've just devoured a huge spread of food Josh had waiting for us in our hotel suite, and I'm feeling fine as wine and ready to role-play.

"So you're feeling good now?" Josh asks.

"Yup. I'm feeling *great*. Heidi Kumquat reporting for duty, sir, any which way you please. So what's your pleasure, sir? Whips? Chains? Donkeys?"

Josh shoots me a sly smile. "You'll see. The outfit I want you to wear for me is laid out on the bed in there." He indicates the master bedroom of the suite.

"Oh," I say, raising my eyebrow. "French maid costume, maybe? Latex? Rabbit suit? Damsel in distress?"

"You'll see soon enough. I packed your makeup and toiletries, by the way—they're in the bathroom." He stands, his eyes blazing. "Meet me back out here in forty-five minutes. I'll get dressed in the other bedroom."

"*Oh*. We're doing his and hers costumes, huh?" I say. "What on earth have you been fantasizing about on the sly, you naughty Playboy?"

"No questions. Just do as your told. This is *my* fantasy—not yours—you're just my plaything today."

"Oooh, I like the sound of that. But, seriously, babe. I want to be sure you get your fantasy, whatever it is. What if I don't know what to do?"

"Oh, you'll know." He pulls me to him and plants a kiss on my lips that's so passionate, I'm certain he's about to bend me over the

260

table and fuck me senseless right here and now. But, nope, he doesn't. Instead, he pulls away and slaps my ass. "Now get showered and dressed, Party Girl. You've got exactly forty-five minutes—don't keep me waiting."

"Yes, sir," I say.

I head into the bedroom, as directed, and gasp when I see what Josh has laid out for me to wear: a formal red gown, red lace bra and undies, black strappy heels, and a small clutch covered in sparkling Swarovski crystals. I look at the label on the gorgeous dress. *Carolina Herrera*. Oh my God. I can't even imagine how much this beautiful creation must have cost. Quickly, I throw off my clothes and slip the gown on, even before showering, just to make sure it fits—and, man, oh man, does it ever—like a glove, baby bump and all.

"Wow," I say out loud, staring at myself in the mirror. "Hello, *Pretty Woman.*"

It's actually astonishing how much this dress looks like a modern update of the iconic red dress Julia Roberts wore in that movie. Of course, Josh wouldn't know that since he's the only human in the Western Hemisphere who's never seen *Pretty Woman*, but, truly, this gown is a dead ringer for that famous dress. I giggle to myself. This is such classic Josh Faraday—even without knowing it, he's managed to fulfill one of my top fantasies.

I slip out of the dress and hop into the shower, singing "Pretty Woman" at the top of my lungs—and just over an hour later (oops, I'm little late), I emerge from the master bedroom wearing my beautiful Julia-dress and gorgeous, strappy heels.

Josh is sitting across the room, looking down at his phone, dressed to perfection in a classic, tailored tux. At the sound of my entrance into the room, he looks up from his phone and his handsome face bursts into immediate flames.

"Wow," Josh says. He hops up and strides toward me. "Look at *you*. Wow."

I twirl. "You like?"

"I *love*." He kisses my cheek and I'm treated to the scent of his delicious cologne. "You're absolutely stunning, Kat," he adds.

"So are you," I say. "You look amazing."

Josh furrows his brow, apparently considering something. He blatantly looks me up and down. "Hmm."

"What?" I ask, suddenly feeling insecure.

"Something's missing."

"Huh?" I look down at myself. "There was nothing else laid out on the bed," I say.

Josh purses his lips. "Ah. I know. Hang on."

He strides with great purpose across the room and grabs a flat velvet box off the bar—and the minute I see that damned box in Josh's hand, I know exactly what's up. *Red gown. Tux. Flat velvet jewelry box.* Holy Julia Roberts, Batman—Josh is re-enacting *Pretty Woman*!

I clamp my palm over my mouth. "Oh my God!" I gasp.

Josh holds up the velvet box, a huge smile on his face, but before he can say a word, I begin jumping up and down and shrieking like a monkey escaping from the zoo.

"Oh my God, I *love* this movie," I shriek excitedly. I take a deep breath and shake out my arms. "You're incredible-amazing-wow-I'm-so-excited-thank-you!"

Josh laughs. "Are you okay? Do you need a minute?"

I giggle like a hyena. "I can't believe you did this! When did you watch it? Oh my God!"

"Are you okay? Are you gonna pass out?"

"I'm good. Oh my God. Go ahead. Holy shit. Okay, I can totally do this—I swear. Do it. Gah! Okay. *Go.*" I bite my tongue to keep myself from babbling further.

Josh smiles. "Ready?"

I nod, still biting my tongue.

Josh slowly opens the box... to reveal the most redonkulous diamond necklace I've ever seen in my entire freakin' life. It's even more spectacular than the one Sarah wore on her wedding day—something I didn't think was possible.

Of course, I know this necklace is just a rental—I've seen the movie twenty times, after all, so I know how this scene goes—but, still, this is so freaking exciting, so *unexpected*, I can barely stand. I can't believe Josh even *thought* to arrange a *Pretty Woman* fantasy for me! I can't fathom how that's even possible.

Josh is grinning wickedly, holding the box open, inviting me to enact what comes next in this scene—and, of course, I'd never, ever disappoint him.

"Can I touch it?" I breathe.

Josh nods, smiling from ear to ear. "I was hoping you'd ask me that."

I shudder with excitement.

"Go on," Josh coaxes. "If you dare."

I giggle. "I'm nervous."

"Dig deep, baby—be brave."

"Whew. Okay." I reach slowly into the box, my Julia-Roberts belly laugh all cued up—oh my God, this is so freakin' *awesome!*— and, as expected, even before my fingers have touched the sparkling necklace, Josh clamps the lid down on my fingers. And even though I had my Julia Roberts impression ready to rip, I surprise myself by bursting into authentic Kat-Morgan, dude-like guffaws, sending Josh into a fit of hysterical laughter along with me.

When both of us have calmed down a bit, Josh removes the dazzling necklace from the box. "Turn around, hot momma," he says. "Let's get this bad boy on you."

I turn around and I'm rewarded with the sensation of my hair being pushed off my neck and Josh's soft lips against my Scorpio tattoo—followed by Josh securing the outrageous necklace around my neck.

I touch the dazzling rocks against my skin, trembling. "Oh my freaking God," I breathe.

"Lemme see you," Josh says softly. "Turn around."

I do.

"Gorgeous," Josh says, his eyes blazing. "Wow."

I touch the necklace again, feeling slightly faint. "Josh?"

"Yes, my love?"

"If I forget to tell you later: I had a really good time tonight."

Josh laughs. "Thank you." He leans forward like he's going to kiss me, but, instead, he presses his lips against my ear. "It's all yours, baby," he whispers, his voice low and sexy.

I stand stock still, holding my breath, positive I've misunderstood him. It sounded like Josh said, "It's all yours, baby." But what would the "it" in that sentence be? That's what my brain isn't comprehending. Josh's heart? The dress? I pull back and stare at Josh with wide eyes. "Huh?"

Josh cups my face in his large palms. "The *necklace* is all yours, my love—my gift to you—because I love you with all my heart and soul."

My entire body jolts. "*What?*" I shriek.

The look on Josh's face is utterly priceless—he's a kid in a candy shop, as excited as I've ever seen him. He moves his hands to my shoulders. "My beautiful Kat, marriage isn't in the cards for us, as you know." He strokes my hair. "So I'm hoping you'll accept this necklace as a symbol of my eternal love for you."

My heart has truly stopped beating. Oh my God, no, wait, now it's exploding. And, now, holy fuck, it's bursting out of my chest and hurtling against the hotel wall.

"*What?*" I say, this time in a hoarse whisper, my eyes bugging out of my head.

Surely, I'm misunderstanding this conversation. The strange words coming out of Josh's mouth sound remarkably like English, but they're being strung together in a nonsensical way.

"You're the great love of my life, Kat," Josh says, still stroking my hair, gazing into my eyes. "I choose you, baby. That's what this necklace means. Not because of a piece of paper, not because of the kumquat, but because I want you and no one else. I choose you, Kat, and I hope you choose me, too. *Forever.*"

I clutch my throat like I'm choking on a big-ass diamond. "Forever?" I blurt. "You choose me *forever?*"

Josh nods.

"You're promising to love me *forever?*"

He nods again.

"And this necklace is *mine?*"

Josh nods again.

"To *keep?*"

"Yes."

I throw my arms around his neck. "I love you, too," I shriek, tears of joy springing from my eyes. "I choose you, too, forever and ever and ever! Yes, yes, yes. I choose you, too, baby! *Yes!*"

And just like that, even before I can say, "Well, color me happy!"—(which I was totally gonna say, by the way, but how the *fuck* could I possibly remember to say my line now?)—my beautiful gown is hiked up, my pretty lace panties are on the floor, and Josh's donkey-dick is sliding in and out of me, filling me to the brim and making me scream. Oh, God, this is insanity. I'm not only screaming with pleasure, I'm crying and howling, too. I'm either thoroughly enraptured or possessed by a freaking demon, it's not clear which.

After several minutes of fuckery that can only be described as "a mini-porno-version of *The Exorcist*," Josh lays me down on my back on a table in the suite and fucks me with breathtaking fervor, whispering into my ear as he does about how much he loves me and how hot I am with my little baby bump and how good and wet and tight I always feel for him—and, within minutes, I'm convulsing with an orgasm that curls my effing toes and blurs my vision (and also makes my green head spin round and round on my shoulders).

When we're both done, Josh hulks over me on the table for a long moment, catching his breath. "Holy fuck," he says, his breathing ragged. "That wasn't according to plan."

I breathe deeply, trying to calm my racing heart. "Are we gonna be late now?" I gasp.

Josh straightens up, his eyebrows raised. "Late for what?"

"For the opera?"

Josh chuckles. "Oh, Kat." He pulls me off the table and wraps me in his strong arms.

"What? That's where Richard took Julia in the red dress—to the opera in San Francisco."

"Yeah, I know—I've seen the movie," Josh says, rolling his eyes. "But this is *my* fantasy, remember?—and I'd rather poke needles in my eyes than go to the fucking opera."

I giggle. "Oh, thank God. I was gonna be a good sport about it, of course, but I'd rather poke needles in my eyes than go to the fucking opera, too."

Josh kisses my forehead. "Don't you worry, PG. You're with *me*, remember? The Playboy—and where I'm taking you today is gonna curl your toes and soak your panties a thousand times more than any stinkin' *opera* ever could." He winks. "I guarantee it."

Chapter 36
Kat

Our limo pulls up to a small airport displaying a sign at the entrance that says, "Boeing Field."

"Are we flying to San Francisco?" I ask.

Josh grabs my hand. "No questions. Your only job today is to *react*—not to try to figure things out."

"Richard took Julia to San Francisco," I say.

"We're not going to the opera, and we're not going to San Francisco," Josh says. "No more questions."

I survey the long line of small jets lined up on the tarmac. "But we're flying somewhere?"

Josh puts his finger to his lips.

The limo winds its way through a gate and stops at a hangar about fifty yards from a small jet with its door opened wide and retractable staircase down.

"Are we going somewhere on that plane there?" I ask, pointing.

"God, you're a terrible listener," Josh says.

"Sorry. But are we going somewhere on a private plane? I've never been on a private plane. Oh my God."

"Ssh."

The limo driver opens our door and Josh gets out first.

"Don't forget our bags in the trunk, please," Josh instructs the driver. He bends down and peeks at me in the backseat. "You ready to make my hottest fantasy come true, Party Girl?"

I shoot Josh a look that says I don't believe for a second we're here to fulfill *his* fantasy. So far today, Josh has dressed me like Julia Roberts, slapped a beachside condo around my neck, and told me he'll love me forever and ever. It really doesn't take a brain surgeon to realize he's fulfilling *my* top fantasies today, no matter what he says. "If you say so, PB," I say, looking at him sideways.

"Oh, I do." Josh pulls me out of the car and threads my arm into his. "You look incredible in that dress," he whispers. He begins escorting me toward the nearby jet.

"Thank you. I absolutely love it. And the *necklace*—oh my God, Josh, it's beyond my wildest dreams." I touch the dazzling rocks encircling my neck, still not able to comprehend they're mine.

"That's good. Because *you're* beyond my wildest dreams, babe."

I abruptly stop walking. "Okay, that's it," I say. "What the heck is going on?"

Josh furrows his brow. "What do you mean?"

"I mean I had to lesbo-out with a bisexual supermodel and hypnotize you with a devious song to trick you into saying 'I love you' not too long ago, and now, suddenly, you're watching *Pretty Woman* and acting like Michael Bublé on steroids?"

Josh laughs and touches my belly. "Kat, just roll with it, baby. Don't overthink it. Your job is to *react.* Nothing more."

"At first I thought maybe you'd arranged all this because you're so happy to be having a daughter named after your mom, but then I realized you had to have arranged all this before we found out the kumquat's gender."

"Don't think, babe. *React.*"

"But, Josh, you watched *Pretty Woman,* for cryin' out loud. Have you gone completely mad?"

Josh brushes the hair out of my face and gazes into my eyes. "Yes, I have. Completely and utterly insane." He smiles. "And I've never been happier."

I bite my lip.

"Now come on, baby—we've got a private plane to catch."

When we reach the jet on the tarmac, a pilot in full uniform descends the retractable stairs and greets us. Josh leads me up the stairs and directs me to a window seat.

"You need anything?" Josh asks as I settle into my seat. "Club soda? A barf bag?"

I shake my head. "Nope. I'm good. I haven't barfed in a few days, actually."

"Hey, give that girl a salami," Josh says, grinning. "Will you do me a favor and hang out here for a minute, PG? I've got to talk briefly to the pilot about the flight plan."

"Is it okay if I send Sarah a photo of my necklace?"

"Of course," Josh says. "It's yours, after all."

"Oh my God," I breathe. "You just made my heart skip a beat."

Josh grins. "I'll be right back, baby." He winks and disappears down the stairs.

I pull my phone out of my clutch bag, take a quick selfie (making sure my dazzling necklace is front and center), and shoot the photo off to Sarah, tapping out a quick message along with it. "OMFG," I write. "I'm sitting on a PRIVATE PLANE wearing THIS!"

"Really? Wow! Amaaaaazing!" Sarah writes back instantly. "Where are you going?"

"I have no freaking clue!!!!!!" I write. "Josh dressed me in a Pretty Woman red dress and gave me this ridicky diamond necklace—TO KEEP!!!!!!—and told me he's gonna love me 'FOREVER' and called me 'MY LOVE'! And he didn't pass out or hurl during any of it! And now we're on a private jet heading to I DON'T CARE WHERE!"

"No way! That's so exciting! WOWZERCATS!"

Even in text, something about Sarah's reply feels canned to me. I shoot a snarky look at my display screen. "Oh, Sarah Cruz," I write. "You're the worst liar ever, even in text. I hope when you're a lawyer you wind up defending only innocent people because, otherwise, your guilty clients are all going straight to prison."

"LOL," Sarah writes. "First off, I'm not gonna practice criminal law—I'll be working for Gloria's House helping women get restraining orders and stuff. Second off, I like the fact that I'm a horrible liar. It's one of my best qualities." She attaches a scared-face emoji to the end of her message.

"You already knew about the necklace, didn't you?" I write.

"Of course. Do you really think I would have chosen working with my mom today over celebrating the big reveal of Gracie Louise Faraday? Come on, girl!"

"Yeah, I thought it was weird you were turning down an opportunity to drink champagne," I write. "So, hey, will you go shopping with me when I get back? I'm suddenly feeling the urge to buy lots and lots of PINK!!!!! Woohooooooo!"

"Hellz yeah!!!" Sarah writes. "I'm already planning to buy my sweet little niece a pair of her very own pink, sparkly boots! Yeehaw!"

I laugh out loud and begin tapping out a reply, but before I can finish my message, a text notification comes in from Josh.

"Raise the blind on your window and look outside," Josh's text says.

"Gotta go," I quickly type to Sarah. "The director of our mini-porno just told me to take my mark. Teehee. I'll give you a full report later, girlio."

"You better," Sarah writes. "Have fun, Kitty Kat!" She attaches a cat emoji and a heart.

"Meow," I write, followed by a salsa dancer (the emoji I always use to symbolize Sarah), plus a heart of my own.

I put my phone back into my sparkling clutch and then, as instructed, slowly raise the window blind and peek outside.

No.

Impossible.

Joshua William Faraday has just killed me. I'm officially dead. RIP Katherine Ulla Morgan. It's been a great life.

Josh is standing below me on the tarmac in his perfectly tailored tuxedo, staring up with a smoldering expression on his handsome face—*and with his arm in a freakin' sling*!

"Stop!" I yell toward the cockpit, even though the airplane isn't moving (and the engines aren't even on). "Stop!" I shriek again, leaping dramatically up from my chair. My brain isn't processing coherent thought right now, it's true, but I don't need conscious thought to know what I'm supposed to do in this scene—I've seen it in *The Bodyguard* twenty times, after all.

I burst down the stairs of the plane as fast as I can manage in my tight-fitting dress and towering heels and sprint (sort of) to Josh. And when I reach him, I throw my arms around his neck, hyperventilating. "Josh," I gasp. "I love you, I love you, I love—"

Josh's tongue slides into my mouth, shutting me up, while his free hand caresses my back—and when he pulls away from our kiss, his eyes are on fire. "Katherine Ulla Morgan," he says, his voice intense. "I. Will. Always. Love. You."

I squeal loudly, completely enthralled.

"I know marriage isn't in the cards for us," Josh says, "since neither of us wants that kind of *hoopla,* as we've discussed." One side of his mouth hitches up. "But I hope you'll accept this gift as a symbol of my eternal love for you." He pulls a skinny, rectangular jewelry box out of his pocket.

"Oh my effing God," I blurt, even before Josh has opened the box. "No, Josh. *No.* Whatever that is, it's too much, honey. *No.*"

"There's no such thing as 'too much' when it comes to you, babe," Josh says.

"No," I breathe. "Baby, no. You can't. Too much."

"Ssh. You can forbid me to give extravagant gifts to your parents," Josh says. "But when it comes to giving gifts to you, I'll do whatever the fuck I want."

I clutch my stomach. "Oh God, I feel like I'm gonna hurl," I say.

Josh flinches. "Not quite the reaction I was going for, babe."

I feel myself turning green.

"Well, shit," Josh says, crinkling his nose. "Maybe take a deep breath? Fuck, Kat. Seriously?"

I take a deep breath, but my nausea doesn't subside.

Josh's scowl intensifies. "I haven't even opened the box yet, Kat."

"Sorry."

Josh exhales in frustration. "Maybe bend over and breathe deeply? I'll hold onto you so you don't fall over."

I bend over and breathe for a long moment as Josh holds me and rubs my back and, soon, thankfully, I've regained my equilibrium. "Okay," I say, standing upright again. "I'm good."

"You sure?"

"Yep. I'm fine. I'm ready."

"You gonna barf if I open this box?"

I shake my head.

"I really like these shoes, Kat," Josh warns. "These are Stefano Bemer shoes, babe—*please* don't barf on them."

"Ooh la la—Stefano Bemers," I say, even though I've never heard that name in my entire life. "I'd never barf on *Stefano Bemer* shoes, baby. I respect Mr. Bemer too freaking much."

Josh laughs. "Okay. Here we go." He opens the box, and, instantly, I'm a goddamned fucking wreck. If my necklace is a beachside condo, then the behemoth of a diamond bracelet sitting inside that velvet box is at *least* a convertible Porsche.

"Oh my *God*!" I shriek, tears pricking my eyes.

Josh pulls the bracelet out of the box and clasps it to my wrist. "I love you, Kat," he whispers. He wraps me in a huge hug and kisses my tear-soaked cheeks.

"It's too much," I mumble into Josh's lips. "Oh my God, Josh. You can't do this. I'm not worthy."

Josh pulls back sharply from me, his eyes on fire. "Don't say that," he grits out, his voice spiking with sudden intensity. "Never, ever say that—do you understand me?"

My breath catches in my throat. I'd only meant that phrase as a figure of speech, kind of like from *Wayne's World*—"We're not worthy! We're not worthy!" Although, of course, I'm truly *not* worthy. Who could *possibly* be worthy of this kind of extravagance?

Josh cups my face in his large hands, heat wafting off him, his eyes burning. "You're my Pretty Woman and I'm your Bodyguard, Kat. You're the great love of my life and the mother of my future daughter." He presses himself into me and the hard bulge between us feels like it was forged in a steel factory. "Babe, have you been listening to me *at all*? You're *mine* now. *Forever.* Mine, all mine. And I'm not just some normal, boring guy—I'm *Josh Fucking Faraday.* And that means you gotta be *dripping* in fucking diamonds when you're on my arm." He slaps my ass, making me jump. "Now, come on, babe. Time to get your tight little ass onto that plane. I'm hard as a rock and ready to initiate my Party Girl with a Hyphen into the mile-high club."

Chapter 37
Josh

"Oooooh, a *white* limo," Kat says, settling herself into the backseat. She shoots me a snarky smile. "Just like in the final scene of *Pretty Woman.*"

"Ssh," I say, pulling the skirt of Kat's gown out from under my thigh as I scoot closer to her in the back seat. "This is *my* top fantasy—not yours, baby. You're here to *react,* not to try to figure things out."

"Okay, well, my *reaction* is, 'Hey, you arranged a white limo just like that awesome final scene in *Pretty Woman.*'"

I roll my eyes. "Smart-ass."

Kat grins.

I glance through the rear window of the limo just in time to see our driver closing the trunk. My stomach somersaults with excitement. *This is it.*

The driver walks along the length of the limo and settles into his seat up front.

"You got everything into the trunk?" I ask, referring to more than just our overnight bags.

"Yes, sir," the driver says. "Everything's there." He winks.

"Fantastic," I say. "Let's blow this popsicle stand."

The limo begins to pull away.

"Where are we going?" Kat asks, looking out the car window at the small airport we're leaving behind.

"Are you hungry, Party Girl?" I ask, completely ignoring her question. "There's a platter here—fruit, cheese, tapenade, crackers, prosciutto."

"Oh, God, yes. Thank you. I'm *starving.*" Kat begins literally stuffing food into her mouth like her very life depends on it. After a moment, she giggles at herself. "Dude, I'm in full Homer-Simpson mode," she says. "Nom nom nom. I can't control myself."

"The kumquat's really hungry, huh?" I ask.

"Pretty much all the time these days. She's a demanding little thing."

I open my mouth to make a snarky comment but Kat holds up her hand.

"Don't say it," she says, mock-glaring at me.

I smash my lips together and we both laugh.

"You know, the two of us are really not behaving in a way becoming of people dressed in formalwear," Kat says, chomping on a piece of cheese.

"Thank God," I say.

"Yeah, sure, it's all fun and games for *us*, but definitely not for the flight attendant," Kat says. "It really wasn't *that* big a plane, poor thing."

"Oh, she'll survive. We can't possibly be the first people to fuck like rabbits on a private plane."

"I wouldn't be so sure," Kat says. She giggles. "Surely other people fuck, but not like *that*—that was pretty *enthusiastic*, even for us, Josh. Dressed in a gown like this, I really should have acted much more like a proper young lady on that plane. Tsk, tsk."

I lean forward and touch Kat's chin. "Promise me something, babe," I say.

"Anything, my love."

"Promise me, no matter what, you'll never, ever act like a proper young lady as long as we both shall live."

A lovely smile spreads across Kat's face. "I promise."

"Thank you."

A few minutes later, after Kat's finished eating like a truck driver suffering from mad cow disease, she scoots closer to me on the car seat and rests her head on my shoulder. "Thank you for this amazing day, Josh," she says. "This is the best day of my life." She clasps her fingers in mine.

"That's sweet," I say nonchalantly. "But your feelings are completely irrelevant, since today is for my benefit and not yours."

Kat giggles. "You're so full of shit."

We silently watch the passing scenery through the car window for several minutes, the Southern California ocean glimmering in the late-afternoon light. "I've never been to San Diego," Kat says. "It's beautiful here."

"Yeah, I love it here," I say. "I usually make it down here a couple times a year during racing season. I've got several good friends who own racehorses."

"Of course, you do. I'm shocked you don't own a couple yourself."

"Meh. I did a few years ago. But it turns out racehorses are fucking money pits to own—a lot more fun when someone else is paying the bills."

"God, ain't that the truth," Kat says, squeezing my hand. "It's what I *always* say."

We look out at the passing scenery again, our hands clasped comfortably.

"I love the ocean," Kat says. "Especially at this time of day when the light is soft and golden."

Just like your hair, I think, stroking the full length of her soft, golden mane—but, of course, I keep that thought to myself. There's only so much poetic babbling a guy can do in one day and I've got to rest up for all the poetic babbling that lies ahead. I stare at the passing scenery for a long minute, stroking Kat's glorious hair, breathing in the scent of her, thinking about what I'm gonna say to her when we reach our destination.

"Staring at the ocean always makes me feel small, but in a good way," Kat says quietly, looking out the window.

"Me, too," I say. "Like my problems don't matter in the grand scheme of things."

"You have problems?" she asks.

I kiss the top of her head. "Not anymore."

Kat nuzzles into me. "I wish I had something amazing to give you—the male equivalent of a Carolina Herrera gown and diamonds, whatever that would be—so you could feel the way I do right now."

"Well, the male equivalent of a Carolina Herrera dress and diamonds would be an Italian sports car—which I already have. But, don't worry, you've already given me something ten times better than that."

Kat lifts her head, apparently about to say something, but yawns, instead.

"Damn, you're hard to impress," I say.

She giggles. "Sorry. It's been an exciting day. I'm duly impressed, I assure you."

I open my arms to her and pat my heart. "Lay your cheek right here, beautiful. Close your eyes for a bit."

Kat nuzzles into my chest. "Where are we headed?" she asks groggily.

"God, you're a terrible listener," I say, stroking her hair.

Kat purrs like a kitten against my chest and in less than a minute, her head droops like a dead weight. I shift in my seat, trying to make her more comfortable, but, inadvertently startle her awake, instead.

"Oh, I'm sorry," I say. "I was trying to make you more comfortable. Go back to sleep, babe. I won't move."

"How long 'til we get wherever we're going?" she asks, her voice thick with drowsiness. "Do I have time to sleep?"

"How much longer 'til we reach our destination?" I ask the limo driver.

"About thirty minutes, sir, depending on traffic," the driver says.

"Plenty of time for a little nap, hot momma," I say. "Go for it."

Kat rests her cheek against me again. "I think I will, if that's okay—just for a few minutes."

Twenty seconds later, Kat's out like a light, passed out with her cheek against my heart, her little belly underneath her red gown rising and falling evenly with every breath she takes. When I'm sure Kat's deeply asleep, I tilt her face up to mine and stare at her stunning features, marveling at God's handiwork. I trace the line of one of her bold eyebrows with my fingertip, brush the back of my hand against her cheekbone, stare for a long moment at her perfectly formed lips.

As evil as Kat's startling beauty is when she's awake, her face is actually quite angelic when she sleeps. This isn't the face of a woman who'd blindside me, is it? After everything that's passed between Kat and me since my first god-awful proposal, Kat wouldn't shatter me by turning me down for a second time, would she?

My stomach flips over. If by some shocking turn of events Kat was actually telling the truth when she said she wouldn't marry me if I were the last man on earth, if she truly doesn't want all the "hoopla" of a wedding, if marriage truly isn't something she yearns for in the depths of her soul—or, at least, not marriage with *me*—then I truly don't think I'd survive the rejection.

My phone buzzes with an incoming text and I pull it out of my pocket.

"The eagle has landed," Henn writes. "The fucker's at his house. Go straight there. No Plan B required."

"Well, how considerate of him to be home in time for my visit," I write.

"Can you talk?" Henn writes.

I look down at Kat. Her mouth is hanging open and she's drooling. "Calling now," I write.

"Yo," Henn says when he picks up my call.

"Nice of the bastard to be sitting at home, waiting for me," I reply softly.

"He's always home at this time of day after a round of golf at the country club. But just to make double-damn sure he was gonna be there for you today, he *might* have received a VIP-invitation to a live chat with his favorite porn star. *Wink.*"

"Fucking genius."

"So I've been told. How close are you?"

I glance at Kat, making sure she's not overhearing any of this, and she's snoozing like she's been cold-cocked. "We're in the limo now," I say quietly. "I'd say we're about fifteen minutes out."

"Cool. The dude's not going anywhere. He's watching a gangbang-*bukkake*-porno on his iPad while simultaneously live-chatting with a porn star on his laptop."

"He's double-fisting porn?" I ask.

Henn laughs. "I think he *might* have an addiction."

"Ya think?" I say.

"So, hey, I went through the dude's computer like you asked me to," Henn says. "You were right—he's totally cheating on his wife. Like, compulsively."

"Yeah, I figured. A leopard doesn't change his spots."

"The guy's a scumbag," Henn says. "I literally *hate* him."

"Welcome to the club," I say.

"I went through his wife's phone and laptop just to get the lay of the land and she's a total sweetheart—a genuinely good person. Clearly, she's got no idea who she's married to."

"Not surprised at all."

"So are you gonna rat him out?"

"I wish I could so badly—but, no, I wasn't planning to, for the sake of the wife."

"Yeah, I guess that's the right call. It's not really our place to ruin her life. But it kills me. They're trying to have a baby—doing hard-core fertility treatments. I hope one way or another she finds out she's married to a cheating scumbag before she gets pregnant with the guy's kid."

"So you think we should rat him out, after all?" I ask.

"No," Henn says. "It's really not our place, man. That's not the mission."

I sigh. "Damn. I would have loved to decimate that cocksucker in every conceivable way."

"Oh, well. I guess even a guy as awesome as you can't have everything, Josh."

I look down at Kat's beautiful, sleeping face. "Actually, I'm beginning to think he can."

"Wait. So you *do* wanna tell the wife about his extracurricular activities?"

"No, sorry. I wasn't referring to ratting him out. Kat's asleep on me. I was looking at her face when I said that."

"Oh, well, I can see why you'd say that, then."

"Kat's totally drooling right now," I say, chuckling.

Henn laughs. "Yeah, but I bet it's really *pretty* drool."

"Actually, it is." I smile to myself. "Okay, yeah, I agree," I say. "We don't tell the wife she's married to the world's biggest scumbag."

"Not today, anyway. I might not be able to control myself tomorrow. I make no promises."

"Hey, you gotta follow your conscience, baby," I say. "I trust you. But just not today."

"Okay. Got it, boss."

"So can we somehow make sure the wife's not there when Kat and I arrive?"

"You should be good. Her iPhone says she's got an appointment at a hair salon ten miles from their house. She left about fifteen minutes ago. Don't women's hair appointments at hoity-toity salons take at least an hour or so? Her appointment's at one of those really fancy places where they give you cucumber water and wash your hair, so she should be gone a while."

"That's your definition of a fancy salon?" I say. "They give you water and a shampoo?"

"Hey, I go to Supercuts, man. What do I know?"

"You do? Oh, I totally couldn't tell that from looking at you, Henn."

Henn laughs. "So, here's the sitch, man. When you get there, the name 'Frank Farmer' is on the approved visitors' list at the guard station. Just text me when you're there and I'll go in and freeze the bastard's hard drive."

"Will do. We're almost there. Sit tight and wait for my signal, okay?"

"Yup. No worries. I'll just be sitting here, watching him watch porn," Henn says. "Don't you worry about a thing except bagging that babe."

"I'll do my mighty best."

"Is that a note of *anxiety* I detect in your voice, boss?"

"Yeah, this is life or death, man—I don't wanna fuck it up."

"Aw, come on. You can't fail. Just dick it up and the babe will be eating out the palm of your hand."

"Gee, thanks for the tip."

"No prob."

"I'll text you when we're there."

"Roger that."

Ten minutes later, the limo pulls up to an exclusive gated community in Del Mar, California—a wealthy seaside enclave north of San Diego—and our driver tells the security guard at the gate the name of the resident we're here to see.

"And what's the visitor's name?" the guard asks.

"Frank Farmer," the driver says, motioning to me in the back seat. "He should be on your list."

"Wait here."

The guard disappears into his guardhouse, presumably to look at his approved visitors' list, and my stomach clenches sharply. But when the guy comes back out, he's all smiles.

"Do you know how to get there?" the guard asks my driver.

"We have the address," the driver replies.

"Well, lemme just tell you: follow the main road here for two miles and then take the third right. Mr. Bennett's house is on the left."

"Okay, thanks," the driver says.

As we cruise slowly down the main drag of the complex, I survey the McMansions lining the street, my stomach bursting with butterflies. In just a few minutes, my life will be forever changed. *And I can't wait.*

My eyes drift down to Kat, still asleep against my chest.

It feels like a lifetime ago that Kat waltzed out of the bathroom at Jonas' house and straight up to me like she owned me—which she did, of course, right from the start. I fought her on it, for sure, but now in retrospect it's clear this very moment with Kat was unavoidable. My fate. A beautiful brick wall I've been barreling toward my whole fucking life.

I nudge Kat gently. "Babe," I whisper. "Time to wake up, beautiful."

Kat's dead to the world.

"Party Girl," I whisper. "It's time to party, sweetheart." I nudge her again and she rustles.

"Hmm?" Kat says. She lifts her head and looks around with dazed eyes.

"It's time to party, honey," I say softly.

Kat wipes the drool off her chin and gazes out the car window, just as the limo turns right onto a street lined with the same cookie-cutter mansions on the main drag.

"Where are we?" Kat asks, stretching her long arms and looking around.

The limo comes to a stop in front of our destination.

"It's a surprise," I say. "Stay here, baby. I'm gonna set something up for us—it'll just take a minute. While I'm doing that, you freshen up—put on some lip gloss, wipe your chin, whatever—and when you hear blaring music, come out of the limo and stand next to me, okay?"

"What?" she asks. "Come stand next to you?"

"Yeah, baby, when you hear blaring music, that's your cue to come out of the limo and stand next to me." I stroke her hair. "Freshen up your makeup, babe—make yourself extra pretty—I want you looking like a man-eater when you step out of the car, okay? And the minute you hear the music, come out and stand next to me."

"Okay," she says. She grabs her makeup bag out of her duffel. "Your wish is my command, sir."

I grab Kat's face and kiss her. "See you soon, my love," I say.

"Josh?"

"Yeah?"

"Um. I'm really sorry, but I have to pee—like, really, really bad. Is this gonna take long, whatever it is? I'm about to explode."

I chuckle. Damn. I didn't think about Kat's constant need to pee these days when I planned this mini-porno-rom-com. I peek out the window of the car. There are definitely plenty of bushes in The Asshole's manicured landscaping, including some fairly large bushes along the side of the house.

"Okay, Party Girl—come with me," I say. "We'll find a place for you to pop a squat."

Kat laughs. "I'm dressed in a Carolina Herrera gown, diamonds, and Manolo Blahniks—and you're asking me to 'pop a squat' behind a bush?"

"Do you have a better plan?"

"Well, no. I just didn't want you to think I'm low-class."

"Babe, you're the classiest broad I know. Now, come on. Let's go take a classy piss behind a bush."

Chapter 38
Josh

"Sir, do you want—?" the driver begins when Kat and I emerge from the backseat of the limo looking for a place to relieve Kat's bursting bladder.

The driver's standing at the back of the car, exactly as instructed, getting ready to set up two speakers currently nestled in the trunk of the car.

"Hang on," I say, putting up my hand and cutting him off. "My baby-momma needs to take a quick piss before we begin. Await further instruction."

The driver smirks. "Yes, sir."

Kat and I creep around the side of the large house and quickly find a suitable bush—and while I keep a lookout, she hikes up her red dress around her hips, squats her tight little ass down, and pisses like a racehorse.

"Ah," she says as a loud stream of urine blasts out of her. "Delicious."

I laugh. "*Delicious?*"

"Yes, *delicious*. When I have to pee really, really bad and finally get to go, it feels semi-orgasmic. Same muscles releasing, actually. *Delicious.*"

"Only you, Kat," I say, zipping down my fly and taking a quick whiz myself.

"Wow, we're a classy pair, aren't we?" she says. She stands almost upright, still hiking her elegant gown up, and shakes her pelvis furiously like a wet dog after a bath.

"What the fuck are you doing?" I ask.

"Shaking the extra pee off my cooch. That's what I do when I don't have toilet paper—the pee-pee-shake. It's not just me, trust me—every girl who's ever gone on a pub crawl or painted her fingernails and then realized she has to pee has resorted to the pee-pee-shake." She straightens up.

"You good now?"

"Oh yeah, I'm gooood." She shoots me two thumbs up.

"Okay, then get your tight little ass back into the limo. Freshen up your makeup—I want you looking like you could eat a douche for breakfast, okay?—and then come out the minute you hear blaring music."

"And stand next to you. I got it, Playboy." She smiles and looks around. "Where are we, by the way? Who lives here?"

"No questions. Now *go.*"

Kat shoots me an adorable smile and traipses back to the limo—and the minute she closes the car door behind her, I powwow with the driver at the opened trunk.

"You want both speakers aimed at the house?" the driver asks.

"Yep," I say. "The song's all cued up on my phone and connected to the speakers via Blue Tooth. Just point the speakers at the house and press play on the song at my signal."

"Yes, sir." He holds his hand out for my phone.

"Hang on," I say. I tap out a quick text to Henn. "In exactly three minutes, do your thing," I write.

"You got it," Henn replies.

"Here you go," I say, handing my phone to the driver. "The song's all cued up."

Three minutes later, I grab my trusty Walmart boom box out of the trunk of the car, position myself on the porch of our host's McMansion, make quadruple sure the ring box is still in my pocket (it is), raise the boom box over my head, and, finally, with a curt nod, cue the driver.

Here we go.

Whitney Houston begins belting out "I Will Always Love You" at full volume—so fucking loud, in fact, my molars feel like they're one high-note away from popping out of my head.

My pulse is pounding in my ears.

My hands are shaking.

This is it. Oh my God. The love of my life is about to come out of that white limo and, hopefully, make me the luckiest man in the world.

The door to the limo opens. And there she is. *Kat*—my fantasy sprung to life, looking as gorgeous as ever... and utterly confused. But when Kat's eyes land on me and she sees the CD player over my head, her face contorts with instant glee. She sprints toward me as fast as her heels will allow, her eyes glistening, her cheeks flushed. Just before she reaches me, I put my makeshift boom box on the ground and open my arms to her.

"I love you," Kat cries, barreling into my arms. "I love you so much."

I kiss her passionately, devouring her, lost in her—until the sound of an aggravated male voice behind us, shouting over the music, breaks us apart.

"What the fuck is this?" the voice shouts behind us. "Turn that music off and get your shit off my—"

"Garrett?" Kat blurts, obviously floored. She looks at me, her mouth agape, apparently trying to make sense of this incomprehensible ghost from her past. "This is *your* house?"

"Kat?" Garrett yells above the blaring music, obviously as shocked to see Kat as she is to see him. "What are you doing here?"

I motion to the driver to cut the music and he does.

"Hey, Garrett Asshole Bennett," I say smoothly, my voice cutting through the sudden silence. "Sorry for the interruption—I know you were busy inside wacking off to gangbang-*bukkake*-porn, but Kat and I have some important business to attend to and it requires your participation. Shouldn't take more than fifteen minutes at the outside."

Garrett looks absolutely blindsided. "*What?*" he chokes out. "Who are you?"

"My name's Frank Farmer," I say.

Kat's face lights up at the mention of my code name. (It should, for fuck's sake—the woman's only seen *The Bodyguard* twenty fucking times.)

"I believe you're acquainted with my baby-momma, Kat?" I continue.

Garrett stares at me dumbly.

"We came here today because there's something important I

want to ask Kat—and I thought it'd be extra special for her if I asked her this particular question in front of you."

Kat lets out a little yelp, perhaps realizing where this thing is headed.

"So I'd really appreciate it if you'd stay put and listen carefully to everything I'm about to say to her," I continue. "And when I'm done asking Kat my important question, we'll leave you alone so you can continue watching your hardcore porn and cheating on your wife with hookers and the bookkeeper at your church and the waitress at your country club."

"Who *are* you?" Garrett blurts, his face ashen.

"I told you, I'm Frank Farmer," I say. "And you're gonna stay put and listen to everything I'm about to say to this gorgeous woman, or I'm gonna make your life a living fucking hell." I look at my watch. "We'd better get started, Garrett. We don't have that much time before your wife gets home from her hair appointment and I have no desire for her to hear any of this."

"Fuck you," Garrett blurts. "Get off my property or I'll call the police."

I take a menacing step forward, my fists clenched, and Garrett flinches.

"You're not in any position to *fuck* me, cocksucker," I say. "If anyone's getting *fucked* today, trust me, it's gonna be you. Now I want you to listen patiently to every word I have to say to this gorgeous creature, especially the grand finale at the end, because if you don't, a certain photo that's frozen on your laptop screen right now will be blasted to every single person on the email lists for your church and country club, not to mention your senator-daddy's campaign-donor list, too. Feel free to run inside and check out the image on your laptop right now if you don't believe me. We'll wait."

Garrett's face twists in shock. He opens his mouth and shuts it again, but he doesn't move from his spot on his doorstep.

"Good boy." I look at Kat and smile. She looks like her head's about to pop off. I take her hands in mine. "Kat, this motherfucker here once said you're not 'marriage material.' But I'm here to tell you that you are. In fact, you're not just 'marriage material' in general for *some* lucky guy, my love—you're specifically marriage material for *me*."

Kat lets out a little yelp and literally wobbles in place.

I grasp her arm and steady her. "You okay?"

Kat shakes her head. She's totally losing it. She clamps her hand over her mouth.

"You gonna barf?" I ask.

She shakes her head again. "Keep going. I'm fine. Oh my God. Keep going, babe. Holy fuck."

I look at Garrett. "Don't go anywhere, fuckwad."

Garrett crosses his arms over his chest, but he doesn't move.

"Katherine Ulla Morgan," I say. "You're the great love of my life. I'll never want anyone besides you, ever, 'til the end of time, forever and ever, and I'm one hundred percent sure of that fact. You're The One, babe. The one and only. It's literally impossible for me to want someone else, ever, because you're sheer perfection in every way." I glare at Garrett. "The reasons I love you are too numerous to count, but let me tell you just a few of them while we've got Garrett's undivided attention."

Kat whimpers.

"You're hysterically funny, baby. Sweet and kind. Caring and compassionate. You take care of those you love with a fierceness I've never witnessed before. Babe, I *admire* you."

She gasps.

"You're a sassy little thing," I continue. "Good lord are you sassy. A fucking terrorist. A demon spawn. A force of nature. To call you *determined* is like calling a pit bull *assertive*."

Kat laughs.

"You're honest, Kat. Oh my fuck, do you call me on my shit. The way you *don't* kiss my YOLO'd ass is one of the best things about you. You're smart, baby. Intuitive. Clever. Bold. When I'm with you, there's no place I'd rather be, no matter what we're doing, even if we're just peeing in a fucking bush."

Kat laughs heartily through her tears.

"You're hell on wheels, Kat Morgan. Totally unpredictable. A heart of gold hidden beneath a layer of pure evil. *And I love all of it.*"

Kat laughs again and wipes her eyes.

"I'll never get bored with you. It's impossible. Never a dull moment." I glare at Garrett. "I'm one hundred percent positive I'll never feel the need to watch gangbang-*bukkake*-porn as long as you're by my side because you're better than any porno—better than any fantasy. With you, life *is* a fantasy. Every single day."

285

Lauren Rowe

Kat makes a weird chortling sound, a combination of a cry and a laugh.

I shoot daggers at Garrett again and then return my gaze to Kat. "Garrett here didn't think you were marriage material because you're so sexual. Let's talk about that, shall we? Because, my love—my beautiful, sexy, feisty, funny, kinky, perverted, wonderful sick fuck—the way your motor runs so fucking hot is definitely one of the best things about you. You're highly sexual because you're so fucking passionate, Kat—because you're relentlessly honest and raw and a fucking beast in every way. You should never, ever be ashamed of your amazing sexuality. It's your superpower, baby." I glare at Garrett again, and, for some reason, a rage rises up and boils over inside me. "Hang on a second, my love," I say to Kat. I drop her hands and take a menacing step toward Garrett, pointing at Kat behind me. "This woman right here is a fucking unicorn," I seethe. "She fucks like a dude and sucks a dick like nobody else."

Kat squeals with glee behind my shoulder.

"In fact, she's quite literally the best dick-sucker the world has ever seen. If there were an Olympic event in the sport of dick-sucking, Katherine Morgan would take the gold, silver, and fucking bronze."

Kat makes a sound of pure joy.

"And the way she fucks? Oh my God. When it comes to fucking, this woman right here is truly gifted. If fucking were *thinking*, Kat Morgan would have a genius-level IQ."

Kat bursts out laughing and so do I.

But Garrett isn't laughing. Not at all. "I'm calling the cops," he seethes.

"Oh, shut the fuck up, Garrett. No, you're not. Because we both know I'm in your computer right now—and what information I've got access to. But, for what it's worth, I promise I'm not here to harm you today. Actually, I'm here to *thank* you—from the bottom of my heart. If you hadn't been such a slut-shaming prick who was more concerned about what Mommy and Daddy would think than letting yourself be truly happy in this one fucking life, if you'd rather secretly beat off while watching porn on your computer than fuck a woman who looks like Kat every day of your life—then all I can say is, you're my new best friend. Because, thanks to you and your tiny dick and even smaller balls, this gorgeous woman is all mine 'til the end of fucking time, praise be to God."

286

Kat makes a strangled sound.

"Which brings me to that question I've got for you, Kat."

I turn away from Garrett, pull the closed ring box out of my pocket, and kneel down. "Katherine Ulla Morgan," I begin, holding up the box, a huge smile on my face.

"Oh my God, oh my God, oh my God!" Kat shrieks.

I pause, thinking Kat's gonna calm down and let me get a word in edgewise, but, instead, she lets out a pained wail like she's a spider and her eight legs are being simultaneously ripped off her body.

"Babe," I say. "Are you okay?"

She nods, but she looks like she's about to keel over.

"Put your hands on my shoulders," I say. "I guarantee you, when I open this box, your knees are gonna buckle, babe."

Kat puts her hands on my shoulders, squealing and trembling.

I take a deep breath. "Katherine Ulla Morgan," I begin again, beaming up at her—but before I can say another word, Kat pivots, buckles over, and barfs all over Garrett's shoes.

"What the fuck!" Garrett yells, jumping back.

I burst out laughing. Oh my God. This is the best day of my life.

"You people are fucking crazy!" Garrett shouts. "Get the fuck off my property!"

I stand, howling with laughter. "You okay, babe?" I choke out, completely ignoring Garrett.

Kat's laughing hysterically right along with me. "Yeah, I'm great." She wipes her mouth. "Oh my God. Now *that's* a story for the grandchildren."

"I'm not gonna say it again," Garrett says. "I don't know who the fuck you think you are, but—"

I've suddenly got anti-freeze in my veins. In a flash, I've got a fistful of Garrett's shirt in my palm and I'm slamming his backside against his front door. "My hacker's in complete control of your computer right now, motherfucker," I growl, "which means he's in complete control of your *life*. Now, if you don't believe me, go check your screen right now—your screen-saver is that selfie you took when you were getting blown by that hooker in Vegas."

Garrett's jaw drops.

"Go look at your laptop if you don't believe me, cocksucker," I grit out. "I'll wait."

Garrett waffles briefly and then slams the door in our faces.

"You need some water, PG?" I ask.

Kat nods. "Sorry. That was so gross." She looks down at herself. "Did I get puke on my pretty dress?"

"Nope. Not a drop. Just all over Garrett." I chuckle. "So fucking hilarious."

Kat giggles.

"You're sure you're okay?"

"I'm great." Her face is positively glowing. "Better than great."

"Hang on. I'll get some water and your toothbrush out of your duffel bag." I sprint to the car, grab a couple bottles of water, Kat's toothbrush, and a tube of toothpaste out of her bag, and race back to her. "Here you go, PG. Do your thing. I'll wait." I wink.

She smiles sheepishly and walks toward the side of the house, but before turning the corner, she stops and turns around. "Josh, please, while I'm gone, for the love of God, don't change your mind about what you're planning to ask me. *Please.*"

"Are you gonna say yes?" I ask.

She clutches her heart. "Of course."

I breathe a sigh of relief. "Thank God."

"Was there ever a doubt?"

"Babe, when it comes to you, I'm never completely sure what the fuck you're gonna do."

We beam massive, excited smiles at each other.

"Now go brush your teeth, hot momma," I say. "I'm gonna wanna kiss you after you say yes."

"Oh. Right. Okay. I'll be right back." She sprints around the side of the house, giggling, and disappears.

I pull out my phone and text Henn. "The Asshole's inside his house, looking at his computer. He was threatening to call the police. Send him a message loud and clear, would you? Make sure he knows he's at my fucking mercy."

"Gotcha, boss. When he comes back out, the tiger will be nothing more than a pussy cat—I promise."

Kat returns from around the corner looking fresh as the morning dew at the same time Garrett opens his front door, his face bright red.

"Motherfucker," Garrett says. "So this is blackmail? You want money?"

I scoff. "No, not at all. This is twenty minutes of payback for you being a total asshole to the love of my life for eight long months. I'm gonna make your life miserable for mere minutes and then leave you alone to cheat on your wife as much as you please. Of course, you deserve to have me fuck up your life irreparably, but by all accounts, your wife is a really sweet lady and totally clueless about you. So I'm not gonna do a damn thing to you, just to spare her from embarrassment. Plus, as a side note, blackmailing a guy worth a mere fraction of my net worth would be a pretty stupid thing to do, don't you think? Yeah, that's right, Garrett, I've seen your bank statements. I could buy you at least a hundred times over, fucker." I point to Kat's necklace. "See that? *Real.*" I hold up Kat's arm like she's a rag doll and point to her sparkling bracelet. "And this? *Real.* Both gifts from me—and that's just *today.* Who the fuck knows what tokens of my affection I might give her for Christmas and her birthday and maybe after she sucks my dick extra nice. And do you wanna know why? Because this woman's gonna be my *wife.*"

Kat lets out a loud wail and throws her arms around me.

I hug her to me, still looking at Garrett Asshole Bennett, my eyes burning with near-homicidal rage. "Make no mistake about it, motherfucker, any wife of mine is gonna be *dripping* in motherfucking diamonds, cocksucker—I promise you that."

Kat makes a very, very bizarre sound—a sound I couldn't categorize if I tried—and presses her body fervently into mine, kissing my cheeks frenetically.

"So," I say, dodging Kat's furious lips, "like I said, if you want us to leave and never come back, then all you've got to do is stand here and watch me pop the question and we'll be on our merry way, off to fuck like rabbits for the third (but not final) time today, never to think about your pathetic, hypocritical, miserable ass ever again as long as we both shall live." I look at Kat. "You ready, my love? It's time for me to ask you to be my wife."

Kat nods, her eyes blazing. "Oh my God."

"But, wait. You know what? One more thing before I do that."

Kat throws up her hands and exhales loudly, flapping her lips together.

I wink at her. "Patience, my love." I look at Garrett and my jaw sets. "Apologize to my future wife for what you did to her, asshole."

Garrett looks flabbergasted.

"It's okay," Kat says, putting her hand on my forearm. "Let's not waste our time on—"

"Ssh. I told you, baby. This is *my* fantasy, not yours." I look at Garrett again, my eyes burning. "Tell my future wife and mother of my child you're sorry for what you did to her. For using her. Lying to her. Slut-shaming her. You gave my future wife a complex about her superpower and now you're gonna tell her you're sorry."

Garrett's nostrils flair. His jaw muscles pulse. He looks at Kat, not a hint of apology in his eyes. "Kat, I think you took things between us *way* too hard. I don't even remember saying you weren't 'marriage material'—"

"Are you calling my future wife a *liar*?" I bellow.

"No," Garrett says quickly, recoiling.

I take a deep, shaky breath. It's taking all my willpower not to beat this little prick to within an inch of his life. "Now apologize to my future wife. Last fucking chance."

Garrett looks like he's gonna cry. "Kat, *if* I said that to you— which I honestly don't even remember—"

I lunge at Garrett and he immediately throws up his hands defensively, cowering. "Wait! Wait! If I said that, which I don't remember—but it's definitely *possible*—then all I meant was that you weren't 'marriage material' for *me* personally. That's all I meant, Kat."

Kat squints. Her nostrils flare. She's turning into the dragon-lady before my eyes.

"That sure didn't sound like an apology, Garrett," Kat says evenly. "I didn't even hear the word 'sorry' pass your lips." Kat grits her teeth. "Did you not hear my future husband? Apologize to me— and make me believe it—so this sexy man can ask me to marry him and I can say 'hell yes.'"

Garrett exhales a shaky breath. "I'm sorry, Kat. You were great and I was an asshole and I'm sorry. I shouldn't have said that to you."

"And not only that, you shouldn't have used me to cheat on your virgin-girlfriend in the first place, asshole," Kat says.

Garrett clenches his jaw. "Yeah, I'm genuinely sorry about that."

Kat's face magically transforms into pure sweetness. "I forgive you, Garrett. But only because I don't give the slightest fuck about you." Kat flashes me a truly angelic smile. "Go ahead, my darling beloved. You were saying?"

I smile broadly. "You're pleased with his apology?"

"Quite pleased."

"All right, then. Let's proceed." I clear my throat. "'My dearest Katherine, if your feelings are the same as you described to me that horrible night in the hospital, then tell me now—one word from you will silence me forever.'"

Kat's face lights up with instant recognition of the scene I'm portraying. She puts her hand on her heart, her face aglow. "Mr. Darcy," she whispers, her eyes watering. "Oh, Josh."

I kneel down slowly, my eyes fixed on hers, and open the ring box.

Kat gasps at the sight of the spectacular rock. "*Josh*! Oh my God! *Josh*!"

I hold the ring up and beam a huge smile at her. "Katherine Ulla Morgan, the love of my life, the mother of my future baby girl, the Party Girl with a Hyphen *and* Heart of Gold: 'You have bewitched me, body and soul, and I love, I love, I *love* you.'"

"Oh my God," Kat breathes.

I take a deep breath. My heart is racing. I'm shaking like a leaf as adrenaline suddenly floods me. "Kat, my love, will you *please* make me the luckiest man in the world and say yes to marrying me?"

"Yes!" Kat shrieks, tears springing into her eyes.

I stand and slip the ring on Kat's finger—and she shrieks at the sight of the massive rock on her hand. She throws herself into my arms, crying and cooing and purring and basically losing her shit completely.

"Can I go now?" Garrett says dryly.

I break free from Kat and wipe my eyes. "Almost, Garrett. We're really close. There's just one more thing."

"For fuck's sake," Garrett says, rolling his eyes. "My wife's gonna be home any minute." He looks at his watch. "Whatever it is, say it already and get the fuck off my property and the fuck out of my computer."

I take Kat's hand and squeeze it. "Kat wanted you and you rejected her," I say. "Big mistake. *Big*." I motion to Kat like I'm giving her the floor but, much to my surprise, she looks at me with wide, blank eyes, not catching my meaning. *"Big mistake. Big,"* I repeat. I motion to Kat again. But she's still clueless. I throw up my hands, totally annoyed. "Aw, come on, babe," I say. "You're totally fucking this up, babe."

"I am? What am I supposed to do?"

"You really don't know?"

She shakes her head.

"Babe. Duh. I'm doing the thing when Julia goes back to the ritzy clothing store in Beverly Hills after the store clerk wouldn't help her the day before?"

"Oh my God!" Kat slaps her palm on her forehead. "I can't believe I didn't get that. My brain's not even functioning right now." She holds up her hand, displaying her massive rock. "Who could blame me—holy shitballs, honey—this thing is causing me brain damage." She giggles. "Okay, cue me again, honey. I'll nail it this time."

"You two are fucking crazy," Garrett says.

"Ssh," I say to Garrett. "Listen up, fucker." I clear my throat, clearly cuing up the script. "Garrett, she wanted you and you rejected her," I say. I motion to Kat, yet again.

A huge smile spreads across Kat's face. "Big mistake," she says enthusiastically. "Big. *Huge.* Now I gotta go do some shopping."

"Are you people *insane?*" Garrett asks. "You show up at my house in fucking formal wear, blast Whitney Houston at me, and hack into my computer—and then you fucking *barf* on me and tell me to— *oh shit.*" Garrett's eyes suddenly bug out of his head. "My wife. Oh, fuck. You gotta get the fuck out of here. Oh, God, no."

We all turn toward the end of the long driveway, just as a sleek black Mercedes pulls in.

"Oh, shit," Garrett blurts, suddenly looking panicked. "Please. I'm begging you. Don't you dare—"

"We won't say a word," I say. "Chill the fuck out, fucktard. I told you. I have no desire to hurt your wife."

A demure brunette walks up to us, a quizzical look on her face, looking every bit the nice girl Kat described, right down to her sweater set and the large cross around her neck.

"What's going on, sweetheart?" the woman asks. She nods at Kat and me. "Who are your friends?"

I put out my hand. "Hi, I'm Kevin. And this is my wife, Whitney. Garrett and I went to school together—we played on the golf team together. Whitney and I were visiting a friend in your neighborhood on our way to a benefit gala so we thought we'd pop by and say a quick hello."

"Oh," the woman says. "Hello."

"I was excited to tell Garrett about our little bun in the oven." I pat Kat's stomach.

An unmistakable shadow passes across the woman's face. "Oh, congratulations. How wonderful. When are you due?"

"Early December," Kat says quietly, clearly picking up on the shift in the woman's demeanor.

There's an awkward beat.

"Oh, gosh. Where are my manners?" the woman says. She extends her hand and shoots daggers at Garrett, clearly chastising him for failing to introduce her. "I'm Maggie Bennett, Garrett's wife. I don't think we've met before?"

"We haven't," I say, shaking her hand. "I was a senior when Garrett was a sophomore, so our paths didn't cross for long. Lovely to meet you, Maggie."

"Would you like to come inside?" she asks. "I baked brownies today."

"No, thank you. Whitney and I have that gala to attend. We just wanted to stop by and say a quick hello and, you know, reminisce about old times for a minute." I shake Garrett's hand. "Great to see you again, buddy. Like I was saying, man, I owe you big. *Huge*. I'll never forget the favor you did for me. Thanks again."

"Oh my goodness," Maggie says, putting her hand on her heart. "What on earth did Garrett do for you?"

"Oh. He gave me some life-changing advice," I say.

"Life-changing advice? Really? What was it if you don't mind me asking?" She looks at her husband like he's got three eyes.

"I don't mind at all," I say. "Garrett told me, 'When you find The One, hold onto her and never let her go. Because all great happiness in a man's life comes from finding his one true love. I should know.'"

"Wow," Maggie says, obviously completely shocked. "*Garrett* told you that? *My* Garrett?"

"He sure did."

Kat pats Maggie's shoulder like she's petting a German Shepherd. "It was so nice to meet you, Maggie. Garrett was just telling us how wonderful you are—and now I see what he was talking about."

"He was?" Maggie says, seemingly dazed.

"Bye, Garrett," Kat says. "Thank you so much for what you did for Kevin. It sure worked out well for me."

Garrett shifts his weight.

"Well," I say, "I guess I'd better tell my buddy we're on our way—he's waiting for us at the gala. Excuse me." I pull out my phone and text Henn: "I bagged the babe. She said YES. Fuck yeah! Exit The Asshole's system now."

"Congratulations!" Henn writes back. "I'll leave without a trace."

I look up at Garrett. "Okay, my buddy says he's gonna quit working now." I look at Maggie. "A mutual friend of ours from school. Great guy. A computer specialist. He says he's leaving work right now to meet us at the gala."

There's a very awkward silence. Clearly, Maggie doesn't know why the fuck I'm telling her this bit of information.

"Okay," she says awkwardly.

"Well, we've definitely taken up enough of your time," I say, grabbing Kat's hand and pulling her toward the limo. "Come on, Whitney—time to party, honey." I kiss Kat's cheek. "Have I ever told you you're really *fun*?"

Kat giggles. "Yes, you have."

"Well, you are. And as far as I'm concerned, that's one of the greatest qualities any man could ever ask for in a wife."

Chapter 39
Kat

I lean back from the table as our private butler clears our plates from dinner and then disappears through French doors leading back into our suite.

"Are you chilly?" Josh asks. He stands, obviously intending to remove his tuxedo jacket for me.

"No. I'm good. It's still pretty nice out. Great idea to eat out here on the patio."

"I wanted to take full advantage of the view in the moonlight."

I look out at the dark Pacific Ocean glimmering in the moonlight beyond the cliffs. "Yeah, this view is absolutely spectacular."

"I was talking about you."

"Aw." I bat my eyelashes. "Sweet-talker."

"You really are gorgeous, Kat. You take my breath away."

"I guess complete happiness looks good on me, huh?"

"You sure you're not cold?" Josh asks. "It's getting a bit chilly out here. I don't want you to catch cold."

"I'm fine. The kumquat must be some kind of internal furnace— I'm never cold these days." I look down at the sparkling rock on my finger and the convertible Porsche on my wrist and touch the beachside condo around my neck. "Plus, it's amazing how lots and lots of ice keeps a girl toasty warm," I add.

Josh laughs.

The butler approaches the table. "Are we ready for dessert?" he asks.

"Yes, that'd be great," Josh says. "Just bring us a sampling of your best stuff. And I'll have some Sambuca, too."

"Very good, sir. Madame?"

I touch my belly. "No Sambuca for me. Just a decaffeinated cappuccino would be great."

"Very good," the butler says, and leaves.

"This is so fun," I say, giggling. "I guarantee you, if Sarah were here, she'd be calling that poor guy Jeeves all night long."

Josh smiles. "And singing that Iggy Azalea song."

I sing the chorus from "Fancy."

"Yep. That's the one," Josh says. "I'll send Jonas the info about this hotel so he can bring Sarah here for a weekend of relaxation."

"Awesome. Maybe the four of us could come here together—a last hurrah before the baby comes?"

"Sure, but only if we get separate suites. No more listening to each other having sex through paper-thin walls ever again, thank you very much."

"Babe, this suite is massive—bigger than my parents' entire house. I'm pretty sure we could share it with Jonas and Sarah and not hear each other having sex."

Josh shakes his head. "Not if you're gonna scream the way you did in Caracas. Jesus, woman, that was the shriek heard 'round the world—or at least throughout South America." He snickers.

I smile. "Yeah, that was a good one."

"Good times," Josh agrees. "I'm getting hard just remembering it. Do you see what you do to me? I can't get enough of you."

"Well, that's good, because you're stuck with me now." I hold up my hand with my engagement ring on it. "No refunds or exchanges."

Josh laughs.

I look at my ring for a long moment, dazzled. "How the heck did this happen? I'm not trying to talk you out of the whole will-you-marry-me-thing, believe me, but what the fuckity happened to the guy who not too long ago didn't even mention he was moving to Seattle?"

Josh shrugs. "It's not a *thinking* thing—it's a *feeling* thing. You're The One and I know it and nothing will ever change that fact as long as I draw breath into this body."

I swoon.

Josh leans forward. "But enough talking about our fucking feelings. Let's talk about the wedding. You wanna marry me before or after Gracie makes her screaming entrance?"

"Oh, before, definitely," I say. "I wanna be Mrs. Faraday when I check into that hospital. Is that okay with you?"

"Whatever you say, hot momma. I'd marry you tomorrow."

I know Josh is saying that as a figure of speech, but, for a brief moment, I actually consider marrying Josh tomorrow down at City Hall and calling it a day. "No, tomorrow's no good," I finally conclude, scrunching up my face. "I want to wear a pretty white dress and I definitely want my entire family there. And not just my parents and brothers—the whole Morgan-enchilada. I've got a pretty big extended family—I should warn you—lots of aunts and uncles and cousins—and some of them pretty effing crazy—and I'd want them all there. Fasten your seatbelt."

Josh purses his lips, thinking. "Hmm. Well, if we're aiming to do this before Gracie arrives, we'd better not wait too long. We definitely don't want you going into labor while we're saying our vows. That would totally fuck everything up for me."

"Fuck everything up for *you*?" I say, laughing.

"Yeah, it'd fuck up my dream wedding." He shoots me a snarky smile. "I've been dreaming of my perfect wedding since I was a little boy."

I burst out laughing and we giggle together for a long time.

"Okay, let's get serious for a second, Party Girl," Josh says. "If we're gonna do this wedding thing before Gracie comes, we really don't have that much time to pull our shit together." He looks up, apparently calculating something. "I'm thinking we've got, what, three months tops before we're potentially butting up against your water possibly breaking as you say 'I do'?"

"Yeah. Sounds about right. Actually, I'd rather we aim for two months, just to be on the safe side. I'd like to have a little extra time after the wedding to relax before the kumquat shows up and fucks everything up."

"Okay. Two months. How many people are we talking about here? I've probably got, oh, I dunno, twenty people I genuinely care about being there? Give 'em all a plus-one and let's say forty."

"For me it's about fifty people, plus give everyone a guest. So a hundred?"

"Okay, so we're talking a hundred-fifty people max, right? Sixty days from now?"

I shrug. "When you say it like that, it sounds impossible."

He waves me off. "Bah. Totally doable."

"You think?"

"Oh, yeah. Easy peasy. You forget—I've got T-Rod in my back

pocket. She can hire a wedding planner and throw gobs of money at the whole thing and it'll happen like magic. No worries. Will you still be allowed to travel in eight weeks?"

"Yeah, I've got twelve weeks—I'm supposed to stay put beginning at thirty-two weeks."

"Okay, perfect. Why don't we do a destination wedding in eight weeks? Plus a two-week honeymoon after that? Then we'll come home and hunker down and get ready for the arrival of Mademoiselle Terrorist."

My heart skips a beat. "A destination wedding? Where?"

"I dunno. A medieval castle in France? A vineyard in Tuscany? The beach in Bora Bora? Bali? Fiji? You pick."

"Oh my God, Josh. Slow down."

"Why? Any of those would be a blast."

I place my hand on my racing heart. "I'm overwhelmed. Gimme a minute."

"Please don't barf, Kat. I love you, I really do, but I'm not sure my love can withstand watching you barf more than once a day."

I squint at him. "Don't tempt me."

He laughs.

"But, seriously, I might hurl if you keep talking about flying a hundred-fifty people to France or Bora Bora in eight weeks. I'm sorry to be Debbie Downer here, but some of my peeps probably don't even have passports. Not everyone is used to gallivanting all over the world on a moment's notice to party with Gabrielle LeMonde's daughter."

He rolls his eyes.

"And, even if my peeps have passports, they wouldn't be able to afford taking off work and getting themselves to France or Bora Bora just to watch me get married."

Josh waves his hand dismissively. "Babe, *duh*. Whatever we do, I'll pick up the tab for everyone, all expenses paid. We'll fly them to wherever and show 'em a great time. We'll take over some resort for an entire week."

"Are you serious?"

"Of course."

"Holy shitballs, I'm crapping my pants," I say. I put my hand on my heart again. "You would do that?"

"Kat, it's our *wedding*. I'm only doing this once. YOLO, baby. Go big or go home. Work hard, play hard. We can sleep when we're dead." He grins. "I'm sure there's another spiffy little catch-phrase that would be even more *apropos* than all those, but you get the gist."

"My family's gonna lose their freaking minds."

"Good. Shit-stained pants and psychotic breaks are what we're going for here."

"But I still think something international is too ambitious," I say. "Just too many logistics. Plus, from here on out, I wanna stay in the U.S. 'til after Gracie's born—just in case she decides to make an early appearance."

"Yeah, probably a good idea. I didn't think about that. Hmm. Well, that really limits our choices for the 'destination' part of our 'destination wedding,' doesn't it?" He pouts.

"Sorry to rain on your parade, Groomzilla." I assess Josh's beautiful, pouting face for a moment. "You know what? Let's just do it in Seattle, babe. It'd be so much easier for everyone."

Josh looks aghast. "Seattle? Fuck no. Jonas just did that. I'm *Josh*. I gotta show that bastard up. Plus, it's my duty to show everyone the Playboy Razzle-Dazzle."

I roll my eyes. "Okay, so how about here in Del Mar, then?" I say. "This resort's spectacular."

"Yeah, we could do that." He shrugs. "Or maybe Hawaii?"

My eyes light up.

"Oh, I see that little gleam in your eye, PG. The idea of Hawaii floats your boat, huh?" He snickers. "You dreaming of doing a little wedding-night hula-dance on my face?"

"Yes, Josh. That's precisely what I was thinking just now."

He laughs.

"Really, we should just do Seattle, babe," I say. "It'll be easier. I have a huge extended family—lots and lots of batshit-crazy aunts and uncles and cousins. Plus, my mom and dad have longtime friends who are like family to me, and I really want them there—"

"Babe, we're not going for easy here—we're going for *awesome*. Case closed. Decision made. I saw the look in your eye when I said Hawaii, and I'm in the fantasy-fulfillment business, remember? Hawaii it is."

I open my mouth to protest.

"It's settled. It's an easy five-hour flight from the west coast; it's still the U.S. but it feels like a faraway tropical paradise; and you said your family's never been. Just give me your list and we'll make it happen. Easy peasy."

I pause. "Seriously?"

"Yeah."

"And you really think we can pull this off just eight weeks from now?"

"Of course. This is exactly why I pay T-Rod an ungodly amount of money. I get the crazy ideas and she makes 'em happen. She'll find us a venue—you really can't go wrong anywhere in Hawaii, so we'll let her pick which island and resort depending on availability. And if we have to do it mid-week or something to book a good place on such short notice, we'll do it. Bada-bing-bada-boom."

I squeal. "Okay. If you really think we can pull it off. Wow. That's exciting. Done." I clap my hands together.

"Shit, that was easy," Josh says. "That was like planning a wedding with a dude."

"I told you right from the start—I'm an honorary dude."

Josh snorts. "Yeah, yet another big ol' steaming pile of bullshit brought to you by Katherine Ulla Morgan." He snorts again. "You *said* that, but it didn't turn out to be *quite* as true as the brochure promised."

I want to be pissed, but it's impossible. I laugh heartily.

"So you got any must-haves?" Josh asks. "Speak now or forever hold your peace. Time's already tickin'."

I think for a minute. "Well, I definitely wanna wear a pretty white dress. I don't care if I'm pregnant, I'm still your virgin-bride, right?"

"Absolutely. I've never fucked you as Mrs. Faraday before. That's virgin enough for me."

"And I want my family and best friends there, of course." I twist my mouth, considering. "If we're doing this in Hawaii, then I'd like to get married on a beach at sunset, right on the sand. And I don't wanna wear shoes. I think it'd be hilarious if I were barefoot and pregnant."

Josh laughs. "Awesome."

"You like that idea?" I ask.

"Of course. I love it. Why wouldn't I?"

"Because if we're gonna do a beach-on-the-sand-thing, you can't really wear one of your fancy suits."

"Whoa, whoa, whoa. Them's fighting words, babe. Why the fuck not? I'm wearing a tux to my wedding, no matter where it is. If it's on the beach, I won't wear shoes—but I'm wearing a goddamned tuxedo to my own wedding. I'm the *groom*."

I giggle. "Sorry, Playboy. Momentary insanity on my part."

"Jesus," Josh says, mock-glaring at me. "Don't even joke about me not getting my dream wedding."

I laugh.

"We gotta look like the bride and groom on top of a wedding cake."

I laugh again. "Wow, you've actually thought about this, haven't you?"

"Hey, I know," Josh says, his eyes lighting up. "Why don't we have everyone go barefoot? The theme can be black-tie barefoot-and-pregnant."

"Dude, you should be a party planner. It's brillz."

"Yeah, I'm liking this," Josh says, his eyes sparkling. "What else, Party Girl?"

"I'd like to have a kick-ass band at the reception. Dancing is definitely one of my bridezilla demands."

"I'll put Reed in charge of getting us a kick-ass band. He'll get someone awesome for us, I'm sure."

My heart is beginning to race with excitement. "Oh, and a fully-stocked, open bar all night long so everyone but me can get shit-faced drunk."

Josh rolls his eyes. "You really feel the need to say that explicitly to me? Do you also feel the need to tell me you want *food* at our wedding? How about toilet paper in the bathroom?"

I get up from my chair and fling myself onto Josh's lap. "Thank you so much. This is the best day of my life."

"From this day forward, my goal is to make you say that every day of your life."

I kiss him. "Thank you. This is amazing."

"Hang on," Josh says, pulling out his phone. "Lemme shoot T-Rod a quick text. If I tell her the gist tonight, by tomorrow she'll have a list of potential venues for us, I guarantee it. And then you can work with her and whatever wedding planners she hires to get everything exactly the way you want it."

I purse my lips. "It's funny," I say. "After all the wedding planning I helped Sarah with, I really don't have any thumping desire to do it all again, even if it's for me this time. I think I just wanna show up, basically."

"Hey, maybe you are a dude, after all," Josh says. He pokes his fingertip into my crotch. "Are you sure you don't have a dick and balls under there?"

"Nope. Definitely a vagina and uterus." I pat my belly.

"Okay, I'll tell Theresa to talk to you about basic vision and whatever's on your wish list and she'll take it from there. Sound good? We'll both show up and look fucking gorgeous and enjoy whatever treats Theresa's lined up for us."

"That sounds really nice."

"It does, doesn't it? That's how I run pretty much my whole life—I just show up looking fucking gorgeous and enjoy the treats."

I nuzzle my nose into his. "You do that really well, Playboy." I kiss Josh's soft lips and I'm instantly aroused. "You know," I purr. "I thanked you for my diamond necklace and bracelet, but I never thanked you for my beautiful ring."

"Oh," Josh says, raising an eyebrow. "Well, shit, we'd better remedy that situation right away."

"Here we are," the butler says, out of nowhere, making us both flinch. He lays down a platter of desserts on the table.

"Change of plans," Josh says abruptly. "Sorry, Jeeves. We've decided we'd prefer privacy for the rest of the night."

"Yes, sir."

"Just bring the desserts inside. I'm sure we'll nibble them later."

"Yes, sir."

The butler picks up the platter of scrumptious looking desserts and quickly disappears into the suite.

The moment we hear the front door open and close, Josh smirks wickedly. "Guess what, my lovely fiancée?"

"What?"

He reaches into his pocket and tosses a poker chip onto the table. "It's time for your bachelorette party."

Chapter 40
Kat

I'm sitting on the edge of the bed in our hotel bedroom, completely naked except for the startling array of diamonds decorating me, while Josh stands before me, still fully dressed in his immaculate tuxedo, looking like Richard Gere *wishes* he looked in *Pretty Woman.* Holy hell, he's an utterly gorgeous man.

"It turns me on seeing you naked and dripping in diamonds," Josh says, reaching out to caress one of my erect nipples. "Now I wanna see you naked and dripping down your thighs."

"I'm already well on my way," I manage to say. But I can barely speak. I've suddenly got the delicious idea that Josh's reference to my "bachelorette party" means I'm about to behold the sexiest man alive re-enacting *Magic Mike* just for me, and I can barely keep it together at the mere thought.

Josh heads over to his laptop and "Kiss Me" by Lil Wayne begins playing.

Immediately, I giggle with nostalgia. This is the song Josh taunted me with (and brought me to orgasm with) on the dance floor during our first night out together in Las Vegas. "A walk down memory lane," I say. "God, that feels like a lifetime ago."

Josh grins mischievously. "That night was when I first realized you're not like anyone else."

I smile from ear to ear. "Are you gonna dance for me the way you did on the dance floor that night—only this time with a lot less clothes on, hopefully?"

"Ssh. No questions. That poker chip gets me *my* fantasy, not yours."

I giggle. "Sure, Playboy. This whole day has been about *your* fantasies."

303

"It has been." He looks me up and down lasciviously and bites his lip. "And if it hasn't been, then it sure as fuck is now. Hot damn, woman, you're giving me a raging boner. Look at you. *Fuck*, you're hot."

I flash him a naughty smile. "Well, send that raging boner my way—I know just what to do with it."

"That's not how this bachelorette party works."

"No?"

"Nope." He trails his fingertip over my necklace. "If you want a show, you gotta earn it. Touch yourself for me—turn yourself on. The more turned-on you get, the more articles of clothing come off. Reach orgasm, and you'll get the fully monty."

"Oh," I say. "So you're a *Magic Mike* wind-up doll, powered by sexual arousal—like how in *Monster's, Inc.* they powered the city with little-kid-screams?"

"Exactly." He bends down like he's gonna kiss me, but instead, he gently licks the cleft in my chin. "Guys in strip clubs work for dollar bills—the Playboy works for orgasms."

I giggle.

"Now come on. No more chitty-chat. It's time to play my game." Josh squares himself in front of me and lowers his chin. "Power me up, baby."

"Yes, sir," I purr. I reach between my legs, my eyes fixed on his gorgeous face.

"Other hand," he commands. "I wanna see my rock sparkling between your legs."

Wordlessly, I switch hands, never looking away from his smoldering eyes.

A few moments later, a soft moan escapes my mouth that seems to flip the "on" switch on my *Magic Mike* wind-up doll. Josh begins swiveling his hips and singing along to the song, his eyes instantly on fire.

"Oh," I say. "Work it, baby. You're so sexy, you should be illegal," I purr.

Damn, this boy can *move.*

Another moan involuntarily escapes my mouth, and, in response, Josh removes his jacket with a sexy flourish.

"Oh yeah, take it off," I growl.

I let out a long, loud moan and Josh immediately begins unbuttoning his shirt, revealing taut muscles, sexy tattoos, and sexy nipples standing on end.

"Oh, Jesus," I say. "You're so freaking hot, babe."

Josh peels off his shirt and throws it across the room, his body gyrating, his eyes devouring me. "Kiss me," Josh sings along to the song, a devilish gleam in his eyes. "Kiss me."

"Oh my God," I sputter. "Come here and kiss me. I can't stand it."

"Make yourself come first."

"Get the hell over here and kiss me," I coo, "and I guarantee I will."

Much to my happy surprise, Josh complies with my request, gyrating his body an inch away from my face to the bass-heavy beat of the music.

Like a woman possessed, I pull him into my face and devour his abs with my lips and tongue, my fingers fumbling frantically with his belt and zipper. Oh God, I'm hyperventilating with desire. He's truly the sexiest man alive, especially when he dances.

When I've loosened Josh's belt and pants, I yank his pants down, desperate for him—and I'm met with the unexpected sight of his huge bulge straining behind briefs emblazoned with... a large Batman logo right on his bull's-eye.

"Holy... *Batman*, Batman!" I breathe.

Josh laughs. "A little present for you, baby," he says. "Happy Bachelorette Party, Party Girl." He leaps back and does a sexy little dance for me, rocking his hips, flexing every muscle on his body, kissing his own biceps—and when I shudder with a little orgasm, he attacks me, sliding his fingers into my wetness and his mouth on my breast.

I stroke the outside of his briefs, grasping frantically at his Batman-bulge—my body boiling over with desire. "Holy Fuck Me Now, Batman," I breathe, pulling down his briefs and letting his hard-on spring out. "Holy I'm Gonna Get Fucked by Batman, Batman. Holy Batman's Got a Donkey-Dick, Batman. Holy... Fuck..."

"Okay, you can stop now," he whispers.

He slides his briefs completely off and hurls them across the room and I lick the side of his enormous shaft like it's a melting popsicle on a sunny day, and then greedily take his glistening mushroom-tip into my mouth like it's liquid chocolate.

When Josh's balls begin rippling against my palm, ramping up for ejaculation, he pulls his donkey-dick out of my mouth, turns me around, bends me forcefully over the edge of the bed, and shocks the living hell out of me by slapping my ass *hard.*

I gasp, paralyzed with shock. Not What I Was Expecting at This Particular Moment, Batman. For the love of all things holy, I'm sitting here covered in sparkling diamonds. The man has asked me to be his *bride.* I'm gonna be this man's beloved *wife*—the saintly mother of his *child*—which is currently growing inside me as surely as Jesus grew inside the Madonna—*and he just spanked the motherfucking shit out of me like a two-dollar whore?*

But Josh is in the zone, apparently bound and determined to show his fiancée just how much he owns her. He spanks me again—this time even harder—and every nerve ending in my body explodes with sudden, outrageous pleasure.

Josh blasts me one more time and I'm gone, hurtling into an orgasm that sends me reeling with vision-blurring pleasure. When my orgasm finishes, Josh grabs my hair, pulls my head back roughly, and enters my wetness powerfully, like a wild stallion mounting a defenseless mare in a freaking pasture. Holy shitballs, he's claiming me as his property—there's no doubt about it. *And I love it.*

Oh, God, yes. This is good. How the hell does this man always know the shortcut into my deepest desires? *Yes, yes, yes.* Before Josh, the men I've been with have treated me with kid gloves—like a very pretty and fragile trophy—and I guess I thought once Josh asked me to be his wife, he'd fuck me differently somehow—with some sort of newfound reverence and awe. But I should have known better. Josh always knows what's gonna get me off hardest at any given moment—and right now is no exception.

Oh, God, *yes.* Delicious. The diamonds around my neck are slapping my skin with each pounding thrust of Josh's muscled body into mine. I reach down and fondle his balls behind me—God, I love the sensation of those suckers slapping my ass as he fucks the crap out of me.

I slowly move my fingertips from Josh's balls to the place where his hard donkey-dick is pounding into me, and my body shudders with indescribable pleasure. This man is all mine. *Forever.*

"I wanna call you Mrs. Faraday," Josh growls out. "I'm gonna make you my *wife*."

I shriek as another orgasm powers through me, twisting my insides violently.

At the sound of my orgasm, Josh pulls out of me, bends down behind me, and begins eating me through the back door, lapping at me, sucking me, gnawing on me—all the while fingering-fucking me, too—and my body responds with complete and utter rapture. Where the fuck did this man learn the stuff he does to me? It's like he's some sort of sexual Jedi. Oh, Holy... Oh, shit. I'm on the cusp of truly losing my mind.

A strangled cry lurches out of my throat. Oh my God.

Josh shifts his fingers inside me and begins flicking at me in a way he's never done before, and it's more than I can bear. I'm seeing pink. Then yellow. Oh, shit.

He does it again and then again—and it's like he's turned a key to a secret room inside me. My skin pricks with goose bumps. My toes curl. I feel like I'm being jolted with an electric current.

Josh flicks inside me again on that same weird spot and, all of a sudden, I feel my entire body unlock for him in a whole new way—a dam bursting inside me—and not figuratively. A shocking torrent of warm fluid absolutely gushes out of me, more than ever before... and pours right into Josh's waiting mouth.

"Oh my God," I sputter, my entire body warping and flailing.

Josh laps at me feverishly for several more minutes, cleaning me like he's licking icing off a cupcake, and finally turns my limp body over onto my back on the bed, slides his massive dick inside me, and thrusts powerfully into me again from this new position. His mouth lands on mine. His warm skin brushes against my breasts and baby bump. Oh God, I'm absolutely enraptured.

This man is my master. I'm his slave—and not as part of a freakin' role-play. I genuinely have no free will left. I'm his to command—mind, body and soul.

"I'm gonna make you my wife," Josh growls into my ear. "I'm gonna give you my name." He kisses me passionately.

"Yes," I choke out.

Josh grips my face, covering me in kisses. His lips find my ear. "Don't leave me, Kat," he says, his muscled body moving against mine, his voice tight. "I need you. Don't leave me."

I grab his muscled ass, urging him to burrow into me even more deeply. "I'll never leave you. I love you. *Forever.*"

He comes inside me, quite forcefully, growling and shuddering as he does—and when he's done, he grabs my face again, his eyes blazing with an intensity I've never seen from him before. "I can't live without you. I can't breathe without you, can't smile or laugh." He doesn't even sound like himself. "I love you. Oh, God, baby, I love you so much, it hurts. I've never risked this much before—I'm risking *everything.* Please, God, don't leave me, Kat. It would destroy me." He clutches me to him fiercely, his chest rising and falling violently, his breathing ragged, his skin drenched in sweat. "I've never loved like this, Kat. *Please.*" His words are tumbling out. He's trembling. He buries his nose into my neck and I stroke his hair, soothing him. "Please, Kat," he chokes out. "Don't leave me. I couldn't overcome it."

"It's okay, baby," I say calmly, stroking his hair. "I'll never leave you. *Never.*" I rub his back, coaxing him to calmness. "You're okay, baby. Ssh. We're gonna be happy, honey. We're gonna have a beautiful family, you and me and a pretty baby makes three. And whenever you don't know what to do, it'll be okay because I'll teach you."

He's shaking. "I love you, Kat."

"I love you, too, baby. Don't you worry about a thing. We're gonna be happy forever and ever. You'll see. We're gonna be a family—a *happy* family. It's gonna be better than your wildest dreams. I promise."

He's calm now. His breathing is regular. He's stopped shaking.

"Okay?" I ask.

He nods into the crook of my neck. "Okay."

I kiss his cheek and continue stroking his back. "I love you, honey. I'm not going anywhere, I promise. If you fuck up, so what? I'll be patient. And when I'm insane, you'll be patient with me. And if you don't know what to do, then I'll teach you. No big whoop. Okay?"

"Okay."

I kiss his cheek again. "I'm gonna love you and take care of you forever, baby. You'll see. You won't need to overcome a goddamned thing. Those days are over, baby. I got you. I promise."

Chapter 41
Josh

"Hey, Uncle William, will you tie Henn's bowtie?" I ask. "I'd do it, but I'm so nervous my fingers won't function."

Uncle William laughs. "Sure thing. Come here, Peter."

"If this bowtie were a motherboard," Henn says, "I swear it'd be my bitch."

"It's hard to tie a bowtie," Uncle William reassures Henn. "Much harder than it looks."

"See, Reed?" Henn says. "It's not me that's the problem—it's the bowtie."

Reed laughs. "Keep telling yourself that, man."

"All the chairs are filled," Jonas murmurs quietly. He's peeking out a crack in the bungalow door toward the beach. "Everyone looks really excited."

"Gah. Don't tell me that," I say. "I'm nervous enough already."

"What do you have to be nervous about, Faraday?" Reed asks. "You're marrying the greatest girl, ever."

"Which is exactly why I'm nervous. I don't wanna fuck this up for her. Hey, Jonas," I call to him at the door. "Were you nervous right before you went out to marry Sarah?"

Jonas shuts the door. "Oh, yeah, I was shitting." He glides toward the group, absently twirling his wedding ring around his finger. "I wasn't nervous about getting married—I was just freaking out I was gonna fuck up my vows."

"*Exactly*," I say. "What if I spontaneously start spewing gibberish up there? Or pass out? Or, worst-case scenario, what if I spontaneously shart in front of everyone?"

Everyone bursts out laughing, except Uncle William.

"What's *sharting*?" Uncle William asks.

"When you think you're gonna fart, but you unexpectedly shit instead," Henn explains.

Uncle William laughs and shakes his head. "*Joshua.*"

"Well, let's look at this logically," Reed says. "When was the last time you sharted?"

"Hmm," I say. "Maybe when I was ten?"

"Okay, then, realistically, the odds are extremely low it will happen within the next thirty minutes for the first time in twenty years," Reed says.

"God willing," I say.

"Unless, of course, it's been so long, you're now statistically *overdue*," Henn says.

"Not helpful, Henn," I say. "In what universe would you ever think that's a helpful thing to say?"

"Sorry."

Jonas puts his hand on my shoulder. "Josh, you got this. If *I* can say my vows without sharting, then you most certainly can." He flashes me a warm smile and I'm struck, as I often am these days, by how genuinely happy my brother seems.

"You know what, Jonas?" I say. "You should wear black-tie more often, bro—it suits you. You've got this Thor-meets-James-Bond thing going on."

Jonas scoffs. "I feel more like I've got an Idiot-Brother-meets-Dancing-Monkey-thing going on."

"All done," Uncle William says, patting Henn on his shoulder. He turns Henn to face me. "Acceptable, Joshua?"

"Suave perfection," I say. "You're Cary-Grant-meets-Steve-Jobs, Henn."

Reed sidles up to me with a bottle of Patron. "A little something to calm the jitters, Faraday?"

"Just a little sip," I say, grabbing the bottle. "Any more than that and I might spontaneously shart from being too relaxed." I take a quick sip and then pass the bottle around.

"Pretty good," Uncle William says when the bottle makes its way to him. "But at the reception, we're all drinking my Scotch."

"Did you bring the good stuff?" I ask.

"Of course. I brought several different bottles to be shared at the party, plus I've got bottles of some forty-year-old stuff for each of you boys to take home."

"Bottles of what now?" Henn asks, his face perking up.

"Scotch," I answer. "From my uncle's private stash. Whatever it is, it'll change your life, I guarantee it."

"Well, don't mind if I do," Henn says. "Thanks, Uncs." He pats my Uncle on the back.

Uncle William laughs. "You're very welcome, Peter. Do you boys know anything about Scotch?" he asks, and when Henn and Reed both admit they're fairly clueless, my uncle proceeds to school both of them on the topic.

"Hey, Jonas?" I say. "Can I talk to you for a second?"

We move to the corner of the bungalow.

"You okay?" Jonas asks.

I nod. "Just a lot more nervous than I expected to be." I shake out my arms. "It's taken me a lifetime to get here. I don't wanna fuck it up."

Jonas looks at me sympathetically. "Just take a deep breath. It'll be over soon."

"No, not the ceremony. The *marriage*. I don't wanna fuck it up."

"You won't. You never fuck anything up."

I scoff. "We both know that's a load of complete bullshit. Got any advice for me?"

"Just imagine everyone naked," Jonas says. "Except Sarah. Definitely don't picture Sarah naked or I'll have to punch you in your pretty face."

"No, don't give me advice about saying my vows—gimme your best advice for a happy marriage. You're the happiest married guy I know."

Jonas shrugs. "Well, I haven't been married all that long—but, yeah, I guess I already know the secret. Put her happiness ahead of your own every single day and it'll come back to you ten-fold."

"You sound like a fortune cookie."

He laughs. "Yeah, just add 'in bed' to anything I say."

"Thank you, Jonas," I say. "That's exactly what I'll do. I'll worship her every fucking day."

"In bed," Jonas says. Emotion washes over his face and he hugs me. "I'm so happy for you, Josh. You've been my rock my whole life, and I don't know what I would have done—"

"Whoa, whoa, whoa," I say, pushing him away. "Bro, we just did this exact thing mere *months* ago at your wedding. Do we really need to talk about our fucking feelings *again* so fucking soon?"

Jonas laughs. "But, Josh—talking lets the feelings out."

We both laugh.

"Honestly," I say, "I love you, bro, I really do, but I don't have a pressing need to articulate every warm and gooey feeling I have about you more than, say, once a year?"

"Fine by me," Jonas says, shrugging. "Once a year sounds good. And, by the way, I love you, too."

"Gah. Stop. What'd I just say? Once a year, bro. How 'bout we do it on our birthday?"

"Great. I'll mark it on my calendar: 'Remember to tell Josh I love him today and that he's the best brother a guy could ever hope for.'"

"I think you just did an end-run around that one-year thing," I say.

Jonas winks. "I'm smart like that. Remember? I'm the smart one, and you're the good-looking one."

"No, I don't think that's how things got divvied up. You're the smart one *and* good-looking one, Jonas. I'm the *charming* one."

"And we're both the *happy* ones," Jonas says.

We share a huge smile.

"Did you ever think life would turn out like this for us?" Jonas asks, shaking his head.

I join him in shaking my head. "Never. Like, literally, *never.* Things weren't looking too good for the Faraday brothers for a while, but we've pulled victory out of the jaws of defeat, haven't we?"

"Definitely."

The wedding planner pokes her head into the bungalow. "We're ready for you gentlemen now. Time to take your positions on the beach." She looks at her watch. "We have to time this with the sunset, so you've got to be in position in five."

"Thanks," I say to her.

Jonas and I hug.

"Congratulations, Josh," he says.

"Couldn't have done it without you, bro—you showed me how to do it."

Jonas flashes a huge smile.

"Thank you, Jonas."

Jonas nods. "My pleasure."

I take a deep breath and turn toward the rest of the guys. "Ready, men?"

Everyone says they're ready and raring to go.

"Reed, hand me that tequila one more time."

Reed hands me the bottle of Patron and I take another huge swig—and everyone does the same thing right after me.

I put my hand on Jonas' shoulder. "Hey, bro, you got a Plato quote for me to think about when I'm up there, just in case I suddenly feel like I'm gonna spontaneously shart?"

"Of course. 'Courage is knowing what *not* to fear.' And the one thing *never* to fear is spontaneous sharting."

Everyone laughs.

"Perfect. Thank you. You're a beast of a best-man, Jonas Faraday." I take a deep breath. "Now let's get out there and get me a smokin' hot wife, shall we?"

Everyone expresses enthusiastic agreement with that plan of action.

"Wife on three," I say, putting my hand into the huddle.

Everyone covers my hand with theirs. "One, two, three. *Wife!*" we all shout together, and then throw our hands up.

"I love you, Josh," Jonas says, slapping me on the back.

"No. Stop it."

"I love you, too, Joshy," Henn says, laying his cheek on my shoulder and side-hugging me.

"Me, too," Reed says, laying his cheek on my other shoulder.

"So do I," Uncle William says, patting my cheek.

"Look what you started, motherfucker," I say to Jonas. I shake Reed and Henn off me and they laugh hysterically. "I love you all, too. You're the best guys I know and I'd be lost without each and every one of you. Now, come on, guys. Quit making me say all this shit. I swear to God if I shart up there, I'm blaming all of you."

Everyone laughs and high-fives and passes the tequila around one final time.

"All right. Enough fucking around. My fantasy-girl awaits. Let's get out there and bag me a goddamned gorgeous wife."

Chapter 42
Josh

The girl walking toward me on her father's arm is literally the most spectacularly beautiful creature I've ever laid eyes on in my entire life, without exception. She's the precise sum of parts I'd order at the Build-a-Wife store if there were such a thing. Her dress is simple and white—the bottom half of the dress cascading over her round belly and floating like a soft cloud down to the sand.

She's glowing from the inside-out, shining brighter than any diamond—which maybe explains why, despite all the ice I've recently showered her with, she's opted to wear only two items of jewelry for her once-in-a-lifetime walk down the aisle: the ring I slipped onto her finger when I asked her to be my wife and the fucking amazing tear-drop sapphire-and-diamond earrings Uncle William gifted her from his late wife's jaw-dropping collection. "Something old and something blue," Uncle William said to Kat when he gave them to her last week. "But definitely *not* something borrowed—they're all yours, sweetheart. Welcome to the Faraday family."

She's gliding down the aisle with her father, floating like a glorious feather, smiling at people in the audience, and beaming at her father.

And then she locks eyes with me—and every bit of nerves I've been feeling vanishes. Why? Because my future wife is looking at me the exact way Sarah did when she walked down the aisle toward Jonas—the exact way I've longed for someone to look at me my whole fucking life, not even realizing it's what I yearned for most.

Thomas and Kat reach me on the sand, and after kissing Kat's cheek, Thomas gently guides his daughter toward me.

"Make her happy," Thomas whispers to me, shaking my hand.

"Forever," I murmur, taking Kat's slender hand.

I kiss Kat's cheek and whisper to her: "I'm the luckiest man alive."

"I love you," she replies.

"I love you, too."

The officiant—a large Hawaiian guy in a white linen suit, sunglasses, and a lei—welcomes everyone and leads us through our very simple marriage ceremony. Or, at least, that's what I presume he's doing—I'm only half-listening. Because, seriously, what mortal man could possibly concentrate on what a Hawaiian dude in a white suit is saying while looking straight into the face of God's most heavenly creation?

"And now, Josh and Kat have prepared vows for each other," the officiant prompts—grabbing my full attention. "Kat?"

Kat takes a deep breath and squeezes my hand. "Josh," she begins. "*Joshua*. You once asked me if I believe in fate—and I said, no, that I believe in kicking ass."

I laugh and so does everyone in the audience.

"But now I know I was wrong about that. You're my fate, my love—my destiny. I truly believe that every minute of my life up 'til now was engineered by a greater power to bring me to this moment— to *you*—so that I could become your devoted wife." She smiles and her eyes twinkle. "One of the things I love about you most is how you take care of everyone you love. As your wife, I vow to be the one who takes care of *you*, Josh. I promise to love you forever, always making sure your needs and greatest desires are satisfied beyond your wildest dreams. Every single day, I vow to make sure you wake up thinking, 'Damn, I'm a lucky bastard,' and every single night fall asleep thinking, 'I can't wait for tomorrow.'"

We share a huge smile.

"I'll love you forever, Joshua William Faraday," Kat continues. "I promise to love and honor you in good times and in bad, in sickness and in health, all the days of my life and never, ever leave your side as long as I'm drawing breath into my body."

"I love you," I whisper to her. "Thank you."

"I love you forever and ever, my love," Kat whispers. "I promise."

Kat looks at the officiant, signaling she's all done speaking.

Lauren Rowe

"Josh?" the officiant prompts.

Those nerves I felt before the ceremony slam into me again. I take a deep breath and take Kat's beautiful face in my palms. "My beloved Kat." I take another deep breath. "Good God, you're *evil*."

She laughs in obvious surprise.

I take her hands in mine. "And not just evil. Stubborn as hell, too." I flash her a huge smile. "But you're also hilarious. Compassionate. Honest. *Passionate*. Baby, you're hell on wheels. And, most of all, you're loving and kind and beautiful." I stroke her golden hair. "*And I love it all—every single thing about you.*"

The bottoms of her eyes fill with tears.

"When I first laid eyes on you at Jonas' house, you waltzed into the living room and marched straight up to me like I'd ordered you out of a catalog—and right then, I knew I was totally screwed."

Kat laughs along with everyone else.

"But a man has never been so happy or *lucky* to be totally screwed in the history of time."

Kat's face contorts with pure joy.

I take a deep breath. "Katherine Ulla Morgan, you've single-handedly taught me how to love—how to be a man in every sense of the word. You're the answer to a prayer I didn't even know I had. And I vow to you, in front of God and all these witnesses, to cherish you every single day—all parts of you, even the heinously diabolical parts—*especially* the heinously diabolical parts—to make your happiness my mission in this life. If someone hurts you, I'll kick their ass, baby. If you're sad, then I'll make you laugh—unless, of course (for some reason only women can possibly understand), you don't *want* to laugh, in which case I'll simply hold you and let you cry on my shoulder."

She sniffles and laughs.

"Kat, I vow to love you and take care of you and our precious baby." I touch her belly gently. "*All* our babies, in fact, because now that I've become a part of your awesome family, I'm hoping God will gift us with an entire minivan full of them."

Kat's eyes pop out of her head and plop into the sand.

Oh, shit. I don't know where that came from. I haven't mentioned my recently discovered desire for a big family to Kat before this moment. Perhaps during our wedding ceremony wasn't the optimal time for me to lay that idea on her for the first time? Oh, well, fuck it. I am what I am.

I clear my throat and barrel ahead.

"And, most of all, my beloved Kat, I vow to you, right here and now, in front of God and all the people we love, which includes Keane, by the way, just to be clear—"

Every Morgan in attendance bursts out laughing along with Kat and me.

When the Morgans have finally quieted down, I continue speaking again, holding her hands in mine. "Like I was saying, I solemnly vow to you, in front of God and all the people we love, that when I'm eighty, I won't have a baby with a trampy twenty-six-year-old gold digger, even though she'll be at optimal child-bearing age."

Kat hoots with laughter and so do I—and so does everyone watching us, even though, surely, no one but Kat and me fully understands the joke.

I cup Kat's jawline in my palm. "YOLO, Kat," I whisper. "Damn, I'm a lucky bastard that I get to live my one and only life with you." I touch the cleft in her chin. "I. Will. Always. Love. You." I reach into my pocket, pull out a poker chip, and covertly place it into Kat's palm. "I promise to make every day of our life together better than any fantasy, baby. *Forever.*"

Chapter 43
Josh

"When Josh asked me to be his best man," Jonas says, speaking into the microphone in his hand, "the first thing I thought was, 'Oh, shit.'"

Everyone seated in the reception room laughs.

"Because I immediately realized I'd have to give this fucking speech—excuse my language—and anyone who knows me will tell you I absolutely *hate* giving speeches, almost as much as I hate hip-hop and One Direction and talking about my fucking feelings—excuse my language again." He grins at Sarah and she beams an adorable smile at him. "*So* I'm gonna try to keep this short and sweet." Jonas raises his champagne flute and everyone follows suit. "Aristotle says love is composed of a single soul inhabiting two bodies. Well, Josh and Kat, when I look at you two together, and the way you fit together like two halves of a divinely designed puzzle, I know in my bones Aristotle's words remain true to this very day. My wish for you both is that you find eternal light outside the cave together. Welcome to the Faraday family, Kat—and thank you for taking my constantly *emoting* brother off my hands." Jonas raises his glass. "To Josh and Kat. Hear, hear."

"Hear, hear," everyone says, taking a sip of champagne.

"Damn, we Faradays rock," Kat whispers into my ear.

Jonas lurches over to Kat and me and hugs us fervently, and then hands the microphone to his adorable wife.

"Kitty Kat," Sarah begins, smiling. "My best friend and now my *sister*—oh, I just gave myself goose bumps saying that." She giggles and everyone joins her. "Anyone can see how beautiful you are on the outside—it's actually quite unfair how truly gorgeous you are, Kat—

but the amazing thing about you, the unexpected thing, is that you're as beautiful on the *inside*, too." Sarah's voice wobbles. "Most people can only dream of having a best friend like you, Kitty Kat—and I'm the lucky bitch who actually does."

Everyone in the reception room laughs.

"I love you so much, Kat," Sarah says.

"I love you, too," Kat mouths, her hand on her heart.

Sarah looks at me, seated next to Kat at the end of our table. "Joshy Woshy. You're quite a beast of a man, you know that?"

Everyone in the reception chuckles and cheers in agreement with that statement.

"Josh, I marvel at your sheer amazingness every day," Sarah continues. "I'm so lucky to be your sister. Thank you for embracing me as part of your family. I love you with all my heart."

"I love you, too," I mouth.

"And to Josh and Kat together—the Playboy and The Party Girl with a Hyphen—the unstoppable duo. The poet Kahlil Gibran said, 'Marriage is the golden ring in a chain whose beginning is a glance and whose ending is Eternity.' It's been thrilling to watch your first glance at Jonas' house turn into the beautiful eternity of today."

Kat rests her cheek on my shoulder and I squeeze her hand.

"But I'd be lying if I didn't admit you two scare the bajeezus out of me," Sarah continues, and everyone in the room chuckles. "Seriously, every time I'm in an enclosed space with you two, I find myself immediately scanning for emergency exits and fire extinguishers."

Everyone laughs again.

Sarah raises her glass. "To Josh and Kat. May you always inspire everyone around you to scan for emergency exits and fire extinguishers. Hear, hear."

"Aw," Kat says next to me, raising her sparkling apple cider.

"Hear, hear," everyone in the room says.

I get up and kiss Sarah's cheek and take the microphone from her.

"Thank you, Sarah. Thank you, Jonas. We love you guys so much. We Faradays are pretty effing cool, I gotta say." I turn toward the smiling faces in the room. "I want to thank you all for joining us, not just for today's celebration, but for this whole past week in paradise. I know you all have busy lives so we thank you for taking so much time to celebrate and party with us this whole week. It's been incredible, hasn't it?"

Everyone claps and cheers.

I glance at Kat and the sight of her makes me completely forget what I was about to say. "Hello, Mrs. Faraday," I say softly, not into the microphone.

Kat blushes. "Hello, Mr. Faraday."

We stare at each other for a beat.

"Better give your speech, honey," she prompts. "People are waiting."

I chuckle and put the microphone to my lips again. "Thank you, dear."

Everyone laughs.

"First off, I'd like to say my first ever toast to Mrs. Katherine Faraday. You rock my world, baby. My greatest joy in this life is the honor and privilege of calling you my wife."

Kat blushes and bats her eyelashes.

"To you, babe. The Party Girl with the Heart of Gold."

Everyone in the room toasts and drinks.

"Oh!" Kat suddenly blurts, her hand on her belly. "Wowza. That was a biggie!"

I lurch toward Kat and she grabs my hand and places it on the side of her belly, and, instantly, I feel someone throwing an upper cut against my hand.

"Whoa!" I shout. This isn't the first time I'm feeling my baby kick, of course—I finally managed to give Little G her first-ever high-five a few weeks ago—but this is by far the strongest movement I've felt. "So cool," I say when Gracie punches me forcefully again. I give Gracie a high-five with my fingertip and she kicks the crap out of my finger, right on cue. I put the microphone to my mouth again. "Sorry about that, folks. Gracie wanted to join the toast to her mommy, I guess. I think she's inside her mommy's belly shouting, 'Hear, hear!'"

Kat pulls the microphone in my hand to her mouth. "We're starting her young," she says, and everyone laughs. Kat hands the microphone back to me. "Come on, babe. These people wanna dance. Wrap it up." She makes a swirling motion with her index finger.

"Okay, just a few more words," I say. "The missus says I gotta wrap it up. I'd like to say a special thanks to my great friend Reed for that incredible surprise earlier. Wasn't that amazing?"

Everyone claps and cheers wildly.

"When Reed asked me what song Kat and I wanted for our first dance, I thought he was gonna arrange for the cover band to play it for us. I truly had no idea he was gonna fly James Bay to Maui." I laugh heartily, thinking about how shocked Kat and I were when James Bay himself waltzed into our reception hall two hours ago and started serenading us on acoustic guitar. I raise my champagne flute to Reed. "Thank you, bro. We'll never forget that moment as long as we live."

Reed points his glass at me and winks.

I guide Kat out of her chair, snake my arm around her ever-growing waist, and pull her to me as I address the room again. "And one last thing. With my beautiful wife by my side, I wanna say a few words of thanks to my new family, The Morgans. There's been a lot of talk about Kat becoming a Faraday today, but, trust me, I got the better end of the bargain. You know that expression 'The apple doesn't fall far from the tree'? Well, that's especially true when it comes to Kat." I raise my glass to Kat's immediate family at their nearby table, and they all return the gesture. "To Tom Tom Club, Momma Lou, Cheese, Captain, Peen, and Baby Brother—and all the Morgans I've met this past week, too—" I raise my glass to the various Morgans seated at tables in the large room. "Thank you for your part in making Kat the incredible woman she is today and for letting me be part of your hilarious and fucking awesome family. Hear, hear."

"Hear, hear," everyone in the room says in unison.

Kat throws her arms around my neck and squeezes me tightly.

"You wanna say a few words?" I whisper to her.

Kat shakes her head. "Hell no. I just wanna *dance*."

"So, okay," I say into the microphone as Kat squeezes the life out of me. "Mrs. Faraday says enough talking about our fucking feelings—it's time to *dance*."

Chapter 44
Josh

"Fucking motherfucker!" Kat shrieks, squeezing my hand. "Jesus Christ Superstar!"

I lean into Kat's sweaty face. "Do your breathing, babe. Breathe in through your nose and out through your mouth."

"Fuck that shit. *You* breathe in through your nose and out your mouth, motherfucker—I want a fucking epidural!"

"Babe, you heard the doctor—everything happened way too fast for an epidural. We missed the window. Just *breathe*. Like this." I lean into Kat's face and model the breathing we learned at our getting-ready-for-childbirth class at the hospital.

Kat's eyes turn unequivocally homicidal. "If you breathe like that again, I swear I'll cut off your balls and make s'mores out of 'em," she growls.

I bite my lip and cease all breathing.

The monitor attached to Kat tells me she's in the throes of another huge contraction.

"Push now, Kat," the doctor says. "Right now."

"I can't."

"Sure you can," I say. "You're a beast—you can do anything."

"Just gimme a second—fuck!" She lets out a blood-curdling scream. "Motherfucker!"

I look at the doctor, my heart racing. "Is something wrong?"

"Nothing's wrong," the doctor says. "Kat's just *expressing* herself. Isn't that right, Kat?"

Kat whimpers. "December second's not for eleven more days—I needed more time to mentally prepare to do this."

"Sorry, Kat. She's decided to come today," the doctor says. "In about three minutes, I'd estimate."

"But she wasn't supposed to be a *Scorpio,*" Kat whines. "She's supposed to be a *Sagittarius.*" She lets out a truly pathetic sound. "Please, God, I'll be good and nice from here on out. I'll never lose my temper. I'll be patient. *Saintly.* Just, please, don't give me a goddamned fucking female *Scorpio.*" She grips my hand fiercely. "Babe, listen to me. Tell them to stuff her back in for another twenty-four hours. *Please.* Tomorrow, she'll be a sweet little Sagittarius. Please. *Pay them, Josh.* Make them listen."

The monitor hooked up to Kat indicates another huge contraction is hitting her—which is something I'd have surmised without the monitor, based on the string of expletives suddenly spewing from her mouth.

"Push now," the doctor says. "Push with the contraction, Kat. You can do it."

Kat bears down and pushes, as instructed, growling and whimpering as she does.

When the contraction is over, I lean into Kat's sweaty face. "Good job, baby. You're doing great."

"Okay, Kat," Dr. Gupta says. "Two more big pushes and the baby will be out."

"I can't," Kat says, her tone pathetic.

I touch Kat's beautiful, sweaty face. "You can do this, babe." I squeeze her hand. "We're so close."

"What do you mean 'we'? Are you gonna do this? Are you gonna pass a fucking bowling ball?"

"Push now, Kat," the doctor instructs. "*Right now.*"

Kat takes a huge breath and bears down, her face turning bright red.

"Good. That's good," Dr. Gupta says. "You're doing great, Kat. Okay. Rest for a moment and then we'll do it one more time."

Kat grips my hand. She's shaking violently. "I'm done," she says meekly. "I can't do any more. Knock me out, Doc. Stuff her back up inside me and cut her out. I don't care. Do whatever you have to do. I quit."

I stroke Kat's beautiful cheek. "You don't know the meaning of the word 'quit.'"

"Yes, I do," Kat whimpers. "I'm not a beast—I want my mommy." She bursts into tears.

"Your mommy's coming as fast as she can. Everyone's on their way, baby. It just happened too fast for them to get here in time."

"I've change my mind. I don't want a baby, after all. Stuff her back in!" she cries. "Make her go away!"

I laugh, even though I shouldn't.

"Here we go," Dr. Gupta says calmly, looking at the monitor next to Kat. "You're gonna push with this next contraction, Kat—one more big push and this baby will be out and you'll be a mommy. Come on."

Kat whimpers pathetically again.

I squeeze Kat's hand. "Come on, baby. Dig deep."

"*You* dig deep, motherfucker," she says, making me chuckle, but, immediately, she bears down, as instructed, grunting loudly with her effort, and not more than twenty seconds later, a tiny, pink angel pops out from between my wife's legs, shrieking like I just woke her up from an afternoon nap in front of the TV by shouting "Boo!"

And, just like that, my heart is no longer inside my body.

My cheeks are absolutely soaking wet.

And I'm exactly the man—the husband and father—I was always meant to be.

Chapter 45
Josh

"Babe! Get in here!" Kat shrieks. "They just introduced him!"

I throw on a pair of briefs, race out of the bathroom still wet from my shower, and leap onto the bed next to Kat, careful not to crush Gracie's blonde head as she sleeps at Kat's breast.

"There he is!" Kat shrieks, pointing with excitement at the TV.

I look at the television screen and, I'll be damned, yep, there he is: Will "2Real" Riley, holding a microphone and launching into a beastly performance of his monster hip-hop hit, "Crash" on *Saturday Night Live*. "Oh my God!" Kat shrieks. "Look at him! He's *killing* it!"

"I feel electrified just *watching* him," I say. "I can't imagine how he must feel."

"Did you know Will was *this* amazing?"

"I had no idea," I say. "He was so funny and chill when we hung out with him. Who knew?"

"I guess we were hanging out with *Will*, not '*2Real*,' huh?" Kat says.

"Indubitably," I say.

We sit and watch Will's entire performance, completely mesmerized, and when it's over, we cheer and clap like we're sitting in the live audience.

I grab my phone off the nightstand and quickly shoot a text to Reed. "Just watched your boy on SNL," I write. "HE KILLED IT. Tell him congrats from Mr. and Mrs. Faraday and Little G." I put my phone back on the nightstand. "Jesus, between 2Real and Red Card Riot this past year, Reed's absolutely slaying it."

"God, I sure hope his streak continues into next year when Daxy's album comes out," Kat says.

"Reed sure thinks it will. He told me just the other day he smells a smash hit."

"Which song?"

"Reed predicts 'People Like You and Me' will be the break-out first single."

"That's my favorite, too," Kat says.

Out of nowhere, Gracie busts out with an ear-piercing wail.

"Oh my goodness, little lady," Kat says, opening a flap on her nursing nightgown and pulling out her engorged boob. "No need to scream, for crying out loud. I'm right here." She sticks Gracie on her nipple and Gracie immediately latches on and starts gulping down milk in hungry swallows. "Wowza, can this kid eat," Kat says, looking down at Gracie's little face.

I lay my palm on the top of Gracie's soft head as she suckles and stroke her white-blonde peach fuzz. "She's passionate about eating, that's for sure," I say softly. "Aren't you, my little angel?"

Kat rolls her eyes. "Don't kid yourself by calling her an angel. We both know she's a demon spawn *disguised* as an angel."

"No. She's just *passionate*, like I say—she simply knows what she wants. Nothing wrong with that." I continue gently stroking Gracie's soft head. "Isn't that right, Mademoiselle Terrorist? You're just *assertive,* that's all."

Kat looks down at Gracie's face as she nurses. "Mark my words, she's a wolf in sheep's clothing, I'm telling you, babe. She's gonna be bossing you around in no time."

"Good. I've always liked 'em sassy," I say. "Don't worry, I know just how to handle her."

We share a smile.

"So what do you wanna do for your birthday in a couple weeks, honey?" Kat asks. "After three months of being marooned in Babyville, are you in the mood to break out of our baby-bondage and paint the town red?"

I lean down and nuzzle my nose into Gracie's soft hair for a long moment, breathing in her scent. "Not really," I say softly. "I'm happy to stay home this year. Why don't we do the romantic-dinner-thing I'd originally planned for the night you poker-chipped me with Bridgette?"

"You sure? Thirty-one's a biggie."

I chuckle. "Thirty-one is meaningless."

"Bite your tongue. You didn't think you'd make it to thirty, remember? And now you're gonna be thirty-*one*. That's a big deal."

I make a face like maybe she's got a point.

"You sure you don't wanna get freaky-deaky and do something really wild and crazy to celebrate your unexpected old age?"

I touch Gracie's hand as she continues to eat and she curls her little fingers around my index finger. "No. I had a huge party for my thirtieth. Jay-Z played, actually."

"Oh, well that wasn't excessive or anything."

"So this year I'm ready to have a quiet celebration, just my wife, my baby, and me—a romantic dinner for two-and-a-half—followed by you and me getting freaky-deaky on the carpet in the nursery again after Little G falls asleep." I wink. "I really like the way that carpet feels on my balls."

Without warning, Gracie pulls sharply away from Kat's breast, milk dripping down her chin, and glares at me like she understood every word of what I just said.

We both burst out laughing at the hilariously pissed expression on Gracie's face—and the sound of our laughter makes Gracie break into gurgling peals of adorable laughter, too.

"Take a video of her giggling, babe," Kat says. "Oh my God. She's hilarious!"

I grab my phone and take the video, followed by a whole bunch of photos of Kat and Gracie together. But after a moment, Gracie begins fussing so Kat tries to get her to feed off her other boob.

"Aw, come on, Gracie-cakes," Kat says. "Don't you want my other boob? You're gonna leave me lopsided, baby."

Gracie breaks into a pterodactyl scream.

"What the heck?" Kat says. "She gets riled up so freaking fast, I swear to God."

"Gee," I say. "I wonder where she gets *that*?"

"Definitely not from me," Kat sniffs—and much to my surprise, she sounds completely serious. But before I can reply to her and tell her she's a delusional loon, my phone buzzes with an incoming call from Reed.

"Oh, it's Reed—I wanna take this." I leap out of bed and sprint out of the bedroom, far away from Gracie's loud shrieks, to take the call.

"Tell him congrats from me!" Kat calls to my back.

"Reed!" I shout into the phone. "Congrats, man! Your boy *killed* it!"

"Oh my God. Didn't he? He hit a fucking homerun, man."

"A grand slam in the bottom of the ninth," I say. "We were screaming at the TV like we were right there in the audience. Was he loving it?"

"Yeah, afterwards, for sure. But beforehand, he was so nervous, he puked into a trashcan. Oh my God—you should have seen him, worse than you were right before your wedding." He laughs. "This is the first major performance Will's given since the whole Carmen thing. She's normally the one who calms him down when he gets really amped."

"What 'whole Carmen thing'?"

"Oh, shit. I didn't tell you? Oh. Yeah. They broke up."

"Oh, really? Aw, she seemed like a sweetheart."

"She is—a total sweetheart. You know how it goes. He's twenty-four. He fucked it up. It's to be expected under normal circumstances, but he's also adjusting to the whole fame thing, you know—women throwing themselves at him wherever he goes. Pretty tall order not to fuck up at least once."

"Too bad."

"Believe me, he regrets it."

"So when are you gonna be on the West Coast, bro?" I ask. "You gotta swing by and see Little G. She's gotten so big since you saw her."

"Not for a while, man. I'm hopping a flight to Thailand first thing in the morning with Will. We recorded a song with this Thai hip-hop group, and—"

"A *Thai* hip-hop group?" I interject. "I didn't realize there was such a thing."

"Yeah. *Thai*me's Up. They're huge in Thailand."

I laugh. "Are you serious?"

"Yeah, they're massive and so is American hip-hop—this song's gonna make me a fucking mint, mark my words. So, anyway, we're shooting the music video with the Thai boys in Phuket for a week and then we're doing a promotional appearance the following week at a nightclub in Bangkok."

"Ah, Bangkok," I say, chuckling. "The scene of the original crime."

"Ah, yes. I remember it well. If you weren't such an old man these days, I'd have invited you to join me for a little walk down memory lane."

"Oh, fuck. No thanks. I'm too old and too happy to do any of that shit now. Almost killed me at eighteen—God only knows what that shit would do to me at thirty-one."

"Oh, yeah. Happy almost-birthday, old man."

"Thanks. So what dates are you gonna be in Bangkok?"

He tells me.

"I think Jonas and Sarah are actually gonna be there during those dates," I say.

"Really? No way."

"Yeah. Jonas is taking the missus climbing in Mae Do for four days—poor, poor Sarah—and then I'm pretty sure he said they're gonna hit Bangkok for a few days after that."

"Well, if the timing works out, tell 'em to come to the promotional thing at the nightclub. I'll put 'em on the VIP list. Will and the Thai boys are gonna perform their new song, plus they'll all do 'Crash' together. The crowd's gonna go apeshit—'Crash' is number one in Thailand right now."

"Where *isn't* 'Crash' number one?"

"In countries filled with stupid people."

I laugh. "Yeah, put Jonas and Sarah on your VIP list, for sure. Sarah loves hip-hop. She'll freak out."

"Okay, cool. I'll text you the details when I have 'em. You can forward the info to your brother."

"Awesome. Thanks. Just be warned, though, Jonas might try to break your pretty face for torturing him—as much as Sarah loves hip-hop, Jonas absolutely abhors it. Plus, Jonas hates nightclubs—so he'll be extra grouchy for you."

"Eh, I'll be okay. If Jonas tries to attack me, I'll sic Barry on him."

"Oh, Barry will be there? Say hi to him for me. I love that guy."

"Will do. So, hey, I gotta go—we're at the after-party with the *SNL* cast—I just stepped outside for a smoke."

"You're already partying? Will just performed a few minutes ago."

"Three-hour-tape-delay for the West Coast, numnuts."

"Oh, yeah. Duh. Well, have fun, man—enjoy every minute of

your success. You deserve it. You're totally winning at The Game of Life, man. It's awesome to watch."

"Hey, that's the idea, man—as you well know. Win, win, win, as much as humanly possible—and then die taking none of it with you. Speaking of winning at The Game of Life, say hi to Stubborn Kat for me and tell Little G her Über-Cool Uncle Reed loves her like crazy."

"I will. Text me the info about Bangkok when you have it."

"Sure thing. Bye, bro. Enjoy changing shitty diapers. Peace."

I hang up my phone and walk back into my bedroom—and I'm met with Arma-fucking-geddon currently in progress: Mademoiselle Terrorist is wailing her head off and Kat is leaping desperately around the room like a kangaroo, bouncing Gracie up and down frantically, obviously trying her mighty best (and failing miserably) to quiet our mini-beast. When Kat sees me, she flashes me a look of such desperation, I almost laugh out loud.

"I don't know what's pissing her off so much," Kat whimpers. "I've tried everything."

"Give her to me, babe." I hold out my arms. "I'll hit her with the Playboy Razzle-Dazzle."

"It won't work," Kat whines. "I fed her. I changed her. I burped her. I sang to her. She just cries and cries and *cries*. Oh my *God*."

"Give her to me, babe. She likes the smell of my skin." I take Gracie's writhing, shrieking body from Kat and hold her against my bare chest—and not four seconds later, Gracie's head does three complete revolutions on her neck and she pukes breast milk all over me.

"Gah!" I shout.

"Whoa, that's a lot of puke," Kat says, laughing.

I look down at my puked-covered chest, grimacing. "Fuck."

"Poor baby worked herself up into a puking frenzy," Kat says.

"Gee, I wonder where she gets that?" I ask.

Kat laughs. "Give her to me so you can shower, babe." She puts out her arms.

"No, just grab me a towel. I'll shower after I get her calmed down."

"Nothing will calm her down, like I said," Kat says, throwing me a burping towel. "I've tried everything, trust me."

"Not everything—you haven't *playboyed* her." I gently wipe the puke off Gracie's chin, right off the little cleft I love so much, and then off the "G-R-A" in my "GRACE" tattoo, and bring Gracie to the makeshift diaper-changing table on top of our dresser. I gently lay Gracie down on her back, stroking her screaming face with my fingertip. "I'm sure my baby just needs a fresh diaper, that's all," I say soothingly.

"No, I just changed it," Kat says. "It's something else."

"Is your diaper bothering you, little one?" I coo to Gracie, ignoring Kat's skepticism. I lean over Gracie's face, shooting her my most serene and soothing smile—and, instantly, Gracie stops crying on a dime, even before I've opened her diaper, and stares at my face, completely transfixed.

"That's right, my little Scorpio," I soothe. "Look into my eyes. That's it, baby girl."

Gracie reaches up and touches my nose and I kiss her little fingertips, eliciting dove-like coos from her.

"No freaking way," Kat says. "I tried *everything*—and one smile from her handsome daddy and she's blissfully happy?"

I touch the teeny-tiny indentation on Gracie's chin and stroke the soft, blonde peach fuzz on top of her head. "She's just a daddy's girl, that's all," I say softly, my voice low and calm. "Isn't that right, Little G?" Gracie gurgles at me and pulls on the scruff on my chin and I rub my nose against hers. "My baby girl just needed a little Playboy Razzle-Dazzle, that's all," I say quietly. "Isn't that right, angel?" I shoot a snarky look at Kat. "It's the same tactic I use to soothe another Scorpio I know when she goes off the rails and starts acting like a demon spawn."

I smile, expecting Kat to shoot me a snarky expression to match my own, but she doesn't. To the contrary, she's looking at me the same way she did when she walked down the aisle toward me on our wedding day—like I'm the answer to her most fervent prayer.

"I love you," Kat says softly, her eyes wide and sparkling.

"And I love you," I say. I begin changing my serene daughter's diaper. "I love you forever and ever and ever, Mrs. Faraday."

Kat's face melts.

"I tell you what, Party Girl," I say. "How about you get yourself into a nice, hot tub in the bathroom while I rock our little terrorist to sleep, and then I'll join you in the bath and let you wash the baby-puke off me?"

"Oh," Kat says. "That sounds lovely." Without hesitation, she pulls her nightgown over her head and throws it onto the bed, revealing her new, sexy curves and dark, erect nipples. "Maybe while we're in the tub together, I'll imagine I'm a mermaid who's recently sprouted legs—and maybe if you're *really* sweet to me, I'll let you teach me what my newfangled *vagina* is for."

I laugh. "So, we're gonna do a porno version of *The Little Mermaid*?"

Kat giggles and winks. "See you soon, Prince Eric. Don't keep me waiting too long." She honks her delectable boobs and sashays into our bathroom, singing "Part of Your World" at the top of her lungs, her ass cheeks swishing to and fro as she moves.

I look down at Gracie. "Damn, you're mommy's sexy," I say. "And very, very silly, too."

I scoop Gracie off the dresser, change her into her Hello Kitty footy-pajamas, and bring her over to the rocking chair that's now a permanent fixture in the far corner of our large bedroom. After settling into the chair with Gracie in my arms, I rock her slowly, looking deeply into her big, blue eyes—the beautiful blue eyes that make me want to be a better man—and I begin to sing my favorite lullaby to her: "You Are My Sunshine."

"You are my sunshine," I sing softly, rocking rhythmically in my chair, staring into my daughter's ocean-blue eyes—and, as always happens in moments like this, I begin thinking about Gracie's namesake, the supernaturally beautiful woman who long ago sang this same, simple song of love to me.

When I reach the end of the song, Gracie's still staring at me with wide eyes, so I sing it again from the top, rocking my sweet little baby slowly, calmly, breathing deeply as I do—until, finally, Gracie's lovely eyelids flutter and shut.

"Gracie Louise Faraday," I whisper softly when my song is over and her breathing has turned deep and rhythmic. "I love you, Little G." I close my eyes, sending a little prayer to heaven to the other Grace Faraday, the one surely watching over us at this very moment. "I love you, Mom," I whisper.

Gracie's rosebud lips part and hang open in complete relaxation. Her body's a tiny sack of potatoes in my arms. I get up from the glider and carefully lay her down on the center of our large bed, and then I head toward my bathroom, my cock tingling with anticipation.

I enter the bathroom and there she is—my beautiful mermaid, soaking in a hot tub, her skin pink, her eyes closed.

"Hey, Ariel," I say softly. "Our little fishy's out like a light."

Kat opens her eyes and smiles. "Thank you, Baby Whisperer. Now take off those briefs and get your YOLO'd ass in here."

I do as I'm told, of course—and, as I'm lowering myself into the warm water, Kat points at my crotch with cartoon-like, wide eyes.

"What's *that*?" Kat asks.

I look down at my naked body. "What?"

"*That*." She points right at my hard dick. "That ding-a-ling thing."

"Oh *that*?" I smile from ear to ear. "It's my *thingamabob*."

Kat giggles. "You've seen *The Little Mermaid*?"

"I told you I was a very nice boy." I stroke her smooth thighs under the warm water.

"You *were* a very nice boy?"

"That's right. Past tense. I'm a very *bad* boy now—a *beast* with a raging boner."

"Ooh, that gives me a faboosh idea," Kat says. "How about you and me do a porno version of *Beauty and the Beast* tomorrow night?"

I chuckle. "So we're gonna do the entire Disney catalog, huh?"

Kat giggles. "Why not? I'd love to see how you'd pull off *Snow White and the Seven Dwarfs*."

"Pfft. Child's play," I say, running my palms over her curves under the warm water. "Six dildos and an apple. Easy peasy."

Kat laughs.

"Okay, Little Mermaid," I say. "We've got probably three hours 'til our little fishy wakes up, screaming and demanding to be fed—so let's use our free time wisely, shall we?"

"Yes, sir." Kat grabs my dick and strokes it with authority. "Let *The Little Mermaid* mini-porno begin."

"You know what?" I say, licking my hungry lips. "I've suddenly got an inexplicable craving for sushi."

I begin lowering my face into the water, but Kat grips my hair, stopping my movement.

"Ariel is mute when she's human remember?" she says. "Her voice is trapped in that necklace thing. So let me say this now: I had a really great time tonight, my love. I love you so much—and, oh, you fucked me brilliantly."

"I love you, too," I say. "Now quit your yapping, Ariel. It's time for me to show you what that *whatzit* between your legs can do."

Epilogue
Josh

I pull my brand new, cherry-red Ferrari FF into my driveway and sit for a moment, singing along to the song blaring through my speakers. It's my current theme song: "All I Do Is Win" by DJ Khaled. When the fucking awesome song finishes, I kill the engine of my fucking awesome car and lovingly caress my steering wheel.

"I love you, baby," I say softly to my beautiful car—my thirty-first birthday present to myself. It's just a little something to celebrate how fucking hard I'm *winning* at The Game of Fucking Life. God-*damn*, I'm a fucking beast. All I do is win, win, win, baby. Fuck yeah, I do. No matter what. Because I'm a *winner*. Truth.

I run my hands tenderly over my steering wheel again, exhaling with near-sexual pleasure as I do. God-*damn*, this is a beautiful fucking car. I get a hard-on every time I get behind the wheel. Fuck yeah, I do. I've got a beautiful fucking Ferrari to match my beautiful fucking Ferrari of a wife and my sweet little baby girl and fucking awesome house ten minutes away from my fucking awesome brother.

And not only that, Climb and Conquer is absolutely slaying it these days—we've already shattered our mid-year revenue projections and we're planning major expansion in seven more markets later this year—plus, our designated charities are all flourishing, too. As it turns out, Jonas' entire business model was pure fucking genius. Surprise, surprise.

And, on top of all *that*, when I got home from work last night, I'd no sooner taken two steps through my front door than my beautiful sick fuck of a wife silently greeted me at the door by unzipping my pants, kneeling before me, and sucking my big ol' dick 'til I exploded into her waiting mouth. God-*damn*, I'm crushing life. Winner, winner, chicken fucking dinner, baby. Boo-fucking-yah.

I pull my phone out of my glove box and quickly scan my texts, and, as expected, there's a message from good ol' fucking awesome and reliable T-Rod, confirming everything's set for my romantic-stay-at-home birthday dinner with my two favorite blondes. "Everyone's already at your house, setting up," Theresa writes. "Chef, waiter, violin, cello. Oh, and I added a viola just for yucks. Have fun, Birthday Boy!"

I shoot off a quick reply. "Thanks a million, T. Just got home. Gonna be a great night."

I tilt my rearview mirror toward my face and survey my reflection. Handsome motherfucker. Lucky bastard. *Winner*. I run my hand through my hair, carefully smoothing a stray, and straighten the knot on my Roberto Cavalli necktie.

I pick up the bouquet of gardenias and the velvet jewelry box sitting on the passenger seat of my fucking awesome car—what better way to celebrate my birthday than giving my wife more ice for her ever-growing collection?—and then I bound happily toward the front door of my fucking awesome house, clicking the heels of my Stefano Bemer shoes, singing the DJ Khaled song under my breath as I go.

But when I get inside my house, it's perfectly quiet. No hustle-bustle; no signs of preparations for a birthday dinner; no wife dropping to her knees as she greets me in the doorway.

I peek into the kitchen. No chef. I check the dining area. No violinist, cellist or viola-ist. (What the fuck do you call someone who plays a viola?)

"Kat?" I call.

But my smokin' hot wife is nowhere to be found.

I head into the nursery and, lo and behold, there's my mother-in-law, sitting in a glider with Gracie, quietly reading her a book about farm animals.

Louise looks up from the book in her hands and her face lights up. "Happy birthday!" she says. "Look, Gracie. Daddy-the-birthday-boy is here!" Louise gets up from the glider, toting Gracie in her arms.

"Hi, Gramma Lou," I say, kissing Louise on her cheek. "Where's my wife?"

"Oh, she went out," Louise says.

"What? We were supposed to have a romantic dinner-for-two-and-a-half here at the house. I had everything all set up."

"Yes. And, I must say, everything you arranged looked *very* romantic, indeed—absolutely stunning. The chef was a real sweetheart, too. He took it *very* well when Kat sent him and the musicians to Colby's house, instead." Louise leans in like she's telling me a secret. "Colby's got a hot date with his physical therapist tonight, so I'm sure he'll greatly appreciate everything you had planned."

I stare at Louise dumbly. "Kat sent everyone *away*?"

"Mmm hmm. She left a note explaining the new plan. It's in the kitchen. I've got a few birthday presents waiting for you in there, too. Come on." She hands Gracie to me and the three of us make our way into the kitchen. When we arrive, Louise hands me a rectangular box off the counter, wrapped in bright yellow paper and a bow.

"Thank you," I say. I hand her Gracie and unwrap the box to find a genuine treasure awaiting me. "Wow. 'Barrique de Ponciano de Parfidio,'" I say, reading the label on the elegant—and rare—bottle of tequila. "Lou, this stuff is *really* hard to come by—a total collector's item. How on earth did you get it?"

She shrugs. "Oh, just a little something called the Interwebs."

"Thank you so much. I've tasted this stuff once before a long time ago and it was fantastic. Thank you." I kiss her on the cheek, and as I do, Gracie reaches for the scruff on my chin so I take her back from Louise.

"It's from the whole family—the boys, too—we all chipped in. Even Keane."

"Even Keane?" I ask, laughing.

"Even Keane. So that tells you where you rank in this family's pecking order. Pretty darned high."

"Wow, I'm totally honored. I'll call everyone and thank them tomorrow—but will you tell them I got it and loved it?"

"I sure will. Ryan said you better save him a couple shots of that stuff, by the way, or he'll never forgive you."

"That goes without saying—not just for Ry, for everyone. Maybe we can do a foosball-tournament-tequila-tasting-dinner later this week?"

"Great. It'll be your belated birthday party. What would you like me to make?"

"Oh, everything you make is great."

"It's your birthday, honey. Pick what you want."

"Spaghetti, then," I say definitively. "My favorite."

Louise smiles. "You got it. Plus extras for the birthday boy."

"Hot damn. You know I love my extras."

Louise giggles and hands me another box. "This one is from Ryan, specifically."

I open the box and it's a crystal shot glass, etched with the name "Lambo."

"Ry got himself one engraved with 'Captain' so you two can sit out on the patio like lovebirds, watch the sunset together, and drink your new tequila." She rolls her eyes. "Ryan's truly talented at giving gifts to others which actually turn out to be gifts to himself, isn't he?" She grabs a gift bag off the counter. "And this one is from me. Just a little trinket."

"This is all too much, Lou," I say. "Really."

"Oh, no. This is just a little nothing. Hardly anything at all. I saw it and thought of you."

Gracie bats me in the face so I shift her in my arms and pull out the contents of the gift bag. A lump rises in my throat at the sight of my gift—a coffee mug, emblazoned with the phrase, "World's Greatest Son-in-Law."

"Thank you," I say, hugging Louise with my free arm.

"Whenever you have a cup of coffee, you'll be reminded how much you're loved, honey."

I bite my lip. "Thank you."

Louise waves her hand. "You're impossible to buy presents for, you know that, Josh? What do you get the guy who has everything?"

I motion to everything I just opened. "All this."

"We all just wanted you to know how much you're loved, that's all."

"Thank you. I feel it. I love all of you, too."

Louise wipes her eyes. "So, enough of that. You never intended to spend your birthday hanging out with your boring mother-in-law. Gimme that baby." She grabs Gracie from me and hands me an envelope off the counter. "Here you go. Kat asked me to deliver this to you exactly at six."

I look at the clock on the kitchen wall. Six on the button.

I open the sealed envelope and immediately smile from ear to ear. There's a poker chip inside—and a typewritten note: "Happy Birthday, my darling, beloved Playboy with a Heart of Gold!" the note reads. "Sorry-not-sorry, but our romantic dinner-for-two-and-a-half has been cancelled and donated to a very good cause (namely, getting Colby laid by the hot physical therapist he's been drooling over for the past two months). The Playboy and The Party Girl with a Hyphen can't stay home like old farts on the Playboy's thirty-fucking-first birthday! Hell no, old man! We can sleep when we're dead! Go big or go home! YOLO! It's time to party like it's 1999! (Well, until about midnight, that is, since that's when Gracie's been waking up lately for a feeding.) So get into your fancy new Ferrari and get your YOLO'd ass to this address, PB." It's an address in nearby Kent. "Because, Playboy, I feel the need—the need for speed! XOXOXOXOX Mrs. Katherine Ulla Faraday. P.S. I've always wanted to fuck the winner of the Indy 500!"

I look up from reading the note, my cheeks hot, my dick tingling.

"Well?" Louise asks. "Good news?"

"Great news." I pull my phone out of my pocket and Google the address on the note and quickly discover it's a professional-grade racetrack about forty minutes outside of Seattle, exactly as I figured. "*Fantastic* news," I say. I kiss Louise and Gracie on their cheeks and gather my car keys off the counter. "Thanks for watching Gracie. We'll be home around midnight, if not before."

"Don't rush home. Kat pumped before she left—we've got plenty of milk to tide us over."

"Thank you so much." I kiss Gracie again. "Bye, Little G. I love you, honey."

"Guh," Gracie says.

I sprint toward the exit of the kitchen.

"Hey, wait, honey," Louise calls to my back. "Aren't you hungry? Maybe you should take a little something to nibble on?"

"Good point." I say. Quickly, I make a couple orgasm-inducing peanut butter and jelly sandwiches—one for me and one for my wife—and throw them into a bag with some apples and chips and bottles of water. "A meal fit for a king and queen," I say. I wink at Louise. "Thanks again for watching Little G."

"Have fun, honey," Louise calls to my back.

"Oh, I will," I yell back.

I race outside, hop into my fucking awesome new car, and peel out of the driveway of my fucking awesome house, my dick throbbing, my heart racing, my skin buzzing; and, once I'm driving smoothly on the highway, I press the button to call Kat through my wireless connection.

"Hey, Playboy," Kat purrs into the phone. "Did you get my note?"

"I sure did," I say. "I'm on my way."

"Are you mad about dinner being cancelled?"

"Hell no. This is a much better offer. YOLO, right, babe?"

"Words to live by."

"Especially for a guy who happens to have 'em stamped on his ass."

"Amen." Kat laughs. "Drive safe, my love. I can't wait to celebrate your birthday in a manner befitting the one and only Playboy with the Heart of Gold. I've got a whole bunch of surprises waiting for you." She snickers. "I sure hope you're well rested."

"Thanks, baby. You're the best. I think you might know me better than I know myself sometimes."

"*Might*? *Sometimes*? Of course, I do—and don't you ever forget it. If there are two things I know in this life, it's PR and Joshua William Faraday."

I chuckle. "Truer words were never spoken, PG."

"Okay, get off the phone, honey. Concentrate on your driving—I need you here in one piece or else you'll fuck everything up." She makes a sexual sound. "Oh, baby, I'm gonna give you a birthday present you'll never, ever forget."

"Oh, yeah, Party Girl?" I ask.

"Oh, yeah, Playboy," she replies. "It's gonna be so goooood."

I laugh. "So that's how this story ends, huh?"

"You don't know how this story ends?" Kat asks.

"Well, yeah, I do—we fuck like rabbits."

"Oh. Well, that's a pretty damned good ending, I'd say."

"And then we live happily ever after," I add.

"Aw, amen, baby," she says softly. "The best ending of all."

"I love you, Kat," I say quietly, my heart soaring. "I love you, I love you, I love you."

"I love you, too, my beloved Joshua. With all my heart and soul." She sighs on the other end of the line. "*Forever*."

Acknowledgments

This book is for The Love Monkeys, my devoted and wonderful readers. What a ride this has been! Thank you for loving my characters as much as I do. Writing this series has been one of the greatest joys in my life, eclipsed only by the joy of sharing it with you. Oooo oooo eeee eeeee monkey shriek! I love you.

Author Biography

USA Today bestselling author Lauren Rowe lives in San Diego, California, where, in addition to writing books, she performs with her dance/party band at events all over Southern California, writes songs, takes embarrassing snapshots of her ever-patient Boston terrier, Buster, spends time with her family, and narrates audiobooks. To find out about Lauren's upcoming releases and giveaways, sign up for Lauren's emails at www.LaurenRoweBooks.com. Lauren loves to hear from readers! Send Lauren an email from her website, follow her on Twitter @laurenrowebooks, and/or come by her Facebook page by searching Facebook for "Lauren Rowe author." (The actual Facebook link is:

https://www.facebook.com/pages/Lauren-Rowe/1498285267074016).

Additional Books by Lauren Rowe

All books by Lauren Rowe are available in ebook, paperback, and audiobook formats.

The Club Series (The Faraday Brothers Books)

The Club Series is seven books about two brothers, Jonas and Josh Faraday, and the feisty, fierce, smart, funny women who eventually take complete ownership of their hearts: Sarah Cruz and Kat Morgan. *The Club Series* books are to be read in order*, as follows:

-*The Club* #1 (Jonas and Sarah)

-*The Reclamation* #2 (Jonas and Sarah)

-*The Redemption* #3 (Jonas and Sarah)

-*The Culmination* #4 (Jonas and Sarah with Josh and Kat)*
    *Note Lauren intended *The Club Series* to be read in order, 1-7. However, some readers have preferred skipping over book four and heading straight to Josh and Kat's story in *The Infatuation* (Book #5) and then looping back around after Book 7 to read Book 4. This is perfectly fine because *The Culmination* is set three years after the end of the series. It's up to individual preference if you prefer chronological storytelling, go for it. If you wish to read the books as Lauren intended, then read in order 1-4.

-*The Infatuation* #5 (Josh and Kat, Part I)

-*The Revelation* #6 (Josh and Kat, Part II)

-*The Consummation* #7 (Josh and Kat, Part III)

In *The Consummation* (The Club #7), we meet Kat Morgan's family, including her four brothers, Colby, Ryan, Keane, and Dax. If you wish to read more about the Morgans, check out The Morgan Brothers Books. A series of complete standalones, they are set in the same universe as *The Club Series* with numerous cross-over scenes and characters. You do *not* need to read *The Club Series* first to enjoy The Morgan Brothers Books. **And all Morgan Brothers books are standalones to be read in *any* order.**

The Morgan Brothers Books:

Enjoy the Morgan Brothers books before or after or alongside *The Club Series,* in any order:

1. *Hero.* Coming March 12, 2018! This is the epic love story of heroic firefighter, **Colby Morgan,** Kat Morgan's oldest brother. After the worst catastrophe of Colby Morgan's life, will physical therapist Lydia save him... or will he save her? This story takes place alongside Josh and Kat's love story from books 5 to 7 of *The Club Series* and also parallel to Ryan Morgan's love story in *Captain.*

2. *Captain.* A steamy, funny, heartfelt, heart-palpitating insta-love-to-enemies-to-lovers romance. This is the love story of tattooed sex god, **Ryan Morgan**, and the woman he'd move heaven and earth to claim. Note this story takes place alongside *Hero* and The Josh and Kat books from *The Club Series* (Books 5-7). For fans of *The Club Series,* this book brings back not only Josh Faraday and Kat Morgan and the entire Morgan family, but we also get to see in detail Jonas Faraday and Sarah Cruz, Henn and Hannah, and Josh's friend, the music mogul, Reed Rivers, too.

3. *Ball Peen Hammer.* A steamy, hilarious enemies-to-friends-to-lovers romantic comedy. This is the story of cocky as hell male stripper, **Keane Morgan**, and the sassy, smart young woman who brings him to his knees on a road trip. The story begins after *Hero* and *Captain* in time but is intended to be read as a true standalone in *any* order.

4. *Rock Star.* Do you love rock star romances? Then you'll want to read the love story of the youngest Morgan brother, **Dax Morgan,** and the woman who rocked his world, coming in 2018 (TBA)! Note Dax's story is set in time after *Ball Peen Hammer.* Please sign up for Lauren's newsletter at www.laurenrowebooks.com to make sure you don't miss any news about this release and all other upcoming releases and giveaways and behind the scenes scoops!

5. If you've started Lauren's books with The Morgan Brothers Books and you're intrigued about the Morgan brothers' feisty and fabulous sister, **Kat Morgan** (aka The Party Girl) and the sexy billionaire who falls head over heels for her, then it's time to enter the addicting world of the internationally bestselling series, *The Club Series.* Seven books about two brothers (**Jonas Faraday** and **Josh Faraday**) and the witty, sassy women who bring them to their knees (**Sarah Cruz** and **Kat Morgan**), *The Club Series* has been translated all over the world and hit multiple bestseller lists. Find out why readers call it one of their favorite series of all time, addicting, and unforgettable! The series begins with the story of Jonas and Sarah and ends with the story of Josh and Kat.

<u>Does Lauren have standalone books outside the Faraday-Morgan universe? Yes! They are:</u>

1. *Countdown to Killing Kurtis* – This is a sexy psychological thriller with twists and turns, dark humor, and an unconventional love story (not a traditional romance). When a seemingly naive Marilyn-Monroe-wanna-be from Texas discovers her porno-king husband has thwarted her lifelong Hollywood dreams, she hatches a surefire plan to kill him in exactly one year, in order to fulfill what she swears is her sacred destiny.

2. *Misadventures on the Night Shift* – a sexy, funny, scorching bad-boy-rock-star romance with a hint of angst. This is a quick read and Lauren's steamiest book by far, but filled with

Lauren's trademark heart, wit, and depth of emotion and character development. Part of Waterhouse Press's Misadventures series featuring standalone works by a roster of kick-ass authors. Look for the first round of Misadventures books, including Lauren's, in fall 2017. For more, visit misadventures.com.

3. *Misadventures of a College Girl* – a sexy, funny romance with tons of heart, wit, steam, and truly unforgettable characters. Part of Waterhouse Press's Misadventures series featuring standalone works by a roster of kick-ass authors. Look for the first second of Misadventures books, including Lauren's, in spring 2018. For more visit misadventures.com.

4. Look for Lauren's third *Misadventures* title, coming in 2018.

Be sure to sign up for Lauren's newsletter at www.laurenrowe books.com to make sure you don't miss any news about releases and giveaways. Also, join Lauren on Facebook on her page and in her group, Lauren Rowe Books! And if you're an audiobook lover, all of Lauren's books are available in that format, too, narrated or co-narrated by Lauren Rowe, so check them out!

CPSIA information can be obtained
at www.ICGtesting.com
Printed in the USA
LVHW02s1731280818
588393LV00005B/932/P